P9-BZW-259

Praise for Angela Hunt

Five Miles South of Peculiar

"Angela Hunt has penned another winner! From the opening scene, she had me wanting to find out what would happen next to the people of Peculiar, peculiar and otherwise."

—Robin Lee Hatcher, bestselling author of *Heart of Gold* and *Belonging*

"Hunt folds into this recipe for family dramedy two men, tangled family history, and small-town dynamics. The result is deeply engaging characters who readers will care about."

—*Publishers Weekly*

". . . this small-town southern story has a big heart and refreshing characters."

—*Booklist*

The Fine Art of Insincerity

"Hunt delves into some serious issues in this family drama centered around three sisters clearing out their grandmother's house, yet still manages to add humor when it's needed most. This emotionally compelling novel is a gem."

—*Romantic Times*

"Angela Hunt's *The Fine Art of Insincerity* is a tale of sisterhood and friendship. She not only addresses serious choices women face, but also will hold readers' interest with Lillian's eccentricity and no-nonsense wisdom. Readers will come away knowing judgment and insincerity lead to heartache, but truth releases forgiveness."

—*Christian Retailing*

"Angela Hunt is a virtuoso of emotion. She is able to not only explore and explain feelings, but draw you into them with a deftness that's nearly magical. All too soon, you're reading these chapters and unable to put the book down. . . . Delightful, engaging, and rich with emotion. If you're looking for a good weekend read or perhaps a book that will help bring you closer to your own family, this one is it. Angela Hunt hits it out of the park."

—Fictionaddict.com

"Only Angela Hunt could write a relationship novel that's a page-turner! . . . From one crisis to the next, the Lawrence sisters are pulled apart, then knit back together, taking me right along with them. I worried about Ginger one moment, then Penny, and always Rose—a sure sign of a good novel, engaging both mind and heart. Come spend the weekend in coastal Georgia with three women who clean house in more ways than one!"

—Liz Curtis Higgs, bestselling author of *Here Burns My Candle*

"Angela Hunt's womanly tale of sisterly affection and protective martyrdom is a well-woven story of self-discovery and personal growth that will melt your heart!"

—Patricia Hickman, author of *The Pirate Queen* and *Painted Dresses*

"*The Fine Art of Insincerity* is a stunning masterpiece. I was pulled into the lives of Ginger, Pennyroyal, and Rosemary—sisters touched by tragedy, coping in their own ways. So real, so powerful. Pull out the tissues! This one will make you cry, laugh, and smile. I recommend it highly."

—Traci DePree, author of The Lake Emily series

The Offering

A Novel

ANGELA HUNT

HOWARD BOOKS
A DIVISION OF SIMON & SCHUSTER, INC.

New York   Nashville   London   Toronto   Sydney   New Delhi

Howard Books
A Division of Simon & Schuster, Inc.
1230 Avenue of the Americas
New York, NY 10020

This book is a work of fiction. Any references to historical events, real people, or real places are used fictitiously. Other names, characters, places, and events are products of the author's imagination, and any resemblance to actual events or places or persons, living or dead, is entirely coincidental.

First Howard Books trade paperback edition May 2013

HOWARD and colophon are trademarks of Simon & Schuster, Inc.

For information about special discounts for bulk purchases, please contact Simon & Schuster Special Sales at 1-866-506-1949 or business@simonandschuster.com.

The Simon & Schuster Speakers Bureau can bring authors to your live event. For more information or to book an event, contact the Simon & Schuster Speakers Bureau at 1-866-248-3049 or visit our website at www.simonspeakers.com.

Designed by Jaime Putorti

Manufactured in the United States of America

10 9 8 7 6 5 4 3 2 1

Library of Congress Cataloging-in-Publication Data

Hunt, Angela Elwell.
The offering : a novel / Angela Hunt.—First Howard Books trade paperback edition.
pages cm
1. Birthmothers—Fiction. 2. Adopted children—Family relationships—Fiction. I. Title.
PS3558.U46747O34 2013
813'.54—dc23

2012037907

ISBN 978-1-4391-8205-5
ISBN 978-1-4391-8208-6 (ebook)

Now after these events it was

That God tested Avraham

And said to him:

Avraham!

He said:

Here I am.

He said:

Pray take your son,

Your only-one,

Whom you love,

Yitzhak,

And go-you-forth to the land of Moriyya/Seeing,

And offer him up there as an offering-up

Upon one of the mountains

That I will tell you of.

—Genesis 22:1–2

From *The Five Books of Moses*,

Translated by Everett Fox,

Schocken Books

The Offering

Chapter One

Marilee and I were trying to decide whether we should braid her hair or put it in pigtails when Gideon thrust his head into the room. Spotting me behind our daughter, he gave me a look of frustrated disbelief. "Don't you have an important appointment this morning?"

Shock flew through me as I lowered the silky brown strands in my hands. Of course, this was Monday. At nine I had a tremendously important interview with the Pinellas County school system.

I glanced at the pink clock on my four-year-old daughter's bureau. I had only an hour to shower and dress, drive across Tampa Bay, and find the school system's personnel office. Somewhere in the mad rush I also needed to rehearse my responses to standard interview questions, calm my nerves, and call the grocery so they'd know I'd be late.

How could I have let time slip away from me on such an important day? Good thing I had a helpful husband.

"Gideon!" I yelled toward the now-empty doorway. "Can you call Mama Isa and tell her I'll be late this morning?"

"Just get going, Mandy," he yelled, exasperation in his voice. "Your coffee's in the kitchen."

I squeezed Marilee's shoulders. "I'm sorry, sweet girl, but this morning we have to go with something quick."

"Okay. Can I wear it like Princess Leia tomorrow?"

I frowned, trying to place the name. Was she one of the Disney princesses? "How does Princess Leia wear her hair?"

"You know." Marilee held her hands out from her ears and spun her index fingers in circles. "She has honey buns on her ears."

I laughed, placing the image—she was talking about the princess in *Star Wars.* "Sure, if you want to have honey buns over your ears, that's what we'll do. We aim to please."

I pulled the long hair from the top of her head into a ponytail, looped an elastic band over it, and tied a bow around the band. Then I kissed the top of her head and took a moment to breathe in the sweet scent of her strawberry shampoo. "Love you," I murmured.

She grinned. "Love you, too."

I returned her smile and hurried into my bathroom.

Twenty minutes later I stood in my closet, wrapped in a towel and dripping on the carpet. What to wear? I had a nice blue skirt, but the waistband had lost its button and I had no idea where I'd put it. The black pantsuit looked expensive and professional, but sand caked my black sandals because I had worn them to the beach last weekend.

"Baby girl?"

"In here."

The closet door opened and Gideon grinned at me, a fragrant mug in his hand. "Aren't you ever going to learn how to manage your schedule?"

I grabbed the mug and gulped a mouthful of coffee. "Maybe I like living on the edge."

"And Mama says *I* have a dangerous job." He waggled his brows at the sight of my towel. "Pity you don't have any extra time this morning."

"And too bad you have to get Marilee to school. So off with you, soldier, so I can get my act together."

Chuckling, Gideon lifted his hands in surrender and stepped away from the closet. "Okay, then, I'm heading out. But you're picking up our little bug from school today, right?"

I dropped the blouse I'd been considering. "I'm *what*?"

"Our daughter? You're picking her up this afternoon because I'm leading a training exercise."

For an instant his face went sober and dark, reminding me of the reason he'd been so busy lately. The military had to be planning something, an operation Gideon couldn't even mention to an ordinary civilian like me.

"Sure." My voice lowered to a somber pitch. "I've got it covered."

He nodded, but a hint of uncertainty lingered in his eyes. "Mandy—"

"I've got it, so don't worry." I shooed him out the door. "Tell Marilee I'll see her later."

Gideon nodded and left the bedroom, his combat boots thumping on the wooden floor.

A snap of guilt stung my conscience, but I had no time for remorse. I needed a better-paying job and Pinellas County needed a middle school cafeteria manager. Rarely did any school have a midyear opening, and this interview could be the answer to all my prayers. . . .

I opened a drawer and pulled out a pair of panty hose, then hesitated. No one wore hose anymore, especially not in the Florida heat, but for this job I'd wear rubber sheathing if they expected me to. I had to look my best, I had to dress to impress, and I had to get across the Howard Frankland Bridge in record time. No one expected a lunchroom manager to look like a fashion icon, but everyone expected her to show up on time.

A brown skirt hung behind Gideon's gun safe. Though the suede material would be hot and heavy, at least the garment had buttons and a hem. I grabbed it, then yanked a utilitarian white shirt from a hanger. Ready or not, I had to get moving.

A few minutes later, as I fastened the buttons at the sleeve, I noticed a reddish stain on the cuff, probably from Marilee's cranberry juice. With no time to change, I rolled both sleeves up to the elbow.

I brushed my teeth and hair, swiped mascara across my lashes, and thrust my feet into a pair of worn loafers. I stepped back for one final look in the mirror, then shook my head. I looked more like an absentminded blonde than a manager, but maybe the interviewer wouldn't mind. I'd impress her with my professionalism.

I ran back into the bedroom, grabbed my oversized leather tote from a hook on the door, and hurried out to my car.

Chapter Two

"I know I'm late and I'm sorry," I called, pushing my way through the door of Mama Yanela's, the Cuban grocery owned by my father-in-law, Tumelo, and his twin sister, better known as Mama Isa.

Amelia, Mama Isa's daughter and my cousin by marriage, stood behind the checkout counter and pretended not to hear me. *"Muchas gracias,"* she told a customer, handing over a bag filled with freshly baked Cuban bread. "Please come again."

I waited until the elderly customer had shuffled out of the building, then I stepped into the rectangular checkout stand in the center of the store. "Gideon called your mom, right? I had to drive all the way to Largo and back this morning—"

"You could have told me. You were supposed to open."

I stared, remembering too late that I'd been entrusted with opening the store. In my excitement over the interview, I'd completely forgotten. "But Gideon called," I whispered in a weak voice, knowing my excuse wouldn't fly.

"He didn't call *me*. And if he called Mama, I didn't get the message."

Amelia's pretty face remained locked in neutral, but when she didn't leave the checkout stand I knew she was royally ticked off.

"You could have told me *before* this morning," she went on, glaring at me from beneath her brown bangs. "I nearly panicked when I showed up at seven fifteen and found the doors still locked. At first I thought you'd been in a wreck or something—"

"I wasn't in a wreck."

"But how was I supposed to know that? All those old guys who come for coffee were lined up outside. Even Jenna was waiting, and she had two cakes to decorate for noon pickups. Now she's hopelessly behind."

"Jenna!" I swiveled toward the bakery at the back of the store, where Jenna Daniels decorated cakes and pastries behind a glass display case. "I'm sorry if I threw you off schedule."

When I turned to Amelia again, her lips had thinned with irritation. "I don't know how you can be so casual about everything. This is not funny."

"I didn't mean to be funny." I sighed and stashed my purse in an under-the-counter niche. "Look, the interview I had this morning was a onetime thing. It was important."

"Sometimes I think you treat the grocery like some kind of hobby."

"A hobby?" I dropped my jaw. "I work my tail off at this place, just like the rest of you. So don't tell me I don't work hard."

If Amelia had been a cartoon figure, steam would be blowing out her ears. "Okay, you work," she said, shrugging. "But working part-time means you breeze in whenever you feel like it and take off whenever the mood strikes you."

"That's not fair. I'm not that erratic."

"But this isn't the first time you've been late. If you're going to open the store, you have to be here before seven. You have to get everything ready, turn on the lights, set up the coffeepots.

I closed my eyes. "I know what I have to do."

"I don't think you do. Because somehow you've managed to reach adulthood without learning how to take responsibilities seriously. It's about time you grew up."

Anger flared in me. Amelia and I were the same age, but sometimes she acted like a worried old woman and seemed to think I behaved like a child. I wanted to tell her that I could be as responsible as she was, but just then the bells above the double doors jangled and Claude Newton, one of our regular customers, shuffled in wearing his usual costume: a Hawaiian shirt, a denim kilt, and bright pink flip-flops.

I covered my smile while Amelia turned and called out a welcome. "*Hola,* Claude. *¿Cómo estás*?"

"*Muy bien.*" He moved slowly toward the canned goods. "Looking for goat's milk."

"Over there, right under *la leche de coco,*" Amelia told him. "You can't miss it."

My anger evaporated as I watched Claude navigate the aisle. How could I stay mad when our one and only resident nudist had popped in for his daily snack run? Working in a Cuban grocery might not be the most exciting job in Tampa, but it had to be one of the most interesting.

"Look." I folded my arms and transferred my gaze to Amelia. "I'm sorry I forgot about opening the store. I'll do better. I promise."

Amelia drew a breath as if she wanted to continue arguing, then she blew out her cheeks. She never could stay mad at me for long.

"From now on, let me know if you're going to be late, okay?" she said. "Mama wants to retire, so she needs to know she can depend on us. If you or Gideon needs to call about store business, call me, not Mama."

"Okay. Got it."

Her gaze softened. "Well . . . did you get the job?"

"I'm pretty sure I didn't." I pulled my apron from beneath the counter and tied it on. "I don't have a college degree, so I shouldn't even have bothered applying. I was hoping they'd be desperate enough to overlook my lack of education, but apparently I'm unqualified to oversee a middle school lunch line." A bitter laugh bubbled to the surface. "I guess my experience here at Mama Yanela's doesn't count for much."

Amelia stepped back to let me move toward the register. "Why did you drop out of college when you were so close to finishing? You invested all that money and time—"

"I didn't plan on quitting in my junior year. I didn't plan on falling in love and getting married, and I didn't plan on getting pregnant—" I stopped when Amelia's face twisted.

I could have kicked myself. I kept forgetting that after four years of marriage Amelia and Mario had no children. I'm sure they had their reasons for remaining childless, but I didn't want to pry.

I shifted my gaze to the front window, granting her a measure of privacy.

"I'll get out of your way now." Amelia backed out of the narrow space behind the counter, then caught my eye and gestured toward the office at the rear of the store. "I'll be at the desk. Mama and Uncle Tumelo are coming in later to go over the new order."

I nodded. "Don't worry. I'll handle things up here."

"If you need a translator, come get me."

I resisted the urge to roll my eyes. Though I didn't speak Spanish nearly as well as Gideon or his family, I'd been working at the grocery long enough to get a sense of what people were saying when they talked to me. Or I could at least guess what they wanted.

"Go on." I waved Amelia away. "I know what I'm doing."

Now, as I look back, I think that may have been the last day I could say those words and even come close to meaning them.

At two, after making sure Amelia had everything under control at the grocery, I drove to the Takahashi Early Learning Center and sat in the carpool lane. The teachers had already begun to lead their students to the front walk, and as soon as a bell chimed two fifteen they began leaning into cars and buckling in their students for a safe ride home.

I eased off the brake and let my car roll forward. Gideon and I had been fortunate to find this educational program for Marilee. Not everyone understood that we had been blessed with an exceptional four-year-old, but ever since we discovered our daughter's musical talent, I knew we had to do our absolute best for her.

I smiled as her teacher opened the rear door and reached for the seat belt. "Hey, sweetheart," I said as Marilee climbed into her booster seat. "Did you have a good day?"

Marilee responded as she always did—with a simple "Uh-huh"—then leaned back and looked out the window as I drove away.

"Did you learn to play any new songs in your piano lesson?"

When Marilee didn't answer, I glanced in the rearview mirror to see if she was paying attention. Her eyelids were half closed and her head nodded like a puppet on a string. Poor kid. Gideon often wondered if we had involved her in too much too soon, but I thought she'd be fine as long as she remained interested and happy. I wanted her to play and have fun like a normal kid, but we needed to nurture her musical gifts, too. Not everyone was born with perfect pitch and total recall.

Now Gideon worried about what we would do when Marilee entered first grade and her tuition payments gobbled up an even bigger percentage of our income, but I had never been able to see the point in fretting. By then, I told myself, surely I'd have a full-time job, something that would pay far better than a part-time stint at the family grocery.

Yet after today's disastrous interview, I was beginning to reconsider my opinion. People kept telling me I needed to get a college degree to snag any job paying above minimum wage, but where could I find the money to go back to school? We couldn't take out a loan when we were already mortgaged to the hilt.

And I certainly couldn't earn that kind of cash in a Cuban checkout stand.

"Whatcha doing, baby girl?" a man murmured in my ear.

"Gideon!" I turned and playfully swatted his bare arm with the newspaper I'd been reading at the kitchen counter. "You scared me to death."

He wrapped his arms around me, nuzzled the side of my neck, then planted his cheek next to mine. "Whatcha reading? Looking for yard sales?"

"Not today." Giving up my search of the classifieds, I dropped the paper and slid from my stool, grateful for my husband's attention. Gideon wrapped his arms around me, his chiseled muscles flexing and bulging in easy rhythm as he drew me closer. I ran my fingers through his dark hair, long now, and curly, a far cry from the buzz cut he'd worn during his early years in the Army. Men who belonged to the elite unit Gideon led weren't supposed to look like they were in the military, but I could spot one of his buddies from fifty yards away. Though they rarely wore uniforms, they carried themselves in a certain way—shoulders squared, backs straight, arms hanging loose, and eyes observant. They were supermen who could survive by eating grass and drinking dew, and they were prepared to take action anywhere, at any time.

Gideon looked around. "Where's our angel?"

"Taking a nap. I put her down when we got home, and she hasn't moved since." I peered up into his dark eyes. "Good day?"

He shrugged. "We're keeping an eye on a developing situation, so we might be heading out soon. But we shouldn't be gone too long."

I took a deep breath to calm my leaping pulse and didn't ask any questions. Gideon led a counterterrorism unit under Special Forces Command, and though I knew he did important work, I didn't want to know what his job entailed. He had always been intent on his training, but lately he had also been tense and cautious. I never knew when he would be called away—sometimes he left in the middle of the night—and he couldn't tell me where or why he was going.

All I knew was my husband wasn't allowed to travel more than an hour away from Tampa's MacDill Air Force Base, home to USSOCOM, the Special Operations Command headquarters. He and his sixteen-man unit frequently disappeared for days, then returned to family life as if they'd never been away.

Though I found Gideon's unpredictable departures frustrating—probably because I'd never been good at saying good-bye to people I loved—I was proud of my husband. He and the other secretive special operators were brave, dedicated, and skilled warriors, and I was always grateful when they came home unscathed.

I, on the other hand, was not an ideal military wife. I wasn't good at saying good-bye, I wasn't brave, and I didn't feel an innate need to be all that I could be. Worst of all, I couldn't sleep when I knew the pillow next to mine would be empty, so Gid had developed the habit of slipping out without telling me he was going. When I woke without him, if his duffel bag lay on the floor of the closet, I knew he had only gone out to the base or to run an errand. But if the duffel bag had disappeared, so had Gideon.

He tightened his arms around me, then nodded at the newspaper on the counter. "Why were you reading the want ads?"

I sighed and stepped out of his arms. "You know I adore your family, but I need a bigger paycheck. I could have had that middle school lunchroom job if I had a college degree. I could do a lot of things if only I had a degree, so I need to go back to school. I was looking through the classifieds and hoping to find some way to pay for it."

Gideon's brow furrowed. "I could talk to Dad about giving you a raise."

I shook my head. "I already make more than the hourly employees. If Tumelo gave me a raise I'd be making as much per hour as Amelia. Considering that I'm only a cashier and she practically runs the place, that wouldn't be fair."

"I could see about earning some money on the side—"

I brushed my fingers across my husband's lips. "You can't do that. I'm sure there's a regulation against it, and even if there isn't, I don't want you worrying about things at home. This will be my way of contributing to the house fund. "

"You already do plenty." His arms slipped around me again. "You're a great mom and a good wife."

"Only *good*?"

His eyes twinkled. "Okay, you're a fantastic wife. And we'll get our own house, I promise. We just have to be patient."

"But being patient is *hard*."

"My team has a saying: The path of least resistance is the path of the *loser*. Good things usually hurt."

I smiled, only slightly amused at his he-man humor. "Have you always dreamed of being Captain America?"

He tipped his head back and laughed, the warm sound filling our small kitchen. "Maybe I have. America is a great country, you know? My grandparents may talk about Cuba all the time, but they wouldn't want to leave Tampa. Neither would my parents."

"Neither would I." I settled my head against my husband's chest, reassured by the strong and steady sound of his heart. "But I'd follow you anywhere."

Chapter Three

¿Cómo está, Claude?" I smiled at our quirkiest and best-tanned customer. "Did you find everything you need?"

The old man dropped a bag of beans on the counter, then scratched at his grizzled white beard. "You don't carry suntan lotion. You should order some."

"Mama Yanela's is a Cuban grocery. We don't carry everything."

"But this is the only place I like to shop. So be a dear, will you, and ask your boss to stock some suntan lotion? I like Hawaiian Gold."

"But this is Florida, not Hawaii."

I waited, expecting him to chuckle at my little joke, but he only crinkled his brow. "Hawaiian Gold, okay? When you tan all over"—he winked, reminding me that he lived in the local nudist colony—"you need the best."

"I'll ask about it," I promised, dropping his beans into a bag. "And, um, then you can tell everyone at the colony that we have the good stuff. Suntan lotion, I mean."

He grabbed his bag and turned for the door, twiddling his fingers in a backhanded wave as his pink flip-flops slapped the floor.

From the canned goods aisle, Amelia snickered.

"*Hola,* Mandy." I looked up as Mario, Amelia's husband, entered the store wearing his butcher's apron. *"¿Está bien?"*

"Bien," I called as he hurried past. "Hope you're good, too."

Gideon's family spoke Spanish almost exclusively at home, making an exception only when they had to stop and translate something for me. Even Gideon's mother, Elaine Lisandra, had learned to speak Spanish fluently, though she was as much a *gringa* as I was. I tried to learn Spanish, honestly I did, but I couldn't see much point in learning when they all spoke English as well. And they lived in America—shouldn't they adapt to us instead of the other way around?

But some of our older Cuban grocery customers apparently believed in the adage about old dogs not learning new tricks. So I tried to maintain a working vocabulary in Spanish, practicing how to meet and greet and count back change, along with reciting the names of fruits, meats, and delicacies such as octopus salad (*ensalada de pulpo*), our special of the week.

I had just scribbled a note to ask Mama Isa about suntan lotion when a hugely pregnant woman came toward the register, one arm holding her shopping basket, the other supporting her back. The woman looked slightly familiar, but I couldn't place her face.

When she lifted her basket onto the counter, I tilted my head. "You look familiar. Do you attend Calvary Chapel? Or maybe you just shop here a lot."

The woman smiled. "I've seen you in the car pool line at the Takahashi school. My little boy goes there."

I nodded. "Okay, now it makes sense. This is my daughter's first year at the school."

"I've noticed her—she's cute. Does she like the school?"

"Marilee loves it. And she's learned so much! I keep telling my husband we may have a budding Mozart on our hands, but he just laughs and tells me to rein in my imagination." I shot a pointed glance at her protruding belly. "I see you're expecting another child. Your second?"

"This?" Her free hand fell protectively on the mound beneath her breasts. "This baby is responsible for my being here—I've a desperate craving for flan. Though I don't know why I'm eating anything. I feel like I'm about to pop."

I studied her belly again. "When's your baby due?"

"Any day—and it's not my baby."

I had been about to lift a can of evaporated milk from her basket, but my hand froze in midair. "Did you say—Wait. What did you say?"

The woman pressed her hand to her back again and grimaced. "This kid belongs to a couple in D.C. As soon as I feel the first honest-to-goodness contraction, I'm calling them so they can fly down. And I don't mind telling you, I'm more than ready to see my feet again."

I lifted a brow, then rang up the *leche evaporada* and a package of flan mix. "So the other couple is adopting your baby?"

She gave me a weary look, wordlessly letting me know she'd been asked the question before. "It's *their* baby—they defrosted a frozen embryo and I'm carrying it for them. A friend of mine convinced me this would be a good gig for a military wife." The woman reached for a bag of merengue puffs and tossed it onto the counter. "Those look good, too."

"They are good." I ran the puffs under my scanner and stuffed them into a grocery bag, glad to hear the woman and I had something else in common. "Your husband's stationed at MacDill?"

"He's in Afghanistan. By the time he gets leave, I should have my figure back."

"So . . . you're a surrogate?"

The woman shifted her weight and leaned forward, bracing her arms on the checkout counter. "That term's gone out of fashion because it usually means the birth mom is supplying the egg. No couple wants Mary Beth Whitehead drama, so most intended parents either supply the egg or buy it from an egg farm."

I shrugged to hide my confusion. "Wow. I had no idea that kind of thing went on around here."

"It goes on everywhere, I guess. Most people just don't talk about it."

"But you do?"

The woman tossed the Cuban version of a Twinkie into her basket. "Lots of women on the base do. Surrogacy agencies love military wives because they know we tend to be independent, we have access to great health care, and our husbands are underpaid. Plus, they're always saying we have an unusual willingness to serve others. While I don't know about *that,* all the other stuff adds up to a lot of willing women."

The word *underpaid* vibrated in my head. "You do this for money," I whispered, thinking aloud.

"Not only for money." A suggestion of annoyance flashed in her eyes. "I'm doing it to help a couple who couldn't have kids otherwise."

"Oh, I'm not blaming you," I added quickly, "because I know how it feels to stretch a dollar until it rips. I don't fault you at all, in fact, I think what you're doing is great. You're doing it to help your family, right?"

"Why else would I go through this kind of agony?" The woman stepped back, looked pointedly at her bulging belly, and gave me a lopsided smile. "Trust me—at first it's all about helping a childless couple, but as the months go by that good feeling fades and you keep reminding yourself that you're doing something good for *your* kids. By the time I hand over this baby, I'll have earned as much in nine months as my husband does in a year. Helping other people is great, but helping your family is better."

I snapped my fingers as a realization took shape. "The base—you must shop at the PX."

"When I'm not shopping at Walmart, yeah."

"Maybe I'll see you again. Marilee and I shop there every couple of weeks."

"Well, I hope I'm skinny the next time you see me. I can't wait to pop this baby out."

My mind bulged with noisy thoughts as I finished ringing up the woman's order and ran her credit card through the machine.

"Good luck with your delivery," I said, handing over her grocery bag. "I hope things go smoothly for you."

"They had better." Her mouth lifted in a smile that didn't quite reach her eyes. "I'm giving these people nine months of my life. That's enough."

I crossed my arms as the woman slowly waddled out of the store. Amelia stepped out from behind a display and followed my gaze as I watched our heavily pregnant customer get into her car.

"Who was that?" Amelia's brow wrinkled. "And isn't she about to drop that kid?"

"Her husband's in Afghanistan, and her son goes to Marilee's school." I turned to face my cousin. "We were just talking about her pregnancy."

"I was wondering if we should call an ambulance. She looks like she's at least a week overdue."

I didn't answer, but stared at my cousin as a series of thoughts toppled like dominoes in my brain. Gideon and I needed money, we were a military family, and I had time and a strong constitution. We wanted other children, but not right away, so I could carry a baby for someone else. I'd have to do some research and convince the family, though, and Amelia knew *la familia* better than I did. I could talk Gideon into almost anything, but the other members of his clan weren't as susceptible to my powers of persuasion. . . .

"What?" Amelia's expression shifted to alarm. "Something wrong with my face?"

"I need a coffee break." I uncrossed my arms. "Want to come with me?"

The question hung in the air between us, shimmering with significance, and Amelia seemed to understand that I didn't really want coffee at all. "Jenna!" she finally called. "Can you watch the register a few minutes?"

"I'm busy."

"Mario?"

"Claro. Un momento."

We waited until Mario stepped out from behind the meat counter, then I led Amelia toward the back of the store.

Amelia and I stepped out into a blindingly bright Florida morning. November had brought cooler temperatures, and with it the promise of something resembling winter, but not even the appearance of decorator pumpkins, dried cornstalks, and harvest scarecrows could convince our tropical sun that autumn had arrived.

Amelia sank into one of the cheap plastic chairs by the back door, Mama Isa's idea of furnishing an employee break room. "So what's on your mind?" Amelia said. "Mama said you might be needing a raise."

"I don't want a raise." I pulled the other chair into the thin strip of shade cast by the overhanging roof. "But Gid and I do need extra money. Marilee's tuition will go up every year, and her teacher has already mentioned that we need to think about buying her a piano. I wouldn't worry about finances if I had the sort of job I thought I'd get after college, but I can't get anything close to that until I finish and get my degree. Going back to school will cost money we don't have."

Amelia propped her sneakered feet on an overturned plastic bucket. "Things are tough all over. Mario and I are trying to tighten our belts, too. Someday this store will be ours, so if we invest in it—"

"Gideon and I can't wait to invest, we need more income now."

Amelia hauled her gaze from the shrubs behind the store and squinted at me. "What's your hurry?"

I shook my head. "We've been married five years and we've never had a home to call our own. I'm sick of renting. And there's Marilee's school; the tuition goes up every year. Finally, we want to have more kids someday, in a house with a real backyard and room for a dog."

Amelia nodded. "Have you thought about a loan?"

"We applied for a loan a few months ago; the bank turned us down."

"You could talk to Mama or Elaine or Abuela Yanela—"

"Gideon doesn't want to borrow money from the family. He says his parents and grandparents worked hard to get what they have, so he's not about to take it from them, not even as a loan."

Amelia pressed her lips together, then shrugged. "If you're planning to ask me and Mario, I hate to disappoint you, but—"

"I didn't bring you out here to ask for money. I came because I wanted to ask your advice about something."

Her mouth twitched with amusement. "I would advise you not to clean out the cash register."

"Don't be silly. I was thinking about that pregnant woman."

"Whatever for?"

"Because she's not pregnant with her own child—she's having a baby for some people in D.C. It's their kid. She's only carrying it."

Amelia gaped at me like a woman facing an IRS audit. "Don't tell me you think *that's* a good idea."

I blinked, momentarily intimidated by the intensity of her reaction. "I don't know what I think. First, I don't know if I could do it. When you're pregnant, you're so aware of everything the baby is doing—you can feel it moving, kicking, and turning around. I'm not sure, but I think I could even tell when Marilee burped. I sang to her, I stroked her through my skin, I was so completely in love with her. . . ."

A warning cloud settled on Amelia's features. "Would you have been in love with her if she belonged to someone else?"

She asked the question I'd been avoiding. "I don't know. I don't know how I'd feel. The idea never crossed my mind until today."

We sat in silence for a long while, then Amelia leaned forward and looked me in the eye. "You're seriously thinking about this?"

"I think maybe I am. The money's good."

She snorted. "It's crazy. Who does that? Ordinary people do not rent out their uteruses. Or uteri. Whatever the word is."

"But apparently it happens a lot these days. Maybe more often than we realize, and right under our noses. It's just not talked about."

"You don't think people would notice if someone showed up with a baby when they were stick thin the week before?"

"Maybe they'd assume her kid had been adopted."

"What about a woman who walked around with a big belly and then—*poof*—she was thin and childless? And flashing a wad of cash?"

"Maybe her belly and her finances are nobody's business. All I know is the money is really, really good. It's enough to solve our problems, at least for a while. And I think it's enough for a down payment on a house."

Amelia leaned back and closed her eyes. "I didn't know you and Gideon wanted more kids."

"Sure we do, but we have to be able to afford them. Right now we can't even afford to eat out more than once a month, so how could we pay for another baby?"

"You have good insurance."

"It's not the hospital expense that kills us, it's the *living* expense. It's schools and college funds and clothing and all the gadgets kids want these days—it adds up. Once I have my degree and a good job we could get pregnant again. Then we might have a couple more kids."

Amelia sighed and appeared to study her hands. "I don't know, *prima*. A baby is a gift from God, so maybe that privilege shouldn't be for sale."

"Couldn't God work through a surrogate? He works through doctors to help people overcome infertility. Why couldn't he work through a surrogate to help a couple have a baby?"

"Okay, but it's so expensive! It hardly seems fair that some people can buy a biological baby when other people try so *hard* to have one—"

"Those would be the people I want to help." I leaned toward her, eager to make her see my point of view. "Infertility is on the rise, haven't you heard? And this is a way to do something for those people. Just think—I could help create a family for a couple who can't have their own babies."

"You want to have a baby for a poor woman? There's no money in that, Cousin."

I stared into space, lost in my thoughts, and then realized that Amelia had risen and was opening the back door.

"I think the idea is *loco,*" she said, her voice drained and distant. "And I think Gideon would hate the thought of his wife being pregnant with some other guy's child. You forget you married a Latin man, *chica.*"

"That's a stereotype."

"Stereotypes exist because they are usually true." Amelia stepped into the doorway, then hesitated. "Better get back to the register. Mario has meat to cut, and he won't be happy if you make him stay too long at the checkout."

"I'm coming." I sighed and stood to follow her, but my thoughts remained miles away.

Somehow I made it through the rest of the morning without spilling my thoughts to everyone who crossed my path. I left the grocery at two, picked up Marilee from preschool, then went home and put her down for a nap. When she had dozed off, I went to the laptop in the kitchen and clicked on the Google icon. I typed "surrogate mother" in the search box, then sat back and watched the screen fill up with links.

I never dreamed I'd find so much information—links to websites about surrogate motherhood, finding a surrogate mother, surrogate agencies, being a surrogate mother, ethical problems with surrogacy, surrogate mothers for hire, cost of surrogate mothers, surrogate parenting, surrogate mothers wanted, affordable surrogacy, gestational surrogacy, surrogate mother compensation . . .

The woman in the grocery was right—surrogacy was more common than I'd realized, and apparently it was happening right under my nose. One website featured state-by-state listings of agencies that arranged surrogate pregnancies, and I was surprised to see the names of several agencies in Florida, including one near me.

Maybe surrogacy wasn't such a big deal after all. Maybe I'd been so wrapped up in my little life that I'd missed the big picture. Even though the listing about ethical problems with surrogacy had raised a warning flag in my brain, surely people had figured out how to make the arrangement work.

Still . . . what would people think if they knew I was carrying a child for someone else? What would they think if I told them the baby in my belly wasn't Gideon's?

I picked up the phone and called my mom.

Ordinarily, my mom wasn't the first person I'd use as a sounding board. Usually I would toss my wild ideas at Gideon, but he was out on a training exercise and I didn't want to interrupt him while he jumped out of a plane or shot at cardboard terrorists. Sometimes I would talk to Amelia or Mama Isa—thoroughly grounded, they usually gave good, godly counsel when I needed it. Sometimes I listened to Oprah, though my life wasn't nearly as dramatic as the issues she usually discussed on her program.

Being a surrogate mother, though, seemed like a fairly dramatic situation.

Fortunately, Mom happened to have her cell phone with her. My mom, who had turned into a social butterfly shortly after I left home, lived ninety-three miles away in The Villages, a golf cart retirement community in north-central Florida. With dozens of ongoing activities for the thirteen thousand mostly retired residents, I rarely managed to reach my mom on the first attempt.

But today, wonder of wonders, Mom answered her phone. Knowing that she probably had a bridge club meeting or some other event to get to, I explained my idea as quickly as possible, then bit my thumbnail and braced for the backlash.

"So," I said after a long moment of total silence, "what do you think?"

"I think you've lost your mind." Mom's voice, calm and cool, rolled over the airwaves. "Honey, have you been working too hard?"

She wasn't taking me seriously. "I'm not working too hard, that's the point. We'll never manage to—"

"You know Gideon would never go for such a thing. He's such a man's man—I can't see him understanding why his wife would want to have another man's baby."

"But I don't want to have another man's baby. I want to carry another *couple's* baby and then give it to them. All I'd be doing is renting out my uterus. Gideon wouldn't see this baby as a threat."

"What about Marilee? How would you explain that situation to my granddaughter?"

I bit my lip, surprised by a question I hadn't fully considered. "She's only four years old. She may not even notice—"

"Good grief, Mandy, you were plenty observant when you were her age. Of course she'll notice, and what are you going to say? How do you explain that you're planning to have a baby and then hand it off to someone else? What's to stop her from thinking that you might give her away, too?"

I flexed my fingers in exasperation. Mom would argue with me if I said the sky was blue, but today she was probably more worried about explaining my condition to her friends than to Marilee. But why should my pregnancy bother her? I wasn't planning to visit The Villages any time soon, so she shouldn't have to explain anything to anyone.

I gulped a breath. "If I do this, I will simply tell Marilee the truth—that I'm having a baby for a couple who can't have a baby of their own. I'm sure she'd understand. Kids are more sophisticated than they used to be, and Marilee's exceptionally bright. She'll understand when I explain that the baby isn't related to us."

"You don't have to be related to get your emotions all in a tangle. Love is a lot more binding than blood, let me tell you."

"Thanks, Mom." I couldn't keep a shade of cynicism from my voice. "I really appreciate your support."

"You asked what I thought, and I'm telling you: I think you'd be borrowing trouble if you went through with this crazy notion."

"Okay, then." I slid from the barstool. "Thanks for offering your opinion."

"You're not going to listen to me, are you? I know you, Amanda, and when you get your mind wrapped around a thing, there's no prying you away from it."

"If I'm stubborn, I must have picked it up from you."

Mom exhaled a heavy sigh. "You must not remember your father at all."

"I remember enough."

"Then you have to remember that he was as contrary as a mule. I could never get him to—"

"I've gotta go, Mom." I turned, ready to be done with the conversation. "Marilee will be waking up soon."

"All right. Just promise me you'll think about this before you go ahead and do something rash. And one more thing—if you convince Gideon to go along with this, you have that man entirely too wrapped around your finger. Men should be more independent."

I lifted my gaze to the ceiling, certain that my wonderful father was watching and laughing at us from heaven. "Okay, I'll think about it. And I'll meet you at the river."

"Yeah, I'll be waiting under the tree."

I disconnected the call and sighed, imagining Mom's reaction if I'd had to leave a message on her voice mail—she would have dialed my number before the recording even finished playing. My mom could be a wonderful advocate when she agreed with a course of action, but when she disagreed, she could be as inflexible as an oak.

Her inflexibility usually drove me to lower my head, dig in my heels, and become even more determined to do whatever she didn't want me to do. Yet when it came down to it, I didn't need her approval to pursue my plans because only one person really mattered. The only person whose opinion could stop me was Gideon.

Mom probably thought I would spring the idea on Gideon as soon as he came through the door, but I decided to keep my thoughts under wraps for a while. I wanted to sleep on the idea, I wanted to do some more research, and I wanted to see how I felt about surrogacy when I woke up to a fresh new day. Why start an argument with my husband if after some reflection I decided that having someone else's baby was a stupid thing to do? So I simply made dinner for my family, Gideon and I watched TV together, and then we went to bed, same as always.

But before we fell asleep, I rolled over and stroked Gid's strong jaw. "Baby?"

"Hmm?"

"I've been thinking about something."

He rolled to face me and caught my hand. "Well, if you're not too tired—"

"Not that. I was thinking about the house we're going to have someday. I think we should look for something with at least three or four bedrooms."

He chuckled. "How many kids you planning on having?"

"I don't know. But you need a place for your exercise equipment, and I might want a sewing room or a study. And it's always nice to have a guest room for when Mom visits. She tries not to grumble about it, but I know she hates sleeping on the sofa bed."

"I've never heard her complain."

"Then consider this—if she were sleeping in a guest room, you and I wouldn't have to clear out of the living room at nine o'clock. And you wouldn't have to tiptoe around when you're making coffee in the morning."

His fingers threaded through mine. "Why are you talking about houses? You know we haven't saved near enough for a down payment—"

"And we never will. Not with all our expenses."

The darkness filled with the sound of his exasperated sigh. "Then we'll just have to rent until I get the store going. If I ask my father to be a silent partner—"

"I love your dad, Gid, but I don't think he ought to invest in a music store. He'll want to help us out, but he's nearing retirement age, so he needs to save his money." I squeezed Gideon's hand before he could sigh again. "But I learned about a potential job today—something I can do without a college degree. Something that might help us get a house sooner than we expected."

He lifted his head to peer at me through the gloom. "It's not some government program, is it? You know how my family feels about government programs."

"It's not any kind of handout. I'll be working for the money, but it's the kind of work I love."

"Are you going to tell me what it is?"

"Maybe tomorrow. I want to sleep on it first." I pulled my hand free of his, then rolled onto my back and tucked the comforter under my chin. "Good night."

"That's not fair, baby girl. You can't leave me hanging like that."

"Don't worry, just go to sleep. If the idea's any good, I'll tell you about it tomorrow."

Obviously too tired to argue with me, Gideon grunted in resignation, then turned over and went to sleep.

The next morning I woke with the idea of surrogacy heavy on my mind. But instead of tarnishing in the stark light of a new day, the notion had taken on a golden glow, an aura of altruism. By having someone else's baby, I would not only be helping my family and another couple, I would be doing something positive in a world that had seen far too much darkness and despair. I would be striking a blow for freedom. I would be taking a stand for a woman's right to control her own body in a way that celebrated motherhood and unborn life.

"Now," Gideon said, coming out of the bathroom with a loaded toothbrush in his hand, "I want to hear about your great money-making idea."

I lifted my chin and let him have the no-frills version. "I could earn a lot of money by having another couple's baby as a surrogate. I love being pregnant, so why couldn't I be pregnant for someone else?"

"No way." Gideon thrust his toothbrush in his mouth and stepped back into the bathroom, brushing like a maniac while voicing his opinion through a mouthful of suds: "No way are you having some other man's kid."

"But it happens all the time. A lot more than we realize." I slipped off the bed and stood in the bathroom doorway, watching my husband's face in the mirror. "The baby won't *mean* anything to us—it will be someone else's kid. But I could earn a lot of money by helping them out."

"Uh-uh." Gideon shook his head, then leaned over and spat into the sink—and on my idea, or so it seemed. I waited until he had rinsed and wiped his mouth, then I walked toward him and wound my arms around his neck. "You do so much for us, babe," I whispered, looking up into his dark eyes. "Why don't you let *me* do something important for our family?"

He caught my arms in his firm grip and removed them from his neck. "You do plenty," he said, smiling as he released me. "And I love having you all to myself. Maybe I don't want to share you with some other man."

What do you know—Mom was right. My Latin male was behaving exactly like the stereotypical Latin male.

"Don't say that," I answered, my voice sharper than I intended. "This is the twenty-first century. You wouldn't be sharing me with anyone; I'd be giving some couple the child they can't conceive any other way."

"No." Gideon flashed a quick smile and planted a kiss on my forehead. "Not interested."

My heart dropped, but I wasn't willing to give up. I knew Gideon had a tendency to react quickly and instinctively. While that tendency undoubtedly worked in his favor on the battlefield, it didn't work so well in our marriage.

That afternoon I set Marilee on a barstool and let her stir a bowl of brownie mix while I pulled a chicken out of the freezer. I wanted to make Gideon's favorite dinner, but the phone rang before I could defrost the bird in the microwave. Gid was on the line, and he only had a minute before he had to catch a chopper.

"Sorry, baby girl," he said, his tone warm and reassuring. "We have to go. I love you."

I caught my breath, silencing the questions any other wife would have asked: where were they going, would the mission be dangerous, and how long would they be gone? But I couldn't ask those questions because not even wives were allowed to peek beneath the veil of secrecy.

So I whispered, "Oh," and tried to swallow the fear and disappointment rising in my chest. Then I said something even more stupid: "I'm making barbecue chicken and Marilee is making brownies."

Since I wasn't supposed to voice the crucial questions in my head, what else could I say?

"Save me some of everything," Gideon said, a smile in his voice.

"I wish you didn't have to go."

"You know the old military saying: You don't have to *like* it, you just have to *do* it."

I slumped against the counter. "Spoken like a true GI Joe."

"Hug Marilee for me. And I'll meet you at the river."

Somehow I managed to whisper my reply: "I'll be waiting under the tree."

The phone clicked and he was gone, leaving me with nothing but a scrap of news and a boatload of worries.

As Marilee hummed and stirred the brownie mix, I stuffed the chicken back in the freezer, then picked up the newspaper and scanned the headlines. I searched for signs of trouble around the world, though in my gut I suspected Gideon and his team were headed to Afghanistan or Iraq, maybe even Pakistan. Or anywhere in the troubled Middle East . . .

A chill shivered the pit of my stomach, as if I had just swallowed a huge chunk of ice.

Closing the paper, I stood at the kitchen counter and whispered a prayer for my husband's safety, then followed with the completely selfish request that he and his team remain stateside for as long as possible. When I finished, I glanced over to see Marilee watching me, her eyes bright with speculation under their long silken fringes. She had stopped stirring.

"Mama"—she tilted her head—"why do you always talk about the tree?"

"Because"—I smiled and kept my voice light—"I don't like saying good-bye."

My daughter pressed her lips together as thought worked in her eyes. "But what are we gonna do under the tree?"

I drew a deep breath and sat on the stool next to her. "When I was a little girl about your age, my daddy told me about heaven. He said it was a huge place with a dozen gates in four big walls and millions of people. The holy city has golden streets and a river flowing straight out from the throne of God. Beside the river, all around it, grows the tree of life."

"Can you fish in the river?"

I laughed. "I don't know. But when I was little I worried about not being able to find my mom and dad in heaven because of all those people. So Daddy told me he'd meet me by the river, under the tree of life. So every time we could have said good-bye, instead he'd say, 'I'll meet you by the river,' and I'd answer, 'Right under the tree.' He always knew what I meant."

Marilee's brow wrinkled, then she smiled. "So I say, 'I'll meet you by the river—' "

"And I say, 'I'll be waiting under the tree.' Or something like that." I kissed her forehead, then ran my finger along the rim of her bowl. "Yummy. Do you want to bake these brownies for supper?"

"Is that *all* we're having?"

"Well, we ought to have some vegetables and meat, too. Or mac and cheese. Or"—I gave her a conspiratorial grin—"we could go see what Mama Isa's cooking."

As Marilee squealed and clapped, I slid from my stool and put ClingWrap on the brownie batter. We'd take it with us and bake brownies in Mama Isa's oven.

Years before, I'd established the habit of heading to Mama Isa's whenever Gideon went out on a mission. Being with family, especially a noisy, happy clan like the Lisandras, took my mind off my fears and helped me feel less alone. The way I figured it, *la familia* was cheaper and more effective than Prozac.

So I put Marilee in the car and we drove to Mama Isa's house. I knew that once we arrived, Isa and Jorge would call Yanela and Gordon, Tumelo and Elaine, Amelia and Mario. Someone would be dispatched to pick up Carlos and Yaritza, who no longer drove. Within an hour or so, the house would brim with *la familia,* food, conversation, and the comforting confusion that didn't allow me time for worry.

And while we cooked and ate and talked and laughed, Gideon would creep through whatever dangers faced him and know his family had united, we were praying for him, and a place had been reserved for him at the table.

Over a generous bowl of *arroz con pollo,* I smiled at my in-laws and tried to maintain a stiff upper lip. The Lisandra family knew plenty about risk, struggle, and patriotism. In 1960 Gordon and Yanela had fled Cuba with nothing but their dreams and the clothes they wore. After a fitful start in Miami they migrated to Tampa, where they met Carlos and Yaritza Fernandez, a childless older couple who welcomed the newlyweds and helped them make a new start. With the support of Carlos, Yaritza, and the Cuban community, Gordon and Yanela established Mama Yanela's grocery in Ybor City.

At sixty-three, Gordon Lisandra still cut a formidable figure. After finishing his dinner, he pushed back from the head of the table and drew Marilee onto his lap. While my daughter giggled, he bounced her on his knee and sang a Cuban song I couldn't understand. Yanela sat by his side, trying to follow various after-dinner conversations and occasionally asking Mama Isa, *"¿Qué dice ella?"*

Mama Isa, who spoke English far better than her parents, watched Marilee and me with compassion in her eyes. Tumelo and Elaine, my reserved in-laws, ignored these pity-filled glances, but I welcomed them, desperate for someone to understand the terror that overflowed my heart every time Gideon boarded a helicopter. I wanted to be brave; I wanted to be as independent as the military wives I met at family support meetings, but my spine lacked the iron others had developed.

But I had Gideon's family for support.

Mama Isa had just passed around a bowl of dessert *pastelitos* when a bell pinged from another room. Jorge excused himself and went into his den; a moment later he returned and gestured to me. "It's Gideon on the computer." A secretive smile softened his mouth. "He wants to speak to you."

Relief and gratitude crested within me as I hurried into the den, where I found Jorge's laptop on the desk. He had opened the Skype program, and Gideon's face filled the screen.

"Gideon!" I sank into the desk chair, thrilled to see my husband's face. "Are you okay?"

"We're fine." A wary look in his eye told me he was guarding his words. "I just wanted to check in and let the family know we're not in harm's way."

"This mission's not dangerous?"

"We're training." His voice lowered as he turned to murmur something to someone nearby, then he turned back to me and grinned while a disembodied hand fluttered near the right side of the screen. "That's Snake. He says hi."

Scott "Snake" Billings was Gideon's right-hand man, a guy who probably spent more time with my husband than I did. I'd made a face when I first learned that my husband's best friend was named after a reptile, but Gideon had explained how the nickname fit: "He's wily, lethal, and he can get anything from anyone at any time. Snake's a good man to have in your corner."

I managed a weak little laugh. "Tell him hi for me."

"I wanted to make sure you were settled. My family taking good care of you and the little bug?"

"Of course." I pressed my hand to my chin to hide its quivering. "I wish you could see what I saw tonight. Your grandpa sang to Marilee and bounced her on his knee."

"Maybe he's the source of her talent."

"Maybe she got it from her daddy."

"I'm nothing special—"

"Come on, Ricky Ricardo, admit that you're good. You probably handle a guitar better than you do a gun."

"Ha! You'd better hope that's not true." Gideon looked away again, then returned to the computer. "I only have about two minutes, so if there's anything else—"

"Nothing here. I love you. I miss you." I touched my fingertips to my lips, then pressed them to the screen.

"Love you too, baby girl."

"I'll meet you by the river."

"Roger that. I'll be under the *árbol de vida.*"

I sat perfectly still, listening to the rumble of heavy trucks, until the transmission blinked out.

Two days later, as I stood in the living room trying to encourage Marilee to play the cheesy practice keyboard on loan from the school, the clump of boots on the porch stairs distracted me. I squeezed Marilee's shoulder. "Guess who's home?"

"Daddy!"

Marilee abandoned her keyboard and ran toward the front door, with me only a few steps behind her. Gideon and Snake stood on the porch, both dressed in camo, both grinning. Gid winked at me. "I hope you don't mind that I brought someone home for dinner."

My heart flipped over like it always did when he looked at me that way. "You could have brought an entire platoon and I wouldn't care. I'm just happy to see you."

Gideon caught Marilee as she leapt into his arms, then stepped into the house to swing her in a circle. She giggled and lifted her hands for more when he put her down, but he reached out and pulled me into an embrace.

"What's gotten into you?" I asked after he kissed me soundly.

"Shh." He glanced over his shoulder and told Snake to make himself at home; he'd be back in a minute. But first he wanted to talk to me.

While Snake sat on the sofa and entertained Marilee, Gideon led me into the kitchen. "Okay, I've been thinking about it," he said, his eyes dark and earnest. "And the way you talked about us having our own house . . . I want that, too. When I get out of the military, more than anything I want a normal life for us and our kids."

"When you get out?" I pronounced the words carefully, testing his meaning. Gideon often talked about the music store he wanted to open when he was free of the military, but he had never given me any idea of when that might be.

"I'm not going to re-up. I'm going to finish the two years I have left, then I'm done. I'm walking away."

I stared, momentarily unable to imagine Gideon as anything but a soldier. His skill, training, and heightened awareness permeated every aspect of his being, so how could he set aside part of his personality?

"Did you hear what I said?" His hands fell on my shoulders and gave me a little shake. "I want out, Mandy, I want to be around to put my kids to bed and make more babies with you."

"Did you say *babies*? As in more than one?"

"Yeah, I want as many as we can handle. So what I'm saying is that I've been thinking a lot about your idea. I even asked some of the guys what they thought about it. I checked out some stuff on the Internet and—"

"What are you saying?"

"I'm saying your idea might be okay. I'm trying to understand how that sort of thing operates."

I caught my breath, surprised by the intensity in his voice. "I've been thinking, too. And I'm not going to pursue it if you're going to hate seeing me pregnant. I need to know you'll be comfortable with the situation."

A wry smile crept into Gideon's voice. "You're sure it's not illegal? Everything's on the up-and-up?"

"It's legal, but not everyone approves of surrogacy." The words came out in a rush, so I paused to let them sink in. "Here's how it works: the baby will be the couple's biological child, but they'll pay me to carry it until it's born. For my part in the arrangement, I'm pretty sure I could earn as much as you do in a year."

Gideon's smile twisted. "That can't be right."

"It is; I've done a lot of research. And we won't incur any expenses, since we're covered under your health insurance. Everything I need will be supplied by the other couple."

Snake and Marilee laughed in the background, but Gideon didn't say a word.

"You don't have to give me a final answer now, Gid. But keep thinking about it, okay? Surrogacy might solve all our financial problems."

"I don't know." Doubt filled his voice. "Don't know what to say, except it still doesn't seem natural. A man wants his wife to carry his own babies."

"In a perfect world, sure," I added quickly, wanting him to understand. "But not every woman can carry babies while people like me carry them easily. Look at it this way—I want to contribute to our family's dream, and you risk your life for us every time you go out the front door. No one could ask you to do any more."

"I'll be done with all that in two years."

"And when you're done, we could leave this rental behind and buy a house with the surrogacy money." I kept my voice light. "But think about what we could do for our family. We could get Marilee a piano and pay her tuition for next year. I could finish college and get my degree. And we could put a huge chunk into our savings account, where it would earn interest until we're ready to move." I laid my hand on his chest, reminding myself not to press too hard. "We'd be working together, Gid, for our family's future."

I left him and pulled together a quick dinner of spaghetti, salad, and French bread. Gideon and Snake relaxed in the living room, but as I listened from the kitchen, I noticed that Snake and Marilee did most of the talking—which meant Gideon had to be deep in thought.

While I watched the spaghetti boil, I wrestled with my own thoughts. Was I wrong to suggest surrogacy to Gideon? I'd known he would be opposed to the idea, but I'd been equally sure I could eventually bring him around to my point of view. But maybe my mom was right—maybe Gideon *was* too wrapped around my little finger. Maybe a good wife should be more inclined to follow her husband's opinions, and maybe a husband should be less vulnerable to his wife's persuasive powers.

No one would dare call Gideon henpecked, but I'd once heard the never-married Snake joke that Gideon was "whipped"—implying that Gid was so besotted he'd do anything I wanted him to do. I loved knowing that Gid wanted to please me, but maybe Snake was right. Maybe I had unintentionally robbed Gideon of some force of will he might one day need to survive. . . .

Dinner was pleasant enough. We talked about the weather, Rays baseball, and the possibility of the Buccaneers ever repeating their Super Bowl win. After dinner, Snake thanked me for the meal, kissed me on the cheek, and pulled Marilee's ponytail before heading out the door.

I was about to go have a long soak in the tub, but Gideon caught me in the hallway. "I've thought about it," he whispered, holding me close while his breath fanned my cheek. "And if it really means so much to you, let's do this surrogacy thing. If I need to sign something, swear something, or say something, just let me know. I'm with you, baby girl. Whatever you want to do is okay with me."

I searched his eyes and saw nothing but eager willingness in them. "Are you sure about this? I'd hate it if you changed your mind when it's too late to turn back."

"I'm sure, baby girl. If you want to be generous, why should I stop you? Some lucky couple is going to thank God for your willingness to help them out."

I studied his face, then smiled. What could possibly be wrong with having a man wrapped around your finger?

I slipped my arms around his neck, then exhaled a long, contented sigh. "You won't be sorry. This is going to be good for us."

"There's just one thing—well, two." He loosened his grip so he could look me in the eye. "First, if this is going to risk your health, I don't want to do it."

"Sweetie, you know I'm healthy." I pressed my hand to his stubbled cheek. "Don't you remember what the doctor said when Marilee was born? She said all the other mothers should be jealous of my easy pregnancy. I told her I wanted a huge family, so maybe that's why I'd been built for having kids."

Gideon grunted. "I don't remember that."

"Because you were too busy passing out cigars. But the doctor said it, and she was right."

"Okay, I'll take your word for it. And the second thing—"

I rose on tiptoe and gave him a kiss. "What?"

"I want a son." An eager, hopeful glint flashed in his eyes. "I will always love daughters, but as long as you stay healthy, I want a son or two to carry on the family name. It's important to me."

I tipped my head back and studied my handsome, intelligent, kind, and undeniably macho husband. "Of course you want a son, and I want to give you one. We'll have another baby—or two or three or four. Once I finish school, I'll get a better job so we'll be able to afford as many kids as we want." I squeezed his arm. "You won't be sorry. This will go as smoothly as any pregnancy on record, then we'll give the baby to its parents and get busy living our dream. But for the first time in a long time, we won't have to worry about money."

"If you say so," Gideon answered. "But you can't take risks with your health. Promise me."

"I promise. But I'm sure everything's going to go perfectly."

I wrapped my arms around him and squeezed tight, determined that he should see how confident I was.

Somehow I kept my mouth shut over the weekend, swallowing my eagerness and offering vague replies when family members asked *"¿Qué pasa?"* at Mama Isa's weekly dinner. We sat around the table passing rice and corn and roasted pork, and every time my eyes met Gideon's I lifted a brow and silently asked if I could share our news. He moved his head sideways and held up a restraining hand, quelling my enthusiasm and urging me to hold off.

But why were we waiting? Now that he'd agreed that I should try surrogacy, all I had to do was find an agency, a couple, and a doctor. And the family should know of our decision beforehand. They would never forgive us if we progressed without telling them, and heaven help us if I became pregnant without forewarning them that we couldn't keep the baby. Gideon's parents might never get over the disappointment.

On Sunday evening I finally convinced my husband that we should tell *la familia* as soon as possible. I stressed all the practical considerations, but truthfully, I wanted to share because I was thrilled about the future stretching out before us. If all went as planned with the surrogacy, in two years Gideon and I would be in a house, with another baby of our own on the way.

I couldn't wait.

No one expected me to arrive at the grocery on Monday until after I'd dropped Marilee at school, but like a kid with a secret she can't wait to share, I let Gideon and Marilee sleep and slipped out of the house before sunrise. Since Mama Isa and Tumelo always arrived at the grocery early on Mondays, I thought I'd get everyone together and make my big announcement.

The approaching dawn spread gray light over the silent highway as I turned into the lot behind the grocery and parked the car. The November morning was cool, not cold, and I barely needed the sweater I'd tossed over my shoulders. I walked through the morning stillness, then opened the back door used only by employees.

Mama Isa's voice and Jorge's laugh rang in the hallway, followed by Amelia's musical murmur as she asked them something in Spanish. She and Mario seemed to be with her parents and Tumelo in the small stockroom, so this should be an ideal time to break the news.

I pulled my sweater closer and walked into the stockroom, then shivered and nodded good morning.

"Mandy." Mama Isa's brows lifted as she stepped forward and kissed me on the forehead, the traditional family greeting. "What brings you in so early?"

"I have news." I looked around the circle, waiting for their undivided attention. Amelia lowered her pricing gun and Mario stopped cutting empty boxes long enough to shoot me a curious look.

"Buenos días." I smiled and tried to maintain a serene expression. "I have an announcement, and thought it would be easier if I talked to everyone at once."

"¡Gloria a Dios!" Mama Isa clapped, and one glance at her hope-filled face told me what she expected to hear.

"Lo siento." I gave her a sad smile. "But Gideon and I aren't having a baby. Not yet, anyway."

Amelia caught my wrist. "You're not quitting work, are you?"

"No."

"Then what?" Mario ripped a strip of sealing tape from the box he'd been breaking down. "We have customers waiting outside."

I lifted my chin and spoke with quiet firmness. "I have decided to volunteer to be a surrogate for a woman who can't carry a baby on her own. Doing this will help us be able to buy a house one day, and I'll be able to do something amazing for a childless couple."

Mama Isa turned to Amelia. "What is she saying?"

Amelia shook her head. *"Ella quiere ser una madre sustituta."*

"¿Qué?"

"You don't want to know, Mama."

Tumelo elbowed Jorge. *"¿Soy un abuelo? ¿Ella va a tener un bebé?"*

Amelia lifted her chin and ripped open a box of plantain chips. "Not if she has any sense, she isn't."

My cousin grabbed the carton of chips and headed to the front of the store, leaving me to face the others alone.

"Well." I spread my hands. "I'm still investigating the application process, so this isn't definite. But I have an agency in mind and everything looks promising. I wanted you to know in case it all works out. I didn't want you to be surprised if I need to take some time off for tests and things."

My heart sank as Tumelo walked away, shaking his head. Maybe I was expecting too much from my father-in-law and the others of his generation. They hadn't grown up with the technology people my age took for granted.

I walked to the checkout stand, ready to begin my day, but as I left I heard Mama Isa ask Mario, *"¿Es ella loca?"*

I didn't have to be fluent in Spanish to know she thought I'd gone crazy.

Though my relatives' lack of support cast a pall over my enthusiasm, ultimately it didn't matter. Let them think me *loca*; let them mutter all they wanted. As young adults in the twenty-first century, Gideon and I were going to take full advantage of the opportunities available to us. I was going to be a gestational carrier, and the sooner I got started, the better off I'd be.

At the stroke of seven, Tumelo unlocked the front door. I took care of a customer who'd been waiting for one of the cellophane-wrapped pastries on the counter, then quietly pulled my cell phone from my purse.

Through an Internet search I'd discovered a surrogacy agency in St. Petersburg, so I wouldn't have far to drive for an interview.

Grasping the last shreds of my courage, I unlocked my phone. Though I knew the agency's office wouldn't be open this early, I hoped to leave a message and request a callback. I punched in the agency's number, then lost my nerve and hung up.

Why was I so nervous about committing to a phone call? Gideon had given his permission, and his opinion mattered more than anyone else's. My mom might never see things from my perspective, but she lived two hours away and wasn't likely to drop in for a visit. She would never have to see this baby or even glimpse me pregnant. She could keep her disapproval to herself while she enjoyed her surreal life in The Villages.

As for Mama Isa and Jorge, Tumelo and Elaine, Amelia and Mario—they might not understand my decision, but they wouldn't condemn me, either. They'd grown up with crazy American ideas, so in time they would shrug and resign themselves to my plan. They might whisper about Gideon marrying a *gringa loca,* but they would also take quiet pride in the fact that one couple in the family had proven themselves unconventional.

If all went well, by this time next year I might be planning to get pregnant with my own baby, mine and Gideon's, giving the Lisandra family plenty to cheer about. Another baby would join Marilee, maybe the son Gideon so desperately wanted, and the family would have planted three generations of Lisandra men on American soil.

They would be so excited about the future, they would forgive the recent past. I knew they would.

I gripped my phone and punched in the agency's number again.

Chapter Four

"So, Mandy—now that we're better acquainted, tell me why you want to be a gestational carrier."

Natasha Bray, whose red hair hung in graceful curves over the shoulders of her dark suit, asked the question as casually as if she were asking my opinion about the weather. I chose my words carefully, though, because I knew my answer might determine whether or not she would confirm me as a participant in the Surrogacy Center's program. In the three weeks I had been working with Ms. Bray, I had completed two phone interviews, an initial medical screening, and a home visit. Only two additional requirements stood between me and official acceptance into the program: this private interview and the results from my psychological screening.

"Gideon and I," I told her, "have enjoyed our daughter so much that we want to give another couple the opportunity to have a child. I carried Marilee with very few problems and had no complications during her delivery. I don't expect things to be any different with a subsequent pregnancy."

"Your statement seems to imply that you did experience some problems—what were they?"

I shrugged. "Nothing unusual. A little spotting in the first trimester, a few days of morning sickness, and a strange craving for

Cheez-Its." Though nervous, I allowed myself to laugh. "I went through boxes of crackers like I was eating for five. But now I'd eat squid before I'd eat a cheese snack."

Natasha smiled and scanned the open folder on her desk. I knew the file contained my application and reference letters from family and friends. I thought about asking Natasha if the references were positive, then decided I didn't want to know what people really thought about me being a surrogate.

"You seem to have made a lot of friends at your church," she said.

"We've met some really nice people there."

"Is faith important to you?"

"Yes." I smiled so she wouldn't think I was part of some grim religious cult. "I became a Christian not long after I met Gideon."

"No religious objections to being a surrogate, then?"

I blinked. "Why should anyone object if I do a good deed for someone else? Isn't that what Christians are supposed to be about?"

Natasha lifted one shoulder in an elegant shrug. "One never knows why some people do the things they do." She turned a page and smiled. "I understand your daughter is quite talented. Does musical ability run in your family?"

I barely managed to keep a giggle out of my voice. "My husband plays the guitar and sometimes pretends to be Ricky Ricardo. His grandfather also plays the guitar and sings."

"So that's where the gift originated."

"Probably." I tilted my head and added, "To be honest, I'm not sure where my daughter's talent comes from, but her teachers at the Takahashi school say it's extraordinary. The money from this program—if I'm accepted—will help us pay for her tuition in the years ahead."

Natasha flipped another page. "You passed your initial medical screening with flying colors, and I really enjoyed our home visit. Your daughter is lovely and your husband is quite charming." She folded her hands on the desk and smiled. "As long as the psychologist didn't spot any problems in the screening interview, you should be on your way."

I pressed my damp palms together, hoping Natasha wouldn't notice my trembling fingers. I'd never been more thrilled, but what if the shrink found faults that wouldn't be acceptable in a gestational carrier? Maybe Natasha would learn that I consistently run late for appointments. Or that I have a tendency to wallow in guilt when I make a mistake. Or that my husband spoils me far more than he should.

Maybe the psychologist had added up all my shortcomings and declared that I wasn't suited for motherhood of any kind, even the traditional variety.

Natasha arranged her papers in a neat pile, closed the folder, and looked over at me. "Did you bring the marriage satisfaction questionnaire? And the personality tests?"

"I have them in my purse." I pulled an oversized envelope from my bag and handed it across the desk. "Was there anything else? I've been so scatterbrained lately and with all the Christmas parties—"

"I have nothing else." Natasha put the envelope in the folder, then pushed the folder aside and picked up her pen, her eyes glinting. "I'll look those pages over later, but now I want to know what you will enjoy most about being a gestational carrier."

I crossed and uncrossed my legs as I searched for an honest but commendable answer. "What will I enjoy? Helping someone. I really mean that. At college I majored in psychology because I've wanted to be a social worker ever since middle school."

Natasha clicked her pen. "Not the typical choice for a middle school girl. Did something specific lead you to social work?"

"I saw a movie—*Radio Flyer,* I think it was called—about a boy who'd been abused by his stepfather. I wanted to help that kid in the movie so much I found myself wishing I could jump through the screen. Maybe that's crazy, but that's when I learned that social workers help kids like that boy. People have always been important to me."

"Did you identify with the child in the movie?"

Recognizing the motive behind the question, I shook my head. "I wasn't ever abused. My dad died when I was six, so after that it was just me and Mom. We didn't always get along—in fact, we're not close even now—but I can't say I was ever abused. I was probably a little spoiled because my daddy would have given me the moon if I'd asked for it. I loved him more than anything, and when I lost him . . . well, it wasn't easy."

"If spoiling a child results in the kind of altruism you're displaying, maybe the world needs to rethink its child-rearing philosophies." Natasha smiled and wrote something on her notepad. "What do you remember most about your dad?"

"Most? I have so many memories, it's hard to pick just one. He sold insurance and worked out of an office in the house, so he was always around when I was little—in fact, I think he changed more of my diapers than Mom did, because she worked at a pet shop in town. He taught me how to count, he read me stories, he would sing silly songs to make me laugh—" I sighed as a flood of nostalgia swept over me. "I miss him even now."

"Did your mother remarry?"

"No. Mom never seemed to have much interest in men . . . or maybe she just didn't have time to date. Between her job and taking care of me, she stayed pretty busy."

"So you grew up as an only child?"

I nodded. "That's why I want to have more kids when Gideon and I can afford them. I've always wanted a big family—that's probably why I love being around Gid's family so much. They're always together."

Natasha glanced at her notes, then looked up at me. "What's the one moment you're dreading most in terms of being a gestational carrier? It's perfectly natural to have concerns and anxieties about the process, so you can be completely honest."

I considered the question. "Everyone seems to think I'll have trouble surrendering the baby, but I don't think that'll be a problem. Maybe I'm being unrealistic, but I honestly feel . . . detached.

It won't be my baby, so I won't bond with him or her. I won't allow myself to get all caught up in feelings I have no right to feel."

Natasha nodded, her expression thoughtful. "If you don't expect to feel maternal, how do you expect to feel? How do you envision your relationship with the child you'll be carrying?"

I smiled, confident of my answer. "I think I'll see myself as a babysitter. As someone who's been placed in charge of a helpless little one, trusted to take care of it and help it grow. And once it's grown and ready to meet the world, I think I'll be relieved to hand it to its true parents. And proud of myself for completing a job to the best of my ability."

A smile lifted the corner of Natasha's thin mouth. "That's an extremely healthy attitude."

"To be honest, though, one thing does concern me . . . but maybe it's no big deal."

Natasha lifted a brow. "I'm listening."

"Well"—I twisted my hands—"I'm a little worried that my husband won't find me attractive if I get all fat with a stranger's baby. I know pregnant females are supposed to look beautiful, but my husband comes from a family of gorgeous women and I don't know what he'll think if I have swollen ankles, a round face, and a big belly. When I was pregnant with Marilee he kept telling me I was beautiful, but he might not feel the same way when it's someone else's baby—"

"That's why it's important you face this situation together." Natasha's gaze softened. "After talking to both of you the other day, I got the impression that your husband is completely on board. I also picked up on the fact that the man adores you."

A rush of blood heated my face. "I am a lucky woman."

"And a very normal one."

We both turned as someone knocked on the door. When Natasha called permission to enter, the blonde who worked at the reception desk came in with a large envelope. "Dr. Dickson just messengered this over," she said, after a quick glance at me. "I thought you might want to take a look."

My stomach dropped at the mention of the psychologist. He'd been a blank wall during my interview with him—I had no idea whether he'd describe me as an altruistic saint or a confirmed lunatic.

Natasha smiled her thanks and opened the envelope. I pretended to study my nails as she pulled out a typed letter. From where I sat I could see dense, square paragraphs on the page, but I couldn't read a word of what the doctor had written.

What if he hated me? What if he didn't like the answers I gave? He probably thought I was a monster because I said I'd been a daddy's girl, so my mom and I weren't really close. I'd tried to follow up and explain that Mom and I loved each other even though we didn't have a lot in common, but my rushed fumbling must have sounded like pure rationalization. Furthermore, he probably cared more about *how* I answered his questions than what I actually said, which meant he had probably written that I would be unsuitable for this program or any other. . . .

Natasha leaned back in her chair, then smiled and lowered the letter. "Good news, Amanda—Dr. Dickson says you're no crazier than any other woman in the program. If you still want to help an infertile couple, we have a green light to proceed."

I pressed my hand to my chest. "For real? That's it?"

"This was the last report I needed. I still want to go over your personality and marriage profiles, but I only use those to help match you with a pair of prospective parents."

"Oh, my." I gulped a quick breath. "I can't wait to tell Gideon."

"I hope he's as delighted as we are. And now, if you'll step into the waiting room for a few moments, I want to review the profiles you brought in today. In about half an hour, I'll ask you to join me again."

"For . . . more questions or something?"

"For something far more interesting than mere questions." Something twinkled in the depths of the woman's eyes. "For something I think you'll enjoy very much."

In the waiting room, I read magazines, studied the wall art (softly focused photographs of smiling couples with adorable naked babies), and attempted to finish a crossword puzzle in a magazine someone had left behind. Too restless to focus on the crossword clues, I hummed along with the Muzak Christmas carols and double-checked my shopping list to be sure I had a gift for everyone I needed to remember. I thought about calling Amelia, just to see how things were going at the grocery, or Mama Isa, to make sure Marilee wasn't being any trouble.

But true to her word, thirty minutes later Natasha opened her door and gestured to me, and I found myself staring at three file folders in a neat row on her desk.

Natasha sank into her chair, crossing her arms and pressing her lips together in the look of a woman struggling to remain impartial.

"I think you'd be a good fit for any of these three couples," she said. "Look them over and see what you think."

"You mean *I* choose?"

"Prospective parents tell me what sort of gestational carrier they would like, and I have matched you to three couples who have indicated a preference for a woman of your age and experience. But the contract will be between you and the parents. I am only the agent who brings the two parties together." She chuckled. "Think of me as renting real estate during a seller's market."

"My uterus is the property?"

"And there are more couples seeking that property than there are willing renters. So yes, you hold the upper hand. You choose."

I ran my fingertips over the nearest folder. For the first time in my life, I held real power in my hands, a godlike authority to change other people's lives with a single word. But I couldn't be comfortable with that kind of control. This felt like too much responsibility.

"I don't want to do this alone." I looked up and bit my lip. "Could you tell me which one you *want* me to choose?"

Natasha shook her head. "I would never presume to make that kind of decision for you. You're the one who will have to work with these IPs."

"IPs?"

"Intended parents. I'm sure you couldn't go wrong with any of these couples, but ultimately, you must make this choice."

I swallowed hard. "It's so much pressure. Can I take these home and let Gideon help me?"

She smiled. "By all means. I'm not saying you have to decide right here and now. These are duplicates of files I have in the office, so don't worry if you spill something on the pages. But they are confidential documents, so I must ask you not to leave them in a public place or show them to anyone but your husband. Read through all the enclosed information, consider the applications carefully, and come back whenever you're ready to name your choice. Whoever you pick, I'm sure they'll be ecstatic to hear that their long wait is finally coming to an end. Your decision may be the best Christmas present one of these couples has ever had."

I picked up the three folders and put them in a large envelope Natasha slid across her desk. I wasn't sure Gideon would care about looking through the information, but maybe this would help him feel more involved. After all, this process would affect our entire family.

"Thank you," I said, my voice hoarse. "I will guard these with my life."

"I don't think we have to go that far." Natasha's smile deepened. "I had a good feeling about you the first time we talked, so I went ahead and prepared a contract—you'll find it in the envelope. Read it over carefully, consult with a lawyer if you like, discuss everything with your husband. And when you're ready to proceed, call the office to set up another appointment. Take as long as you need, but don't forget that these couples have been waiting a long time.

The sooner you make your decision, the sooner we can begin, and the sooner you will receive your initial payment. The payout details are on a sheet in the envelope along with the contract."

I smiled. Charity was a marvelous thing, but so was an additional paycheck.

Because I got caught in heavy traffic on the Howard Frankland Bridge, the sun had set by the time I walked through our front door. A blanket of stillness lay over the house, an unusual quiet that alarmed me at first. But as I tiptoed through the living room and neared the hallway, I heard the rumble of Gideon's baritone and followed it to the threshold of Marilee's bedroom.

"I'm sorry your throat hurts," I heard him say. "And I'm going to ask God to make you feel better."

"Can you ask God to help Auntie Amelia, too?"

"Something wrong with Auntie Amelia?"

"Uh-huh. She read *Curious George* to me the other day, but in the middle she started cryin'. And that's not a sad story, Daddy."

I leaned against the wall outside Marilee's bedroom and wondered what had bothered Amelia. She seemed perfectly fine when I talked to her Saturday night at Mama Isa's, so why would she cry while reading Marilee's story? Maybe she got something in her eye and Marilee misinterpreted those tears. . . .

I folded my arms and waited in the hallway as Gideon prayed for Amelia and for Marilee's sore throat. Without looking, I knew he was kneeling by our daughter's bedside, his big, strong hands clasped over hers. In a moment he would pull up the covers and tuck them under her chin, then he would turn on the ceiling fan and wish her a good night. . . .

"Sleep tight, precious," I heard him say, right on schedule. "I love you."

"Daddy?"

"What?"

"I'll meet you by the river."

A moment of surprised silence followed, then Gideon replied in the way he'd answered me so many times before. "I'll be waiting for you under the tree, baby girl."

Later that evening, I pulled Gideon from the talking heads on ESPN and led him to the kitchen table, which I'd covered with the three folders and the contract from the Surrogacy Center.

"What's this?" A frown line creased his forehead. "This had better not be bad news from the IRS."

I tweaked his nose. "These are folders from prospective parents. We get to choose whose baby we carry."

"*You* carry," he corrected, but he sat and flipped the cover of the first file.

I sat next to him and skimmed the page as he read. I'd devoured each couple's information as soon as I came home, which meant we settled for a dinner of microwaved fish sticks and cold potato salad.

The first couple, Forrest and Jennifer Jeffrey, lived in Orlando, less than two hours away. They were in their midthirties and had been married ten years. "We have tried everything to have a child," Jennifer wrote on the application. "We've tracked my ovulation, Forrest has worn boxer shorts for months, we've done everything the doctors and the old wives' tales suggested. We even tried IVF, but none of our babies implanted after transfer and we felt guilty about using up so many living embryos. When our doctor suggested we contract with a gestational carrier, we didn't take the idea seriously at first, but I want a baby more than anything in the world. So we're going to wait for you, dear volunteer, and hope you will be willing to carry our child to term. Time is of the essence, of course, because Forrest and I aren't growing any younger. We don't want to pressure you, not now or ever, but we have a lot of time, love, and resources to share with you and with a baby."

"Resources." Gideon tapped the page. "That's code."

"Code for what?"

"They're rich. I guess it's the most tasteful way to say they'll pay anything if you'll do this for them."

"At least they were subtle about it."

I handed him the second folder. This couple had sent an eight-by-ten color photograph of themselves, and Gideon blinked when he saw a picture of two middle-aged men. Andre and Hugh had been together six years and planned to marry as soon as the option became legal.

Gideon read the letter aloud: " 'We're now living in Vermont, and we'd go anywhere to have another baby. We are currently raising Samantha and Stephanie, twin girls from China, and more than anything we want the girls to have a brother. So we are looking for a gestational carrier who would be willing to transfer at least three embryos—"

Gideon frowned at me. "Where do they get the embryo?"

"From their sperm and an egg donor, I guess."

"Who's the egg donor?"

"I don't know. Men make deposits in a sperm bank; women must sell eggs to an egg farm—er, bank."

He shook his head. "Abuela won't believe any of this. And they're asking you to carry triplets? Isn't that a lot riskier than a typical pregnancy?"

"I think triplets are a long shot, but I don't know. I'll have to ask Natasha about it."

Gideon kept reading: "—transfer at least three embryos and then selectively terminate any female fetuses. We are a committed couple, dedicated parents, and want to bring more love and joy to this world. What better way to do that than to have more babies?"

My husband scowled. "Did I read that right? They want to terminate females?"

"I've already scratched them off my list." I took the file and pushed it away. "I'm surprised Natasha gave me that couple. I thought she knew I would never terminate a pregnancy."

Gideon said nothing as I opened the third file and handed it over. The photo paper-clipped to the first page featured an unusually striking couple. The husband was tall and big boned, his blond hair full and shining, his beard perfectly clipped. Though the man could have been anywhere from forty-five to sixty, the woman couldn't have been more than forty. She stood tall and pencil thin beside her husband, her pale face unlined and her brown hair long and flowing. Both of them had large blue eyes and the look of people who had never broken a sweat. I had no trouble imagining them in a penthouse on New York's Fifth Avenue or in a country mansion in some exotic locale.

"Damien and Simone Amblour," Gideon read. "From the Loire Valley, France."

"My turn." I scooted closer to read the letter aloud.

"Dear Friend:

"My husband and I live in France, in the beautiful Loire Valley on the western coast. Our home is called Domaine de Amblour—it is a working vineyard and maison d'hôte. *My husband inherited the estate from his father, who inherited it from his father. Altogether, I am told, six generations of my husband's family have lived on and worked this bountiful soil.*

"Damien and I have been married five years with no children. He does have two girls from a previous union, but I am sad to say the girls want nothing to do with the estate or their father. We desperately want a son or daughter to live with us, to bless our home and learn how to live off the bounty and beauty of this land. I was born and raised in Paris, but since coming to the Loire Valley, I cannot imagine living anywhere else. This place is a paradise on earth.

"Though our vineyard is abundantly fertile, our union has not resulted in a child. Surrogacy is not legal in France, so we have turned to the United States for help. If you choose to work with us, we will come to the U.S. to meet you, as we will come

if you need us for anything. We are most eager to care for you, provide for you, and to be present for the child's birth. If you choose us, we would appreciate being notified the moment you suspect birth is imminent. We will have to fly over, but we will make every preparation to arrive as soon as possible.

"I hope you will be the one through whom God answers our prayers.

Most sincerely, Simone Amblour."

I felt Gideon's gaze on my face as I finished reading.

"Wow," he said, rubbing his jaw. "All the way from France."

"I didn't realize surrogacy was illegal over there," I added. "I thought Europe was a lot more liberal about issues like this."

"Apparently they're not more liberal about everything." Gideon slumped in his chair. "What a life—growing up in a vineyard? They sound superrich."

"*All* these people sound rich," I pointed out. "Most couples have already spent a fortune on medical treatments before they even consider surrogacy. And they know they're going to need lots of money for this—I found a financial estimate in the envelope."

I pulled out a list of expenses the intended parents would have to pay. "Look at this—almost twenty thousand dollars for the agency fee, twenty-five thousand for the surrogate's living expenses, another twenty-four hundred per month for the surrogate's miscellaneous costs, two thousand for the medical screening, a thousand to buy the surrogate maternity clothes, up to twenty-four thousand for medical expenses, a thousand for the psychological screening, five thousand for the attorney, four hundred for life insurance on the surrogate mother, money for a criminal background check, and the list goes on, depending on the surrogate's needs. I added it all up. At the very least, a couple who applies at this agency will be shelling out one hundred thousand dollars."

Gideon whistled. "Life insurance, huh? How much do you think they'll take out on you?"

I gaped at him, horrified he'd even notice that particular expense, then saw the twinkle in his eye.

"You are a bully." I tried to punch him—always a mistake, because his reflexes were lightning fast and his muscles like steel. He caught my fist and pulled me off my chair, then settled me firmly on his lap.

"That's better." Encircling me with one arm, he picked up the fee schedule with the other. "Did you figure out how much you'll earn?"

I nodded. "If the pregnancy is successful, it'll add up to more than sixty thousand dollars. And I can be frugal—I don't need maternity clothes; I still have things from when I was pregnant with Marilee. So I could keep most of the money from the clothing allowance."

He crinkled his nose as he read the fine print details I hadn't mentioned. "What's this support group payment?"

"They have a monthly support group for the pregnant women. When I get pregnant, I'll get a hundred bucks a month for going to the meeting."

"Are you sure you'll have time for that?"

"I'd make time, Gid. Imagine being paid a hundred dollars just for sitting in a room. And they'll give us money for health insurance we won't need because we're already covered through Uncle Sam. Tricare takes care of everything that's pregnancy-related."

Gideon picked up the contract and sucked at the inside of his cheek for a moment, his brows angled downward. "This is what you sign?"

"Yes."

"After you cut through the legalese, what are you required to do?"

"Cooperate, mostly. Natasha wrote in clauses to cover issues I feel strongly about."

"Such as—"

"Well, I agreed to have up to five separate IVF transfers of up to three embryos each, but I refused to participate in selective reduction. If I get pregnant with triplets, triplets is what I'll carry. I won't let them terminate one of the babies just because I might have to go on bed rest."

His brows drew together. "You said you wouldn't risk your health. And how are you going to get anything done if you have to go on bed rest?"

I pointed to the contract and gave my worried husband a sweet smile. "The intended parents will supply a housekeeper if I end up in bed, so I won't have to risk anything. Every detail has been spelled out, including the financial arrangements. At regular intervals I'll be paid from an escrow account the agency oversees. Natasha insists on that so no one can accuse the agency of selling babies. The couple will be paying me to carry their child, *not* to hand over a baby after nine months."

Gideon lowered the contract. "You've already made up your mind, haven't you?"

"About doing this, yes. I know I can do it, but I don't *want* to do it if you don't approve."

"And which couple would you want to work with? The people from Orlando or the French folks?"

"I don't know. Want to choose for me?"

He laughed. "Not so fast, baby girl. Some things you have to decide for yourself."

"But it's so hard! I mean, okay, couple number two is out, but couples one and three seem like they could be wonderful parents."

A look of inward intentness grew in my husband's eyes, then he reached out and tapped the last folder. The French couple's file.

I clapped. "I was hoping you'd pick them."

"Why?"

"I don't know. They just seem sort of . . . elegant. And they're older, so if they don't get a baby soon, they're probably not going to get one at all."

Gideon pressed a kiss to the nape of my neck. "Right now, I'm not so worried about other couples. I'm thinking you and I should spend some quality time together."

I giggled and slipped my arms around his neck, laughing as he picked me up and carried me to our bedroom.

A week away from Christmas, Mama Yanela's grocery looked as though it had been caught up in a festive frenzy. Jenna offered free samples of pastry and Cuban cider at the bakery counter while Mario arranged a row of suckling pigs belly up in the meat display case. Mama Isa wore a bright red Christmas sweater and gold spangles in her dark hair and Tumelo occasionally stepped out of the stockroom in an oversized Santa suit.

Thrilled to know I'd been approved by the Surrogacy Center, I was tempted to pull a length of garland from the window display, drape it over my shoulders, and dance to the Cuban-flavored Christmas songs playing over the intercom. But my happiness had little to do with the holiday and everything to do with the contract I had signed and returned to Natasha Bray.

Earlier that morning I had called Natasha to tell her that Gideon and I wanted to work with the French couple. She was delighted by the news, and promised to call the Amblours to arrange a meeting.

"I suppose they'll want to wait until after Christmas," I said.

"Oh no, they'll come right away," she answered. "They have their own jet, and I know they're eager to get started. What a Christmas present you're giving them!"

And what a gift they were giving us. No more financial worries, no more cheap practice keyboards for Marilee, no more stay-cations because we couldn't afford to go anywhere. With the money from this effort, we might finally find ourselves on firm financial footing.

And we could finally buy a house.

Obeying an impulse, I stopped at an office supply store and bought a package of file folders. Later in the afternoon, while Marilee played outside and Gideon worked on the base, I would open the package and lovingly label each of the folders: Living

Room. Dining Room. Master Bedroom. Marilee's Room. Bathrooms. Guest Room. Exteriors.

I knew we couldn't buy a house right away, but I figured I might as well use my waiting time to collect ideas, photos, and color samples. Over the next several months, I would look through catalogs and decorator magazines, ripping out photos of rooms that inspired me and filing them in the appropriate folder. I would spend Saturday at Home Depot and Lowe's, gathering up paint chips and free brochures. And I would watch the Home & Garden Television channel until I knew the lineup by heart.

By the time we signed the mortgage for our own home, I'd know the final color of every wall and the location of every piece of furniture, even if it didn't yet exist.

I had just finished showing Consuela Rodriguez where to find the *tostoneras,* or plantain smashers, when I returned to the register and found Amelia kneeling behind the counter.

I bent to help her search the floor. "Drop something?"

"It's nothing." Amelia wiped her red nose with a tissue, then stood and pointed down the aisle. "Did you help Consuela?"

I refused to be misdirected. "She's fine. What's wrong with you?"

"Nothing."

"Come on, now." I crossed my arms and glanced around to be sure no customers stood within hearing range. Amelia would never open up if a customer hovered nearby.

Her chin wobbled. "It's nothing I want to talk about."

"Last night Marilee mentioned that you'd been crying. She prayed for you." I lowered my voice. "Are you in trouble with your mother? Or did you and Mario have a fight?"

"I'm not fighting with anyone." Amelia swabbed her nose, then lifted her gaze to the ceiling and sighed. "And if you must know, I got my period yesterday."

I almost laughed. "And that upsets you?"

"It would upset anybody who'd been trying to get pregnant for almost two years." Her voice dropped to an intensely quiet note.

"I keep praying, and every month I think the Lord has answered my prayer, but then I get my period and faith seems to be nothing more than a cruel joke."

I stared, shocked speechless. If Amelia could call prayer a cruel joke, she was more discouraged than I'd ever been. I swallowed and tried to think of something to say. "Amelia, I'm so sorry. I knew you didn't have kids and I kinda thought you might be trying to have them, but I didn't realize—"

"I can't talk about it now." She sidled past me and eased out of the checkout stand. "Excuse me, but I need to get some fresh air."

I caught her hand before she could get away. "Why didn't you say anything before this?"

"Like what?" She stopped and met my gaze, her eyes brimming with fresh tears. "I thought getting pregnant would be easy. I wanted to surprise everyone with a big announcement at one of Mama's dinners. I kept hoping it would happen one month, then the next, then the next, and now we've been trying so long I'm almost certain it's not going to happen at all."

I opened my mouth and then clamped it shut, abruptly aware that I probably wasn't the best person to comfort my cousin. For the past few days I'd been babbling about how I got pregnant so easily that carrying another woman's child would be the simplest thing on earth. I'd been inadvertently rubbing salt into Amelia's wound.

"I feel terrible." Reluctantly, I slid my gaze into hers. "I'm so sorry. I didn't realize."

"How could you? Infertility isn't the sort of thing people carry on about."

Ouch. I'd been bragging about my fertility over the last few days.

She turned and strode toward the back of the store, shoulders slumping beneath the weight of unmet expectations.

I braced my hands on the counter and watched her go. We argued occasionally and didn't always get along, but except for

Gideon, Amelia was my closest friend. How could I have been so blind to her pain and struggle over the past few months? Because I'd been too focused on my own plans, that's how. My mom would have called it self-centeredness, and she'd have been right.

A thought occurred to me—one that would never have entered my head if not for my investigation into surrogacy: could I carry a child for Amelia? I could have a baby for her, one member of the family doing something amazing for another. But while that might be a loving gesture, it wouldn't meet my family's financial needs or help our dreams come true. And the prospect of a substantial payday was why I'd investigated surrogacy in the first place.

Besides, Amelia would have mentioned something if she wanted me to consider carrying a baby for her. After all, she'd heard me talking about surrogacy, so it would have been easy for her to bring up the subject. She hadn't, so her silence probably meant she didn't want to have a baby via gestational carrier. She wanted to feel a baby growing under her skin. She wanted to walk around in maternity clothes and beam when people asked about her due date. She wanted the entire experience, and I couldn't blame her. What woman didn't?

So having a baby for her . . . was unfortunately out of the question.

Chapter Five

On Friday, December 21, Gideon and I took Marilee to school and then drove across the bay to the Surrogacy Center. We were supposed to arrive at ten, but Gideon and I pulled into the parking lot a few minutes early. The blond receptionist ushered us into a small conference room and asked if we wanted coffee, but I was too jittery to even think about ingesting caffeine. We sat on one side of a rectangular conference table, and Gideon, who usually seemed preternaturally calm, leaned back in his chair and jiggled his legs—first up and down in a frantic rhythm, then from left to right like a hyperactive adolescent.

I placed my hand on his thigh to calm him, then wondered if his nervousness didn't stem from something other than this interview. He never discussed his work with me, but for all I knew he might soon be leaving to rescue some American hostage being held in a foreign embassy.

I gave him a narrow-eyed look, and got a slow blink in response. "What?"

"Nothing," I answered, shaking off the vague sense of foreboding. "If you're okay, I'm okay."

"I'm okay." He nodded to reinforce the point, then went back to jiggling his legs. I pressed my lips together, wondering if he was being hyperactive or figuring how much ammo he had to pack for his team's next mission.

My thoughtful husband had taken the day off to be with me, but I had the feeling he'd rather be training with his unit.

When the conference room door opened again, I squeezed his knee as my heart leapt into the back of my throat. Natasha led the way into the room, followed by the elegant couple we'd seen in the photograph. Damien and Simone Amblour appeared even more perfect in person, but Damien had shaved his beard, leaving his face round and solid. His complexion was tanned and leathery, but hers as pale as blank newsprint. She looked a bit older than she had in the photo, and I suspected that she'd experienced a sleepless night. Maybe they were as uneasy as we were.

"Amanda and Gideon Lisandra"—Natasha gestured to us—"I'd like you to meet Damien and Simone Amblour. Damien and Simone are the couple whose file you selected, Mandy."

As if I needed reminding.

Gideon and I stood and extended our hands across the table. "So nice to meet you both," I said. "Welcome to Tampa Bay."

Simone and Damien shook our hands, smiled a welcome, and sat opposite us. Like a judge, Natasha sat at the head of the table with a stack of printed documents at her right hand. "These," she said, pressing her palm to the mountain of paperwork, "are for later. Right now I want to give you two couples a chance to get to know one another."

Since no one else seemed inclined to break the ice, I spoke up. "First of all," I said, a blush heating my cheeks, "I want to admit how nervous I am. I don't know why, but I feel like I'm on trial or something."

"Me too." Simone pressed her hand to her chest and laughed. "Thank you for being honest, but please do not feel anxious. We are not here to judge you. We want to know you better, but most of all, we want you to know how grateful we are. We have waited so long for a child; we have made so many attempts and tried so many things. . . ."

Her voice trailed away, but her husband picked up her thought. "It is most important to our family that we have a child—boy or girl, it does not matter. Our vineyard is our life's work, and our child will inherit a historic estate—the Domaine de Amblour is famous for its hospitality and beauty, and our wine has been lauded for generations. We are eager for our child to continue our work and claim the heritage that will rightfully be his."

Gideon and I nodded as if we understood, but how could we? I knew practically nothing about my family history, and Gideon's people had been living in Cuba only two generations before. As citizens of a country only two and a quarter centuries old, how were we supposed to relate to Damien's talk of a multigenerational heritage?

I caught Gideon's eye and smiled, guessing at his thoughts. As a military family, we'd be lucky if we managed to spend three years in the same city.

"Your home sounds beautiful." I crossed my arms. "I've never been to France, but I've seen movies. If it's anything like the country in *Under the Tuscan Sun*—"

"Tuscany is Italy," Simone corrected, her voice gentle. "But I daresay you would find many areas that appear similar. If you have seen any vineyard, you would understand what our home is like. From a distance, the fields look as though they have been stitched with neat rows of vines, plotted with extreme care and patience."

I smiled at her artistic description and hoped she didn't think I was a complete ignoramus. I'd never been to Tuscany or France, so how was I supposed to know which was which?

Damien shifted in his seat. "You have other children?"

Polite of him to ask, since I knew he'd studied my folder and had to know I had a daughter. "We have a four-year-old, Marilee. She's beautiful." I fumbled in my purse, then pulled out my phone and pulled up a picture. Simone and Damien leaned across the table to look at it, then nodded in appreciation.

"Lovely," Simone said. "She looks healthy and strong."

"She is." I smiled at the photo, then dropped my phone back into my bag. "She's perfect in every way."

"Simone, Damien"—Natasha turned to face them—"why don't you tell Mandy about some of the requests you wanted to ask of your gestational carrier."

Simone turned to her husband, who took the lead. "We believe in healthy living," he said, the parentheses around his mouth settling into a look of firm resolve. "So we hope you don't smoke."

"I don't," I answered, grateful to get at least one answer right. "And neither does Gideon. I don't drink, either."

Damien's mouth curved in a rueful smile. "As a vintner, I am sorry to hear that."

"But happy for the baby," Simone added, laugh lines radiating from the corners of her blue eyes. "I know the risks, and I am glad you are willing to be careful."

"I had an easy pregnancy with Marilee," I said, trying to put them at ease. "No hypertension, nothing like that. Not even much weight gain, really. Suddenly it was time for her to be born, and there she was. I think I was lucky, but my mom says my hips were designed for having babies. They're nice and roomy."

The tip of Simone's nose went pink as she released a polite laugh. "I am glad to hear it. We want things to be easy for you."

"I assume you'll want the usual battery of tests," Natasha said, pulling a page from an orange folder. "The test for Downs at thirteen weeks, amnio at twenty—"

"We do not care about tests," Simone interrupted, a thread of alarm in her voice as she straightened in her chair. "They do not matter. If the child has Downs, we would not want to terminate the pregnancy. We do not want to risk the baby's health with amniocentesis, nor do we want to do anything to inconvenience Amanda."

I glanced at Gideon, who had lifted his brows in pleased surprise.

Simone settled back in her chair, lowering her gaze, and her husband reached for her hand. Something passed between them, something I didn't understand, but Natasha had clearly touched a nerve.

"All right," she said, shoving the schedule of tests aside. "We won't require testing at any point. Is that agreeable to you, Amanda?"

Always willing to steer clear of needles, I nodded. "No problem here."

"Very well, then."

We sat for a moment in a quiet so thick the only sound was Gideon's rhythmically squeaking chair, then Simone tapped the table with her long nails and looked at me. "There is something else—I wondered if we might ask a favor?"

"Sure," I said.

"At the appropriate point in the pregnancy, if I emailed you a recording—or sent a tape, whatever is easiest—could you play it for the baby every night? I think it is important for a fetus to hear its mother's voice, especially since this baby will be surrounded by French speakers."

I blinked, then smiled as understanding dawned. She wanted me to hold headphones or a tape player up to my belly. "I could do that. As soon as we know the baby has ears."

Damien propped his arm on the back of his wife's chair. "Our child will probably not learn English until he or she goes to school."

"I don't suppose"—Gideon spoke up for the first time—"you'd consider teaching him Spanish?"

The Amblours looked at each other, clearly baffled, while I kicked my husband's shinbone. "You'll have to excuse him." I forced a smile. "My husband is *cubano,* so he was making a little joke."

"Oh." Simone pursed her lips and nodded slightly. "I see."

"Any other questions or concerns?" Natasha looked from one side of the table to the other. "If not, we have paperwork to sign.

Will you please look over these pages, initial each at the bottom, and sign on the last page. When you've completed one set, pass them across the table so the other couple can do the same thing. Gideon, the Amblours' contract will be with your wife, but you may sign as a witness. You'll see the proper spot on the final page."

I sat up straighter and took the pages Natasha offered me. Gideon and I had already studied the contract, so it held no surprises. In short, I was to do everything necessary to facilitate the success of the embryo transfer. After a positive pregnancy test I was to do everything necessary to ensure a healthy baby and successful delivery. I would not be asked to participate in selective termination of any fetus unless the pregnancy directly threatened my health.

For my efforts to help the couple achieve a successful pregnancy, I would be paid two hundred dollars a month, beginning today and continuing until the baby's delivery. I would also receive one hundred dollars each time I attended a monthly surrogate support group.

Once my doctor confirmed a fetal heartbeat, I would receive twenty-four hundred dollars per month until the baby's birth, and at the beginning of the second trimester I would receive one thousand dollars to cover the purchase of maternity clothing. If at any point my doctor prescribed total bed rest, the Amblours would hire a housekeeper for my family and compensate me for my lost wages at the grocery. In addition, the Amblours would purchase a one-year term life insurance policy—in the unlikely event something went fatally wrong, Gideon and Marilee would receive one hundred thousand dollars.

When we had signed all the documents, Natasha handed me an envelope containing my first check—two hundred dollars to cover parking, mileage, meals, and anything else I might spend as I went about the work of getting pregnant with the Amblours' baby.

"All right, then." Natasha piled the copies of the contract into a neat stack, then smiled at us. "Simone, I understand you are going to see a reproductive endocrinologist here about egg retrieval, correct? And, Mandy, when the time is right the RE will put you on Lupron to prepare your uterus for the transfer. At this stage of the procedure, I step out of the way and let the doctors manage the tricky work of making sure the egg donor and recipient get their cycles synchronized. Any questions about anything we've discussed?"

Relieved to have come to a bridge and successfully journeyed over, I looked across the table at the woman who still seemed terribly tense. I couldn't imagine why she was jittery—after all, she and her husband had money, power, position, a private jet, and a potential surrogate, so what could she possibly lack?

A baby, of course. Until she held her little one in her arms, she would probably worry about every detail.

An inner voice warned me not to get too close, but still my heart went out to her. I had never yearned desperately for a baby, but I had once yearned for Gideon. I could remember being completely convinced that I would never know true happiness unless I had his love.

Simone Amblour was no love-starved romantic, but she was a woman. And something told me that we women loved, hated, and desired with an intensity many men would never experience.

While I waited to hear from the reproductive endocrinologist about how I should begin preparing for the embryo transfer, holiday festivities continued at the grocery. Three days before Christmas, a busload of residents from a retirement center pulled into the parking lot. *"Ay, caramba,"* Mario muttered loud enough for me to hear. *"Me olvidé de las personas mayores."*

He hurried to attend to something behind the butcher counter while I watched the old folks step from the small bus, their careful movements reminding me of the elderly Carlos and Yaritza Fernandez.

"What's this about?" I asked as Mama Isa came over to check out the new arrivals. "We have tourists now?"

She nodded, her eyes intent on her potential customers. "The activities director promised to bring twenty-four people, and it looks like they all made it. Mario and Jenna prepared box lunches of a traditional Cuban Christmas dinner, so the old folks are coming to visit the grocery, then they're taking their boxes and eating at the park across the highway. It won't be exactly traditional, but at least it'll be something different for them."

Mama Isa sashayed toward the door while I watched the seniors gather in the parking lot. Their faces shone with expectation, and I could only hope our little shop didn't disappoint. What memorable gems did they expect to find in a Cuban grocery?

A moment later Mama Isa pushed the front door open and welcomed them in a cheerful voice. "*¡Hola, bienvenido!*" She nodded toward a tall gentleman who inched forward with small, cautious steps. "*¿Cómo está, señor?*"

"No speak-o Spanish-o," he said, offering his arm to one of the women following him. "English only."

"Then welcome to our grocery." Mama Isa stepped back so he could enter. "If you have any questions, don't hesitate to ask."

A moment later Amelia came out of the office and joined me at the register, but I hadn't exactly been bombarded with folks rushing to purchase Goya beans, packaged cockles, or suckling pigs.

"They've already paid for the box lunches," Amelia told me, looking at an old man who kept smiling at her. "So unless they buy something else . . ."

I folded my arms and watched a woman sniff a can of coconut milk. "Looks like they're more interested in looking than buying."

"What do you think?" Amelia smiled at me as she leaned against the counter. "Will we be riding a tourist bus one day?"

I shrugged. "We'll be lucky to live so long."

Amelia straightened as a woman plucked something from a

nearby vegetable bin and lifted it into the air. "What's this thing?" she yelled. "It says *boniato—*"

Amelia hurried to the woman's side. "Ma'am, that's a sweet potato."

"Well, why didn't you say so?" The woman dropped it back into the bin and turned toward the door. "I can't read any of the signs in this place. What time is lunch, anyway?"

I turned toward the cash register, hoping one of them would at least buy a candle or a bag of plantain chips, but kilt-clad Claude Newton was the only customer coming toward the checkout stand. He dropped a pack of gum onto the counter and grinned at the seniors around him. "They should come hang out with my posse," he said, winking as I rang him up. "Maybe they'd feel a few years younger."

After a few minutes the seniors' activities director, a young woman in navy slacks and a white blouse, walked to the center of the store, blew a whistle, and announced that her group should head toward the front door. Claude shuffled out with them, but instead of boarding the bus, he hopped on his bicycle and peddled off to wherever he hid when he wasn't lounging around with the nudists.

The driver of the seniors cranked the engine as the last strains of "¡Feliz Navidad!" faded from the radio, then the announcer's voice cut in. Something in the man's tone snagged my attention, and when I heard the words "jetliner" and "terrorist," my heart congealed into a small lump of dread.

"Two Florida men were arrested today," the announcer said, "for allegedly attempting to carry Tasers aboard an American Airlines jet leaving Tampa International Airport. No one was injured during the scuffle at the security checkpoint, but the men screamed out threats as they were led away, increasing fears and tension during this busy holiday season."

I looked out the window as my heart began to thump almost painfully in my chest. Fools like those two men were going to get my husband injured or killed in some stupid international incident. I hated worrying about Gideon, but I simply couldn't bear it if he were hurt or disabled. The military was pretty good about taking care of its own, but what would become of our dreams if Gideon spent the rest of his life in a wheelchair or a hospital bed?

A darker prospect loomed as well, but I couldn't think about that. Losing Gideon would be horrible for me, but even worse for our daughter. So I refused to consider the possibility.

I watched the young activities director hold out her hand and herd the remaining senior adults onto the bus. Those people had enjoyed a long life, but with crazy people making threats every week, was my generation going to be able to do the same? How could I help my daughter thrive in a world where the man seated next to her on a plane might be determined to kill everyone on board? Or when the next piece of mail she opened might be filled with some variety of powdered poison? Gideon and his men were risking their lives to keep our country safe, but they were only a few men, and the world brimmed with lunatics. . . .

The little bus had just pulled out of the parking lot when angry voices shattered the sudden stillness in the store. After checking to be sure none of the seniors lingered in the aisles, I left the checkout stand and walked toward the back. I found Amelia and Mario standing in the stockroom, their faces tight with frustration.

"You can't blame me," Mario yelled, apparently not caring that they were no longer alone. "It's not my fault you're not pregnant." He followed with a stream of Spanish so intense I couldn't catch a word.

Anger blossomed in Amelia's taut face. "Oh, yeah? Maybe it *is* your fault." She switched to Spanish, too, and spoke so precisely, so sharply, that I caught something about staying out too late and leaving nothing for her.

"Maybe I should find a woman who sees me as a man and not a stud service." Maybe Mario spoke in Spanish; maybe English, I don't know. But his meaning would have been clear in any language.

Knowing I could be setting myself up for a full dose of Cuban fury, I stepped between them and held up my hands. "Hey, guys." I looked from Amelia to Mario. "Anything you want to talk about . . . outside?"

Amelia turned away, her lower lip quivering, while Mario stormed out the back door without even looking at his wife. I watched him go, then moved to comfort my cousin.

"Hey." I squeezed her shoulder. "Things are gonna be okay."

She shook her head. "I don't see how they can be. I love Mario, honestly I do, but sometimes he can be so bullheaded."

"So—this is about getting pregnant, right?"

She laughed hoarsely. "I guess it's no longer a secret, huh? Mario yelled it out for the entire world to hear."

"No one heard. The store is pretty much empty now. Your mama went outside to say good-bye to the old folks."

"Then we were lucky, because these days Mario isn't thinking before he speaks." Amelia looked up, her eyes damp with pain. "Mama knows about our problem, but I don't want her to hear us arguing. The frustrating thing is we both want a kid, but all this trying and waiting is driving us nuts."

"Maybe you two need to relax. Go on a vacation, take a second honeymoon. Have fun and don't even think about getting pregnant."

Amelia gave me a sour smile. "Like we've never heard that before. 'Relax,' Mama says, 'and it'll happen. Wait for God to answer.' Well, we've tried relaxing, and it hasn't happened. We've tried taking my temperature every morning and Mario's been wearing baggy underwear, which he despises. I've even asked Yaritza about old wives' tales. I've prayed for a baby until I feel like I'm just repeating useless phrases, and I've even been tempted to get one of those talisman fertility candles. . . ."

"Don't waste your money on superstitious junk," I whispered. "And I know God hears your prayers. He wouldn't be God if he didn't, right?"

"Mama says if I feel like I was meant to be a mother, he's probably not saying *no*. He might be saying *wait*. But wait for *what*?" Amelia swiped tears from her face, then crossed her arms and gazed into private space. "I've been waiting a long time. I'm twenty-seven, and I'm not getting any younger. I want to have kids while I still have enough energy to chase after them." She sniffed when the bells on the front door jingled, then jerked her thumb toward the register. "You should get back in there."

"That was probably your mother coming in." I took a step closer and lowered my voice. "Have you thought about investigating other options? There's in vitro fertilization and artificial insemination. You should talk to your doctor about other ways to have a baby."

"Mario's old-fashioned." Amelia pulled a tissue from her jeans pocket, then blew her nose. "He will barely talk about this, and he won't admit that any part of it could be his fault. If the doctor asks him to—" She shuddered. "Never mind. I think he'd cut off his nose before he'd go in for an exam. And those other things you mentioned are expensive. Our insurance would never cover those kinds of elective procedures."

The bells above the front door jangled again, and this time Amelia stepped away. "I've gotta get some cartons unpacked. Don't mind me. There's nothing you can do, anyway. And please don't say anything about this to Gideon. Mario would die if he thought the men in the family knew he couldn't get me pregnant."

Amelia's heavy sorrow seemed to spread until it crossed the space between us and mingled with my own anxiety about a terror-filled future. During that awful moment, I wondered if darkness might manage to erase all the light in the world.

Chapter Six

Christmas finally arrived, complete with a chilly breeze that blew down from Canada and forced us to haul our sweaters out of storage. I think my cardigans were grateful to come out of the closet, and Marilee absolutely loved the fuzzy red sweater I bought her for Christmas and allowed her to open early. The pullover was a little big on her, but it had a treble clef embroidered on one side and a bass clef on the other, so she rolled up the ribbed cuffs and promised that it fit perfectly.

Gordon and Yanela had brought many traditions with them from Cuba, but their love for the Catholic church's nativity service topped the list. Out of respect for the elders, the entire family came together every Christmas Eve to celebrate the Misa del Gallo, or Mass of the Rooster, at St. Joseph's Church. As usual, we paused in Mama Isa's living room so Yanela could tell Marilee why midnight Mass was named for a barnyard bird. "The only time the rooster crowed at midnight," she said, wagging her finger as she smiled at Marilee, "was when the Baby Jesus was born."

My mom had driven down from The Villages to spend the holiday with us, so she accompanied us on our traditional visit to church and to Mama Isa's house afterward. Mom stayed in the pew during the service, her Protestant conscience unable to sanction taking Communion from a Catholic priest, but I had come to adore the beauty of the service and figured I could partake of the Lord's Supper with any group of believers that would let me.

After Mass, we climbed into our respective vehicles and drove to Mama Isa's house, a modest home only a block from the grocery. The house had originally been constructed with concrete block and jalousie windows, a style typical of old Florida, but over the years Isa and Jorge had added Latin touches. A knee-high concrete block fence, topped by white wrought iron and bright Christmas lights, enclosed the property, and Jorge had added a front porch supported by a row of square columns linked by arches. The entire house had been enclosed in pale orange stucco, and though a riotous thicket of purple bougainvillea grew by the side fence, over the years Jorge had turned the front lawn into a concrete parking lot.

Once when I asked Mama Isa if she missed seeing grass outside the window, she responded with a shrug. "Grass I have to cut and water, but concrete never complains."

My mom had been horrified the first time she saw the stone forms spread over the lawn like a patchwork quilt. Personally, I had grown fond of the multisectioned slab—in it I could trace the family's past, from the original driveway at the left side of the house, the narrow two-strip drive that came later, the double parking pad installed when Amelia bought her first car, and finally the "everything but two flower beds" paving Jorge had surrendered to in the end. My neighbors in Town 'n' Country would stage a revolt if Gideon and I were to substitute concrete for landscaping, but no one on St. Louis Street dared rebuke Mama Isa.

As the cold wind quickened our steps and the moon played peek-a-boo in the clouds, Gideon carried Marilee into the house. I followed with our gifts and my mom.

After a delicious Christmas dinner and the subsequent cleanup, all of us went in search of places to sleep for a few hours. Marilee had nodded off during dessert, so Gideon carried her into one of Mama Isa's guest rooms and Mom and I followed. Gideon dozed in an overstuffed chair while Mom, Marilee, and I lay down on the bed, covered with only a thin quilt. I knew Yanela and Gordon would sleep in the master bedroom, while Amelia and Mario would nap in the living room. Tumelo and Elaine actually went home to sleep, but they only lived a few blocks away. I never knew if or where Mama Isa and Jorge slept. They were always awake when I went to bed and awake when I woke up.

We didn't need a rooster to wake us at sunrise on Christmas morning; we had Marilee. She ran from room to room, banging on doors and announcing that Santa had come once again. I emerged from the guest room with rumpled hair and bleary eyes, but the house shone with bright lights and glowing candles. Fragrant pastries and fresh-brewed coffee beckoned us to the kitchen, where Mama Isa stood in her holiday apron, her eyes bright and her cheeks flushed.

Maybe, I mused, she never slept at all on those holiday nights. Or maybe she was energized by the Spirit of the holiday.

After filling a plate with the bounties of Mama Isa's breakfast buffet, I tried to prepare Mom for the traditional Lisandra gift exchange. The extended family rarely gave expensive presents—tradition dictated that we draw names, then find something inexpensive, funny, or especially appropriate for the recipient.

With our plates in hand, we moved into the living room and settled on the sofa or pulled kitchen chairs into a circle near the Christmas tree. Tumelo, Gideon's father, began the exchange by calling my name and asking me to open my gift—a *tostonera,* as it turned out, a hinged wooden device used for flattening plantain chunks so they could be deep fried. I knew what a *tostonera* was, of course, since we sold them in the grocery, but I played dumb and wondered aloud if the gadget was some sort of musical instrument. I tried flapping the device as if it were a castanet, but my efforts only elicited howls of laughter from Gideon's mother, Elaine, who had probably been gifted with a *tostonera* in her younger days.

Her laughter made me smile. Elaine and I had never been close, and not even five years of marriage to her son had managed to crack the ice between us. I had always sensed that she didn't think I was good enough for Gideon, and while that might be true, Gideon didn't seem to care that he'd married beneath his mother's standards.

I had drawn Mama Isa's name, and spent days racking my brain for the perfect present. I finally found a garlic slicer in a kitchen store—and since Cuban chicken calls for loads of garlic, I thought she'd appreciate it. The gift wouldn't be particularly funny, but if anyone could put a garlic slicer to good use, she could.

After opening my gift, Mama Isa spent a full minute staring at the shiny silver tube. *"¿Qué es?"* she finally whispered to Jorge. *"¿Puedo ver a través de él?"*

"*Esto es un* garlic slicer," I hurried to explain. "You put a clove in the bottom part, snap the two sections together, and turn. Sliced garlic comes out the other end."

She gave me a sweet, tolerant smile. "*Muchas gracias,* Amanda."

The other women asked to see it, probably out of sheer politeness, and I sat, my cheeks flaming, as Gordon passed a wrapped present to Mario.

I snuggled closer to my husband as Mario made a big fuss over the beautiful package Gordon had given him. The old man beamed, a twinkle in his eye, and the older folks snickered when Mario opened the box and pulled out a pair of candy cane boxer shorts. Mario tried to smile, but a flush colored his face. Beside him, Amelia's chin quivered and she lowered her gaze.

My heart twisted for both of them. Grandpa Gordon wouldn't have known about their infertility; he had undoubtedly bought the boxers as a gag gift. Unfortunately, those randy shorts were the last thing Mario wanted to exhibit in front of the family.

"Gideon." I nudged him. "Quick, take your present to Yanela."

Bless my husband for not asking why. As Mario stuffed the shorts back in the box, Gideon leapt up and with great fanfare presented a gift to his grandmother—all in an effort to draw attention away from the miserable couple next to us.

"For you, beautiful Abuela"—Gideon fell on one knee in an exaggerated display of gallantry—"because without you, none of us would be here."

Smiling, the old woman absently touched the mound of beautiful black and silver hair piled on the back of her head, then accepted the box—another gift I had chosen after days of frustrated shopping. With glacial slowness she unwrapped the paper, smoothed out the wrinkles, and finally removed the lid.

"Oh!" She lifted the hair ornament I'd ordered from an online site, then her gaze slid around the circle and met mine. *"Que hermosa."*

I'd bought her a *temblique,* an ornate hair ornament typically worn by women in Panama. I had no idea whether Cuban women ever wore such things, but since Latin American culture pervaded the Caribbean, I hoped she'd at least know what to do with it.

Yanela murmured something to her husband, then smiled at me again. "I wore one of these at my wedding." She pressed the delicate, feathery ornament to her heart. "Beautiful. *Muchas gracias, mi querida niña.*"

As Yaritza and the other women admired the *temblique,* Mom jabbed her bony elbow into my ribs. "What is that feathery thing? It looks like something you'd sew on an overdecorated nightgown."

I thought about ignoring her, but didn't want to be rude. "It's an ornament," I whispered, watching Jorge deliver a gift to Amelia. "You wear it in your hair."

"Awfully fussy, isn't it?"

"It's *supposed* to be a little over the top."

My mom harrumphed. "Gaudy is more like it. I can't imagine ever wearing anything like that."

"No one's asking you to, are they?"

Why did Mom have to comment on everything, and why did her opinions have to be right? I sighed and slipped my arm around Marilee, then caught Gideon's sympathetic gaze.

While I celebrated the holidays with my mom and Gideon's family, Simone and Damien observed Christmas at home in France. Natasha called to explain that the couple had gone home for the holiday, but were due to return to Florida the next week. Because Simone had to be involved in all the steps to harvest eggs for in vitro fertilization, they'd probably rent a hotel suite for as long as it took to establish a pregnancy.

"Apparently the grape harvest is finished so this is a good time for them to be away," Natasha told me after setting the date for my first appointment with the reproductive endocrinologist. "They've had bad luck in previous situations, so they're hoping everything will work out this time."

The first Monday after Christmas, when most of the world went back to business as usual, Gideon and I went to see Dr. Harvey Forrester, the RE who would be taking care of me and Simone as we prepared for the embryo transfer. My husband and I sat in the doctor's office and listened to his explanation of the procedure, then shook our heads when he asked if we had any questions.

When the doctor looked down to write something on my chart, Gideon leaned closer. "If you need a daily shot in the backside," he whispered, a teasing note in his voice, "I don't think I'll mind watching."

"Down, boy," I countered, patting his arm. "The doctor said we can't fool around until *after* we get a positive pregnancy test."

I had lowered my voice, but apparently I didn't lower it enough.

"Speaking of pregnancy tests"—Dr. Forrester looked up and nodded at the nurse waiting nearby—"we have to draw blood for the preprocedure beta test. We have to make absolutely sure you're not pregnant before you begin the hormone injections."

While the nurse tied a rubber strip around my upper arm, Gideon stood and walked to the wall, where he pretended to study diagrams of fetal development. A memory flickered through my mind—he had also turned away from the sight of a needle when I went into the hospital to have Marilee. Could my warrior husband be nervous about needles?

"All finished." The nurse capped the blood-filled vial and carried it toward the doorway. "This will only take a few minutes."

I held a cotton ball on the tiny spot where the syringe had broken my skin. "Why couldn't I have peed in a cup?"

"Because urine tests aren't nearly as reliable as blood tests," the doctor said. "But let's go ahead and talk while we're waiting for confirmation."

I shot Gideon a questioning look as he sat again, but he kept his gaze on the doctor.

"I'm giving you prescriptions for an estrogen patch, progesterone cream, birth control pills, and Lupron," Dr. Forrester said, "as well as a handy little calendar to help you remember when to start and stop each. You'll take Lupron for the first seventeen days, birth control pills for the first four, then on the ninth day you'll begin to wear the estrogen patch, which you'll use for the rest of the month. On the eighteenth day we add progesterone to the mix to stimulate the lining of your uterus."

I squeezed Gideon's hand. "Sounds complicated."

"It'll all make sense when you look at the calendar." Forrester's gaze darted toward Gideon. "You, sir, might have to help your wife, at least in the beginning. She'll need the Lupron shot in her tummy twice a day. Do you think you can handle that?"

"Stab a needle into her *stomach*?" My brave husband, who had rappelled from helicopters, climbed mountains, and seen countless battle injuries, went slightly green. "I'm not sure I can do that."

"Just pretend I'm one of the guys in your unit," I suggested, knowing he had handled far more dangerous things than needles. "If you can use a thorn to stitch up Snake's arm, you can stick me with a tiny needle."

His square jaw tensed. "Snake is not my *wife.* Somehow it seems different when it's you."

"Remember what you always tell your men," I reminded him. "You don't have to like it, you just have to *do* it."

The doctor grinned and held up a thin syringe. "The needle's not big. But the shot is important because we need to stop your wife's current cycle in order to sync her hormones with the egg donor's. Once we get you two on the same page, so to speak, we can proceed with the embryo transfer."

Dr. Forrester transferred his gaze to me. "As we shut down your current cycle, you may experience symptoms of menopause—maybe a few hot flashes and night sweats."

I made a face. "No one mentioned that."

Forrester chuckled. "Don't worry, it won't last nearly as long as actual menopause. After the donor's eggs are harvested, we'll give you estrogen so you'll bounce back to normal in no time. We'll restart your reproductive engine, as it were."

"Doctor?" The nurse thrust her head into the room. "That test was negative."

"Not pregnant." Forrester smiled at me. "Very good. We have a green light to proceed."

The doctor peeled a protective wrapping from another syringe, thrust it into a small bottle, pulled back on the plunger, and filled it with a small amount of clear liquid. After squirting a tiny bit through the needle, he extended it toward Gideon and me. "Which one of you wants to do the honors?"

I blanched. "Can't you do the first injection?"

"I'd really like to be sure you can handle it." Forrester lifted a brow. "So? What do you say?"

I turned to Gideon and gave him my best helpless-female expression. But for the first time in my life, my husband didn't melt.

"Uh-uh." He shook his head. "You have to learn how to do it. I may not be with you every day."

I pressed my lips together, hating to admit he had a point. If he went out on a mission, I would have no one to administer the shot.

For an instant I considered asking Amelia to do it, then I remembered that I'd be rubbing more salt in her wounds.

"Oh, give me the stupid thing." I took the syringe from the doctor, lifted the hem of my blouse, and thrust the thin needle into the small roll of fat at my belly.

Gideon looked away, his hand tightening on the chair's armrest. "Is it over?"

Dr. Forrester laughed. "It's over. She passed with flying colors." He slanted a brow in my direction. "How did this tough guy handle the birth of your daughter?"

"He stood by my head," I answered, grinning. "So he wouldn't have to look at anything but my face."

"You didn't have to bring that up." Gideon gave me a weak smile. "But I think I proved my point. You can do lots of things without me."

"That's what *you* think."

"We'll want you to come into the office once a week or so for the next month," the doctor said, propping his elbows on his desk, "for blood work and an ultrasound to make sure a sufficient endometrial lining is developing. But you're young and healthy—I don't foresee any problems."

I exhaled in relief. "That's good to hear."

"Let me get some information for you"—Dr. Forrester moved toward the door—"and we'll get you on your way. Be back in a moment."

Gideon and I sat in silence, then he leaned toward me and wrapped his arm around my shoulders. "You didn't mention the needles when you were trying to convince me this would be a good idea." He pressed a kiss to my forehead. "But I love you, beautiful girl, and I think what you're doing is a generous and incredible thing. Trouble is, thinking of your generosity and incredibleness makes me want you—"

"You're gonna have to want me from afar for a while." I tapped the end of his nose, then gave him a peck on the cheek. "You're gonna have to discipline yourself—take a cold shower, play with Marilee, or jog around the block. You know what you're always telling me—good things usually hurt."

"Whaddya know—I was right."

I shifted to look directly at him. "I never knew you got queasy around needles. How is that even possible?"

He gave me a rueful smile, then shrugged. "I don't care if it's one of my men getting stitched up or whatever. But when it's a woman . . . I think it brings back all those memories of my sister. I saw enough needles back then—"

To last a lifetime. He didn't have to finish his thought; I saw it in his eyes. I squeezed his hand, understanding and loving him all the more.

Gideon didn't often talk about the sister who'd died from leukemia at sixteen, but her life and death had profoundly affected him. He'd been her older brother and he had tried so hard to help her, but he couldn't save her. And wasn't that what older brothers were supposed to do?

He never said as much, but I think that feeling of helplessness was the goad motivating him to become an elite warrior. Wherever he met evil, whether on the battlefield or in a dark urban alley, as a special operator he could use his wits and skills to defeat those who would terrorize and murder innocent people.

Gid released me, then slid his hands into his pockets and strolled over to revisit the fetal diagrams on the wall. When the doctor returned, he gave me a plastic bag, wished us well, and sent us on our way.

On the drive home, I opened the bag and found brochures, prescriptions, a few samples, and a small laminated calendar on which the days of the month were marked with symbols representing the specific hormone or drug I was supposed to take. After a month of Lupron injections and days of birth control pills, estrogen patches, and/or progesterone, I would report to the fertility center for the embryo transfer.

According to what I'd been told, Simone would be following a laminated calendar of her own, taking hormones to make her produce more egg-containing follicles than usual. If all went well, once the doctor had harvested as many mature eggs as possible from Simone, those eggs would be fertilized with Damien's sperm. The developing embryos would be watched for five days, and the best-developed embryos—*blastocysts,* they were called at that stage—would be transferred from a lab container into my uterus. After nine days, I would report to the doctor's office to have blood taken for another beta pregnancy test. If the embryo had safely implanted, I'd be officially pregnant.

And Gideon's stint of self-denial would be over.

Chapter Seven

The first month of the new year passed in a blur of needles, prescriptions, and calendar watching. I went about my usual schedule, caring for Marilee and working at the grocery, but I dreamed of syringes at night and picked at my fingernails during the day. By the end of January, I had bruises on my belly and bald fingertips.

Though I was fairly obsessed with fertility, I couldn't help worrying about Gideon. The papers were full of news about unrest in the world—tribal warfare in Kenya, bombings in Iraq, the Taliban wreaking havoc in Afghanistan. I tried not to read the papers, but those headlines drew me the way a fire truck attracts a crowd. Any one of those stories could be about Gideon's next mission and the place where he would next risk his life, and something in me had to understand what was going on.

For the next few weeks I watched Gideon with narrowed eyes, convinced that at any moment he and his duffel bag would disappear because he had to go save the world. But though he did spend more time than usual at MacDill, he didn't go anywhere else.

As we moved into February, I kept my cell phone with me, hoping to hear that we were ready for the embryo transfer. But though I expected to hear from Dr. Forrester or his nurse, they weren't the person who finally called.

"Amanda?"

For a moment I struggled to place the throaty voice, then the answer came. "Simone?"

"I am afraid I have bad news, my dear." She turned the catch in her voice into a discreet cough and continued. "I hope you will not mind being inconvenienced another few weeks."

I lowered the lid on the rice I'd been boiling and slid onto a stool at the kitchen bar. Had something gone wrong? Was she about to cancel our agreement?

"Simone"—I cleared my throat—"what happened?"

She drew a ragged breath. "I have just returned from Dr. Forrester's office. My ultrasound showed six enlarged follicles, so I was filled with hope, but only one of them was a good size; the others were too small. The doctor felt that proceeding with the harvest would only be wasted effort, so he canceled my procedure. I am so sorry, Amanda. I know you were hoping we could move ahead."

"No, no, it's okay," I said, responding to the desperation and disappointment in her voice. "What does this mean? Are you and your husband going to stay in Florida, or are you going home?"

"We have not decided, but I think Damien is ready to search for an egg donor. He has asked the doctor to investigate suitable candidates even now, so—"

"I'm so sorry, Simone. I know—" I hesitated, thinking of Amelia, and realized I had no idea how Simone felt. "I imagine you're disappointed."

"Ah, well. *C'est la vie.*" Her brittle laugh sounded more like a cry of anguish. "I should have known I would have problems."

I turned toward the living room, where Marilee was banging out a song on a barely functioning practice keyboard. I wanted to focus on my conversation, but it was hard to concentrate on anything with so much noise in the background. "Why would you have problems, Simone?"

"Because I am old." She released another humorless laugh. "I am forty-two, and the doctor reminded me that fertility drops significantly after age thirty-five. I am well beyond that."

My thoughts raced as I considered the possibilities remaining for the Amblours. The last month had been difficult enough for me and Gideon—my stomach was tender from all the injections, and more than once I had awakened in the middle of the night drenched in sweat. My inner thermostat had stopped working, I suffered from mood swings, and I'd given blood so many times my arm was beginning to look like a junkie's. But I'd go through all of it again if it meant we could continue working with Simone and Damien. I had endured too much to give up after earning only two hundred dollars.

My hand tightened around the phone. "You're not going to quit, are you?"

She hesitated, then sighed. "Damien will not quit, no matter what. Sometimes I think that if I fail in this, he will find another woman who can give him what he wants."

I dropped my jaw, then snapped it shut, grateful she couldn't see the horrified surprise that had to be evident on my face. I'd heard rumors about French men and their mistresses, but I never imagined that a man would cast his wife aside because she couldn't give him an heir. Then again, wasn't that exactly what Henry VIII had done? Maybe things hadn't changed all that much over on the Continent.

"I'm sure Damien is as committed to you as he is to having a child." I injected confidence into my voice and smiled into the phone. "I know this is going to work; I can feel it. We may have suffered a setback, but we're far from out of the race, right?"

Again, silence, then a soft laugh with a trace of hope. "You and your American optimism. No, we are not out of the race. Damien will find an egg donor, and we will begin again. But I am sorry for you. I know you have made sacrifices and your husband, too. I know you are a young couple, very much in love, and it must be difficult for you—"

"We're all right, Simone, we're fine. And I'm so sorry the egg harvest failed. I know every woman wants to have her own biological child, if it's at all possible." I spoke on presumption, rattling off sentiments I wanted to share with Amelia, but hadn't yet been able to. The words sounded hollow to my ear.

"Thank you," Simone answered, her voice stronger than it had been when we first began to talk. "And now I must go. We will be in touch, or Natasha Bray will call you. Right now, I need to rest."

"That sounds like a good idea." I smiled into the phone again. "And don't worry. We'll simply move into another month. I'm sure everything's going to be fine."

"By the way"—Simone paused—"do I hear an electronic piano?"

I groaned. "It's a cheap little practice keyboard. Marilee brought it home from her school, but I'm afraid it frustrates her more than it helps."

"That little song is from a four-year-old?" Surprise rang in Simone's voice. "She plays so well."

I couldn't help smiling at this bit of unexpected praise. "She plays even better on a decent piano. Gideon and I aren't quite sure where she inherited her ability, but we're grateful for her talent."

"You have been given quite a gift." I could almost see Simone's wistful smile. "You are blessed."

I agreed with her, and as I hung up I thought about Amelia and how desperately she also wanted children. Then, without explaining why, I went into the living room and wrapped my daughter in a heartfelt hug.

I hoped Gideon's duffel bag would remain in our closet for a while, but he and his Special Forces unit left the morning after Valentine's Day. As usual, Gideon didn't tell me where he was going or when he'd be back, but he kissed Marilee, then held me close and whispered, "I'll be waiting at the river."

"I know." I choked back a sob. "I'll look for you under the tree."

I didn't know exactly where he was headed, but I knew I'd be lost until he came home again.

After Gideon left, I barely felt the needle pricks of my daily injections because tension wreaked havoc on my body. My stomach churned with anxiety and my chest felt as if it would burst with every breath. My attention span shrank to nothing, I couldn't remember where I left things, and I put Marilee to sleep in our bed so I wouldn't have to look at Gideon's empty pillow.

A rise of panic threatened to choke me in mid-February when I joined a horrified world in watching a video of a bound American reporter being beaten by his terrorist captors. I sent Marilee out of the room when clips from the tape began to play on the news, and I wept at the sight of the man who was being tortured simply because he was American. The entire time I watched, I kept wondering if this man was the reason Gideon had to leave us—was this reporter someone so significant that Gideon's team had been tasked to find and rescue him? Was he CIA? The kidnapping had occurred in Kenya, though the terrorists had reportedly come from Somalia.

As March roared in like a lion, we learned that the reporter had been rescued. Amelia and I sat in my living room as a newscaster announced that journalist Ben Huggins was on his way home, thanks to a military team that had gone in to rescue him.

"You know he was no ordinary reporter," Amelia remarked, lifting a brow. "The government doesn't send soldiers to snatch up members of the media who get into trouble overseas."

"I was thinking he might be a spy," I answered. "Either that or he's related to someone in Congress."

I was just about to change the channel when the newscaster added that one of the soldiers in the rescue team had been killed in the operation.

I flinched as though a spark had arced between me and the television, but Amelia shook her head. "It wasn't Gideon," she said, her voice flat and final. "We would have heard if something had happened to him."

Knowing she was right, I turned off the television and tried to concentrate on the battle facing me—it was finally time to get pregnant with the Amblours' baby.

As anxious as a girl on her first date, on the morning of March 18 I took Marilee to Mama Isa's and then drove myself to the fertility clinic. According to Damien, the Amblours had located an egg donor, a pretty little Kansas coed with an IQ of 150. After a month of hormone treatments, several of the young woman's eggs had been successfully harvested, flash-frozen, and shipped to Florida. Six days ago, the eggs had been fertilized with Damien's sperm. The fate of the Amblours' child or children now rested with Dr. Forrester. If all went according to plan, it would soon rest with me.

Sometimes, I mused as I parked the car, it took a village to *conceive* a child.

I signed in at the reception desk, then took a seat in the crowded waiting room. Though my thoughts were ping-ponging from one concern to another, I picked up a magazine and pretended to be engrossed in an article. I was so intent on pretending, in fact, that I didn't look up when someone else entered the office. I didn't realize the other person had come to be with me until she sat and touched my arm.

I couldn't have been more shocked if she'd hit me with a Taser.

"Simone!" I dropped my magazine. "I didn't know you'd be here."

She folded her hands and looked at me, her face pinched in an almost guilty expression. "I didn't have to come," she said, her eyes crinkling at the corners, "but I couldn't stay away. I won't invade your privacy; I only want to sit here in the waiting room while you undergo the procedure."

I blinked at her, uncertain how to respond.

"I want to be nearby when my child is conceived," she went on. "Damien thinks I am being silly, but really, is it too much to ask?"

"I don't think so." I shrugged, not caring where she sat. I didn't want her in the exam room, but if she wanted to wait out here, why shouldn't she?

Though I knew the Amblours had viable embryos, I thought I'd make small talk while we waited. "Did everything go smoothly with the extraction?"

"Everything went beautifully. We have six embryos." Simone gave me a pleased smile. "All are healthy and of a good size. Damien and I have decided to keep four in storage and transfer two. Our agreement calls for the transfer of no more than three, but we wanted to be considerate of you. Carrying three babies would be, I imagine, quite strenuous, no matter how healthy the volunteer."

I laughed. "Carrying *one* baby can be strenuous, so I appreciate your thoughtfulness."

I shifted my gaze and stared at the carpet as a realization bloomed in my brain. Today they would transfer two embryos. I might soon be carrying twins. Two little flag-waving French citizens.

"I would love twins," Simone said, happiness warming her voice. "But who can say whether both eggs will implant? But if they do, yes, twins would be wonderful. If they do not, we will pray that at least one survives. Damien's dreams and all our hopes depend on it."

I nodded, though I knew Gideon wouldn't be thrilled by the idea that I might actually carry multiples. We had known all along that the doctor could implant up to three embryos, but Gideon was adamant that I not risk my health. If I found myself pregnant with twins, he'd make me hire a housekeeper and stop working at the grocery. He'd want me to check my blood pressure every day. He'd be watching my diet and making me put my feet up every ten minutes. In short, he'd turn into a royal pain in the tuchus.

I set the magazine back on the table while Simone picked up another one and used it to fan herself. "I cannot get used to the heat here. We will return to France tomorrow, but we will keep in touch with you. We can come back if we are needed. All you have to do is send an email, and we will return as soon as possible."

I didn't have a chance to comment because at that moment the inner door opened. A nurse stepped out, file folder in hand, and looked straight at me. "Amanda?"

I squeezed Simone's arm. "Say a prayer for me, will you? We need everything to go right this morning."

Simone didn't answer, but her eyes filled as I released her. I managed a falsely confident smile and followed the nurse, trembling with every step.

The nurse led me into an exam room and closed the door behind me. "Everything off; gown opens in front." She pointed to the folded paper garment on the exam table. "The doctor will be in shortly."

I stepped out of my shoes. "Do I get some kind of medication for this? Maybe a Valium?"

"You won't need anything." A half smile crossed the nurse's face. "This is no more painful than a Pap smear. You just lie there with your feet in the stirrups. The doctor does all the hard work."

I drew a long, steady breath and unbuttoned my blouse. The nurse could talk all she wanted about the doctor's hard work, but he wasn't the one who'd been enduring shots every day for two and a half months. The cute little egg donor and I had been the hardest-working parties, though I supposed someone in a lab had to add Damien Amblour's sperm to a petri dish containing the eggs and then count the developing cells. But that person, whoever he was, didn't have bruises on his arms and stomach.

Wrapped in the thin hospital gown, I climbed onto the table and lay back, the paper mat crinkling beneath me as I tried to get comfortable. Someone had tacked a child's drawing of a palm-tree-studded beach onto the ceiling, so I was trying to imagine myself at the seashore when Dr. Forrester came into the room.

"Hello, Amanda. He sat on his little stool and rolled toward the business end of the exam table. "Ready to get pregnant?"

I sighed. "As ready as I'll ever be."

"I've confirmed the names and double checked the file numbers," the nurse said. "Amblour to Lisandra. We're all set."

All business, the nurse handed the doctor some kind of gadget—I only glimpsed it from the corner of my eye—and squirted ultrasound jelly on my abdomen. A wave of déjà vu swept over me—I'd been in this situation before, when I was first pregnant with Marilee and terrified by the thought of having a baby. I was terrified this time, too, but not about having a child. I couldn't say exactly why my heart was rattling like a trip-hammer and my arms had pebbled with gooseflesh. Maybe this anxiety sprang from fear of the unknown. Or of possible complications in this brave new world of baby making.

As I tried to keep from shivering, the nurse rubbed an ultrasound transducer over my abdomen.

"This is a basic procedure," the doctor said, my view of him obstructed by a paper drape spread over my bent legs. "Nancy will use the ultrasound to give me a good image of the uterus and help me keep the tip of the device in the center of the endometrial cavity. This gives the embryos the best chance of implantation. After placing the catheter in exactly the right spot, I will squirt the embryos into your womb. Just think of me as the man with the turkey baster."

I managed a fake laugh. "You make it sound so simple."

He chuckled. "It's not quite as simple as basting a turkey, but I like to put my patients at ease."

"Do you transfer both embryos at the same time?" Not knowing what to do with my hands, I gripped the side of the table. "Simone said there were two."

"I'll insert them simultaneously," Forrester said, "but after I remove the catheter, we'll do a microscopic examination of the tubing to make sure we didn't miss one. If we find cells remaining in the device, we'll simply go through the routine again."

I winced as the doctor inserted one of his instruments—no doubt about it, that was a speculum and this felt like a Pap test. I closed my eyes and felt vague interior movements that elicited a cramp, then nothing. A moment later, the nurse carried something to the microscope on the counter. Finally, she nodded at the doctor. "All clear."

"Then we're about done here." After the doctor removed the intrusive speculum, the resulting metallic clatter told me he had tossed it on a tray of instruments. "Great job, young lady," he said, rolling away from the exam table. "We're all finished."

I lifted my head. Finished? The procedure had taken no more than ten minutes.

The doctor stood and pulled off his latex gloves. "Now, Amanda, Nancy is going to make sure you're comfortable and you're going to lie on your back for about an hour. You can sleep if you want. After an hour you can go home, but we want you to limit your physical activity for the rest of the day—no running on the treadmill, no weight lifting, and above all, no intercourse with your husband. We've just given you the perfect excuse to camp out in the living room and be a couch potato for the rest of the day."

"What about tomorrow?" I asked. "And the rest of the week?"

The doctor smiled and crossed his arms, folding his hands into the armpits of his lab coat. "You may resume your normal activities tomorrow. But I would not recommend jogging, strenuous exercise, or any vigorous activity until after the pregnancy test. Once the embryo or embryos have safely implanted, you can behave like any other pregnant woman—and since you've had a baby before, I trust you know what that entails."

"I do."

Dr. Forrester smiled, but before leaving the room, he stopped by the side of the exam table to shake my hand. "I think you're doing a generous thing. Not every woman is able to be a gestational carrier."

I managed a wavering smile. "You might want to hold that thought. I haven't done anything yet."

"But you will." The doctor gave me a cocky grin. "You look like the sort of woman who accomplishes whatever she sets out to do."

Did I? No one else had ever seen me that way.

As Nancy the nurse cleaned up the instrument tray, I folded my hands on my stomach, stared at the ceiling, and hoped Dr. Forrester was right.

The clock's minute hand had slid well past the hour when I ran into the grocery the next morning. A light spring rain had slowed the carpool lane at Marilee's school, but Amelia didn't even seem to notice my tardiness. Without even glancing in my direction, she stood at the register chatting up two white-haired men who were buying pastries and coffee. I slunk past her, half expecting to hear a jibe tossed at my retreating back, but instead I heard her laugh. Amelia, *laughing*? Something unbelievable must have happened, because Amelia rarely laughed these days.

I halted in midstep. Could she be pregnant?

Buoyant with hope, I stashed my purse in the office, poured a cup of coffee, and strolled over to take my place in the checkout stand. Amelia didn't scold me for being late; she simply surrendered the register and smiled as she ambled back to the stockroom with a dreamy look on her face.

She *had* to be pregnant. What else could elicit that kind of euphoria?

I took my place at the register and gave Mama Isa an *I'm sorry* smile as she walked by. "The rain slowed me down," I told her, not mentioning that I'd also overslept by half an hour. I hadn't felt guilty for oversleeping, figuring my body needed the rest. I was sleeping for two now, or maybe even three. When the time came to announce a pregnancy, Mama Isa would understand.

For some reason I felt extra protective toward the tiny embryos inside me. Yesterday I ate an extra helping of green vegetables, last night I climbed the stairs more slowly than usual, and this morning I took a tepid shower because I didn't want to shock a pair of blastocysts with an abrupt change in temperature.

I sipped from my coffee mug and studied Mama Isa's face, wondering when I would hear about whatever had transformed Amelia from a morning grump into a glowing angel.

I didn't have to wait long. Mama Isa leaned over the counter. "Have you heard Amelia's news?"

I smiled. "What's up?"

Mama Isa caught a breath as if she would spill the secret, then some motherly instinct must have stopped her. She shook her head. "She should be the one to tell you. I'll send her over to give you the news."

"Is she expecting?" I called to Mama Isa's retreating back.

She only lifted her hand and waved, prolonging my frustration.

Other morning customers entered the store and wandered the aisles, thumped the fruit, and argued with Mario over the price of pork. I rang up several orders, filled the cigarette boxes behind the counter, and organized the candy bars, which seemed to have vaulted into other brands' boxes on my day off.

During a lull, I spotted Amelia beneath the Cuban flag at the back of the store. She was simply standing in one spot, her eyes wide and distracted, so I hurried over.

"What's this big news of yours?" I tugged on her sleeve to snap her out of her daze. "Not fair keeping me in the dark, cuz."

She glanced around, then leaned toward me. "Mario and I did it."

"You're pregnant?"

"Not quite." She tapped my wrist in light rebuke. "If God closes a door, he opens a window, right? So we've been praying, and we felt led to make an appointment with a social worker. I think we're going to get a baby through an adoption agency."

This wasn't the news I'd hoped for, but I managed to work up enough enthusiasm for a tentative squeal. "Honestly? You're going for it?"

"Shh." If Amelia was disappointed about missing out on pregnancy, I would never have guessed it from the way her eyes sparkled. "I called the public agency over in Clearwater. They handle adoptions of all kinds of kids and all ages. They don't work with international agencies, but that helps keep the costs down. Mario and I have our first interview with them next week."

"That's really wonderful." I gave her a quick hug, then squeezed her shoulders. "I'm so excited for you both. We might be pregnant at the same time—sort of. We'll both be expecting babies, but you'll get to keep your figure."

"I'll get to keep the baby, too," Amelia quipped, then she bit her lip. "I'm sorry, Mandy. That was probably a thoughtless thing to say."

"Don't worry—when it comes to being insensitive, I think I've already won that prize. And I know having a kid is a lot more important to you than keeping your figure."

"Yeah . . . well." She gave me a rueful smile. "Look at us, pioneers in parenting. Who'd have thought we'd both explore such unconventional options?"

"Yanela and Gordon must be thinking we're crazy." I forced a laugh. "But the sooner I get through this surrogacy arrangement, the sooner Gideon and I can begin to plan our family's future. We don't want Marilee to be an only child, and Gideon really wants a son. We want our kids to play with *your* kids."

Caught up in a flood of optimism, we hugged each other like middle school girls on a hormonal high.

"There's one thing I need to ask you." Amelia released me, abruptly curbing her enthusiasm. "We need letters of reference from three adults who know us well. We're not supposed to use immediate family members, but since you're a cousin by marriage, I think you'll qualify. Would you please write a letter for us and say we'd make decent parents?"

"I would be delighted." I grinned at her, happy I could do something to help. "Just tell me where and when to send it."

"You can mail it anytime and the agency people will put it in our file. I'll bring the social worker's contact information tomorrow—there's so much stuff whirling in my brain I can barely remember my own name. But I do remember hers—Helen. Helen Something-or-other."

I stepped into the center aisle and checked the register to be sure I had no customers waiting, then I leaned against the stockroom doorway. "How does the adoption process work, anyway? I've always wanted to be a social worker, but I've never had an opportunity to see how things actually operate."

Amelia drew a deep breath. "This is how they explained it over the phone: Mario and I will have six meetings with Helen. In the first, we'll talk about our marriage and how we got together so the woman can understand us as a couple. In the second, we'll talk about Mario. In the third, I guess, we'll talk about me. In the fourth, we'll discuss what kind of child we want to raise, and in the fifth, she'll come to our home and make sure it's suitable for a kid. In the last meeting, I guess, we'll tie things up and she'll explain how she'll go about finding a baby for us." Amelia paused, breathless. "It sounds simple when you spell it out, doesn't it?"

I flashed back to the day before, when the doctor had finished the embryo transfer and called it *simple*.

"Nothing says parenthood has to be complicated," I answered. "And I hope everything goes smoothly for you. Just think—in as little as six weeks, you could be a mommy."

Amelia's eyes widened. "*¡Caramba!* Sort of sobering when you think about it in those terms."

I squeezed her hand. "I know you'll be a good mom. And let me know when the baby's on his way because I want to throw you a shower. I'll even serve Cuban food, if you want it."

"You'd better, if you want the family to come." She backed into the stockroom, a smile trembling over her lips. "*Gracias,* Mandy. Thank you for understanding."

Of course I understood. We were both pregnant with hope, waiting for the confirmation of a child.

Sheltering whatever life might lie inside me, I dropped my hand to my abdomen and watched her walk away.

Chapter Eight

Four days after the embryo transfer, Gideon stomped across the front porch and walked through our front door. Marilee and I both dropped what we were doing and flew to his side, amazed and grateful that he'd come home safely.

When I looked up that afternoon and saw my husband sitting across from me at the kitchen table, I could almost pretend we weren't waging a war against illusive and lethal enemies. I could smile and ask how he liked his chicken pot pie, ignoring the fact that not even Gideon and his Special Forces comrades could ever defeat the sort of terrorists who valued destruction and the murder of innocents more than their own lives.

Though I wanted things to appear normal, I was still tiptoeing through the house as though I were a fragile bubble. I refused to lift Marilee lest I strain an abdominal muscle, and I didn't even try to budge the big box UPS left on our porch Friday afternoon. Gideon brought the heavy carton in the house, and inside we discovered a large basket of gourmet French foods: pastries, cheeses, macaroons, chocolates, truffles, pork sausage, fancy mustards, Petits Trésors, and cornichons.

"I don't even know how to pronounce some of these things," Gideon said, helping me unpack the basket. "What the heck is a cornichon?"

I studied the jar. "Tiny cucumbers, I think."

Gideon removed boxes of crackers and mustards, then he chuckled. "Did you notice what's not here?"

I looked over the crowded countertop. "What could possibly be missing?"

"There's no wine. Nothing alcoholic for the expectant mother."

"For the *possibly* expectant mother. And I appreciate Simone's thoughtfulness. I wouldn't want to be tempted."

I didn't want to raise anyone's hopes, including my own, but I had been feeling a bit out of sorts ever since the transfer. Maybe I was imagining things, but Thursday I experienced some mild cramping and almost panicked. The cramps subsided by Friday morning, so after lunch I reached under our bathroom sink and pulled out a home pregnancy test I'd picked up at Walgreens. I did the test and felt my heart sink at the negative result, but maybe it was too soon to tell.

The doctor had scheduled a beta pregnancy test nine days after the transfer, but I didn't want to wait until next Wednesday for an answer. So I lounged around over the weekend and did another home pregnancy test on Monday morning: still negative.

I stared at my reflection in the bathroom mirror and tried to convince myself that the tests weren't accurate because I was testing too soon. But if the result was correct, how could I break the news to Simone and Damien? I didn't even want to tell Gideon if the procedure had failed. He'd made sacrifices, too.

I decided to keep my mouth shut. I would leave all the announcements to Dr. Forrester, who was paid to be right about such things.

Tuesday afternoon, the day before my beta test, Gideon packed his duffel bag, hugged me, and told me he'd meet me at the river. I knew he had to go; I knew something had come up and his unit needed him.

But this would be the worst parting ever. Not only was he flying off to fight only God knew who, but how was I supposed to face disappointment if the pregnancy test was negative? Who would comfort me if all our sacrifices proved to be for nothing? No one in the family even knew I'd been through the embryo transfer, so whose shoulder was I supposed to cry on?

Wednesday morning, tired and red-eyed, I took Marilee to school, then drove to the reproductive endocrinologist's office. I sat in the waiting room, but dropped my magazine when a television on the wall flashed an urgent news update: In what they were calling "the Passover Tragedy," a suicide bomber had just killed twenty-nine people in Israel. The terrorist, dressed as a waiter, had walked past security and into a hotel's dining room, where more than 150 people were celebrating the Seder. Many of those present were Holocaust survivors.

Horrified by the news, I remained quiet when nurse Nancy called my name and led me back to a desk where she drew blood. Ice spread through my stomach as I thought about how the evil and hatred that ignited the Holocaust had never really gone away. Today it had blazed forth from another channel.

And who stood against that hatred? Millions of people, including men like my husband, who, for all I knew, might have been in Israel at that moment.

"You're awful quiet," the nurse said, loosening the rubber strip around my upper arm. "Are you feeling queasy?"

"I'm fine." I forced a smile. "Just thinking about the sad state of the world."

"A lot of that going around." Nancy slid the needle out of my arm and pressed a cotton ball on the insertion point, then gestured for me to apply pressure.

After the nurse applied a Band-Aid, I picked up my purse and told the receptionist I'd be home in the afternoon if they wanted to call with the results. Then I drove to the grocery, worked my usual shift, and left at one-thirty to pick up Marilee from school.

The phone was ringing as we came through the front door. I hurried to grab it, said hello, and heard Nurse Nancy singing "Be My Baby."

I swallowed hard and sank into a kitchen chair. "Does this mean—"

"Congratulations, Amanda. Your test was positive."

Positive. A baby. Maybe two. The home pregnancy tests hadn't been able to pick up the HCG in my urine, but my blood told the truth. I was going to have the Amblours' baby.

"What happens next?" I croaked, barely recognizing my voice.

"Call your surrogacy counselor, then make an appointment with your OB/GYN. From this point forward, you're an ordinary pregnant woman. Good luck, honey."

I thanked her and hung up, then sat absolutely still as the happy realization twirled in my head. All our sacrifices—mine and Gideon's and Simone's and Damien's—had been worth it.

The dark visions that had occupied my imagination for the last few hours faded away. How dark could the world be if people still longed to care for innocent babies? Every time God sent a new baby into the world, he was giving mankind another chance to make things right. Babies were a bundle of hope.

Marilee strolled into the kitchen, then stopped and stared at my face. "Mommy?"

"Yes, darling girl?"

"You look funny."

How long had it been since she saw pure happiness on my face? "I probably look happy."

I slid out of my chair and wrapped her in an embrace so tight she complained. "You're squeezing my breath out."

"Then I should let you go." I released her, then pointed to my cheek. "How about a kiss?"

She gave me a polite peck, then ran off to practice her piano while I climbed back into my chair and picked up the phone.

I knew I should call Natasha Bray first, but I pulled out the little notebook in my purse and dialed France. I was so eager I forgot to figure out the time in La Roche-sur-Yon, the small town where the Amblours lived. The phone rang three times, then a woman answered: *"Allô?"*

"Simone?" I glanced at my watch and hoped I wasn't interrupting her dinner.

"May I say who is calling?"

"Mandy—Amanda. From Florida."

"One moment, please. Let me fetch Madame."

I waited, tapping my foot, and finally I heard Simone's familiar voice: *"Allô?"*

"Simone, it's Mandy." Without indulging in pleasantries, I drew a breath and gave her the news: "We're pregnant."

"Are you—are you certain?"

"I am. The doctor said so."

"Merveilleux!" Her voice rang with the happiness of pealing bells, then she broke into a sob. "*Dieu merci,* I am sorry, but I am so overcome—"

"I'm not sure what all that means, but I'll take it as something good," I said, laughing. "Please give my congratulations to your husband."

"I am so sorry, I spoke without thinking." She sniffed. "Thank you for telling us. And . . . is it one baby or two?"

"I don't know," I admitted. "I'm not sure we'll learn that until I see my OB—or during the ultrasound, which I'll have in a couple of weeks. Don't worry, I'll let you know everything as soon as I learn it."

"You will email me a photo?"

"I will email you pictures, notes, anything you like."

"*Merci beaucoup,* Mandy. You have done so much for us."

"My pleasure. I'm just so happy everything worked out."

As I hung up the phone, I realized that helping the Amblours had filled me with an unexpected joy. In the midst of war, during a time I would usually be worried sick about my husband, the awareness that I was doing something good for someone else was . . . empowering.

Unless I was simply basking in an abundance of pregnancy hormones.

The next morning I found an email from Simone in my inbox.

My very dear Amanda:

You may never know how your happy news affected Damien and me. When I disconnected the call, I sat for a long time and imagined how it would feel to finally bring a baby into our home. My emotions felt paralyzed—joy and fear, in equal measure, held me hostage.

Yet I will always remember every detail of yesterday—the way the fire crackled to chase away the chill even as the mimosa trees outside my window budded with new life. If I went into the village, I knew, I would see the first colorful Easter candy displays in the *patisserie* window. For years I have avoided those displays, knowing they were designed for children, but this year I will study them with hope in my heart. Next year we will have a baby to charm with Easter eggs and cakes, and this wonderful expectation is all due to you and your kindness.

You may have realized how disappointed I was to learn we would have to use a donor egg—I was heartbroken at first, but I've decided not to expend so much emotional energy on things that cannot be helped. My heart has been broken many times, but this time, I am sure, all will be well.

I wanted to tell you more about our background when we met on the day of the transfer, but we did not want to share anything that might taint our budding relationship. I probably sounded a bit tense when Natasha mentioned testing, but I had my reasons for concern.

As you may have heard, you are not the first surrogate we have contracted. The first was a young woman in California who told us she did not drink alcohol or use drugs. We believed her, but Damien kept feeling uneasy, so during the sixth month of the pregnancy we asked the agency if they would test her for drugs. When they did, we discovered that she had miscarried a month earlier. We suspected her drug use had been the reason she lost the pregnancy; she blamed my egg and said the pregnancy was doomed from the start.

So we resolved not to make the same mistakes again.

The second time we contracted a surrogate, we engaged an older woman, a mother who already had children, so we felt we were working with a more experienced and mature surrogate. We also asked the agency to require frequent testing—ultrasounds every other week, amniocentesis at appropriate intervals, surprise drug tests for the mother.

She got pregnant and we waited by the computer for test results after every medical appointment. She lost the pregnancy in the fourth month, however, and she also blamed us—she said we had been too demanding and required too many tests.

Again, Damien and I decided to revise our approach. No tests, unless medically necessary. No pressure that might affect our carrier's health.

So if in the months ahead you think Damien and I seem pensive or unusually concerned about details, please be patient with us. We have already lost two babies because our gestational carriers did not understand how much we valued the precious cargo they carried. We are striving to balance our trust in you with our concern for our child. It is not an easy thing to do.

However, I have a sense about you . . . maybe it is because your husband gives so much to serve his country, or perhaps it is because I can see how you adore your lovely daughter. But you have demonstrated such concern that we are sure you will carry our child as if it were your own. And for that, I am unspeakably grateful. I wish I could think of a unique way to show our gratitude—financial support doesn't begin to express what we are feeling.

So while I was initially disappointed that my egg harvest failed, this will be the child who was not born under my heart, but in it. He or she will be the sum of our expectations and our hope for the future. Damien is especially pleased to know his heritage will be passed on to another generation.

I cannot imagine what sort of impression you have of my husband—perhaps you think he places too much emphasis on the estate and his family's status in this district. But he is not a bad man, I can assure you.

He is, in his way, quite tender, and I know he will be a good father. A quiet father, perhaps, but a dutiful parent.

Damien, you see, has the gift of seeing potential other people miss. When we met, somehow he looked beyond my lonely expression, my torn jeans, and my paintings—all of which were tinged with melancholy in those days. Somehow he saw the woman within, the soul languishing for love, and he married me. You do not know me well—and you'll find none of these thoughts in our file at the Surrogacy Center—but I sense that you and I might be friends. Fate has brought us together, and united we will accomplish something wonderful.

I pray the happiness and fulfillment you experience in these next few months somehow equals the joy I will revel in for the rest of my life.

By loving me, Damien helped a melancholy girl become a wife. By feeling compassion for us, you have helped a grief-stricken woman become a mother. I will never be able to thank you enough for what you have done.

(Do you think me melodramatic? Perhaps it is the artist in me, but I feel things . . . deeply.)

And now begins the waiting and the preparation. While you endure the months of physical labor—and do not think I am unaware of what you will be going through—I will prepare the house for our child. I will hire a nanny (or two, if we have been blessed with twins), and I will finally finish decorating the room I have reserved as a nursery. I wish you could see it—a tower on the south side of the ancient house has been vacant for years. Damien says his mother used to store her shoes in that space, but ever since seeing it, I have known that any child would love to have it as his or her private fortress. The magical space features a high ceiling; tall, curving windows to channel sunshine and starlight; and smooth, plastered walls forming an almost perfect circle.

I will place the cradle in the center of the room, because from this day forward, my life and Damien's will revolve around this child. He or she will be our reason for living—and if all goes well, we may use the frozen embryos to provide our firstborn with a sibling.

Our children will be our purpose, our future, and our hope. And we, dear woman, will always be grateful to you and to God.

Sincerely,
Simone Amblour

For two days I kept my pregnancy a secret from the family, then Gideon called from the base. "I'm on my way home," he said, his voice husky. "And I'm hoping you have good news for me."

"I do." I turned away from Marilee so she wouldn't notice the excited light in my eyes. "I'm taking Marilee over to Mama Isa's. She's going to spend the night over there and tomorrow they're going to McDonald's for breakfast."

"So we'll be all alone?" Gideon chuckled. "I can't wait to see you, baby girl."

"I'll be here."

I didn't care where he had been or what he had done; all that mattered was that Gideon was home.

The news I couldn't wait to share was an added bonus. We were on the brink of a new adventure, the beginning of the rest of our lives. In a few months we would have a financial nest egg, and soon we'd have our own home. Gideon could establish the store he'd always wanted, and I could have the babies we'd always longed for. . . .

I had candles glowing on the table by the time I heard the familiar sound of his boots, followed by the thunk of his duffel bag dropping onto the wooden foyer tiles. "Mandy?"

"In here," I called from the kitchen. I smoothed my hair and adjusted my dress as I listened to his approaching steps. I had taken great pains to look as good as or better than the cheesecake waiting on the counter.

Gideon inhaled the mingled aromas as he came into the room, then he stopped, his dark eyes glinting with masculine interest. "Something sure looks delicious—and it ain't on the table."

I laughed. “Hang on a minute, soldier.”

Aware of the hunger in him, I dimmed the overhead lights and smiled at my husband through candle-cast shadows. Two place settings gleamed on the table, two steak fillets waited in the oven, and two loaded baked potatoes dripped with cheese and butter on my best serving dish. I had set a beautiful table, but all I wanted to do was wrap my arms around Gideon.

I was lucky to have him home.

Gideon glanced at the food, then he smiled at me, his gaze as soft as a caress. “I take it this is a special occasion?”

“It is.” I slipped out of my high heels and padded toward him, then slid into his arms. “We have the house to ourselves for the next twenty-four hours and it’s official—I’m pregnant.”

His smile broadened. “You mean—”

“Yessir, soldier, we’ve been given permission to fool around. We can eat this yummy dinner and then go to our room—”

Grinning, Gideon lifted me into his arms. “Or we could go to our room *first.*”

“What about the steaks?” I ran my fingertip over his three-day stubble as he carried me into our bedroom. “And those lovely baked potatoes?”

“They’ll keep. And if they don’t—who cares.” He lowered me to our bed, and I hoped the yearning that showed in his face wasn’t quite so obvious on mine. A woman, my mom always told me, should play at least a *little* hard to get.

“By the way,” I whispered, “welcome home.” Smiling, I reached for the lamp and turned out the light.

The next Sunday, as the family gathered at Mama Isa’s after church, I stood with my arm around Gideon’s waist and announced that I was pregnant with a French couple’s baby. In return I received several polite smiles, a couple of confused looks, and a weak “Congratulations . . . I think,” from Amelia.

"When are you due?" Elaine asked, looking at me as though I might explode at any moment.

"December first." I stretched my mouth into a smile. "It'll all be over and done by Christmas."

I hadn't expected them to be thrilled with the news, but I did want them to know so they wouldn't make incorrect assumptions when I started to grow a baby bump.

Five days later I pulled myself out of bed and arrived at the grocery before sunrise. A wave of nausea crested in my gut as I fumbled with the back door key, but I managed to calm my stomach with deep breaths and sheer determination. Once I got inside, I reminded myself, I could be as sick as I wanted to be, but I needed to get the store open by seven. For Amelia's sake.

She had called the night before and begged me to open for her. "Our social worker is coming tomorrow for the home visit," she said, her voice jagged with nerves, "and I need the morning to clean house. So if you could open for me, I'll come to work as soon as Helen leaves, I promise."

How could I refuse?

A thick silence lay over the dimly lit grocery as I locked the back door behind me and hurried past the stockroom. A single overhead fluorescent glowed over the cash register, and as I made my way to the office I glanced at the wide front windows and wondered if criminals lurked in the semidarkness outside. I couldn't see anything but my own reflection, so I tried to forget about my roiling stomach and stick to the morning routine. First on the to-do list: turn off the alarm.

After punching in the alarm code, I hesitated by the restroom and rechecked the state of my stomach: holding steady so far, and I could always grab crackers from the snack aisle. I might just make it.

From their black-and-white portraits next to the Cuban flag, Gordon and Yanela's unsmiling eyes watched as I moved to the coffee station and prepared the morning brew. Customers would begin to arrive soon, so the coffee and *tostadas* had to be ready.

I had just put the coffee on when someone slammed the back door. I froze, terrified by the thought of an intruder, then I recognized Jenna's voice. "Hello? Amelia?"

"It's me," I called, remembering that Jenna now had her own key. "I'm filling in for Amelia today."

Jenna went to the bakery counter to stash her purse, then strolled toward me, tying on her apron as she came. "Let me give you a hand with the *tostadas.* You buttered the bread yet?"

I shook my head, nauseated by the thought of butter. So . . . oily.

"I'll do it. If I have time, I might make some *croquetas* today. They went over real well the last time I made them on a weekday."

I swallowed hard. "Don't you make those every day?"

"Only on weekends. But hey, it's Friday, so we're nearly there." She wound an elastic band around her long hair, then pulled a tub of butter from the small fridge beneath the counter. "The expats love the *croquetas.* One of them told me he hadn't had anything so good since he ate lunch at the Hotel Nacional de Cuba."

"Oh." I always felt a bit lost when the old folks talked about Castro and the revolution, but I was grateful Jenna had taken charge of the breakfast bar. "I'll leave you to it, then. I need to unlock the safe and get some cash—" I stopped, covering my mouth as my stomach lurched.

Jenna peered at me. "You okay? You look a little green."

I nodded without speaking, drew a deep breath, and waited for my stomach to stop flip-flopping.

Truthfully, I loved being pregnant. I loved feeling new life inside me, I loved the stretchiness of maternity pants, and I loved flashing other pregnant women a "Me too" smile. I loved the condition of my hair and nails and the way my skin glowed from the life-giving hormones. I loved having older men offer me their seats in church, and seeing Gideon's conservative father blush whenever anyone patted my expanding tummy. Without a doubt, being pregnant was one of my most rewarding life experiences.

But morning sickness—which cast a dull shadow over months one through three—was the rat turd in my sugar bowl of happiness.

"I'm okay," I finally told Jenna, wiping sweat from my hairline. "Just an upset stomach."

"Better hurry up with the cash, then. A couple of guys are already waiting outside. And they look hungry."

I glanced out the glass doors. The brightening day revealed two older men in Guayabera shirts and Panama hats—two of the expats who came to the grocery to mingle, eat, and talk about the glory of Cuba before Castro.

I hurried into the office and knelt to open the safe behind Mama Isa's desk. Keeping one eye on the clock, I took out some change and a hundred dollars in small bills. Being on my knees reminded me of Amelia's desperation, so I whispered a quick prayer for her and Mario. I didn't think they'd have any problems with their home visit, but Amelia sounded panicked when we talked.

Once I unlocked the front door, the morning passed in a blur. I stayed behind the register and noticed that several of the bakery tickets included charges for Jenna's *croquetas* as well as the usual *tostadas.* For a *gringa,* Jenna certainly knew her customers.

I was feeling better when Mario and Amelia breezed in, her face lit by a smile as wide as Texas. "We did it," she said, leaning on the checkout stand. "We got through the interview and showed the house without a single disaster."

I crossed my arms and laughed. "I knew you'd do fine."

Amelia glanced left and right, then leaned closer. "I thought Helen would pull on a white glove and run her finger over my bookshelves, but she didn't do anything like that. She just looked around to get a general idea about the house. Then she asked where we would keep the baby, so I showed her the room that'll be a nursery when—*if*—we get the call. Mario had to move a few boxes and the treadmill in order for her to see the space, but she seemed to think it would work."

"Of course she did." I leaned back against the counter, confident in my cousin's ability to impress a social worker. "Your home is perfect for children."

"By the way"—Amelia's eyes narrowed and focused on my belly—"how are you feeling these days? Everything okay?"

I understood the reason for her question. IVF recipients tended to have a higher miscarriage rate than natural pregnancies, so I might still lose this baby. But I not only *felt* pregnant, I sensed that this little one was determined to stick around.

"I'm good," I told her, meeting her gaze.

She must have seen something in my face, because her eyes softened. "Were you sick this morning?"

"Just a little queasy, so I managed."

"Then I *really* appreciate you coming in to open for me." The corner of her mouth twisted. "You know, you said we could both be expecting at the same time."

"Looks like I was right."

"It hardly seems fair, though. Getting pregnant for you is as easy as robbing a blind man."

My temper sparked. "It wasn't easy. I had to take shots and hormones for two months."

"How awful." Amelia slapped her cheek in pretend horror. "I'm surprised you survived the ordeal."

I knew she had good reasons for being sarcastic, but I wasn't trying to hurt her. "Can we move past this subject and get back to work?"

She arched a brow, then her gaze shifted and thawed slightly. "Have you told anyone outside the family yet?"

"Only the Amblours and the woman from the Surrogacy Center. I haven't mentioned anything to my neighbors because so much can go wrong in the first trimester. And at this point I'm not sure I want to answer a lot of questions about who the parents are."

"Don't worry. I won't say anything to the customers."

I nodded. "I appreciate it."

"And I'm sorry for being difficult. You can't help being Fertile Myrtle."

I squeezed her hand. "But I'm glad we're cousins."

I thought everything was okay between us, but as I stepped out of the checkout stand to walk to the ladies' room, Amelia called after me: "By the way, what are you going to say when people ask why you didn't offer to help me and Mario?"

I pivoted on the ball of my foot, disturbed by something I heard in her voice. "What?"

"Someone's bound to ask why you didn't volunteer to carry a baby for us. How are you going to answer?"

I drew a breath, saw the searing anguish in her eyes, and slowly turned away, my gaze drifting toward safer territory. I knew the answer; of course I did.

But I couldn't bring myself to say it aloud.

On a beautiful Saturday morning, Marilee woke me by yelling in my ear. "Mommy, wake up! Is it Easter today?"

I struggled to lift my heavy eyelids, but couldn't manage it—bizarre dreams had awakened me several times during the night and left me exhausted. I groaned. "I don't think it's morning yet."

"Uh-huh. The sun's up."

Was it? I lifted a single eyelid, glimpsed daylight around the window blinds, and squinched my eyes shut. "Ask Daddy to get you some breakfast."

"Did the Easter bunny come again?"

"No, sweetheart." Gideon rolled over and leaned on my shoulder as he answered Marilee. "Easter was two weeks ago. We have to wait another year before Easter comes again."

"Oh." Disappointment filled Marilee's voice. "Then what are we gonna do today?"

"We're gonna let Mommy sleep late." The bed frame groaned as Gideon stood and reached for his robe. "And while Mommy sleeps, you and I can eat breakfast. Come on, little bug, let's go in the kitchen and make some pancakes."

I smiled, grateful for Gideon's consideration, but though I wanted to sleep, the sight of daylight had flipped a switch in my head. I was fully awake and needed to pee in the worst way.

Sighing, I flipped off the covers and lowered my feet to the floor, then staggered to the bathroom. Sitting on the toilet, I stared blankly at the wall, and grabbed a handful of tissue to finish up.

Then I saw blood.

I closed my eyes, hoping I'd imagined it. I was seeing things, my eyes were blurry, it was a trick of the light. I wasn't bleeding, I couldn't be.

I opened my eyes, grabbed another wad of tissue, and saw another bloody streak. Enough to make me wonder if I was about to miscarry the baby or babies inside me. I looked at my underwear and saw spots of blood there, too.

No wonder I'd had horrifying dreams.

I stared at the bright stains, overcome by a sense of loss beyond tears. I'd invested so much and been so careful. I had done everything Dr. Forrester told me to do.

And Simone would be devastated if I lost this child.

"Gideon!" Since he was in the kitchen, I raised my voice. "Gid!"

He came running into the bathroom, an apron around his waist and his eyes wide. "What? What's wrong?"

"I'm . . . I'm bleeding."

"Oh, baby." He sank onto the edge of the bathtub and pressed his hand to the back of my head. "I'm so sorry. What can I do?"

"It may be nothing," I said, clinging to hope. "After all, I bled a little when I was pregnant with Marilee. That turned out to be nothing."

"You should call your doctor. I don't want you taking any chances." Gideon stood, then bent to kiss my hairline. "Call the doctor and take the day off. Don't clean anything. Don't go to Mama Isa's. I'll bring you something for dinner. You stay in bed, prop your feet up, and take it easy."

I nodded, weakly agreeing with his suggestions.

I grabbed my cell phone, then fell back against my pillows. Call a doctor—which doctor? I hadn't yet met with my OB, so the only doctor familiar with my case was the reproductive endocrinologist.

So I called Dr. Forrester's answering service. Tracking him down on a Saturday wasn't easy, but I finally reached him and explained my concerns. "I'm not too worried, because I experienced some spotting with my first baby," I told him. "So this could be completely normal, right?"

"It could be," he said, his comment accompanied by a chorus of birdsong. Apparently I'd interrupted him on the golf course. "But be sure to call again if the bleeding gets heavier. If it does, I want you to head to the ER for an ultrasound so we can see what's going on."

I spent the rest of the day in bed, just as Gideon suggested, yet the bleeding persisted—a few drops here, a smear there. I pulled an old box of sanitary napkins from beneath the bathroom sink and stuck one to my underwear, then lay back down and forced myself to watch TV. I refused to look at the pad any more than once an hour, and every time I went into the bathroom I prayed that the stain hadn't grown.

At three o'clock I decided to call Gideon if things were worse by four. But the bleeding had slowed by that time, and by six it had stopped completely.

So . . . the baby—or babies—should be fine. They *had* to be fine.

Later that night, when I received a newsy email from Simone, I decided not to tell her about the bleeding. Why should I worry the woman about something that couldn't be helped?

I would simply do my best to take care of myself and the littlest Amblour.

My obstetrician, Dr. Rita Hawthorn, had scheduled me for an exam and ultrasound exactly one month after the embryo transfer, but the morning of my appointment I received a phone call from her receptionist—a car had struck a telephone pole near her office and a transformer had blown, leaving the medical building without power.

"Dr. Hawthorn is only seeing emergency patients, and she's seeing them at the hospital," the receptionist explained. "Are you having an emergency?"

I sat hard on a kitchen stool and thought about the bleeding I'd experienced nearly two weeks before. Since that day, I'd had no problems at all. "No," I told her. "I'm fine."

"Then you'll understand if I reschedule you." The receptionist's tone warned me not to protest. "Dr. Hawthorn's next available appointment is in three weeks."

I grimaced. "Are you sure you can't squeeze me in sooner? My IPs are eager to know if I'm carrying twins."

"Excuse me?"

"Intended parents. My chart should say I'm a gestational carrier."

The telephone line hummed for a moment, then the nurse cleared her throat. "All right, then, I'll put you on a waiting list. But if Tampa Electric takes a couple of days to get out here, we'll see you May eighth at nine thirty."

I thought about asking for a referral—after all, other doctors had ultrasound machines, and I could probably make another appointment with Dr. Forrester if I needed to—but if I insisted on an ultrasound from a different doctor, wouldn't I alarm Simone and Damien? They had gone through so much with their previous surrogates and I didn't want to give them any reason to worry.

Besides, I wasn't a first-time mother and I knew what to expect. In approximately seven months I would give birth whether or not I had an ultrasound that afternoon.

I would see my OB/GYN as soon as I could get an appointment.

Chapter Nine

As April showers paved the way for blooming plumeria and the fragrant jasmine vining around Mama Isa's wrought-iron fence, I checked my jeans and noticed that they weren't as tight as I expected them to be. Shouldn't my belly be bigger?

Maybe my perceptions were skewed. I hadn't realized I was pregnant with Marilee until well into my second month, so I seemed to balloon all at once. This time, I'd known about the pregnancy from the first minute. No wonder this first trimester seemed so long.

On the first Monday in May, Gideon announced that Mama Isa had invited the entire family over for supper. We always gathered at her home on Saturday nights, but what had sparked this invitation for a Monday? Gideon didn't know.

The entire clan had arrived by the time we did, the men huddling on the front porch to smoke cigars. The women were undoubtedly inside, congregating around the fragrant dishes in the kitchen.

I took Marilee's hand and led her through the cigar smoke and into the company of the women. *"Hola,"* I called, stopping to hug Yanela and Yaritza, who sat in matching rockers near the window. *"¿Cómo están?"*

The others called greetings, but Amelia leapt up from the table and grabbed my hand, pulling me into the narrow hallway that led to the bedrooms. "Come here, I have something to show you," she said, drawing me into the pristine guest room.

I widened my eyes. "Your mom is going to kill you if we mess up her guest room."

"We're not going to mess it up. Even if we did, Mama wouldn't mind because we're celebrating."

"What are we celebrating?"

"You'll see."

Amelia dropped onto the guest bed and I sat next to her, wondering why her eyes glittered like dark sequins. Had Mama Isa decided to retire and turn the store over to Amelia and Mario? Or was this about something else?

I realized the source of Amelia's excitement when she unfurled the magazine she'd rolled up in her hand. "It's for adoptive parents." She smiled as if she'd recently been initiated into a secret club and these pages unlocked the entrance. "Our social worker gave it to us."

"You had a home study interview today?"

"Our last. We're done. We're going on the list as soon as Helen gets our file uploaded to her network. But I wanted to show you this."

She riffled through pages until she reached the back of the publication, then she pointed to a section titled "Some Children Wait." More than a dozen grainy photos filled the page, most of older children. A caption beneath each picture listed the child's name, age, and a fact or two: *Johnny is six and likes to paint rainbows. He's waiting for his forever home.*

A lump rose to my throat. "Good grief, how can you stand to read those bios?"

"I know, aren't they heartbreaking? I asked why people aren't beating down doors to adopt these kids, and Helen said the situation isn't as simple as you might think. These kids might be angels, but some of them come with real baggage, and you can't just stick them in a home and hope for the best. Plus, most young couples are like us—they want kids, but they want to start with a baby or a toddler. It's hard to find people who have what it takes to adopt one of these older kids."

I pressed my hand to my stomach as I studied the pictures. I knew hundreds of kids languished in the foster care system because their parents either couldn't or wouldn't take care of them, but I couldn't help wondering why people like the Amblours wanted to go through all the trouble and expense of finding a gestational carrier when so many kids needed homes. France had to have waiting kids, too. I could understand if Simone and Damien wanted genetic offspring, but they had to use an egg donor, so the child inside me would be genetically related only to Damien. Why not consider an already-born child who needed a home?

I looked up at Amelia, who was gazing at the grainy black-and-white photos as if she'd open her arms to every kid on the page. If I showed the same magazine to Damien Amblour, I didn't think he'd react in the same way.

Still, who was I to judge his motives? Amelia and Mario had been comfortable with adoption, but not every couple would be. Gideon and I never had to make that decision, so maybe I had no right to say what someone else should do.

I tilted my head. "I know you didn't want to try IVF because it's expensive, but why did you write it off so quickly? Wouldn't Mario love to have a son who was a chip off the ol' block?"

The light in Amelia's eyes dimmed a degree. "I did some reading on IVF before we decided to go with adoption. I read that doctors create lots of embryos and then freeze some, knowing that half the frozen babies aren't going to survive the defrosting. That felt wrong to me. Why freeze a lot of babies knowing that something you'll set in motion is going to kill half of them?"

My stomach twisted. "I didn't realize. I . . . hadn't thought about it."

Maybe I didn't *want* to think about it.

"Well, you can't expect IVF facilities to emphasize that aspect of the procedure. And what do you think happens to the embryos that don't develop as well as the others? They're alive, but if they're not used for transfer, they're abandoned and they die. I couldn't stand knowing that. Embryos are human beings, Mandy, no matter how small they are."

"Hey." I lifted both hands in a "Don't shoot" gesture. "I'm not telling anyone to do it, I just wondered why you didn't consider the option."

Amelia pressed her lips together, then shook her head. "I simply couldn't go through with it. If we could find a doctor who would harvest only two eggs and create only two embryos and promise to transfer both of them, then, okay, I could believe we'd done the best we could for those two little ones. But it's not financially profitable for doctors to operate on such a small scale, so they harvest a lot of eggs and create as many embryos as possible. More bang for the buck, you know. And I couldn't reconcile saving a few bucks with allowing human embryos to die."

My gaze fell on the magazine and the pictures of black, white, tan, blond, brunette, petite, gangly, and round children. At one point all of them had been helpless babies; all of them had been embryos blessed with an opportunity to grow.

I couldn't imagine anything more tragic than parents walking away from their child, be he full-size or microscopic.

Amelia and I looked up when someone knocked on the door. Mama Isa's round face appeared, then she gestured to her daughter. *"Te necesito en la cocina,"* she said. *"Apúrate."*

Amelia stuffed her magazine into the back pocket of her jeans, then hurried toward the kitchen. Mama Isa didn't follow, but came into the bedroom and closed the door.

I watched, blinking, as she sank onto the bed beside me. "You know"—she patted my arm—"Amelia has finished the home study."

I nodded. "I know."

"And Amelia, she hopes to get a baby soon."

"I know that, too. I've been praying it happens quickly for her."

"Ah, yes. We are all praying. Many prayers. And we are confident God will answer." Mama Isa leaned forward and looked at me from the corner of her eye. "You still have the cradle from Tumelo and Elaine? That Gideon used when he was a baby?"

I nodded again, but more slowly this time. When Marilee was born, my in-laws had been kind enough to give me Gideon's baby bed. The beautiful oak cradle had been hand carved and stained in a rich, warm color. Someday I hoped to pass it down to Marilee and her children.

But the gleam in Mama Isa's eye set off my internal alarm system.

"Would it not be nice"—Mama Isa leaned closer—"if you gave Amelia the cradle for her baby? She would love to use it, I know."

I stiffened. Give away Gideon's cradle? It had come from *his* side of the family, not Isa's, so it belonged to us. Gideon had been rocked in it, and so had Marilee. The next baby to use it should be from my branch of the family tree.

"Um, maybe Amelia would rather have her own cradle—something she could give to her children. Or maybe you have Amelia's bassinet up in the attic? Maybe Yanela has your old cradle stashed away someplace—"

Mama Isa shook her head. "My *madre* kept us in a dresser drawer when we were babies, and I never had a cradle for Amelia. Elaine, she had money, so she bought a cradle for Gideon." Isa's expression took on a wistful look, and I knew she wanted a promise from me. But how could I give up something so precious? The cradle belonged to me and Gideon, and within a couple of years I hoped to lay our son in it.

"I tell you what." I forced a smile and patted Mama Isa's hand. "When Amelia gets word about her baby, we'll see if she still needs a cradle—maybe she won't, if the child she adopts is older. But if she needs one, we can have a baby shower and pitch in to buy her a cradle. That way she can have an heirloom for her children."

Mama Isa nodded, but the spark had gone out of her eyes. Apparently my suggestion was a sorry alternative.

But that heirloom cradle belonged in my family, and I wouldn't—couldn't—give it up for love or money.

Much to my dismay, apparently every woman in Tampa kept her appointment with Dr. Hawthorn during the last weeks of April. The receptionist never called to tell me about an available opening, and when I called to see if anyone had canceled, the receptionist just laughed. I was in no hurry to go back to the doctor, but Simone was eager to know if they should expect one baby or two.

"I don't want to pressure you," she told me on the phone one afternoon. "But surely you can understand our longing to know if you're carrying twins."

"Oh, I understand," I assured her. "But I don't know what to do about it, unless you want me to change doctors."

"No, no," Simone answered quickly. "If this is the doctor you know and like, then you should stay with him."

"It's a *her,*" I said. "And she delivered Marilee, so I know she's good."

"Then I will try to be patient. As will Damien."

I told Simone good-bye and hung up, knowing she was thinking of their second surrogate, the woman who said they were too demanding. The Amblours had asked very little of me so far, and I knew they were terrified of stressing me to the point where I might lose the baby. I didn't think they had to worry—my stomach was still queasy and my breasts still tender, so I was certainly still pregnant—but I understood their reluctance to press me unnecessarily.

Yet I was also curious. Was my still-flat belly home to one little baby or two?

On the eighth of May, the date of my OB appointment and ultrasound, I groaned when Gideon shook me awake. The room spun around me, my stomach churned, and I knew that if I attempted to speak or stand, I'd throw up. I could barely lift my hand to warn Gideon away.

No wonder I'd spent the night dreaming that I lay on a bobbing, spinning life raft.

"I can't . . . go anywhere," I whispered, carefully portioning out my words. "Call Amelia . . . won't be in."

Gideon dropped to the edge of the bed, compressing the mattress and unintentionally threatening my fragile equilibrium. "Won't you feel better in the afternoon? Or is this something other than morning sickness?"

I barely had the strength to answer. "Don't know . . . but *sick.* Leave . . . don't . . . make me talk."

"Can I get you anything? Do you want something to eat?"

Gideon learned a lesson that morning: never mention food to a woman with an unsettled stomach.

My strength had returned by that afternoon, so I showered, dressed, and went to my OB's office. Dr. Hawthorn met me in the exam room and smiled as we listened to the quick, pulsing heartbeat of an unborn baby.

"Are you sure there aren't two heartbeats?" I asked, thinking of Simone's longing for twins. "They implanted two embryos."

The doctor shot me a sideways glance. "Were you hoping for twins?"

Until she asked, I hadn't realized how much I *had* been hoping for twins. Simone and Damien wanted children, so why not give them two at once?

I sighed and leaned back on the table, realizing that the spotting I had noticed might have resulted from the death of the second fetus. I couldn't know for sure, but the timing seemed about right.

"I only want a healthy baby." I bent one arm to pillow my head. "One is fine."

Gideon would be glad to hear I was definitely carrying a singleton. "One would be so much easier for you," he'd told me that morning. "I don't want you doing anything dangerous. Leave the risk taking to me, will you?"

I blinked the memory away as the doctor reluctantly shook her head. "I'd show you on the ultrasound, but our machine is out of commission at the moment. I'm only hearing one heartbeat, but it's nice and strong. How are you feeling?"

I shrugged. "Like any pregnant woman, I suppose. I'm more tired than usual, I have strange cravings, I have to pee all the time, my breasts are tender, and my mood can turn on a dime."

Dr. Hawthorn chuckled. "Sounds like you're feeling normal. Anything unusual?"

"I had some spotting a couple of weeks ago," I confessed, gripping the edge of the exam table. "Scared me to death, but it only lasted a few hours. And I had spotting with Marilee, too."

"Apparently it was nothing to worry about." The doctor made a note on my chart, then told me I could sit up. "I know any kind of unusual bleeding is scary, but everything looks and sounds good." She moved toward the counter where she would write out her notes. "I'll have my office call the Surrogacy Center to report a heartbeat. I know that milestone is important to your clients."

I thanked her as I sat up, realizing that the Amblours and I had reached a financial checkpoint: my monthly surrogacy payment would rise to twenty-four hundred dollars once the doctor confirmed a fetal heartbeat.

Good news indeed.

The day before Mother's Day, I sent a cute e-card to Simone. In the message box I typed, *Wishing you a Happy Mother's Day this year and for many years to come.*

Gideon and Marilee made me a delicious breakfast in bed the next morning, then my husband and his duffel bag disappeared. This time, I knew, he'd be gone several weeks. According to the news reports, our work in Afghanistan was far from finished, so he and his team would be going back to continue working against enemies of truth, justice, and the American way—or whatever their shadowy bosses ordered them to do.

I spent the rest of May trying to be a good military wife. Marilee and I quietly tied a yellow ribbon around the skinny tree in our front yard and tried to carry on. We spent a lot of time at Mama Isa's, where the family accepted our presence as if we belonged there.

At dinner one night someone mentioned a rumor that had surfaced in the grocery store: the expats had heard Castro was dead. Gordon and Yanela were thrilled by the report, but Tumelo didn't believe it.

"Nothing in the press about Castro being on his deathbed," he said, saving a newspaper before Gordon's eyes. "If it were true, it'd be on the headline news. No one has confirmed anything."

Not wanting to explain Castro's atrocities to Marilee, I sent her into the living room to play Mama Isa's old upright piano. As she plunked the yellowed keys, I propped my elbows on the table and tried to follow the conversation. Neither Gideon nor I reacted as passionately to news about Castro as the older generation did, but we hadn't lived under his regime.

"None of us knew Castro was a communist when he took power," Gordon proclaimed. "We thought he was a patriot, a nationalist. But then he and the government took control of everything, beginning with big industries. Then they came for the small merchants, then they came for our homes. Soon he had turned a proud and prosperous people into slaves. Those who did not agree with him were imprisoned . . . or murdered."

"*¿Te acuerdas?*" Yaritza spoke up, her eyes glowing with the distant light of happy memories. She spoke quickly in Spanish, her voice wavering with emotion as Mama Isa translated for my benefit. "Cuba was so beautiful in those days. The Teatro Nacional was outlined in lightbulbs and lit up the night. Havana was famous for its exotic nightclubs, cabarets, and shopping. The Paseo de Martí was as pretty and modern as anything you'd find in Chicago or New York."

"Recuerdo." Gordon nodded. "But these young people"—his hand swept across the table, taking in me, Mario, and Amelia—"they have no idea. Living in a free country has spoiled them. So many riches here! And so few appreciate them."

We who had never lived under Castro or communism maintained a respectful silence as Gordon's hot eyes raked over us. "Castro is as much a tyrant as he ever was. Eleven million people his family keeps in slavery." His snapping eyes trained on me. "Did you know his regime keeps ninety-eight percent of the money from foreign contracts and gives only two percent to the workers?"

I swallowed hard and shook my head. Experience had taught me that Gordon could not be distracted when the subject of Castro came up, but I had to admire the man's passion.

Business at the grocery picked up over the next few days as Cuban expatriates stopped by to talk about Castro, his brother, and the faded glory of Cuba. And as I listened to them reminisce, I experienced an epiphany: to the expats, Cuba before Castro was an Eden, a beautiful place that had been spoiled and from which they were exiled.

My generation had its own Eden: America before September 11, 2001. We had taken so much for granted before terrorists destroyed our illusion of safety, and we would never be the same. Like my family's Cuban friends, we would always be exiled from those innocent days when we breezed through airport security with our soft drinks in hand. We now lived with what Gideon called our "new normal."

If terrorism did not exist, my husband would not need to be a warrior. But Gideon would not always carry a gun. In eighteen months he would be finished with his tour, then he would walk away from the military and be a normal husband and father. I could be an ordinary civilian wife and not have to worry about him being tortured and killed in some obscure region. I could cut up that blasted duffel bag and burn it on a trash heap.

As the days of May slipped away, Marilee's school year came to a close. The Lisandras and I attended her year-end recital on a Tuesday evening and sat patiently as other young musicians struggled through various classical pieces. When Marilee played a simplified version of Bach's *Minuet in G Major* on the school's grand piano, I applauded politely while Mario, Jorge, and Tumelo stomped and whistled their approval. But afterward I made Marilee stand next to the huge piano so I could snap her picture and email it to Gideon.

When we got home, I called Natasha Bray for my weekly check-in and sent a pleasant email to Simone Amblour. I had nothing new to report to either of them, but they were happy to know I was still doing well.

But after I put Marilee to bed that night, my world darkened when Fox News reported that an American contractor's body had been discovered in a shallow grave just outside Pakistan's borders. The corpse had been chopped into pieces.

I sat alone in the living room, shocked silent by the news, and couldn't help wondering if I would soon hear this kind of report about Gideon. I knew his work was dangerous, I knew he and his team members were elite warriors, but I also knew anything could go wrong during a mission. His jaunty little sayings—*Lead from the front, not from the rear* and *The more you sweat in training, the less you bleed in battle*—had once made me smile, but now they colored my thoughts with gloom. I kept seeing Gideon running up a mountain at the head of his squad; I imagined him hit by rifle fire, I visualized him tumbling into the hands of ruthless captors who would beat him senseless and videotape his torture and murder for all the world to see.

Then I went into my bedroom, closed the door, and quietly went to pieces.

I tried to be strong during the long days when Gideon was away, but more than once that month I cried myself to sleep. On the mornings I showed up at work with anguish in my eyes, Amelia would ask how I was doing. I always told her I was fine, but feeling a bit hormonal.

But I would have you know the truth. On those days, during those hours, I felt as though a vicious tumor had unfurled in my chest, taking up the room I needed to breathe. Only Gideon, only *normalcy,* could shrink it enough to fill my lungs with life-giving air.

I tried to soldier on, but every tear only proved once again that I wasn't cut out to be a warrior's wife.

On my way to my second OB appointment—when by my reckoning I had entered my second trimester—I picked Marilee up from Mama Isa's house and drove straight to Dr. Hawthorn's office.

"Ultrasound today?" the receptionist asked, her glance cutting from me to Marilee. "Do you want your little girl to go in with you or stay in the waiting room?"

Grateful that the ultrasound machine was working, I looked at my daughter and smiled. Maybe this would be a great way to describe what would be happening in the coming months. Marilee might not understand exactly how I came to have another couple's baby in my belly, but as the weeks passed I could explain the situation bit by bit.

"I think I'd like to keep her with me during the scan. She can wait out here during the exam."

I sat and listened as Marilee told me about her day until a nurse called me into the ultrasound room. I took Marilee's hand and walked in with her, then asked her to sit in a chair with her storybook while the lady examined my belly. Without asking any questions, Marilee sat, but her book remained closed as I climbed onto the table and unzipped my jeans.

"Mommy, is something wrong with your tummy?"

"No," I assured her. "But though you can't see it yet, there's a baby in my belly."

Marilee's brows drew into a frown, but she didn't say anything as the ultrasound technician entered and sat on her stool. "And how are we feeling today?" she asked, squirting gel onto my mostly flat stomach.

"Pretty good." I tensed as the chilly goop raised gooseflesh on my skin. "Except for a few days of major morning sickness."

The tech smiled at Marilee, then clicked the keyboard at the ultrasound machine. "Your second time around?" She pressed the transducer against my abdomen and rolled it back and forth, searching for the fetus. After a moment, she paused and glanced at my chart. "How far along are you?"

"Fourteen weeks."

"Congratulations on making it through the first trimester. But are you sure about the date?"

"Absolutely. I'm a gestational carrier, and the embryo was transferred March 15."

"Excuse me a minute, please."

I frowned as the technician stood and left the room, leaving me alone with my daughter.

"Are you okay, Mommy?"

I shifted my gaze to Marilee, who was holding tight to her book. "I'm fine, sweetie. I'm sure the lady just had to check something."

Marilee nodded. "Maybe she needed to go potty."

"Maybe."

I lay in the silence for a moment, then the door opened again. The technician reentered, followed by Dr. Hawthorn. "Good to see you again, Mandy." She walked over to the table and smiled at me, then turned to greet Marilee. "Oh, my. Is this the little angel I helped bring into the world?"

"That's her." I smiled as Marilee stared up at the doctor with wide eyes.

"She's growing up into a beautiful little girl. Now—" The doctor turned and focused on the ultrasound monitor. "Let's see how this new little one is coming along."

The ultrasound technician didn't speak, but her lips drew into a thin line as she pressed the transducer to my abdomen.

I tilted my head and watched the monitor as the doctor pointed toward a small, nebulous shape. "Okay—there's the fetus," she said, concern lacing her voice as the technician probed more firmly with the transducer. "I see eyes . . . and an earlobe. The fetus is small, but everything appears normal."

I shivered in a sudden tremor. "What do you mean by *small*?"

"Somebody might have mixed up their numbers. Or this baby might be a bit of a slow starter."

I caught my breath as ripples of alarm began to spread from the spot where the transducer pressed against my skin. If this baby was undersized, there ought to be a reason—a logical, innocent reason.

"The intended mother told me the egg donor was petite—the woman's like, five feet or something. Very tiny." I knew very little about the biological mother, only what Simone had reluctantly shared. The donor—twenty-four, young, and desperate for ready cash—had been healthy, brunette, blue-eyed, pretty, intelligent, and only five feet tall.

Dr. Hawthorn tilted her head. "I suppose that could explain it. Because this is a tiny baby." The technician tapped on her keyboard and snapped a picture, then another, as I lifted my head again.

"There's the heartbeat—see it beating?" The doctor stepped aside so Marilee could see the pulsing on the screen. The technician turned a knob and we all heard the quick, squishy thumping of a heart perfectly synchronized to the tiny glowing image. "That's a nice strong rhythm."

"See that, honey?" I smiled at Marilee. "There's the baby growing inside Mommy's tummy."

Marilee's eyes widened as she stared at the ghostly picture. "I don't see a baby."

"It's still very small, but it's going to grow. Soon my belly will get big, and that's how we'll know the baby is growing, too."

Marilee abandoned her book and walked over to the exam table for a closer look at my stomach. "How'd the baby get in there?"

The technician shot me a curious glance, but I'd been anticipating the question. I smiled and squeezed Marilee's arm. "Some doctors put the baby inside. It belongs to a mommy who can't grow babies in her own belly, so one day we'll give it to her."

Her lips pursed. "Why can't we keep it?"

"Because it doesn't belong to us. You know how sometimes you spend the night with Mama Isa? She takes care of you, right? I'm doing the same thing for another mama. When the baby runs out of room in my belly, it will be born, and its mama will come to pick it up, just like we pick you up from Mama Isa's house."

Marilee studied my stomach with a look that told me her brain was working hard to decipher the situation. "I still want a baby of our own," she finally said, meeting my gaze. "A little brother would be okay. Or a puppy."

"One day Daddy and I will have another baby. Maybe a brother, maybe a sister. But definitely someone you can play with."

Marilee shifted her gaze to the screen and the amorphous flickering blob. "That doesn't look like a baby."

"I know, honey, right now it looks more like a sea monkey. But one day it will look like a baby." I met my doctor's gaze. "Can you see enough to determine the sex?"

She peered more closely at the screen. "I'm afraid this one's not feeling cooperative today. Maybe next time."

I drew a deep breath and tried not to be disappointed. I knew Damien wanted a son, but he'd accept a daughter because he and Simone had other frozen embryos. If this pregnancy produced a boy, however, I wasn't sure Damien would want other children.

So what would happen to the frozen babies he had stored in a tank?

None of my business.

I squeezed Marilee's shoulder again and turned to the doctor. "So . . . we're good?"

"We're good, but we're not finished." She gave me a paper towel to clean the goop from my skin, then turned and spoke to Marilee. "Sweetheart, my nurse is going to walk you to the waiting room while I take some measurements and talk to your mommy for a few minutes. Can you wait out there for your mom?"

Marilee's dark eyes darted toward me, then she nodded slowly. The ultrasound tech stood and took Marilee's hand, then led her out of the room.

As I slipped out of my clothes and into a gown, Dr. Hawthorn asked routine questions that I answered as best I could. Then I got up on the exam table while she measured the distance between the top of my pubic bone and the top of my uterus. "A lot of doctors don't bother to measure the fundus anymore," she said, "but I'm old-fashioned and I'm concerned about the baby's size. Charting the fundal height will give us reliable evidence the baby is growing as it should be."

I bit my lip, remembering her concerned expression as she studied the ultrasound. "Did you see something . . . wrong?"

She gave me a reassuring smile. "Not wrong, just small. So be sure to take your vitamins and eat a balanced diet. I'd like to see you in another month, so we can be sure the tadpole's developing properly."

"I can do that."

"You have decent insurance?"

"Tricare."

"Ah—the best. See you in a month, then. Take care of yourself."

I sat up and gave her a wry smile. "I will—I have all kinds of people looking out for me."

As the doctor left the room, the technician came back in. As I dressed, she printed copies of the photographs for me and promised to email copies to Simone.

I planned to hang my copies on the refrigerator for Marilee's benefit. If she could see the baby's gradual growth, maybe the situation would begin to make sense to her.

Right after we arrived at home, I went into the living room and called Simone. She had already received the photographs, and while she was thrilled with the picture of her baby, she shared my disappointment in learning I was definitely carrying only one child.

"Twins would have been wonderful," she said, "but one is what we truly wanted. We are delighted, and perhaps we will do better with only one child in our lives. He or she will have our undivided attention."

I told her that one child could certainly keep a mother busy, and promised to check in as soon as I received any other news.

But for now, I assured her, everything looked perfect.

Weeks flew by—long days and silent nights without Gideon. I left our laptop powered up on the kitchen counter in case he was able to Skype us, but sometimes the computer stayed quiet for days. I knew Gid and his men sometimes had to remain incommunicado for security reasons, but every day without hearing from him felt like torture.

How did other wives handle the silence? I asked another operator's wife when I saw her at the PX, and she said she didn't handle it at all. "I take all those feelings," she explained, "and put them in a jar, and put the jar up on the shelf. Every once in a while, when I just can't stand it, I take the jar down and have myself a good rant or a good cry. Then I bottle everything back up and back on the shelf it goes."

I don't know what a psychologist would say about her approach, but I preferred to find other ways to cope. Instead of looking around and feeling sorry for myself, I decided to look forward.

That's when Marilee and I began to play the New House game. The idea came to me one hot Saturday afternoon when I cleaned her room and saw her dollhouse sitting on top of the toy box. She had loved the dollhouse when she received it last Christmas, but she hadn't played with it in what seemed like ages.

I went into my bedroom to get my stack of folders packed with decorating ideas and paint chips. I carried them all into Marilee's room, then sat on the floor, opened the "dining room" folder, and tried to visualize the toy dining room painted in periwinkle blue.

Marilee dropped her storybook and peered over the top of the little house. "Are you playing dolls, Mommy?"

I shook my head. "I'm trying to see if I'd like this dining room painted in"—I held up the paint chip—"this color."

"Oh!" Marilee came around and sat next to me, bending to look inside the toy house. "Why don't you paint the room and see what it looks like?"

I opened my mouth to reply that we couldn't do that, then stopped in midbreath. Why not paint the little room? Home Depot sold tiny paint tester bottles. And practically everything that could go into a real house had been reproduced in toy sizes. . . .

"Come on," I told Marilee, "we're going shopping." As we walked through the aisles of various toy and home improvement stores, I shared our dream with our daughter. "Very soon, when Daddy gets out of the military, we're going to buy a house of our own. You'll have your own bedroom, and we'll have a big backyard—"

"Can we get a puppy?"

I smiled. "I don't see why not."

And as we painted and decorated and repainted and changed our minds again and again, I think I enjoyed the New House game even more than Marilee did. This was play with purpose, and by the time Gideon and I were ready to move, I'd have everything figured out. I'd know my colors, what furnishings we still needed to buy, and how many bedrooms our new home should have. If the new house had rooms proportionately sized like the dollhouse, I'd even know how to arrange the furniture.

Yet Marilee's dollhouse didn't offer everything we really needed. With only a living and dining room downstairs, and only two bedrooms upstairs, the dollhouse had no bathrooms, only a tiny attic, and no nursery.

And a nursery was the one room our new home simply had to have. Being pregnant—feeling the changes in my body and my moods—made me crave another child of my own. I hadn't begun to do anything so foolish as to covet the child growing inside me, but I filled a separate folder with all sorts of ideas for a little boy's room, a nursery done up in light blue with splashes of yellow.

When all this was over—my surrogate pregnancy and Gideon's term of duty—I wanted a son more than anything.

When my fat jeans officially refused to zip, I pulled them off and reached for the cardboard box high on my closet shelf. Natasha Bray had sent a check for maternity clothes after I entered the second trimester, but I'd saved the maternity things I wore with Marilee. Even though they were no longer the most fashionable style, I figured they'd be fine for wearing at work and at home. Besides, a lot of my ordinary clothes were roomy enough to wear throughout the second trimester. We were heading into the hottest part of a Florida summer, perfect weather for comfortable sundresses and loose-fitting cotton tops.

Marilee hadn't said anything about my growing tummy, even though I kept the ultrasound picture on the refrigerator and mentioned the baby several times a week. I wanted to be careful about what I told my daughter because I didn't want her to think all tummy babies had to be given away—what would that do to her sense of security? At the same time, I wanted her to know that giving a baby to someone else wasn't terribly unusual. In some ways, surrogacy was not much different from adoption.

I couldn't help feeling concerned about other people's opinions, too, and one July morning I caught Mama Isa eyeing my belly while I rang up a woman who was buying boxes of sparklers. Mama Isa waited until I finished, then she walked over. "Mandy"—she kept her voice low—"can I talk to you? Amelia can fill in as cashier."

A dozen warning flags in my brain snapped to attention. Mama

Isa was a pillar of the Cuban community—plus she was family, my boss, and the hostess who invited us to her home every week—but rarely did she pull me aside for private conversations. The last time we talked, I disappointed her when I couldn't agree to let Amelia have Gideon's baby cradle.

I gripped the edge of the counter. "Is something wrong?"

"No, no." She smiled and opened the little gate of the checkout stand, now draped with red, white, and blue bunting for the upcoming holiday. "Let's get a coffee and talk."

I cast a sideways glance at Amelia, who waited by the register with her brows raised and her eyes wide. Apparently she didn't know what was on her mother's mind, either.

The warning flags in my brain flapped like mad as I followed Mama Isa. She poured two cups of coffee at the coffee bar, then nodded toward the wooden benches on the sidewalk outside. The thought of drinking coffee in the middle of a stifling summer morning sent a drop of perspiration trickling down my spine, but I took the cup she offered and followed her to the benches. Fortunately, they lay in a narrow strip of shade.

After I'd taken a perfunctory sip, Mama Isa leaned toward me.

"I asked our priest about what you are doing," she said, lifting a brow as she studied me. "I wondered if this thing could be a sin, and Father Jose said it could possibly be a very generous act. As long as no babies were destroyed, this procedure could work for good."

I swallowed the lump that had risen in my throat and stared at two middle school boys who were riding skateboards in the parking lot.

"To be honest, I didn't know much about surrogacy when I began all this," I admitted. "But I can promise you that Simone and Damien—the couple who hired me—did not want to destroy anything. They just want a baby."

"But they created . . . how many *embriones*?"

"Six, I think."

"What happened to the others?" Her wide forehead knit in puzzlement. "You are carrying one. Did they send five babies to heaven?"

I could barely think under her steady scrutiny. "I don't know. I mean, who can say when life actually begins?"

"Bah." She waved the question away. "Life does not begin, it *is*. The egg is alive, the sperm is alive, the *embrión* is alive, no? Life is a gift from God, and is passed on from mama and papa to the *bebé*."

I nodded, unable to argue with her logic.

"So I ask again, did they send five *bebés* to heaven?"

"Um . . . they froze four so they could be used later. And one of the babies was transferred into my womb, but it didn't implant. So it died."

And I saw its blood on my underwear.

Mama Isa pressed her lips together. "Would it have died if it had been formed in its mother's womb?"

"Most likely." I responded in a firm voice, glad I knew the answer to at least one of her questions. "Simone is unable to carry babies. She's miscarried every time she's been pregnant."

"How can you know God would not have saved it?"

"Well . . . no one can know that, I suppose. But doesn't God use doctors to help people overcome their medical problems? He could be using me to give this woman a baby."

Isa tilted her brow. "So this baby inside you—you saved its life?"

"I guess. Yes, I suppose we did. With the doctors' help, of course."

Mama Isa patted my arm. "Then this is a good thing. I can tell Father Jose about this, and he will give you a blessing. I will say a prayer for you and this baby the next time I go to Mass. I will also pray for Amelia and Mario, that God would hurry to send the baby they want so much." She gave me a teasing smile. "If you are not using that cradle, your cousin might like to borrow it for a while. But we can talk about this later."

I exhaled the breath I'd been holding as Mama Isa stood. "Take your time, enjoy your *café*. I must go back to work."

But as she sailed away, my mind supplied the question she had failed to ask: I may have saved this baby's life, but what about the other four? If I was carrying a son for Damien Amblour, those little ones might remain on ice indefinitely.

The hot days of summer fell into a fairly ordinary pattern of humid mornings, rainy afternoons, and sticky evenings. Gideon remained away throughout June, but I had plenty of company—Marilee, Gideon's family, and a steady stream of email messages from France. I had a feeling the Amblours had deliberately restrained their eagerness until I passed the second trimester milestone, but with that behind us, communications began to flow like a rain-swollen river. My doctor assured me that the second trimester was the easiest part of pregnancy, but she had never dealt with two hypervigilant intended parents. Simone and Damien may have decided not to pressure me about medical tests, but they weren't shy about making other requests.

Simone's emails were nearly always apologetic, but more and more often they contained "wishes" I interpreted as *demands*. Furthermore, I had a feeling that these orders didn't originate with Simone, but with Damien, who seemed far more rigid than his wife. Though Simone always cloaked the requests in apologies and gentle language, an unspoken message clearly came through: *We've hired you to do this, so mind how we want the task done.*

The Amblours wanted me to steer clear of harsh cleaners with bleach and to avoid red meats, shellfish, pork, and raw eggs. To help me comply with their wishes, the couple sent cleaning supplies from France, books filled with healthy recipes, and a weekly maid service from Happy Housekeepers. When one email requested that I refrain from pumping my own gas, Amelia joked that the couple might soon deliver an electric car.

As much as I liked Simone and Damien, I was beginning to

wonder if they would ever run out of things they didn't want me to do.

My favorite request arrived via email during the first week of July. I was eighteen weeks pregnant and just easing into maternity clothes when Simone sent a digital recorder filled with Simone and Damien reading stories and poems in French. The enclosed note asked me to play the recordings for at least an hour every night, "preferably through headphones resting on your belly."

Marilee laughed the first time she saw me trying to position a pair of headphones around my gentle baby bump, so she helped by resting her head in my lap and holding the headphones to my stomach. Unfortunately, Marilee had a four-year-old's attention span, so ten minutes later she wanted to go play. In a token effort to comply with the Amblours' request, I propped my arm on Gid's pillow and read a few chapters of *What to Expect When You're Expecting* while Simone sang a French lullaby to my belly button.

She phoned two days later to make certain I'd received the package. I assured her it had arrived safely and that I had begun to play the recordings.

"You may think we are being silly"—I could almost see her blushing—"but this is one of the things I would do if I were carrying the child."

"Really, it's no bother," I told her. "But I'm glad you waited to send it. I didn't have much of a belly before this month."

She laughed. "We waited because the baby can't hear before nineteen weeks. But he's listening now, and I want him to recognize his parents' voices."

My heart did a funny little flip-flop at her comment. I completely understood the longing she felt for someone who was miles away, the anxiety that kept her awake at night, and the helplessness that made her feel small when she realized she had absolutely no control over events that might injure someone she loved dearly. I felt all those things whenever I thought of Gideon, so my heart was also twisted in a knot of frustration and yearning.

But for some reason it felt wrong for her to say "his parents' voices." Which meant my feelings were wrong, because this was definitely *not* my child.

This was a job, I reminded myself. A contract. I was babysitting, nothing more.

I tried to maintain a respectful distance from the Amblours, but sometimes I couldn't help thinking of Simone as a close friend. We were in nearly constant contact, and I couldn't blame her for wanting to reach out to me. If the situation were reversed and she were carrying Marilee, I'd have camped out on her doorstep.

"I understand how you feel," I assured her. "And I'm so sorry we weren't able to learn the baby's gender at the last ultrasound. The little monkey didn't want to cooperate."

"Children rarely do," Simone said, a smile in her voice. "And now, sweet friend, get some rest. *Bonsoir et au revoir.*"

Chapter Ten

"Did you see the big fireworks display last night?" Dr. Hawthorn looked up from my chart and smiled. "Or were you busy cleaning up after your Fourth of July picnic?"

I slipped off the exam table and made my way toward the small dressing alcove in the obstetrician's exam room. "I took Marilee to my aunt's house, and she stayed up to watch the fireworks. I fell asleep on the sofa in the living room."

Dr. Hawthorn chuckled and jotted something on my chart. "You should be able to feel the baby moving now. Experienced any kicks?"

I thought about it, then shook my head and closed the small curtain. "Not really. Unless what I've been calling indigestion is actually the kid practicing his judo."

"Maybe he's one of those sleepy babies. Have you been bothered by anything in particular?"

I drew a deep breath and took my blouse from the hook I'd hung it on. "Everything's fine—except my sleep. I keep waking up in the middle of the night after having the wildest dreams."

"Strange and unusually vivid dreams are perfectly natural," the doctor called. "First, you're getting up during the night more than usual because you have to urinate frequently. You're waking right after a dream, so you remember it. You probably dream just as often when you're not pregnant, but in the morning you don't remember anything about them."

I fumbled with the buttons on my blouse. "The dreams feel so . . . unusual. And weird."

"You're not the first to tell me about bizarre dreams, Amanda. Most of them are easily understood."

I laughed and reached for my maternity jeans. "I didn't know you interpreted visions, too."

"It's not as complicated as you might expect. Think of dreams as a convenient way for your subconscious to send you a message. You go through huge changes when you're pregnant, and you have a lot to think about. Your subconscious works overtime to make sure you're handling everything that comes your way. You can chalk it all up to raging hormones."

When I opened the curtain again, she gave me a knowing smile. "Let me guess—you're in the second trimester, so you've probably been dreaming about cuddly puppies, carrying suitcases, or giving birth to your husband."

My jaw dropped. "Are you psychic? I haven't dreamed about giving birth to my husband, but last night I gave birth to the intended father. And he's huge, so that's no small task."

She chuckled. "I'd love to say I've been reading your mind, but these images are common. You probably dreamed of giving birth to the intended father because dealing with him seems easier than dealing with a helpless baby. You dream about cuddly puppies or some other animal when you're feeling maternal. Women who worry about their mothering skills might dream of being threatened by clinging, infantlike creatures—monkeys, for instance." She tilted her head. "Are you dreaming of animals?"

"I dreamed about puppies a couple of nights ago," I confessed. "I came home and found a litter of poodles behind the refrigerator. I went out on a crazed search to find families for them before Gideon got home."

The doctor raised a brow. "Given your circumstances, you don't have to be a psychologist to figure out that one. You found poodles? *French* poodles, by chance?"

I gasped as the connection became clear. "Wow."

"You wanted to find homes for the poodles because you're concerned about placing the baby you're carrying in its proper family. As to your hurry to get rid of them before your husband came home, does he still support your decision to be a surrogate?"

I shrugged. "He hasn't said anything negative. But he's been away, so we don't get to talk much."

"Perhaps you're worried that he's hiding some degree of resentment. Or maybe you're just worried—about him, about the baby, about life in general. I wouldn't blame you if you were anxious." She smiled. "But don't let yourself worry too much, Amanda. Why don't you start keeping a pregnancy journal and write out your dreams? Once you get them down on paper, you may be able to see what your subconscious was trying to tell you. Dream interpretation can be remarkably easy with a little help from hindsight."

"I've been keeping a diary, so it'd be easy to add my dreams to my notes."

"Write the dreams down right away, or you're likely to forget them. You might try keeping your journal on the nightstand."

"I can do that. And let me see if I'm any good at this—if I dream of carrying suitcases, is that because I'm carrying extra weight?"

"You *are* good at this." She closed my chart and moved toward the door. "Anything else you need from me? If not, shall we meet again in a couple of weeks? It's about time for your midterm ultrasound."

I picked up my purse and checked my reflection in the mirror. "I don't see why not."

In mid-July, Simone and Damien flew in for my twenty-week ultrasound. I expected to enjoy the usual easy conversation with

Dr. Hawthorn, but this time she directed nearly all her comments to Simone and Damien. Like a third wheel I lay on the table and heard my doctor announce that I was carrying a baby boy. "He's still small"—she peered at the screen—"but I can see everything I'm supposed to see. Arms, legs, eyes, ears, and, of course, the little boy bits. Congratulations, Mom and Dad."

Simone turned to Damien and gripped his hand. Damien kept his gaze fixed on the glowing monitor. *"Un fils,"* he whispered, his voice filled with awe. *"Dieu merci! Merveilleux!"*

Simone pressed her free hand over her heart, then smiled at me with affection and gratitude.

In that moment, I stopped feeling like a mindless vessel and became someone who was deeply appreciated. I had to bite my lower lip to keep from bawling right there on the table.

After the ultrasound, the Amblours invited my family to lunch, but Marilee was spending the day with Amelia and Gideon was still away, probably in Afghanistan.

"I'm sorry," I told Simone and Damien. "Seems like my family is scattered everywhere."

"Then we will take *you.*" Simone slipped her arm through mine and playfully led me toward their rented car. "Tell me your favorite place to eat, and we will go there. It is not enough to repay you for what you're doing, but perhaps it is a start."

I went along, bemused by her attitude. Had she forgotten that they were paying me by the month? They didn't need to do anything else, but I didn't want to appear ungrateful for their kindness.

I led them to The Frog Pond, a small café near the beach, and I wasn't surprised that Simone and Damien had never discovered it on any of their trips to Florida. The café lay in a strip mall well away from the usual tourist haunts, but the establishment served a wonderful breakfast and lunch, then closed for the day. I suspected the owner was a working mom who wanted to spend evenings with her family. If that was the case, I couldn't blame her.

After we enjoyed a delicious salad and quiche, Damien went off to buy a newspaper while Simone and I strolled through some of the stores in the little shopping center. One shop featured children's clothing, and I was delighted when Simone asked if I wanted to look inside. We went in together, then split up as I veered toward the girls' clothing and Simone beelined for the boys' section.

I couldn't believe the adorable outfits and gadgets offered in the baby boutique. Infant items had become much more useful and creative in the years since Marilee's birth.

I paused by a beautiful crib set. The bumper pads and quilted coverlet featured sea creatures—a smiling octopus, a happy whale, several colorful fish, and an embroidered big-eyed crab. The set was far too expensive for someone like me, but the exorbitant price wouldn't be a problem for Simone.

I ran my hand over the soft cotton fabric. Since we lived near the beach and I'd heard that the Amblours did, too, I thought Simone might appreciate the blending of both our locales as a nursery motif. I turned and waved to get her attention, then lifted the comforter as she approached. "Isn't this darling? They're making such beautiful items for children's rooms these days."

Simone gave me a perfunctory nod, but the set clearly didn't charm her as it had me. I lowered the blanket, my smile fading as a sharp sense of disappointment replaced my enthusiasm.

What was wrong with this crib set? Did she not like my taste? Or was it not good enough for her? She didn't even take a good look at the design—

I brought my hand to my forehead and told myself to calm down.

What was *wrong* with me? Simone and I weren't best friends, not really, and this wasn't my baby. I was carrying her son and of course she wanted to decorate her own nursery. Once I delivered, I might never see the baby, Simone, or Damien again. We would not be permanently connected, so I'd be foolish to think she would seriously consider my suggestions about her nursery.

On the other hand, would it have killed her to say something nice about the stupid comforter? She could have said any one of a dozen things or even placated me with an "Isn't that lovely," but instead she simply nodded and walked away.

I drew a deep breath and tried to shake off my growing resentment. I had to be hormonal; that's why my mood kept swinging from ecstatic to indignant and back again.

"Not my baby," I murmured as I walked toward a display of high chairs. "This is not my baby, so I don't care what kind of crib he sleeps in. Simone will buy his bed, his high chair, his clothes, his shoes. She *wants* to buy for him, she wants to care for him, and she may even resent my suggestions because I'm doing something she desperately wants to do—"

Obviously oblivious to my muttered monologue, Simone stopped at the front door and turned to look for me. "Amanda, are you ready to go?"

I nodded and hurried after her, eager to leave my irritations behind.

On a hot Sunday night in August, well after I'd put Marilee to bed, a story from Massachusetts dominated the news: in the wealthy enclave of Martha's Vineyard, two ten-year-old girls had gone out for ice cream and disappeared. Local citizens and police were scouring the area to determine what had happened to them.

The news showed a picture of the two girls, both smiling, both wearing bright red windbreakers and dark shorts. In a few years, Marilee might look just like them.

I turned off the TV and sat in an unnatural silence, broken only by the sound of the refrigerator dumping ice into the freezer bin. Inexplicably, my uneasiness swelled into alarm. Was this near panic the result of restless hormones, or was it some kind of premonition that something was happening to Gideon?

I swallowed to bring my heart down from my throat. I was

spending too much time alone in this house. I had too much free time and too active an imagination. At times like this, the house was far too quiet.

With Gideon away, Marilee and I had no one to protect us—maybe we needed a dog now. Maybe we should go to the animal shelter and see if they had a big dog that would love us and fight off an intruder.

Or maybe I should buy a gun.

I turned off the lamp and moved to the window, lifting the louvers on the shutters so I could look out and see the dimly lit street. Nothing moved in the darkness, and my neighbors' vehicles had been neatly tucked into garages and parking spaces. This was a safe neighborhood, or at least as safe as a neighborhood could be.

Still, a chill climbed the ladder of my spine.

What was wrong with me? I would drive myself crazy if I kept looking for trouble. I should go to bed, let myself drift away on a soft tide and awaken in reassuring daylight.

I moved toward the hallway and my bedroom, but paused to pick up my cell phone from the kitchen counter. I could try to reach Gideon, but I'd feel foolish if I asked someone to track him down just so I could hear his voice.

None of the other military wives were this skittish. I saw them at the PX; I heard them talking about how they argued with auto mechanics, climbed on rooftops to repair leaks, and delivered puppies without help from anyone. They had all their fears bottled up and put away on shelves, and nothing seemed to faze them.

But everything bothered me. Especially the evening news.

The darkness around me felt heavy and threatening as I hurried into my bedroom, slid beneath the covers, and pulled the comforter up to my nose. I peered out, searching for signs of trouble, but nothing moved, not even the curtains. The air conditioner clicked on, then a current of cool air stirred the dust trails hanging from the ceiling fan.

My mouth twisted in a wry smile. Would the Amblours allow

me to clean my fans, or would they rather I leave that chore to the Happy Housekeepers?

After several minutes, my pulse rate slowed and I was able to sleep.

My fingers grasped handfuls of dew dampened grass, my sneakers slipped as I struggled to find my footing. I was lying on my back, blinking at a star-spangled sky, but I wasn't alone. From somewhere off to my left I heard a vague mechanical tick, accompanied by low moans.

"Daddy?"

I rolled onto my belly and looked around. A long stretch of asphalt sliced through the woods and our Pontiac lay upside down on a patch of gravel. I saw vacant windows, crumpled metal, and red plastic shards glinting in the moonlight. Then someone groaned again.

"Daddy!" I crawled forward, tiny rocks cutting into my knees as I inched toward the sound. Sparkling glass pebbles mingled with the scree. My father's hand was visible inside the car, the fingers twitching. He was alive.

"Daddy!" I hurried forward on hands and knees, then lowered my head to peer into the gloomy space. I saw my precious father's dark jacket, the ghostly whiteness of his shirt, and his face, painted red like a devil mask.

"Mandy." A weak smile flitted over his mouth as our eyes met. "Honey, you need to get away from the car. Go sit on the grass. And stay there."

"I don't want to leave you, Daddy."

"You have to, honey. You have to obey me, right now."

"I can't leave you!"

"I want you to go, now.*" His voice firmed. "And don't worry. I'll meet you at the river."*

I knew what he wanted me to say next; I could feel the words on my tongue, but I couldn't say them. "Don't leave me, Daddy!"

"Get away, honey."

"Daddy!" I grabbed his hand and pulled until I heard him cry out, but I couldn't move him more than a few inches. "Daddy, help me. Please."

"Mandy." A note of fear entered his voice, chilling my bones, and an instant later I saw the flickering light. "Mandy, get away from here, right now!" He screamed at me, his voice rougher and louder than it had ever been, and the shock of his panic forced me back.

I scooted away, scarcely aware of the glass and gravel slashing my palms. My tears had given birth to sobs, but something in me knew I had to obey. "I'll meet you at the river!" he yelled, his voice ragged with panic. "I'll look for you!"

I pressed my hands to my face, unable to say the words he wanted to hear.

While I sat motionless, paralyzed with panic, the car erupted into flames. A hair-raising scream swallowed up my father's voice, and blazing heat sent sweat streaming over my face.

"I'll be under the tree." I hiccupped the words, hoping my belated obedience would somehow set things right. "I'll be waiting at the tree, I'll be waiting, Daddy, I'll be waiting—"

The scene dissolved and I sat up clutching a sheet to my chest, aware of the dampness of perspiration between my breasts. My breath came in gasps and my arms were covered in gooseflesh.

I reached for Gideon, but my hand closed around empty space.

"You're doing very well." Dr. Hawthorn smiled at me as she concluded my August checkup. "At twenty-three weeks you haven't gained too much weight and your blood pressure is steady. How's your sleep? Is the baby keeping you up at night?"

"He moves a lot these days." I forced a smile. "But it's not the baby keeping me up at night, it's the dreams."

"Still?" She arched a brow. "Let me guess—are you dreaming of a trip to a foreign country where you don't want to go?"

I shook my head.

"Dreaming of your baby's face, but he looks like some kind of animal?"

"I have dreamed of the baby's face, and he looks like Gideon. But that's not keeping me awake. I'm having a recurrent nightmare. I had it Sunday night, then I had it again last night."

"Did you write it down?"

I nodded.

"Tell me about it."

I pressed my lips together, reluctant to revisit the nightmare even in the dull reality of Dr. Hawthorn's exam room. But since she'd asked . . .

I wrapped myself in resolve. "I dream I'm little again, and I find myself lying on a patch of grass. My family's car is upside down, and my father is still inside. I go to him, wanting to get him out, but I can't move him. He tells me to get away, then the car bursts into flames. That's it." I shrugged and turned my head, not wanting her to see the tears that had begun to blur my vision. "If that's a message from my subconscious, I don't know how to interpret it."

She waited, and because nature abhors a vacuum, the absence of sound pulled a sob from me. I cried for a minute, fanning my face as if I were a boiling pot, then Dr. Hawthorn handed me a box of tissues.

When I finally had my emotions under control, I looked up to find her watching me with a slightly perplexed expression, as if she'd thought of a question but didn't want to ask it. "Is your father . . ." she finally said, ". . . still living?"

I shook my head. "He died when I was six."

"May I ask how?"

"Car accident."

"Ah." She glanced at my chart, then looked back at me. "Nearly all pregnant women deal with anxiety, Amanda, and you're probably repressing a boatload of stress. Your husband's overseas, you're dealing with a surrogacy, and for a while, at least, you're functioning as a single parent. You may not be aware of it, but you're probably feeling a high degree of unconscious worry, and your mind has linked it to that traumatic period in your childhood. My advice is for you to schedule some time for personal relaxation. Find a way to release some of that stress, and you'll be fine. Your pregnancy is proceeding just as it should, and you're as healthy as the proverbial horse. So relax and get a massage. Enjoy your family. Ask for help when you need it. And think about how happy your intended parents are going to be because of your generosity."

I let out a long exhalation of relief, then gave her a heartfelt smile. "Maybe I'll take my daughter out for pizza tonight. She'd like that."

"That's the spirit." As I stood to get dressed, Dr. Hawthorn clicked her pen and turned to write on my chart. I hoped she wasn't writing, *Be alert for possible nervous breakdown.*

Chapter Eleven

On several occasions Simone had mentioned that the grape harvest took place in the fall, so everyone at the vineyard would be busy during that season. So it was with great and guilty anticipation that I bid adieu to August and welcomed September, hoping I'd be able to enjoy a few days without international phone calls or daily emails to inquire about my burgeoning belly.

I didn't begrudge Simone the opportunity to vicariously experience this pregnancy—honestly, if I'd had the power to empathically transmit each of my twinges, cramps, and episodes of heartburn, I'd have done so in a New York minute. But I'd been hired to complete a task, and I was working hard to complete it to the best of my ability. At some point, surely, the employer needed to give the employee some breathing space.

I prayed it would come in September.

Payments from the Amblours allowed me to enroll Marilee in the Takahashi program again, so the Monday after Labor Day I sent her off to school, grateful she'd have something to take her mind off missing her daddy.

At my monthly obstetrics appointment I learned that I had officially entered the third trimester, so I'd be seeing Dr. Hawthorn every two weeks instead of every month. I winced at the news, knowing Simone would gently request complete reports on every checkup and weigh-in.

"I'm concerned," the doctor said, studying my latest sonogram. She swiveled on her stool to better see the image. "At twenty-seven weeks, a baby should be the size of a head of cauliflower. Your little passenger is more the size of a spaghetti squash."

I smiled. "I've seen some pretty big spaghetti squash."

"Next week he should be as big as a butternut squash, but your baby will probably be the size of a large mango."

Her references to fruit and vegetables confused me. Didn't human beings come in different sizes? "We've always known he'd be small. We've been told the egg donor was petite."

"Yes . . . but a twenty-seven-week fetus should weigh twice what yours does. If you were the typical patient, I'd assume you got the conception date wrong, but you're not the typical patient." Her brow wrinkled. "I'm wondering if we ought to consider amniocentesis."

I grimaced. I'd endured so many needle pricks back in the Lupron phase that the thought of having a sharp instrument stabbed into my uterus made me feel faint. Amnio also carried a risk to the developing baby, and I didn't think Simone would want to take that risk.

"I think we should talk to the intended parents before deciding," I said. "They're supercautious about medical tests. They may not want me to have amnio."

The doctor clicked her tongue against her teeth, then shook her head. "I suppose we might as well stick to our wait-and-see position. I'd be more concerned if the baby wasn't growing at all. He *is* developing, just more slowly than usual."

"A slow starter," I said, echoing what she'd told me weeks ago. "Some babies don't want to be the first ones out of the gate."

"Perhaps." The doctor closed my chart, then swiveled toward me. "Anything bothering you? Any more bad dreams?"

I nodded, reluctant to tell her about my continuing nightmares. "I'm still dreaming about my dad in the car wreck. And every once in a while I dream about water—I'm swimming and breathing under the surface, I'm in a river, I'm in the ocean, or living in a swimming pool. I'm not drowning, though I'm pretty sure I'm about to."

"Water is a common element in pregnancy dreams," the doctor said, smiling. "Think about it—the baby is swimming in amniotic fluid, and every time he moves you're reminded of that. Perfectly natural."

"And the car wreck?"

A corner of her smile twisted. "Your husband's still away and you're still anxious. Remember to make time to relax. Now that we're in the third trimester, you're heading for the home stretch. Take good care of yourself, and I'll see you in a couple of weeks."

I hadn't run many races in my lifetime, but I knew the home stretch could be the toughest part of the race.

The warm, muggy days of September slid slowly into October, and October brought a welcome surprise—Gideon came home. He didn't know how long he'd be able to stay, but his unit would be working out of MacDill's Special Operations command headquarters for a while, and that was good news for our family.

My baby bump had become more pronounced while Gideon was away, but my fears about him finding me unattractive while carrying another man's baby proved to be unfounded. I saw a new light in his eyes when he gazed at me, a glow that looked like appreciation.

"I guess absence really does make the heart grow fonder," I told him one night as I stepped up to his chair and ran my fingers through his curls. "I think you actually missed me while you were away."

"I wouldn't want you anywhere near the places I've been, but I can't count the times I've wished I were back here with you." His gaze traveled over my face and searched my eyes. "And I've never seen you looking more beautiful." He lowered his head and pressed a gentle kiss to my stomach. "You're a brave one, to do all this for our family."

Brave? I coughed rather than release the laugh that bubbled to the surface. If only he knew how I cowered when he was away.

One Saturday soon after his return Gideon went with me to Mama Yanela's grocery to help the family take inventory. From the corner of my eye I glimpsed kilted Claude Newton speaking to him in the canned goods aisle, then Gideon looked at me and smiled. I finished checking out another customer and sent her on her way. What were Gid and our local nudist talking about?

A few minutes later, Gideon strolled toward the register.

"You know Claude?" I tilted my head toward the man now browsing the vegetable bins. "You two seemed to be having quite a conversation."

Gideon laughed and hopped up on the counter. "He asked if I was part of Yanela's family, so I said yes. Then he asked if Mama Isa was my mother, so I told him no, I was Tumelo's son. Then he asked if Amelia was my wife, so I said no and pointed to you."

"He was probably sorry he asked. Instead of a simple answer, he got the entire family tree."

"That's not the best part." My husband's eyes warmed as he smiled. "Once he realized you were my wife, he congratulated me on the coming baby. I said the baby wasn't ours; you were a having a baby for another couple. The guy looked confused, then he asked how I could let my beautiful wife sleep with another man."

I snorted. "I'm not at all surprised. For one thing, Claude's not . . . conventional. And when I get the same thing—people who congratulate me until I explain the baby's not mine—most of them look shocked and ask how I could possibly give my baby away. I thought people understood surrogacy, but apparently I was wrong."

"Maybe"—Gideon tweaked the end of my nose—"when someone congratulates us, we should just say 'Thanks.'"

"I think you're right."

Though the Amblour vineyard was in the midst of a busy harvest season, Simone's emails continued to arrive as dependably as the sunrise. I endured them as graciously as I could, usually choosing to answer them at the end of the day, when any follow-up questions could be postponed until the next night.

In the meantime, I tolerated the presence of Happy Housekeepers in my home on Wednesdays, used only the "green" cleaners Simone sent when I had to clean, asked grumbling service station attendants to pump my gas, and ordered chicken when I really wanted steak. I cut back my hours at the grocery to the point where one morning Mario clutched his chest and feigned a heart attack when I came through the door.

"I don't know why you even bother to come in," Amelia said, a bemused look on her face as I waddled toward the register. "Aren't you earning a paycheck just by being pregnant?"

"Maybe I miss the joy of the job." I tossed a teasing smirk in her direction and stashed my purse beneath the counter. "Maybe I come to work just to see *mi familia.*"

In truth, I couldn't imagine giving up my work at the grocery. If I didn't go in for at least a few hours every week, I would feel as though I had cut myself off from the world. My mom hadn't visited in months, and I had no other close relatives. The Lisandras were my family now, and I couldn't imagine not seeing them every day.

As much as I enjoyed working at the grocery, I told Amelia I wouldn't be in on October 12, Marilee's birthday.

"You know my mom's driving over tomorrow," I told Gideon as we climbed into our big four-poster the night before Marilee's big day. "She wouldn't miss a special occasion like this."

"I remembered." Gideon stretched out and draped a protective arm over my stomach, then he yawned. "Are you going to play Simone's recording tonight?"

I glanced at the headphones on my nightstand and groaned. "I'm too tired, and there's too much going on tomorrow. We have the birthday here, the party at Mama Isa's, and I'll have to deal with Mom. . . ."

Silence slipped between us, then Gideon drew me closer. "What is it with you and your mother? I thought women were supposed to be tight. Like soul sisters or something."

Too tired to go into explanations I didn't like to think about, I closed my eyes. "I love my mom."

"But you're not close. Sometimes I think you're closer to Mama Isa than to your own mom."

I sighed heavily, hoping he'd take the hint and let me drift away. "I don't know. Sometimes women can drive each other crazy."

"But she's your *mother.*"

"So? Maybe we're too much alike."

"I don't think you're alike at all. And you're pregnant—I thought other women thrived on discussing that stuff. When we had Marilee I expected her to be over here to give you advice every weekend, but she hardly ever came."

"My mom's . . . modest. If you ask her, she'll say the stork brought me."

"She's never struck me as being that old-fashioned. I just don't understand why you two aren't close."

I opened my eyes and frowned into the darkness. "I don't know, Gid, and I'm really tired. Can we go to sleep, please?"

Around us, the room lay quiet, as if listening, then Gideon chuckled. "Get your rest, baby girl. Didn't mean to play the shrink at this hour."

"That's okay, sweetie. I love you."

I rolled onto my side, away from him and his confounded questions.

Sunlight had only begun to fringe our window blinds when my daughter's voice jarred me into full wakefulness. "Mama, wake up! Daddy, *please* wake up!"

Thankfully, Gideon answered her. "I'm comin', jelly belly. But let's let your mama sleep a little longer."

"But, Daddy, it's my *birthday*!"

Marilee's anguished plea—along with a relentless pressure on my bladder—forced my eyes open. A few days ago Gideon had dubbed me the Pee Queen, and I couldn't blame him for making fun. The near-constant need to find a bathroom was annoying, but at least I'd only gained twenty-four pounds. By this point in my last pregnancy, I was packing on a pound per week.

"I'm up," I mumbled.

Unlike Gideon, who seemed to sleep with one eye open, I needed a good ten minutes before my eyes focused and my brain slipped into gear. But Marilee had been anticipating this special day for weeks.

When my surroundings finally shifted from soft blurs to discrete shapes with edges, I saw my adorable daughter dancing in the bedroom doorway, her ruffled purple tutu around her waist and her stuffed monkey under one arm. "Come on, Mommy, get up! It's time to open presents!"

I braced myself on the edge of the mattress. "I thought we were going to wait until the party to open your gifts."

"Do I have to?"

"I dunno." I leaned back on my elbows and peered at Gideon, adorably rumpled and propped against the headboard. "Does she have to wait until the party?"

"I think"—Gideon grinned—"this is a good time for her to open the gifts from us. The family will bring other stuff later, so she can save those presents for the family party."

Proving once again that she had Gideon wrapped around her little finger, Marilee clapped and twirled.

I dropped back onto the bed, my head missing Gideon's thigh by inches, and folded my hands atop my soccer ball belly. "I think the birthday girl and her daddy should make a nice breakfast for the mommy."

"Whaddya think, bug?" Gideon stood and tied on his robe. "Should we make French toast or pancakes?"

"Toast!" Marilee danced away, leaping toward the kitchen.

Gideon paused to plant a kiss on my forehead. "Sleep a little longer if you want. I'll call you when breakfast is ready."

"No, I need to get up." With an effort, I pushed myself upright. "I'm going to shower and dress. I'll see you in a few minutes."

By the time I made it into the kitchen, Gideon and Marilee had done a passable job of making French toast, eggs, and sausage. I couldn't help noticing that Marilee's toast had raisin eyes, a cinnamon-powdered nose, and a chocolate chip smile. "Nice touch, five-year-old girl." I winked at her. "Was that your idea?"

"Daddy's." Marilee bit the end off a sausage link and grinned. "He said birthdays are for chocolate chips."

"I think every day should be for chocolate chips." I sighed as Gideon set a plate in front of me. "Maybe every day should be for Daddy to do the cooking."

Gideon hooked his thumbs behind the straps of my cupcake apron and grinned. "I don't know about that, but I *could* be persuaded."

"We'll talk about that later." I took a heaping bite of the syrup-drenched bread, then closed my eyes. "Umm, that *is* good. I'd be happy to consider your terms."

I had taken no more than three bites when Marilee hopped off her stool and addressed us with unusual solemnity. "I'm finished. May I open my birthday presents now?"

I glanced at Gideon. "Do you know where they are?"

"I have a pretty good idea." He bent forward, his hands on his knees, and tugged a hank of Marilee's hair. "Why don't you sit on your stool and wait for me? I'll be right back with the goodies."

As she hurried to comply, I forked up a bite of sausage and chewed slowly, aware of the extra weight at my center. If Gideon didn't return soon, I was going to have to take yet another bathroom break.

I heard the closet door open and close, then Gideon strode back into the kitchen, two small packages riding atop a huge box in his arms. Marilee's eyes widened. "All that, for me?"

"For you, birthday girl."

Gideon set the smaller boxes on the counter and left the big one on the floor. "Have at it, kiddo."

Marilee opened the two smaller presents first, thanking us for the doll and the new ballerina outfit as soon as she opened them. Then she set those gifts aside and jumped from her stool, approaching the big box almost hesitantly. "Oh my goodness, what is it?"

I propped my chin on my hand. "Open the box and you'll see."

Marilee tore the top fold of wrapping paper away, then squealed so loudly that I thought she might hurt her throat. "Oh my goodness, oh my goodness, a piano!" She turned the half-wrapped package so I could see the box. "Look, Mommy, a piano!"

"I know, sweetie—do you like it?"

"I *love* it!"

I grinned at Gideon, who leaned against the counter, watching us with fondness in his dark eyes. "Here." He bent to help her. "Let me get that thing out of the box for you."

The expensive pink piano was a far cry from the full-size practice keyboards they used at her school, but it was a kid-sized instrument and came with a matching pink stool. I knew it wouldn't do much to enhance Marilee's music lessons, but she'd be able to play it in her room—for fun, not for practice. Sometimes I worried that we were forcing too much on her too soon, and I wanted her music to remain a source of pleasure. If a toy piano helped her retain that sense of fun, it'd be worth the extravagance.

Gideon kicked the box out of the way and lowered the pink piano to the kitchen floor. Marilee dragged the little stool over and sat on it, her fingers stroking the appliquéd flowers, the curving painted lines, and the decorative etching. Finally her fingers caressed the keys, then she played one of her favorite songs, "Blow the Man Down." The tone was a little thin and stringy, but I had never enjoyed a concert so much.

When she finished, she hopped off her stool and ran to me, throwing her arms around my neck. "You are the best mommy in the whole world! Thank you so much for my piano!"

I kissed her cheek, then watched as Marilee gave Gideon the same enthusiastic thanks. At moments like this, I decided, blinking away tears, parenting was worth every gut-wrenching labor pain.

I had just finished clearing away the breakfast dishes when a knock on the door followed the sound of commotion on the street. "Gid?" I called up the stairs to the spare bedroom, where he was working out. "Are you expecting someone?"

Gideon came jogging down the steps, bare chested and sweaty with a towel around his neck. "Someone out there?"

"Will you check? I don't have any makeup on."

Gideon walked through the foyer and stepped out the front door. When he didn't return after a few minutes, curiosity got the better of me. Telling Marilee to stay inside, I ran my fingers through my messy hair and peeked out the front door.

A delivery truck had backed into our driveway, and someone had lowered the automatic lift at the back. Gideon stood on the lawn, his arms crossed as he watched two men struggle with a large shrouded object.

"What is that?" I called, but Gid couldn't hear me over the loud whine of the mechanical lift.

I tiptoed out and squeezed Gideon's arm. "Did you arrange this?"

He shook his head.

"Then who are these men, and what's in the truck?"

He turned, giving me a warning look that put an immediate damper on my curiosity. "You won't believe it."

"What?"

"You'll see."

The men lowered the object on the lift, then wheeled it toward our front door, the wooden dolly creaking beneath the weight.

"Gid—" I tugged on the towel around his neck. "Tell me now."

"They said it's a gift," he said. "From the Amblours."

My thoughts scampered in confusion, then settled on a fragment of a recent email conversation I'd had with Simone. Once again she'd said she didn't know how to thank us, but apparently she had found a way.

I didn't identify the large object until the dolly passed me, then I recognized the harplike shape beneath the cargo blanket. The Amblours had sent us a piano—and not just any piano, but a baby grand.

My mind went blank with shock. I followed the deliverymen and sat speechless on the sofa while they screwed legs on the body, brought in a tufted leather stool, and shifted my furniture to accommodate the instrument. We now had no open space in the center of the living room, but, by golly, we had a grand piano.

When they had finished, I turned to my husband. "We can't accept this. I should probably call the agency and tell Natasha; there might be some kind of rule—"

"Please, lady." One of the workmen straightened and wiped his dripping brow with a handkerchief. "This is the wrong time to be sayin' things like that."

"I'm sorry, but I didn't realize . . . I couldn't believe it."

Gideon eyed me with concern. "Do you want to send it back?"

I might have said yes—I was about to—but just then Marilee came downstairs and froze on the bottom step, her eyes as wide as dinner plates. "Oh my goodness!" Her squeak of excitement reached a register I'd never heard before. "Oh my goodness, oh my goodness, oh my goodness gracious! This is the best gift ever!"

After that, what could I say?

After the big family celebration at Mama Isa's, where once again I tried to remain in the shadows so still-waiting-for-the-social-worker's-call Amelia wouldn't have to stare at my belly, Gideon and I came home and put our exhausted birthday girl to bed. My mom, who had arrived that afternoon to share the day with us, fell asleep on the sofa, reportedly exhausted from her two-hour drive to see us.

I slipped into my nightgown and went downstairs to drape a blanket over my mom, then stared at the Knabe grand piano, now shoved into a corner of our living room. "I have to admit it's beautiful," I whispered to Gideon, who had crept up behind me, "but it's probably against the rules or something. I should call Natasha and tell her about it."

"You can wait until Monday." Gideon's hands fell on my shoulders and began to knead my tight muscles. "In the meantime, let's go upstairs and relax. I'll bet you could use a back rub."

I followed him up the stairs, then dropped onto our mattress and felt my mouth twist when the bed groaned beneath my weight. I was getting bigger, no doubt about it. Dr. Hawthorn might enjoy comparing pregnant bellies to fruits and vegetables, but I saw my stomach as variations of a ball: a golf ball, a tennis ball, a soft ball, a soccer ball. Only two stages remained for me—basketball and bowling ball. I wasn't looking forward to either one.

"Know what?" I turned and put my feet in Gideon's lap. "What I'd really like is a foot rub, if you're up to it."

Gideon leaned against the headboard and grinned. "I think I can manage that. Just let me turn on the TV."

He powered on the television with the remote, then set to work massaging the ache out of my tired feet. I propped my head on a bunched-up pillow and closed my eyes, content to remain in that spot for as long as he wanted to work on me. . . .

I tuned in to the voice on the television when Gideon's fingers stopped moving.

"Over two hundred foreign tourists were killed and another two hundred injured tonight as terrorists exploded bombs in the Tel Aviv shopping district," a reporter said, speaking in the low tone reserved for dreaded topics. "Emergency personnel are scrambling to help the injured in what will go down as the deadliest act of terrorism in Israeli history."

I opened my eyes to study Gideon's face. I didn't see how he could even be aware of me, so intense was his focus on the flickering scenes of carnage. He was thinking about bombs and weapons and how the attack could have been prevented, what he would have done if he and his unit had found themselves in that situation. . . .

His phone would ring soon, and once again he'd be called out into the darkness. If not tonight, then tomorrow or the next day, the duffel bag would again disappear from our closet.

And Marilee and I would be left alone to play house.

Chapter Twelve

Sunday morning I awoke to find a note on Gideon's pillow: *I'll meet you at the river.* As I suspected, the duffel bag had disappeared.

Marilee and I went to church, then we showed up at Mama Isa's house uninvited. But it didn't matter. Isa and Jorge took one look at my face and opened their arms, welcoming us to Sunday dinner at the family table. After a few hours in their company, I knew I could go home and carry on a little while longer.

Though I knew I'd break my daughter's heart if I returned her birthday gift, Monday morning I called Natasha Bray to ask if she had any problem with me accepting a grand piano from my intended parents. I was halfway hoping she would gasp and tell me that such an expensive gift could be considered unethical, but she said nothing of the sort.

"Why, that's wonderful!" Her voice brimmed with surprise and pleasure. "I'm always happy to hear that my intended parents appreciate their gestational carrier. Their approval gives me confidence in my matchmaking abilities."

So . . . the piano could stay.

Throughout the next few days I managed to restrain the urge to express my resentment toward the Amblours' overly generous gift, but I couldn't stop thinking about that piano. Like a pebble in my shoe, thoughts of it rubbed against me, mocking me, reminding me that the Amblours held the upper hand in our relationship.

On those nights I went to bed without playing Simone's recordings for the baby. Monday afternoon I poured out the fancy French cleaner and used good ol' Soft Scrub on my kitchen sink, happy to see it gleam for the first time in weeks. Tuesday I stopped at Burger King on the way home from preschool and ordered hamburgers for Marilee and me. In a red-meat-eating frenzy, we gobbled them up on the drive home.

I knew I was being childish and petty, but I didn't care. I wasn't hurting the baby—no matter how peeved I got, I could never intentionally do that—but I desperately wanted to thumb my nose at his overprotective, controlling parents. They had been much more relaxed during the first trimester, when they worried about me losing the baby. Now that I had safely passed through the most crucial period, they were speaking their minds all too freely.

I wanted to talk to someone about my frustration, but Gideon was gone and I didn't think Amelia would understand. I tried to tell Mom how I felt about the shiny baby grand in my living room, but she looked aghast when I mentioned that I hadn't been pleased when the surprise showed up at our front door.

"You weren't *thrilled*?" She blinked, her mouth falling open before she recovered. "This couple sends you an expensive gift—exactly what you need and want—and you aren't happy about it? Have pregnancy hormones affected your brain?"

I blew out a breath. "It's completely inappropriate. They're paying me to carry their child; they have no business giving me expensive gifts."

"But they're grateful you're doing such a good job. Trust me, Amanda—it's hard to find people who take their work seriously, no matter what that work is."

"I'm carrying their baby, Mom. It's not like I'm doing something as difficult as curing cancer."

"Not everyone takes responsibility so seriously. If these people want to show their appreciation in a tangible way, I think you should write them a gracious note and thank the good Lord that you've been blessed."

Relief settled over me when Mom drove back to The Villages on Thursday.

I did send the Amblours a nice email, thanking them for the lovely piano that arrived on Marilee's birthday, but I couldn't bring myself to write out a proper card. How can you honestly express gratitude for a gift you don't want? But when the next Saturday approached and with it a reminder that I would be paid for attending the Surrogacy Center support group, I put a blank card and envelope in my purse, telling myself I'd write the Amblours' note in group if the speaker droned on and on about the obvious.

I had attended seven meetings since achieving pregnancy. I didn't pretend to enjoy the group, though I did learn a few things about surrogacy in the first three or four sessions. Everyone knew we were bribed to attend, so we all showed up with bored expressions and bellies in various states of prominence. One of the girls always brought her knitting (by my count she'd made four baby blankets—one pink, one blue, one light green, and one yellow); another brought her iPad and spent the hour answering emails and playing Angry Birds. But we received a hundred dollars for every meeting we attended, so we came.

Today's speaker wasn't a nurse, a nutritionist, or a midwife, but a former surrogate. Natasha introduced her as "Millie," and gave the pretty brunette a chair in the circle. About my age and still thick from her pregnancy weight gain, Millie flashed an awkward smile, then opened her hands, revealing wadded-up tissues in each fist.

"I knew I'd cry," she said, glancing around the circle. "So I wanted to be prepared. Maybe it's hormones, but I can't talk about my experience without crying."

I suppressed an inward groan. Was she one of the unfortunates who bonded with her baby? The subject of attachment almost always came up at these meetings, along with the warning that we should never, ever forget we were only babysitting. We knew the babies within us belonged to someone else; we knew we could never keep them. So we steeled our hearts against any sort of attachment; with every kick and movement we told ourselves that someone else's child was restless or attempting the backstroke.

"I want you to know," Millie said, tears spilling from her eyes, "that being a surrogate was the most amazing experience of my life. I cried and cried when I said good-bye because I was so proud of what I'd accomplished. The baby's father came over, held my hand, and thanked me, saying that he'd never imagined himself as a daddy because he'd been told he would never be one. The mother hugged me and thanked me, too."

I shifted my weight, wondering if her IPs had ever sent her anything as wildly extravagant as a grand piano.

"Then I watched them take the baby and try to give it a bottle," Millie continued. "A nurse had to show the dad how to hold a newborn because he was clueless. But he got the hang of it right away. Then the mother fed the baby, and a nurse took pictures. Natasha took pictures, too, and the nurse snapped a few shots of Natasha with my IPs. They asked if I wanted to be in the shot, but I told them no—I was a mess, and didn't want the baby to grow up thinking that the woman who carried him always looked like a disaster."

Her smile wavered as she touched a tissue to her streaming eyes. "I cry whenever I tell this story because it was such an emotional experience. I developed a real bond with my intended parents, and I plan to maintain our relationship—not anything intense, but a letter or two every year. They've promised to send pictures in a Christmas card. I don't want to intrude on their lives, but it would be nice to see how their son is growing up. Because I know one thing for sure—he wouldn't be here if not for me. And realizing that makes me incredibly happy."

She looked down, her chin quivering as she studied her fisted hands. "The dad told me he was going to spend the rest of his life thanking God for me. If I hadn't found the Surrogacy Center and signed up to do this, I don't think I would have done anything really significant with my life. So I'm the one who's grateful."

She looked up, smiling and batting tears away, as Natasha reached over to squeeze her hand. Then Natasha looked around the circle. "Do any of you have questions for Millie? Anything you want to ask about your relationships with your IPs? About labor and delivery? Anything at all?"

One of the skinny girls asked about the schedule for her OB checkups, but I studied Millie and wondered about her personal life. Did she have a husband and child of her own? How had her surrogacy affected them? Did she ever want to reach through the telephone lines and smack her intended parents?

But I didn't feel comfortable asking those questions, no matter how confidential the meeting might be. And, unlike Millie, I hoped my lifetime would hold far more significant feats than having someone else's baby.

I was going to build a home with Gideon. We were going to have a large family. And we were going to be happy for the rest of our lives.

Given how I felt about that piano, I suppose it was inevitable that something would shift in my relationship with the Amblours as the pregnancy dragged on. My email replies to Simone's questions became terser and my attempts at small talk disappeared. Yet if she realized that my attitude had changed, she didn't let on.

Maybe she thought I was feeling grumpy because I was tired and huge—at least that's what I told myself.

I knew the third trimester would be the hardest on my body—not only was I carrying a soccer ball out in front, but the top of my uterus was crowding my ribs and frequently left me breathless.

Pressure from the baby funneled fluids to my legs, resulting in a major pair of cankles. My rounded belly became a hand magnet, drawing perfect strangers who invaded my personal space to poke and pat my midsection.

At my first November appointment, Dr. Hawthorn asked me to start coming in every week so she could check the baby's position and make sure my cervix had begun to thin. "He's still small," she said, checking her chart after measuring me. "About the size of a pineapple."

"With or without the leaves?" I joked from the exam table.

She eyed me over the top of her glasses, apparently unamused. "I want to see you again next week. Keep eating. Keep taking those vitamins. And strap on your seat belt, because the home stretch is filled with all kinds of uncomfortable stuff."

I pushed myself up and groaned, knowing what she meant.

"The rest of the journey isn't pretty," she reminded me. "Back pain, near constant urination, burning feet and heartburn—I could go on, but you probably remember what it's like. Fortunately, this stage doesn't last long."

"I'm ready to be done," I answered, giving her the perfect truth. "More than ready, actually."

Amazing that I could feel so ambivalent about a baby in my own belly. Sometimes, like when I sat on the sofa stroking a protruding foot or arm, I wanted to fight to keep him; at other times I couldn't wait to hand him over to the Amblours. I chuckled at his movements and smiled at his hiccups, but during the night he lay heavily on my midsection, his weight a stone that threatened to squeeze the life right out of me. I told myself that my ambivalence was rooted in my feelings toward Simone—they, too, had waxed and waned over the months.

I couldn't explain exactly why, but ever since the day Simone and I had gone shopping together, a rift appeared between us. A tiny tear opened up in that baby boutique and grew wider as the weeks passed. When the piano arrived, the rift became a major fault line. Marilee was delighted to have a grand instrument, of course, but *I* wanted to be the one who bought a piano for my daughter, and I wanted to wait until she was sixteen or seventeen. If I had worked and sacrificed to provide her with a nice instrument, maybe she would appreciate it more.

But with one thoughtless stroke, Simone and Damien ripped that possibility away.

"You're looking good." The doctor's words snapped me back to reality. She finished her exam and told me to hang in there, the baby was intent on taking his time. Apparently he wasn't the least bit eager to leave.

"And he's still undersized," she added. "He might surprise us, but he'll probably weigh under six pounds and we want to give the little ones all the time they need to develop. Don't worry, Mandy, he'll come out when he's good and ready."

Darn that petite egg donor. If she'd been a bigger woman, maybe this kid would have already run out of room.

"I won't worry," I promised Dr. Hawthorn. "I'll take my vitamins, I'll try to get some rest, and I'll prop my feet up whenever I can. But that won't be easy with my husband away." I slid carefully off the exam table, then waddled toward the cubicle where my clothes waited. "I'll do anything I can for the little pineapple."

"Before you leave today," Dr. Hawthorn called, "have you filed your birth plan?"

Safe inside the dressing area, I stared at my reflection and blinked. I had taken care of Marilee's birth plan early on, but this time I hadn't even thought about filling out the doctor's questionnaire. Was I really so unattached to this child?

"Um, no," I called, reaching for my jeans. "I haven't."

"No worries; we can handle that today. When you come out, you'll see that we've made it easy for you."

I had no idea what she meant, but finished dressing as she wished me a good day and left the room.

When I came out, I found an iPad waiting on the exam table. A sticky note on the surface provided the code to wake the tablet out of hibernation. I followed the directions and watched, thunderstruck, as an electronic form opened, complete with check boxes for various answers to dozens of different questions—all of them pertaining to my impending labor and delivery.

Make sure you type your name at the top, the screen informed me. *When you click Submit, your responses will be sent to our computer and relayed to the hospital of your choice.*

I sat on a small stool, typed in my name and address, then drew a deep breath. Basic information: done. *Name of birth coach?* I bit my lip and finally typed *Simone Amblour.* Since I didn't think anything short of an armed guard could keep her out of the delivery room, I might as well have her do something useful. She could remind me to breathe as well as anyone.

Labor: Did I want to have an enema upon admission to the hospital? Did I want to wear my own clothes instead of a hospital gown? Did I want to play my own music during labor? Did I want to labor in a birthing tub or shower?

On and on the questions went, ranging from the general (Did I want people to knock before they entered the room?) to the intimate (Would I rather tear than have an episiotomy or would I rather have an episiotomy than tear?).

I checked the simplest procedure in each category, particularly in the anesthesia section: *I would like to have an epidural as soon as permissible.*

And anything else they wanted to give me.

I paused, however, when it came to the section on delivery: Who did I want to catch the baby? Did I want the baby placed on my stomach immediately after delivery? Who did I want to cut the cord?

Did I even have the right to answer those questions? Or should the baby's parents decide those things? And if I dared to check the box for wanting to see and hold the baby against my skin, would Simone overrule me?

Would such a decision even be wise?

The last few sections dealt with newborn care and breastfeeding, so I ignored them. But those topics in between—who decided?

I finally left the questions blank and decided to let the situation unfold naturally. This child wasn't mine, and if Simone and Damien wanted to arm-wrestle for the privilege of cutting the cord, I'd let them. I'd simply lean back and drift away on a sleepy narcotic tide.

I wasn't being paid to referee.

Though the baby was due December first, on November fourteenth Dr. Hawthorn mentioned that my cervix hadn't even begun to thin out. "I don't want to worry you," she insisted, "because babies keep their own timetables. I just thought I'd mention it so you won't worry about this little guy coming in the middle of your Thanksgiving dinner. In fact, I wouldn't be surprised if he chooses to make an entrance a week or so after his due date."

I drove home, irritated by the thought of being pregnant longer than I wanted to be, then a new email from Simone annoyed me further. She and Damien had decided to come to Florida early, she wrote, so they were going to rent a house on the beach before the baby's birth and stay until they felt comfortable with the essentials of infant care.

"We need some time to relax," she said, "so we thought we might take a vacation and soak in the sun before the busy day arrives. We do not want you to feel like a watched pot, of course, but if we rent a place we will be only minutes away from the hospital when you go into labor. We thought the news would put your mind at ease—we will arrive on time, so you should not worry about us flying over the Atlantic. We will remain in Florida a few weeks, since the grape harvest is finished and there is no urgent reason to return to Domaine de Amblour. In any case, our doctor says a newborn should not fly until he is at least a week old. Too much exposure to germs in that closed environment."

Though I would never ask the question outright, I wondered if their decision to linger in Florida had anything to do with alleviating the public impression that the couple had taken an overnight trip and returned with an instant baby. If they remained away from home several weeks, some of their neighbors might even wonder if Simone had been pregnant and given birth while abroad—or maybe I was being paranoid. Surrogacy was no longer the deep secret it had once been, and why should I care about what they told their friends and neighbors?

I wanted to hand over their baby, receive my final payment, and wave good-bye as they flew back to France. I wanted to welcome my husband home and start preparing for a son of my own.

After delivering the baby, I wanted to get busy living the rest of my life.

By the time I sank onto a bench outside Macy's, I knew I had to be out of my mind.

It was all my mother's idea, of course. She'd driven over for Thanksgiving, endured the big holiday dinner at Mama Isa's, and then insisted we do something the next day with "just our side of the family." That meant that she, Marilee, and I got up at 5:00 a.m. and went out to commemorate Black Friday . . . while I was a week shy of full term.

After three hours of standing in long lines, fighting the crowd, carrying heavy shopping bags *and* a bowling ball out in front, I felt as exhausted as a runaway dog.

Mom dropped beside me on the bench, a bag in each hand, and gazed at me with wide, innocent eyes. "Are you tired?"

I glanced at Marilee, who was dancing with curiosity because both of Mom's shopping bags contained gifts for *her.*

"I'm wiped out," I answered, resisting the urge to employ a little sarcasm. "The honeydew melon I'm carrying keeps kicking my kidneys. It *really* doesn't like all this walking."

"Nonsense. Exercise is good for everyone, especially expectant mothers. Besides, you should be walking to bring on labor. After all, aren't the French people already in town?"

"They're here. They've rented a place on Sandpiper Drive, but I'm not driving by the house because I'm done for the day. But if you want to take me home and keep shopping, Marilee might want to join you."

"Ice cream!" Marilee clapped and grinned at her grandma. "Can we get ice cream?"

"Of course we can, precious." Mom tweaked Marilee's cheek. "But we can get it on the way home."

I lifted a brow. "At nine thirty in the morning?"

"If she wants it, why not?"

I sighed, knowing it was useless to protest. Ordinarily we'd be hard-pressed to find an ice cream shop open at this hour, but no one kept normal business hours on Black Friday.

"Well, look who's here."

I looked up when the familiar voice startled me. Amelia and Mario were coming toward us, both of them looking a lot fresher than I felt.

I pressed my hand to my belly. The little guy inside was judo-chopping my ribs—I had probably disturbed his midmorning nap.

"Finding many bargains?" I asked.

Amelia shrugged. "Found a few things in the men's department. And there's a great housewares sale at Dillard's. I came out here, though, because I wanted to get a book that's supposed to be good."

"What's it about?" I asked, hoping she'd found a novel that would take my mind off this pregnancy.

"International adoption. These days I'm reading everything I can find on the subject."

Mom tugged on my sleeve, her eyes shining. "Mandy, honey, would you mind waiting here while I check out the housewares sale? I've been looking for new dishes."

I blew out a breath, grateful for the opportunity to rest a bit longer. Even the walk back to the car seemed daunting. "Go ahead."

"Are you sure? You're not having contractions or anything?"

"Not a twinge. Go, and take Marilee with you. But she's slippery, so keep an eye on her."

Mom's mouth tightened. "You talk like I don't have any experience with children. I won't let her get away." She held out her hand to Marilee, who took it and skipped in time to my mom's slower pace.

Mario pointed toward a sports store down the mall, then said something in Spanish. Amelia nodded. *"Hasta luego."*

I waited until he walked off, then patted the bench next to me. "Have a seat. I've a feeling empty benches will be hard to find in an hour or so."

Amelia sat and took a long swig from the soft drink in her hand. "I like your mom, but you must take after your father. She's nothing like you."

I snorted. "Have you looked at us? Mom and I have the same pointed nose and the same sharp chin. Even Marilee inherited the chin, but thank heaven she got Gideon's nose."

"I meant your personalities are nothing alike. She seems so regimented, and you're so"—she shrugged—"not."

"I think"—I hesitated, wishing she'd drop the subject—"maybe I'm more like my dad."

Oblivious to the quaver in my voice, Amelia sipped her drink again, then tilted her head. "By the way, how's your mother handling your pregnancy? Is she still against the idea?"

I pressed my hands to my lower back and tried to stretch. "Mom is conveniently ignoring my belly. She never mentions the pregnancy unless I bring it up."

"Really?"

I shrugged. "In a way, I don't blame her. If this were my baby, she'd be all excited about having a grandson, but what's she supposed to feel when it's someone else's child? It's weird, that's all.

And Mom's always been old-fashioned. When I was a kid, she never wanted to talk about human reproduction."

"So you grew up thinking that storks brought babies?"

"Until Sally Hinson told all the girls in fifth grade phys ed that babies grew in bellies and daddies planted the seeds."

Amelia fizzed with laughter while I stood to encourage blood flow to my lower legs. When Amelia finally stopped chuckling, she took another sip from her straw, then grinned up at me. "Did your mom enjoy Thanksgiving yesterday?"

"I guess. I don't think she understood much of what was happening, though. She doesn't speak Spanish."

"But neither do you."

"I don't speak *much.* But being around you guys has done a lot to improve my skills of interpretation. For instance, I had no idea what Mario said a minute ago, but I knew he told you he was going to the sports store and he'd be back soon."

Amelia snorted. "You know us too well."

I shrugged. "But Mom doesn't know you at all. So she couldn't help feeling a little left out."

"Sorry. We tried to be friendly."

"I know, but my mom isn't the type to put herself out there. You either meet her on her turf or"—I shrugged again—"you don't meet her."

"That's too bad." Amelia shook her cup, rattling the ice inside, then looked at me, her eyes shining with affection. "It's a good thing you're not like that, or you'd never have met Gideon. And you wouldn't have me for a cousin-in-law."

I sat and leaned back, bracing my weight on my arms as I smiled. "And you'd never have a cousin who's a gringa. Speaking of *la familia,* what's the latest on the adoption front? Have you talked to your social worker lately?"

Amelia stood to toss her cup into a trash can. When she sat again her smile held a touch of sadness. "I talked to her a couple of days ago. I called to check in and Helen was nice, like always.

But she hasn't placed any children this month, and there aren't any suitable kids available for us. That's why I wanted to pick up that new book—to see if there were any new avenues for finding kids."

"With all the children needing homes, you'd think—"

"It's not that easy. And I can guess what our file says: 'Mario and Amelia are a young Hispanic couple with no parenting experience but a good support system. They prefer an infant, but would accept a child up to age three with correctible medical conditions.'" She crinkled her nose. "Sounds awfully clinical and not terribly appealing. But no, we haven't heard anything."

I nodded. After a long moment, I added a postscript: "I'm sorry."

"It's okay." She crossed her legs and straightened as she stared into the crowd around us. "All we can do is wait."

I wanted to suggest that we were in the same boat, but I knew we weren't. My time of waiting had a definite end in sight, but hers stretched into the unknown.

So we sat on the bench together, both of us waiting on a child.

Feeling like an overstuffed sack of skin, I had just settled in front of the TV to watch something mindless and entertaining when Gideon came into the room, his duffel bag slung over his shoulder.

"Gid—no." The sight of his gear never failed to send a tremor up the back of my neck, but this time dread lodged in my throat, making it difficult to speak.

"Mandy, baby—"

"You can't go now. I could go into labor at any time."

"I'm sorry, baby girl." Gideon knelt on the carpet and caught my hands. "I know this is a lousy time to leave, but I should only be away a couple of days, three or four at the longest. I've spoken to my mom, and she'll stay with you if you want. Or you could call your mother—"

"But the timing! Surely your commander—"

"The doctor said you had a couple of weeks, right?"

"She said babies keep their own timetable. I don't know when it's going to come." I stared at his face, at his eyes, which asked me to trust him.

So I would.

I lowered my voice. "Your mission isn't dangerous, is it?"

"Nothing's dangerous for Captain America."

"I'm not kidding, Gid. If you got hurt, I don't know what I'd do—"

"Have I been hurt before? Now stop worrying; it's not good for you. I want you to be strong so you can deliver this kid and we can get on with making our own babies and finding a nice house to raise them in. I still want a son, you know."

I drew a breath, then kept silent. Gideon was right, of course. He knew his job, and I knew he was completely competent. His unit was one of the best; that's why they were called out to handle tough situations.

I even knew why he didn't ask for permission to stay home—over the past several years other family men, scores of them, had gone to war and missed their anniversaries, their children's birthdays, and their babies' births. . . .

"I'll miss you," I said, my voice gentle. "And if something goes wrong at the hospital, I'll be waiting at the river."

"Nothing's going to happen to you, honey. And if you need any help, ask *la familia.* They'll be here before you can say *Ayúdeme, por favor.*"

"I'll be waiting at the river, Gideon."

His eyes softened and melted into mine. "Okay, have it your way. Though I don't think anything's going to happen to either of us, I'll meet you under the tree."

And then, as moonlight streamed through the open window and painted a rectangle of light onto that blasted grand piano, Snake Billings rolled up in the driveway and honked the horn. Gideon kissed the top of my head, then picked up his duffel bag.

"Give Marilee a kiss for me," he said, his smile deepening the dimple in his left cheek.

I batted away a recurrent gnat of worry as he walked to the front door, blew me a kiss, and disappeared into the night.

I rolled off the couch and hurried after him, then opened the door and stared into a yawning black hole that should have been our front porch. The darkness swirled and moved, pulling me forward, threatening to drag me from the house and take me under—

Caught in the riptide between sleeping and waking, I closed my eyes and swam upward. When I lifted my eyelids again, I was lying spread-eagle on our bed, pinned to the mattress by a bowling ball belly. My arms were splayed, my legs tangled in the sheets, my skin slick with sweat.

No need for Dr. Hawthorn's help with dream interpretation tonight. Some nightmares, like road signs, were painfully easy to decipher.

Waddling from side to side like an old woman with arthritic hips, I stopped by the grocery on Friday, the sixth of December, just to hear the sound of friendly voices. Contact with Mama Isa, Tumelo, Amelia, Mario, and Jenna so cheered me that I decided to fill the house with people on Saturday. Gideon had spoken the truth in my dream—I had access to all kinds of help if I wanted it; all I had to do was ask. So I called Amelia and Mario, Tumelo and Elaine, Mama Isa and Jorge, and then I called the elders, Yaritza and Carlos, Yanela and Gordon. "I thought we'd have a potluck while Gideon's away," I said, shoehorning a bright note into my voice. "Bring a dish and come for dinner, please. I can barely move and I'd appreciate the company."

Apparently my nonchalant invitation didn't fool any of them. They came early, bearing cleaning supplies and fruit baskets and casseroles steaming with Cuban delicacies. They filled my dining room table until it threatened to buckle, and after lunch they cleaned the house.

Yanela and Yaritza sat on the sofa and told the younger people what to do. Amelia tackled the windowsills the Happy Housekeepers hadn't touched; Tumelo tied on an apron and dusted, even climbing on a chair to wipe the tops of our doorframes. Mama Isa cleaned out my refrigerator, Elaine alphabetized my spice rack, and Jorge roasted enough pork to feed an army. "You will want it for later," he said, tilting his head toward the refrigerator. "Freeze it; it will keep. With pickles, ham, and Swiss cheese, it makes great Cuban sandwiches."

"You need some Christmas decorations." Amelia stood in front of me with her hands on her hips. "Are you going to put something up? At least a Christmas tree?"

I shrugged and braced my lower back. "I haven't had the energy. Plus, the decorations are in the attic, and I can't climb the ladder like this."

"I'll get them down." Amelia set her bottle of all-purpose cleaner on the kitchen counter and moved toward the hallway and the attic ladder, then she paused. "Do you have a tree up there, or is it just small stuff?"

I pressed my hand over my lips to stifle an undignified burp. "It's, um, mostly small stuff. Some ornaments, ribbons, and maybe a wreath—"

"Don't worry, we'll get you all fixed up. Tio Tumelo, come help me get into the attic, will you?"

Delighted with all the company, Marilee played a mini concert on her piano ("Working music," Mario called it), then basked in the family's applause. After Marilee's performance, someone popped a CD into the player, and Tumelo began to sing along with a Cuban trio.

My in-laws filled the house with festivity and food, and all I had to do was sit with my feet up.

Surrounded by so much life and laughter, I finally began to

relax. As the medicine of loving care worked its magic, I decided I'd been silly to harbor negative feelings toward Simone and Damien. After all, what crime had they committed? They had simply tried to show their gratitude for all the extra trouble I went through for the sake of their family. The problem—the rift in our relationship—had existed only in my perspective.

By the time Yanela finished rubbing my feet, I was feeling so generous I vowed to be friendlier to the Amblours. I should invite them over for dinner, I told Yaritza, and let Marilee play for them. They ought to know she would put the piano to good use.

I accepted a glass of punch from Mama Isa and shifted to make room for her on the couch. Inviting the clan over had been a wonderful idea, I told the ladies; I should do it more often. The next time I spoke to Gideon, I would tell him all about the family's visit. He'd be thrilled to hear that I'd invited *la familia* for lunch. He was always urging me to be more independent, to step out and take charge like so many other military wives. . . .

I was sitting on the sofa and nibbling on a *buñuelo* when I glimpsed a dark car outside. When it pulled to the curb and parked I thought its occupants might have come in search of Mama Isa or Elaine, then I recognized a military dress uniform through the car's window.

I dropped the pastry as my heart went cold and still.

I stared as one of the uniformed men stepped out, tugged on the bottom of his dress coat, and adjusted his cap to shade his eyes. I couldn't tear my gaze from him, and under my breath I urged him to stay with the vehicle, to remain outside in what had become a family parking lot.

But on he came with his partner, up the walkway, until he rounded a corner and moved out of my sight line. I closed my eyes, hoping for the impossible, yet still the doorbell rang.

Somehow I stood and took a staggering step toward the door. I didn't want to open it; I wanted to block it, maybe move the piano so no one else could open it, either.

Amelia's voice cut into my awareness. "Mandy? Are you okay?"

"Don't answer . . . door."

A cold shiver lifted the hair on my arms as I remembered my nightmare. Darkness had lain behind that door, a suffocating, dark emptiness.

"Why? Is someone out there?" Moving faster than I could, Amelia stepped forward and turned the doorknob. I closed my eyes and gripped the nearest stationery object—the piano—as I heard Amelia's anguished cry. "No. Please, no."

Her heartrending wail silenced the voices, the music, the clinking of silverware and dishes.

I clenched my free hand, wishing I could rewind time and delete the inevitable ending of this scene.

Is this why Gideon visited me in a dream? Perhaps I'd been bracing for this moment ever since waking.

Maybe I'd been preparing for this since the day I fell in love with a soldier. Or maybe God had taken a lifetime to prepare me for this, the worst hour of my existence.

Mama Isa hurried to my side as the uniformed officers stepped into the house. They removed their hats, rocked uneasily on their feet, and stared at the circle of wide, waiting eyes.

Though none of us wanted to break the silence and ask why they'd appeared at this home, we all knew why they'd come.

I shook my arm free of Mama Isa's grip and tried to reason out an alternative ending. Maybe they were searching for another house. Maybe they had come to give me good news; maybe Gideon had earned a medal. Maybe they got dressed up and came over for no good reason at all. Maybe they'd heard the Lisandra family was hosting a dinner, and everyone on base knew how the Lisandra clan loved to feast—

I approached the officer with the most medals on his chest. Looking up, I saw myself reflected in his dark eyes.

Because I couldn't, he spoke first. "Mrs. Gideon Lisandra?"

I barely managed to nod.

"Ma'am, I have news concerning your husband. Would you like to speak privately?"

I shook my head, then found the breath to utter three words: "We're all family."

Understanding filled his eyes, followed by remorse. "Then, Mrs. Lisandra, I regret to inform you that your husband, Lieutenant Gideon Lisandra, was killed last evening while serving his country. The time and place of his death are classified. If you need any assistance . . ."

He must have said more, but I didn't hear it. My knees buckled and down I went, my fall broken by Mama Isa's embrace. A woman screamed, one of the men howled, and a little girl cried, but I remained silent as Mama Isa and Amelia led me back to the sofa. Isa began to pray in a stream of passionate Spanish while Amelia sat beside me and wept.

What was God doing to me? I closed my eyes, feeling nothing but emptiness within, and lifted my thoughts to heaven. *God, if Gideon's with you now, why didn't you give me more warning?*

I waited for the blissful numbness that reportedly arrived at moments like this; the painless paralysis that would see me through everything that had to happen before life could move forward. But that legendary state of insensibility never arrived. I felt my heart shatter, I heard the clean, sharp sounds of my life falling into shards around me, and I saw, even through lowered eyelids, anguish and despair take possession of Marilee's heart-shaped face.

And then, in a blinding moment of brightness, I saw Gideon standing behind a white balustrade. He was smiling at me. "You're going to be okay, baby girl." His eyes shone with love and quiet confidence. "You are stronger than you realize."

"Gid?"

"I'll be here," he answered. "I'll meet you at the river."

I nodded, and in the next instant, he disappeared. Then loving arms caressed my shoulders while female cries and quiet sobs enveloped me, accompanied by the low moans and sharp curses of men who don't cry but must express something because their hearts simply cannot hold such agony.

I bowed my head as the baby within me pressed hard on my pelvis. A contraction tightened my belly, forcing me to inhale sharply through my teeth.

Today wasn't supposed to be Gideon's death day. He was supposed to finish his tour and help me pick out a house; we were supposed to open a music store and make another baby together. A sob slipped from my throat as the future we'd envisioned faded away like morning fog.

Cocooned on the couch, I realized the cushion beneath me had become wet. This wasn't surprising, as my heart, joints, and muscles had turned to water and I had to be spilling out into the room.

Logic reared its pragmatic head, reminding me of the heavy obligation I carried—the promise holding insensibility at bay.

I pressed my hands to the bowling ball as the shock of discovery rammed me from yet another direction.

Ready or not, the baby had decided to leave me, too.

Chapter Thirteen

I groaned as a fresh surge of pain erupted someplace near my spine and radiated through my body. Even my feet hurt.

"*¡Dios tenga misericordia de nosotros!*" Wailing, Mama Isa leaned forward to rub my back. "I am so sorry. How could this be? First Gideon, and now this. How are you supposed to bear it?"

I wanted to scream that I *couldn't* bear it. With Gideon gone, how was I supposed to bear anything? I had lost my husband and best friend, my daughter had lost her daddy, and we had both lost our future hopes and dreams.

Familiar voices echoed in the hallway outside my hospital room as relatives crept from the waiting area to check on me. Apparently the entire Lisandra clan had left my house and come here, their contagious joy supplanted by unimaginable sorrow. They'd brought Marilee with them, and I knew she'd be well tended by loving arms, hugged and kissed and comforted as Gideon's only child. I couldn't make out all the Spanish phrases flowing in the hallway, but I knew what they were saying about my daughter: *Poor thing, she is all we have left of Gideon.*

How long had they been outside? The clock on the wall read two thirty, so I had been trying to have this baby for at least twelve hours. A half day that felt more like an eternity.

I grabbed Mama Isa's hand and squeezed as another pain threatened to draw a black curtain over my eyes. Truthfully, I wanted to pass out. I wanted to unplug my brain and leave the swollen body that would never again sleep next to Gideon or bear the son he had always wanted. Why should I stay on this earth? Marilee would be fine with *la familia,* and this baby would be safe with Simone and Damien. And Gideon waited for me beneath the tree of life, and I had an appointment to meet him at the river flowing from the throne of God.

No one on earth needed me, no one wanted me. I might as well drift away.

Another pain flashed through my midsection, eliciting a cry of speechless agony. I dug my nails into Mama Isa's hand, pushing my pain onto her, but she didn't complain. She straightened and held her breath along with me, exhaling only when I did.

Where were my drugs?

"You will get through this, *chica,*" Mama Isa said, her voice low and intense. "Soon the doctor will be here and this will be over. Soon you will be free to mourn our Gideon."

I turned my head as tears coursed over my cheeks. My eyes had been leaking ever since we arrived at the hospital—I'd been so distracted by pain I couldn't even say I'd been *crying.* Misery and distress were seeping out through my eyes, my mouth, and even my womb.

I heard murmuring outside the door and recognized Amelia's voice. If she and Mario were still here, who was going to open the grocery tomorrow? I looked at Mama Isa and saw dark circles beneath her eyes. She shouldn't work tomorrow, and neither should Amelia.

"The grocery." I gripped Mama Isa's hand. "You ought to get some rest, and so should the others. If Yanela and Yaritza are out there, someone needs to take them home—"

"Silencio." Mama Isa pressed gentle fingers to my lips and silenced me with a stern look. "We will not open the store tomor-

row. We will remain with you until you are resting, then we will go home to rest. The store will wait."

I braced for another pain, then gripped Mama Isa's hand as it set my teeth on edge. I wasn't sure how much longer I could do this. . . .

Dr. Hawthorn swept into the room and greeted me with a quick smile. She glanced at the machine keeping track of the baby's vitals, then she looked under the drape over my legs. "Okay, Mandy," she said, giving me another falsely cheerful smile. "You're fully dilated, so I think it's time to push. Are you ready?"

I gritted my teeth. "What happened to my drugs?"

She lifted a brow. "You didn't get the epidural?"

I shook my head.

"Too late now, I'm afraid. Something must have happened to your birth plan. But now let's concentrate on getting the baby out."

"Where are Simone and Damien? I'm supposed to give them the baby."

A shadow of annoyance crossed my doctor's face. "Do they know you're in labor?"

Did they? I struggled to remember if someone had called them, but my memories of the past few hours were fuzzy. I'd been told to call Natasha and the Amblours when I left for the hospital, but nothing had gone the way I planned. I was supposed to be calm at the delivery. I was supposed to have Gideon on my left side and Simone and Damien on my right, standing by my head. Simone was supposed to be my coach and I was supposed to have an epidural and plenty of narcotics. . . .

Another contraction, another blast of pain, and suddenly I didn't care about what was supposed to happen. I wanted to get rid of this baby and get back to my own house, where I could be surrounded by memories of my husband. "I've got to push."

"Good girl. You're crowning." The doctor sat on the rolling stool at the foot of my bed. "Okay, Mandy. With the next contraction, I want you to push with all your might. The baby's in a good position, you're more than ready, and this shouldn't be a problem."

Of course it shouldn't be a problem, but this day had produced a tragedy of unspeakable proportions, a black hour of such intense shock and grief that my body had rebelled, expelling the baby who might or might not be ready to come, who might still be as small as a pineapple or mango—

No matter. The baby was coming and I was ready to let him go. I closed my eyes as the next contraction rose and crested within me. Holding my breath, I rode the wave, squeezing Mama Isa's hand, tears flowing down my cheeks, sweat dampening my hair. . . .

The door opened. And as the doctor pulled a new life from me, Damien and Simone rushed in, breathless and wide-eyed, stylish and perfectly groomed beneath their thin sterile gowns. Simone stared at the baby, her hand catching her throat as she choked out a cry. Damien grinned and wrapped his arms around himself, probably in an attempt to keep from leaping forward to hug my doctor.

I swallowed hard, disturbed by the way this event was unfolding. Simone and Damien weren't supposed to be *down there,* they were supposed to be standing by my head and preserving my privacy.

My gaze slid reluctantly from the Amblours to the child. He was pale and blue, shiny with fluids, but his little arms were flailing. And then, while I watched, his lips parted and a lusty cry filled the room.

Holding the baby in her gloved hands, Dr. Hawthorn turned to the Amblours. "Who wants to cut the cord?"

While I blinked in confusion, Damien stepped forward, took a pair of scissors from a nurse, and cut the pulsing cord that bound the baby to me.

I cried out, too.

The nurse looked at me, surprise flashing in her eyes, as I covered my mouth and stifled another cry. I had left this section of the birth plan blank, but the scene before me felt completely wrong.

"Calm yourself, *hija,*" Mama Isa murmured, pushing my wet hair from my forehead. "Everything is all right."

I watched through blurred eyes as the nurse took the pinkening infant and rubbed him with a towel, then suctioned his nose and mouth. She swaddled him in a blanket and hesitated, her eyes wary above her mask, her arms tilting between the woman in the bed and the woman by the door, both of whom were weeping. . . .

In the absence of an official birth plan, Dr. Hawthorn broke the stalemate. "Mandy, would you like to see the baby you've worked so hard to carry?"

Unable to bear the sight of the child I was about to lose, I turned my head. "I'll see him later," I whispered, my voice strangled.

Without another word, the nurse crossed the room and placed the baby in Simone's arms. When Damien gripped his wife's shoulders and gazed at his son, I knew that corner of the room had become their private universe.

I couldn't watch them. As the doctor and nurses worked on me, I fisted my hand and bit my knuckle until I registered the coppery taste of blood.

I hadn't expected to feel a connection with that baby. I had known the little boy would never be mine, but I hadn't realized how my heart and mind would howl when he was taken from me. That agony had nothing to do with the physical pangs of childbirth.

From the moment he left me, I wanted that baby like a thirsty woman wants water. Though I couldn't understand why I suddenly needed that child, if I'd been stronger I would have rolled out of bed and snatched him from Simone.

A suffocating sensation tightened my throat at the thought of watching the Amblours carry him away. I covered my face with trembling hands and wept, overcome by the agony of loss.

I had lost too much in the last twenty-four hours: the love of my life, my daughter's father, and the child my body had been unwittingly loving for the past nine months.

"Mi querida hija," Mama Isa crooned, pushing my wet bangs away from my face. "It is okay. You will be okay."

"Will I?" My voice trembled, tears choking off all the things I wanted to say.

I had lost the opportunity to have another child with my husband. The little boy we had always wanted would never exist. Marilee would never know a brother.

I would never grow old with Gideon. I would curl back into myself, just as I had after I lost my beloved father. Venturing out hurt too much.

Choking back a sob, I lowered my hands and forced myself to look across the room. Simone was stroking the baby's chin as Damien cooed, a nurturing, womanly sound I never expected to hear from him. Oblivious to my suffering, they would go home as a new family, and their lives would never be the same.

I had changed, too, but not in the way I expected. Marilee and I would go forward as a family, but I would go home a widow.

An orderly wheeled me to a room on a quiet floor away from the obstetrical ward. I knew they wanted to avoid reminding me of the child I'd just surrendered, but I wouldn't have cared if they put me in the morgue. Without Gideon or the baby, I felt hollow.

Somehow I slept, waking only when someone slipped a cuff around my arm. "Sorry about that," a nurse whispered, taking my blood pressure in the semidarkness. "Are you awake? Because there's someone outside who'd like to see you."

I glanced at the clock on the wall—6:30 a.m., so unless my visitor was a doctor, he or she was ignoring the rules about visiting hours. But since my visitor could be Marilee or one of the relatives, I raised the head of my bed and tried to clear the cobwebs from my brain.

Natasha Bray strolled into the room, a congratulatory grin on her face. She tempered her expression when she realized I wasn't smiling with her.

"Amanda." She stood next to my bed and tentatively touched

my shoulder. "I was so sorry to hear about your husband. A terrible tragedy for the nation, but especially for you."

A lump rose to my throat and fresh tears stung my eyes. I was leaking again, teetering on the verge of a crying jag, but Natasha hadn't come here to talk about Gideon.

"I wanted to thank you for your service to Simone and Damien." Natasha patted my shoulder as if I were a small child who had correctly solved a mathematics problem. "The baby is beautiful. Eighteen inches, five pounds, two ounces. Ten fingers, ten toes. A perfectly gorgeous little boy."

I swiped my tears away. "Have—have the Amblours left the hospital?"

"They're waiting for the birth certificate, so they'll be around at least until the records office opens at seven. After that, I'm not sure what their plans are. I think they're going to stay in Florida a day or two, then return to France. They're eager to show off their baby, of course."

Were they? I blinked as confusing memories warred in my brain. At some point—last week or last year, or maybe in another lifetime—I had heard that they wanted to stay for some time. Something about newborns not flying because of the risks of exposure to the potentially harmful air on an airplane.

I sat up straighter, glimpsed the hospital wristband on my arm, and shook my head. "I need to go home."

"Don't you want to rest? You deserve it."

"I want to go home. I'm not sick, and Marilee needs me. I have things to do." Tears to weep. A daughter to comfort. A funeral to plan.

Natasha's brows flickered. "But are you sure you're ready? How are you feeling?"

"I'm a little tired and sore, but I'll be fine."

Natasha bit her lip, then nodded. "I'll see if I can page Dr. Hawthorn. She was still here a few minutes ago, and I know she'll have to sign you out. But let me get ahold of her."

Natasha left the room. Fully awake, I pushed the tray table out of the way. Someone had stashed my clothing in a closet by the window, so I climbed out of bed and pulled out my things, eager to get away from everyone involved with the surrogacy. Like a dog that runs home after being hurt, I wanted to crawl into a quiet corner and lick my wounds for a while.

I found my purse at the bottom of the closet and pulled out my cell phone. Amelia wouldn't enjoy being awakened before sunrise, especially if she'd been here when the baby was born. But she'd come get me if I asked. She was family.

A few minutes later I was buttoning my blouse when a footstep snapped against the tile floor. "Amanda? Are you up?"

"Up and dressed, Dr. Hawthorn."

My doctor stepped around the curtain and lifted a brow. "Well. I suppose you *are* ready to go home."

"No sense in waiting around, is there?"

"Maybe not, but someone might want to see you before you go. Would you like to have a look at your baby before you take off?"

I stared out the window and considered the risk to my heart. Why not go see the little guy before I had to face my new reality? He was probably in the nursery, one sleeping infant in a row of identical bassinets. Seeing him in that clinical environment might not rip open a recent wound.

"Okay. I'll see him."

"Good." Dr. Hawthorn turned toward the hallway. "You all can come in now."

Before I could object, Damien and Simone entered, the baby sleeping in Damien's arms. I was so stunned by the ambush—why weren't they asleep somewhere?—that I couldn't speak.

"Dear girl." Simone hurried forward and wrapped me in an embrace. "You have done a wonderful job. Such a beautiful boy, and you made it look so easy!"

A trembling rose from somewhere at my core as I forced myself to meet Simone's gaze. The sounds of the infant—the gasps, snuffling, and grunts unique to a newborn—were enough to threaten my composure. I didn't dare look at him.

"You are so brave, so generous!" Simone went on, gushing like a fire hydrant. "You have done so much for us we can never begin to thank you. And after such a personal tragedy." She stepped away and gave me a sympathetic look that threatened to shred my heart. "You are precious to us, *mon amie.* Damien and I will never forget you."

I swallowed as words formed a logjam in my throat. If I tried to speak, my voice would break and I'd end up blubbering, so perhaps I shouldn't say anything at all.

Simone gestured to the baby. "Would you like to hold him?"

Hold him? When he was wrapped in a blanket she had purchased and wearing clothes she had provided? Then again, maybe it would be easier to hold him while he was wearing something other than my life's blood.

I held out my hands. Damien stepped closer, never taking his eyes off his son, and placed the infant in my arms.

My heart pounded as an unwelcome glow flowed through me. A blush heated my face as I peered at the creature that had so recently lived inside me.

I had never held an infant so tiny. I kept my gaze fixed on his shiny tender head until the baby lifted fringed eyelids and looked straight at me. His eyes were dark and deep, just like Marilee's, and the tip of his nose turned up at an adorable angle. He wriggled his little fingers and worked his rosebud mouth as I bit hard on my lip, torn between laughing with delight and sobbing at the heartbreak I was about to feel all over again.

"You'd better take him." I turned to Simone as my self-control wavered. "I'm a little out of practice."

Damien took the child, probably realizing that I was about three seconds away from tossing him to the nearest pair of arms.

How much loss could one woman endure in only a few hours? How many good-byes could I be expected to say in a single day?

"Are you going to keep in touch?"

I startled at the sound of Amelia's voice. Grateful for the distraction, I turned to see my cousin watching the Amblours with a cold expression, her eyes dark and faintly accusing.

"Do you *want* us to keep in touch?" Simone's brows arched. "I don't remember what we decided—"

"A picture on his birthday might be nice." Amelia moved from the doorway into the room. "After all, Mandy might want to see how the kid's growing up. Since she gave him his start and everything."

"A birthday card, of course." Simone smiled at me. "And a Christmas gift. It is the least we can do for our friend. We will look forward to sending you something every year, and we will pray for you every night."

"Please—no gifts. I don't need presents from you." My gaze traveled again to the baby. That sweet little pineapple-honeydew had slept inside me, grown inside me, fed and kicked and hiccupped inside me.

He had progressed from blastocyst to newborn with Marilee's music in his ears. He'd heard me read to him and felt the pressure of Gideon's protective arm. He might be only an infant, but he'd spent the last nine months as part of my family.

And as much as I wanted to deny it, I loved him. Handing him over—

Good things usually hurt. Yes, they did.

"What did you name him?" My voice emerged as a rough croak.

"Julien," Simone said. "Julien Louis Amblour."

I nodded. "It's a nice name. Very French."

"We like it," Damien said. "My grandfather was also Julien Louis."

We stood there, silence stretching between us, until I couldn't bear the quiet. "He's so small," I said.

"Not a big boy." Damien smiled with confidence. "But he will grow. We will make him stout with fresh foods from the garden."

The sound of quick steps broke the heavy silence as Natasha, her cheeks pink, came back into the room. "How fortunate to find you all still in one place. We were lucky—since we had a pre-birth order, the records office printed this without any trouble." She pulled a manila envelope from her briefcase and handed it to Damien. "In there you'll find your son's birth certificate, on which you are named the father and Simone the mother. Your baby will have dual citizenship—American, by virtue of being born here, and French, because of his French parents."

She had taken care of everything.

"Mandy?" Amelia gave me a pointed look. "Are you ready to go?"

Through tears, I told all of them good-bye.

"The more you sweat in training," Gideon often said, "the less you bleed in battle."

The day of Gideon's memorial service, I revised his axiom: *The more you cry in private, the less you weep in public.*

For reasons I didn't want to consider, I wasn't allowed to see Gideon's body. His remains were flown to Dover Air Force Base, then transported to Washington and buried at Arlington National Cemetery. Someone from Special Operations Command invited me to fly up to the graveside service, but Dr. Hawthorn advised against my traveling so soon after giving birth. So I stayed home to help Elaine and Tumelo memorialize their only son.

At the memorial service, a representative from Gideon's unit stood before a display of bright poinsettias and said my husband died a hero and saved several lives with his unthinking sacrificial action. "Gideon Lisandra was the epitome of the word *warrior,*" the man said. "He had the courage to defy fear, the sense of duty that allowed him to throw the gauntlet down, and the honor to scorn compromise in the face of death. Gideon was one of the most noble and brave souls I have ever had the honor of knowing.

If not for his courage"—the man looked straight at me—"ten other families would be holding funerals today. He is a shining example for the rest of us."

I smiled, appreciating his statement, but his words did nothing to explain how or why my husband died.

Snake Billings filled in the details. He showed up at the house hours after the memorial service, after Marilee had gone to bed and the family had gone home.

I let him in without a word. We stared at each other for a long moment, two pairs of wet eyes exchanging wordless pain and sympathy, then I stepped into the circle of his arms. His embrace felt nothing like Gideon's, but I took comfort from knowing he had been with Gid on my husband's last day.

"Snake"—I finally managed to whisper—"what can you tell me?"

He released me and together we walked to the couch. We sat, both of us erect and facing the opposite wall, then he took off the old baseball cap he always wore when out riding in his truck.

"We were going in to rescue a hostage," Snake said, staring at my silent television, "and we were creeping along this bushy creek bed. We'd surveilled it during the day and it was clean, but someone must have come in and planted the IED right before we moved forward. Gideon was on point. He saw the device and stopped us, but then this little girl from the village comes walking along from the west, and when Gid sees her she's about two feet from the trip wire."

I closed my eyes, intuiting the end of the story.

"The kid—" Snake's voice broke.

"Stop." I dropped my hand on his arm. "You don't have to say any more. And I know you probably shouldn't have told me that much."

"Just know this," Snake said, unshed tears glimmering in his eyes. "I loved Gid like a brother and he will always have a place in my heart. If you need anything, Mandy, don't hesitate to call me. I will never forget Gid, and I will never let you down if you need something."

I thanked him, gave him another hug, and walked him toward the door.

I didn't ask about the outcome of the mission. I didn't need to, because with pulse-pounding clarity I understood the only fact that mattered—my husband had pushed the wandering child away and thrown himself on the explosive device.

When it came to little girls, Gideon had always been a push-over.

The day after Gideon's service, I found myself possessed by an odd restlessness. I knew I was expected to stay home and receive visitors, casseroles, and sympathy cards, but I couldn't sit still and didn't want to linger in the house where I saw Gideon every time I rounded a corner. Knowing how he died had answered my questions, but the knowledge did nothing to ease the empty feeling inside me.

Reminders of the baby also haunted me. Maternity clothing filled my closet while prenatal vitamins and stretch mark preventatives littered my bathroom counter. The kitchen calendar bore scrawled notes about doctors' appointments, and a Post-it on the computer displayed Simone's email address.

Everywhere I looked, I was reminded of my losses.

Mom had driven over to be with us, so I asked her to watch Marilee and greet visitors while I went out. Without waiting for an answer, I grabbed my purse and headed toward the garage.

"Where are you going?" Mom called, alarm in her voice. "When will you be home?"

"I don't know." Since a brisk wind had begun to blow, I grabbed Gideon's favorite hoodie from a hook by the back door. "But I'm not going to jump off a bridge, if that's what you're worried about."

I knew it was a stupid thing to say, but at that point I didn't know where I wanted to go. Yet as soon as I slipped behind the wheel, my subconscious yearnings crystallized into a coherent directive: I had to see the baby again. I had to hold him one more time before the Amblours carried him to France.

To steady my nerves, I pressed my nose to the thick fabric of Gideon's hoodie and breathed in his scent. Gideon would understand my feelings. He would tell me to go see the Amblours, say good-bye, and then get back to being Marilee's mother. To comfort me he'd whisper, *Good things usually hurt.*

Hard experience had taught me how true that saying was.

I dug through my purse and found the slip of paper where I'd written the Amblours' Florida address. I never thought I'd have a reason to visit their rental, but the morning we parted at the hospital I'd been so exhausted and grief-stricken that I barely looked at the baby. All I remembered was rosebud lips, a light spray of brown hair, and tiny fingers, but that description would fit half the infants in any hospital. It wasn't enough. I wanted to examine Julien, I wanted to hold him and say my own special good-bye before he was gone for good.

I pointed my car west and drove. Because Julien was only four days old, I suspected his parents were still trying to figure out how and when to feed him, what his cries meant, and how to get a decent amount of sleep. They were bound to be at the house on Sandpiper Drive, and might even welcome a visit from an experienced mother.

I wasn't surprised when the GPS led me to a home only a block from the beach—the Amblours could afford to rent near the water. My heart pounded as I pulled into the driveway, then parked the car and walked up to the front door. The drapes were open and a rolled-up newspaper lay on the sidewalk, so I picked it up, thinking they might appreciate hand-delivered news. I tried on a smile and rang the bell, then waited for a long moment. When no one answered, I took a few steps back and studied the front of the building. Nothing moved at the windows, no sound came from within. So the family was either sleeping or ignoring the bell.

"Can I help you?"

I flinched at the sound of an unfamiliar voice and turned to see a man in Bermuda shorts approaching from a neighboring home. "I'm looking for the Amblours, the couple renting this house."

"I met them." The man smiled at me, interest flickering in his eyes. "They're gone. Packed up and flew home two days ago."

"They went home?" My jaw dropped. "But—but their baby is only a few days old. He's too young to fly."

"I don't know anything about that." The man gave me the once-over, taking in my puffy figure and maternity top. "But maybe they decided to spend the holidays at home, 'cause they're definitely gone. I have the keys, if you know someone who would like to rent the house—"

"Thank you, but I don't know anything about renting houses."

I stumbled back to the car, somehow placing one foot in front of the other when all I wanted to do was drop onto the front walkway and weep. How could they have gone without telling me good-bye? Without calling? Without stopping at the house to let me hold the baby one final time?

How could they have gone home even before Gideon's memorial service?

I could almost hear my mom's voice: *What'd you expect, lasting friendship?*

No, I didn't expect friendship. But from people who kept going on and on about how they could never thank me enough, I had expected more kindness and compassion.

I had expected one final opportunity to kiss the baby good-bye.

Chapter Fourteen

As a college psychology major, I had been thoroughly schooled in the stages of grief: denial, anger, bargaining, depression, and finally, acceptance. I had also listened to enough purveyors of pop wisdom to know that after a loss, I should begin with denial and move through the stages as quickly as possible in order to Get On With Life.

The trouble was, I didn't want to get on with life. I wasn't suicidal—I loved my daughter too much to consider such a selfish act—but I didn't want to move through any of the required stages, no matter what the TV gurus advised. So I bucked the system and freely admitted that my husband was gone. I gave his books to Tumelo and boxed up his trophies for Marilee. I moved his photos from my bureau to a special shelf in the living room; I piled his clothing into bags and hauled them to our church's thrift store, keeping only a flannel shirt I liked to sleep in. On Sunday mornings I looked around the congregation and wondered if I'd see a pair of Gideon's pants walking by.

I gave Gid's truck to Snake, knowing that's what Gideon would have wanted. On the few occasions Snake dropped by to check on us, I glimpsed the truck through the curtains and felt my heart fling itself against my rib cage, the result of some inexplicable cellular conviction that Gideon had come home.

Yet my mind knew better. My husband was gone, the baby was gone, life as I had known it was gone forever. The rational part of my brain wondered if I was experiencing the results of postpartum depression, but the emotional part of me stared out at a world that had shifted from color to gloomy shades of gray.

Mom watched wide-eyed as I cleared out Gideon's things, then she told me that refusing to go through the stages of grief was the mother of all denials. "Can't you see what you're doing?" Her face twisted into a human question mark. "This isn't normal, Mandy. I'm worried about you." When I wouldn't listen, she shook her head, urged me to see a therapist, and drove home to The Villages.

Mama Isa and Elaine worried over me, too—I could see concern in their faces—but they did their best to make sure life for me and Marilee remained consistent.

After about a month, I went back to work at the grocery, smiling and behaving as though my world hadn't been completely devastated. When regular customers asked how my new baby was doing, I said I'd been a surrogate, so the child had gone home with his parents. After hearing this, the person who'd asked always gave me the compassionate look they'd give someone who'd just lost their dog.

Sometimes I left work early and went to the mall, where I walked around and studied new mothers with their babies in carriages or strollers. I knew they'd come to the mall because they were desperate to put on makeup and get out of the house—I had done the same thing when Marilee was an infant. I never spoke to the mothers, but peered at their babies' faces and wondered if I'd spot a little boy who looked like Julien. I knew *my* Julien was living in France, but I yearned to see something of him in another child's face.

Despite my best intentions, after three months I realized I couldn't stay in the rental house Gideon and I had furnished together. I glimpsed his shadow on the stairs, heard his voice in the hallway, and listened for his steps on the front porch every night.

His empty pillow seemed to mock me on our big bed, and I had trouble sleeping.

His family seemed to understand my need to relocate, and Mama Isa offered her home as a way station, a place of healing and rest. "Jorge and I do not need so much space," she told me, opening her hands wide to indicate the empty bedrooms. "You and Marilee come live with us for a while. You help me, I will help you, and we will keep *la familia* together."

Accepting her offer was one of the easiest things I'd ever done, though my mom couldn't understand why I seemed so eager to give up my independence. "You're not a child," she told me during a phone call. "You need to learn to stand on your own two feet."

I snorted, baffled by her belief that I had somehow been coerced into making the decision to move. "Why should I live alone? It takes a village to raise a child, haven't you heard?"

Later, though, I realized that I wanted to move in with Jorge and Isa because being with them brought me closer to Gideon. He wasn't in the house, but I felt him in his *family*. His eyes lived in his father's and aunt's faces, his voice rumbled from his grandfather's throat, and his smile frequently flashed on Mama Isa's mouth. Everyone in the family spoke his melodious language. As long as Marilee and I remained close to *la familia,* we would never feel far from Gideon.

And I knew there'd be no room for ghosts in Mama Isa's guest room's narrow bed.

The family helped me move on a Saturday. Mama Isa came over the day before to help me pack, and I could tell she was stunned to see me dumping papers, bills, and drawer contents into packing boxes without first going through them. "You might be able to throw much of that stuff out," she said, gently making her point. "You will save money if you do not store so much."

"I don't have time to go through everything," I answered, dumping yet another stack of Gideon's meticulous files into a packing box. He had managed our important papers, our taxes, our canceled checks. One day I *might* go through them—but probably only if the IRS came knocking at my door.

I sold the furniture we no longer needed (including the grand piano) and squeezed our lives into cardboard boxes. We sent some of our furnishings to a rented storage unit and moved everything else into Mama Isa's empty bedrooms.

Living with Isa and Jorge helped me feel less alone, and I know Marilee enjoyed their company. She never complained, but I suspected that she thought her mother had turned into some sort of zombie.

And why shouldn't I? Gideon had been such a huge part of my life that without him I felt like a quadruple amputee. His in-and-out schedule had allowed him to take charge of our bills, make most of the decisions, and even handle a lot of the grocery shopping. He accepted every responsibility I didn't want, and managed everything so smoothly that I never realized how helpless I would be without him.

When Mama Isa took us in, I gratefully surrendered my responsibilities to her. I helped around the house, of course, but she washed our clothes, prepared our dinners, and made sure we were up and out the door every morning. She was stronger than I had ever been, and though I admired her, I didn't think I could ever be like her.

After one family dinner, Amelia asked if I still planned on going back to college, but what would be the point? I had wanted to get my degree so I could get a better job to provide for Marilee's schooling and allow us to enlarge our family. With Gideon gone, I no longer needed extra money.

Our finances, you see, had also been affected by Gideon's death. Due to payments from Gideon's life insurance, the military death benefit, and my surrogate work, Marilee and I had more money than we needed.

Yet thanks to *la familia,* we didn't need anything. And at Mama Isa's house we were always surrounded by people who loved us.

Six months after my husband's memorial service, the president invited me, Tumelo, and Elaine to the White House to receive Gideon's posthumous Medal of Honor. My in-laws went, but I sent Marilee in my place. Even at the ripe old age of five, she had more military steel in her spine than I did.

At about the same time, Natasha Bray invited me to share my experience with one of her surrogacy support groups. I turned her down without a second thought. Sitting in front of pregnant strangers to describe my experience would be like ripping the skin away from my pounding heart and assuring them the experience didn't hurt.

Days without Gideon stretched into weeks and months. Marilee remained at the Takahashi school, and we continued to enjoy Saturday family night dinners at Mama Isa's. I stayed behind the cash register at the Cuban grocery, and Claude Newton of the Hawaiian shirt and flip-flops kept shuffling in every morning. Marilee and I went to church on Sundays, sat in our usual pew, sang the praise choruses, and lifted our prayers. God must have grown tired of hearing mine because they were always the same: *Lord, why did you take Gideon?*

I prayed another prayer, too, but this one I whispered only in the privacy of my bedroom: "Lord, bless that baby boy. Wherever Julien is, keep him safe and help him be happy."

Around the family, I never mentioned the baby I'd carried—I didn't think they'd understand why I mourned the loss of a child who wasn't mine, especially after I'd insisted that carrying a baby and handing it over would be a simple, uncomplicated matter. And while Gideon's loss colored every moment of every day, the loss of that child tinged my nights with despair. The vivid dreams I'd experienced in pregnancy persisted, leading me to wonder if my surrogacy had been a life-altering mistake. Would I never be free of the shadowy remnants that haunted my sleep?

I might have missed the baby less if the Amblours had kept their promise. In the months after Julien's birth, I didn't hear a word from Simone or Damien—not a picture, email, or card. I tried to tell myself their forgetfulness was a mixed blessing and that I wouldn't long for the child if I couldn't visualize him or know how he was growing up. Still, the Amblours' silence surprised me.

In November, nearly a year after Gideon's death, I quietly marked the date that was supposed to usher in our new life. If he had lived, Gideon would have finished his military service and come home to celebrate with a barbecue. The next morning he would have slept late, then gone out to search for the right place to open his music store. Then we would have met for lunch and gone out together to look at prospective houses—*all* of them located more than an hour away from MacDill Air Force Base. Marilee's decorated dollhouse would come to life as I implemented all the plans and dreams I had compiled over the months of my pregnancy.

But with Gideon gone, no one in the family even mentioned his retirement date. They had either forgotten or they were keeping quiet to spare me pain.

As if they could.

Another year passed. A somber Valentine's Day, a reserved Mother's Day, another birthday. I looked in the mirror after my thirtieth and saw a widow with a thin, shadowed face in which dull blue eyes occupied most of the available space. No wonder. I felt like a soulless, barely animate creature of mud and clay.

I might have remained in that unfeeling state for many more months, even years, if Amelia hadn't meddled in my private affairs.

Amelia and Mario continued to work at Mama Yanela's grocery, but for the two years following Gideon's death they focused on the pursuit of parenthood.

After spending several months on an adoption waiting list, they followed a friend's suggestion and took in a foster child, a three-year-old boy named Sydney. Even at three, Sydney was prone to inexplicable fits of rage, but after a few months with my cousins he seemed to settle down. Amelia began to smile again, and I often saw Mario walking with little Sydney on his shoulders, the boy's hands entwined in Mario's collar-length hair.

I was happy for them, and selfishly grateful that they'd taken in an older child—because Sydney slept in a regular bed, Mama Isa had no need to ask about Gideon's cradle. With Gideon gone, the cradle had become even more precious to me. It sat in storage, waiting for the day I would give it to Marilee for my grandchild.

After a year of loving and caring for their foster son, Amelia and Mario filed a petition to adopt Sydney. Their inquiries led a social worker to contact the boy's birth parents and ask that they formally relinquish their rights. Reminded that they had a son, the parents—both of whom had been in and out of jail on drug charges—decided that they wanted to care for their child.

And blood, apparently, trumped every other consideration.

Instead of celebrating Sydney's adoption, Amelia and Mario had to surrender the boy to a social worker, who picked up the screaming, kicking toddler and placed him in a dilapidated house with virtual strangers.

I had never seen Amelia so devastated. As the social worker left with Sydney, Amelia went to pieces while Mario held her, helpless to do anything but rub her back. Later that night they sat at Mama Isa's dinner table and clung to each other as if they expected another official to barge through the door and tear them apart.

I don't know if I could have continued to pursue adoption were I in Amelia's situation. I might have given up and tried to enjoy my childfree status. But Amelia refused to surrender her dream. She asked her social worker to hold their adoption file six months, then put them back on the active waiting list. They needed time to grieve, and during those six months they managed to fortify themselves and recommit to their goal.

I don't know how they did it.

As 2010 drew to a close, the sparkle returned to Amelia's eyes.

She and Mario would be back on the list in January, potential parents once again.

But on the first Saturday in December, as Tumelo sprayed fake snow around the grocery's front windows and the family braced for tragic holiday memories, discouragement filled Amelia's expression again. I understood why when I noticed the tabloid newspaper in her hand—the cover story was an article about a New York actress who had traveled to China to adopt a baby girl. Amelia had investigated Asian adoptions, too, but she and Mario simply couldn't afford the international fees.

"Hey." I waved for her attention, then crooked my finger to call her over.

She shook her head. "Not now," she said, keeping her voice low as she walked by. "Later, we'll talk."

After dinner, she came into my room at Mama Isa's, dropped onto my mattress, and tugged at the tufts on my chenille bedspread. "I wonder"—her forehead creased—"if it just wasn't meant to be."

"What are you talking about?" I asked, though I was pretty sure I knew the answer.

"Maybe I'm not meant to be a mother. Maybe God knows I'll be a lousy mama, so he's keeping children from me. Or maybe my kid would have died from cancer, been hit by a car, or grow up to experience something tragic."

Like dying on a secret mission in a foreign country? Gideon's death may have been tragic, but his life wasn't a mistake.

"Or maybe I would have been distracted by my kid and I would have hit someone else's child while I was driving," she went on, unaware that my thoughts were drifting, as always, toward Gideon. "Maybe there's a purpose in all this frustration. Maybe God has good reasons for preventing me from being a mother."

"I don't know why God does all the things he does." I gentled my voice. "I don't think he wants to keep us from suffering. Maybe he allows us to suffer. Maybe he *plans* for us to suffer, 'cause I know he's not asleep when terrible things happen. And if nothing bad ever happened to us, what would we be like? Spoiled rotten, probably. And lazy."

Amelia laughed, but I heard no real humor in her voice. "You're tired, cuz. You never make sense when you're exhausted."

"I'm always tired." I stretched out across the bed and propped my head on my bent arm. "You'll be a good mama when the time comes. I watch you with Marilee, and sometimes I think you're a better mother than I am. You have so much more energy."

"You'll get your energy back."

"And you'll get your baby."

She barked a short laugh. "Yeah. Like, when I'm fifty, and too arthritic to chase after the kid. Of course, if I were rich and famous, I could buy a baby anytime I wanted."

I sighed, knowing she was still annoyed by the actress who'd traveled such an apparently easy road to adoption.

"I mean"—she turned to face me—"why should it cost so much to do a loving thing? They pay foster parents to take care of children. Why can't someone arrange it so ordinary people don't have to mortgage everything they own in order to adopt an orphan? I'm not asking for a handout, just something to make things easier. It shouldn't cost so doggone much to share your love with someone who needs it."

But good things usually hurt.

As Gideon's voice echoed in my brain, I shook off the haunting memory and tried to focus on Amelia. I had already offered to cover her adoption fees—partly because I had more money than I needed, and partly because I still felt guilty for not offering to carry a baby for my cousins. But Mario said he could never take money from me; it would be like taking from Gideon.

"You keep everything you have," he had urged me. "Marilee will need to go to college, and you may want to buy your own place someday. I couldn't take a dime from you, no matter what."

"I'm sorry," I told Amelia, letting my head fall on my pillow. "Sometimes life hurts."

Amelia leaned over and kissed my forehead, a Lisandra family gesture I'd come to appreciate. "Thanks, cuz. You, me, Mario—we're going to be okay."

"Oh, yeah? When will that be?"

"Soon, I hope." She stood and stepped toward the doorway. "Mama says dessert will be ready in ten minutes. Are you coming?"

"I'm stuffed." My pillow muffled the words, so I lifted my head. "Will you watch Marilee and make sure she doesn't eat herself sick? Dessert is her favorite thing."

"I'll watch her."

She slipped away and I closed my eyes, content to let the world continue without me.

I asked my father-in-law for two days off during the early part of December—I wanted the sixth off because it would be the second anniversary of Gideon's death. I asked for the seventh off because I knew I'd need time to recover from the sixth.

I woke on Tuesday the seventh with a pounding headache, a hangover from my mourning and melancholy. A thick quiet hung over the house, so I opened my bedroom door and padded to the kitchen. Jorge had already gone to the store; Mama Isa would have followed him after taking Marilee to school. I was home alone, and I would have the sprawling house to myself for at least a few more hours.

I had eaten practically nothing the day before, so I toasted a couple of bread slices, then spread them with strawberry jam. I popped a little tub into the individual-serving coffee machine, then leaned against the counter as the fragrant brew began to stream into a mug. After breakfast, maybe I'd take two painkillers and go back to bed. Or turn on the TV and flip through the channels so I could again be amazed at how few programs were actually worth watching.

When the coffee finished dripping from the dispenser, I picked up my mug, set my toast on a paper towel, and carried both into the family room. Still in my pajamas, I sat cross-legged on the sofa and ate my breakfast as the crew of *Good Morning America* giggled their way through the final hour. Since when had the morning news become so entertaining?

I looked up when movement outside the jalousie windows caught my eye. The mail carrier, one of the few who still walked a route, was putting mail into Mama Isa's narrow box. I waited until he walked back down the driveway before I opened the front door and pulled out a handful of envelopes. I dropped everything on the foyer table, but one envelope drew my attention. The letter had been addressed in a slanted, thick handwriting, it bore a foreign postmark, and the stamp was . . . French.

I picked it up and felt its weight on my palm. A letter from France with my name on it.

The sight of a familiar name—Domaine de Amblour—strummed a shiver from me.

I carried the letter into the family room, fell onto the sofa, and ripped at the envelope. As I opened the enclosed velum card, several items fell into my lap—two photographs and a hank of dark brown hair, tied with a blue ribbon.

I read the note:

Dearest Amanda:

As we look forward to celebrating Julien's birthday again, we cannot help but be grateful for what you did for us. So we send our love and prayers, with every wish for your health and happiness.

Sincerely,
Simone, Damien, and Julien Amblour

The first picture was a family photo—Simone and Damien and their little son, who sat between them on a garden bench. The sight of the boy elicited a sense of déjà vu that bloomed into prescience when I studied the second photo, a close-up of Julien Louis Amblour.

I looked into the boy's brown eyes and felt something cold trickle over my backbone, leaving in its aftermath an odd feeling of unease—Mama Isa would have said she felt someone walk across her grave. I held my breath as other remembered images pushed and jostled for space in my brain. Two-year-old Julien looked exactly like Marilee had at that age: the same dark eyes, the same turned-up nose, same facial structure. The same color hair. Same build. Matching rosebud lips.

With pulse-pounding certainty, I knew that if I were to stand this child next to a two-year-old Marilee, they would appear nearly identical. The only difference lay in his hair—Julien's was curly, Marilee's straight. But they certainly looked alike.

Alike enough to be siblings.

Brother and sister.

Dear Lord—I caught my breath—*what have I done?*

I spent the afternoon pacing through the house, Julien's picture in my hand and a thousand questions in my head. Could a mix-up occur in surrogacy? With so many safeguards was it even possible? In the history of surrogacy and in vitro fertilization, spectacular mistakes had been made. I remembered reading about cases in which women were implanted with the wrong embryos—it happened to one woman in Michigan, another in Great Britain. Another American woman gave birth to twins, one white and the other black.

Yes, mistakes did happen with in vitro fertilization, but mine wasn't strictly an IVF case. I had been implanted with an embryo that did not originate from within my body, yet this child looked almost exactly like my firstborn. In order for that to happen, the first embryo would have to die and the second would have to be conceived later, when my body began another cycle.

Was such a scenario theoretically possible? I'd been taking so many hormones during those months, my reproductive system could have been off balance. Gideon and I had refrained from sexual intimacy while we waited for the embryo transfer, but after the pregnancy test we had been told we could enjoy normal relations, so we did. Which meant this child, if he were ours, had been conceived during one of those encounters.

I stumbled to my desk drawer and pulled out all the stuff I'd dumped inside when we moved. I shuffled through scraps of paper and folders, searching for the old calendar I had used to keep track of dates, drugs, and injections.

Finally I found it. The embryo had been transferred on March 18. I received a positive beta pregnancy test on March 27. Julien was born on December eighth, only a few days past his due date. Nothing unusual about that, except I gave birth to a smaller-than-usual baby. He'd been only eighteen inches, only five pounds. More like a honeydew melon than a full-term infant.

I reached for the chair to steady myself. With every ultrasound and measurement, the doctor had made some sort of comment about the baby's small size. I ignored those comments because I'd heard the egg donor was petite. But what if the donor's size didn't matter? What if the baby had appeared small because he was conceived not in March, but in April?

Tears blurred my vision as I walked over and flung open my closet door. The journal I kept during the pregnancy lay in a box buried beneath a stack of containers I hadn't yet unpacked. I yanked on boxes, pulled them out, and spilled their contents. I found the journal in a box with our tax returns, and thanked heaven for my packrat tendencies.

I hugged the slender volume to my chest, crawled over to the desk, and climbed into the chair. In a small cone of lamplight, I opened the book and flipped to the early pages.

I read about the embryo transfer . . . Amelia's decision to adopt . . . the beta pregnancy test . . . and the first email from Simone. I turned more pages and read about the day I began spotting . . . and the canceled ultrasound appointment.

I closed my eyes. Spotting can be insignificant, but it can also be a sign of miscarriage. Later I assumed the bleeding occurred because the first twin didn't implant, but I might have miscarried both babies and remained completely unaware of what had happened. Then my hormone-charged body, prepared and ready to nourish a baby, welcomed a fertilized egg resulting from my union with my husband. The embryo implanted and the baby began to grow.

My baby. Mine and Gideon's.

With my heart in my throat, I flipped more pages in the journal. On May eighth I missed an ultrasound because the doctor's machine was down, but we heard a heartbeat. More proof that I was indeed pregnant, so I assumed everything was fine with the surrogate pregnancy.

Another of Gideon's maxims came back to me: *Never assume.*

By the time I made it into Dr. Hawthorn's office, she'd heard a heartbeat, all right—she could have heard *my* baby's beating heart. And what did she tell me later? I flipped through my journal to find her words: *This baby might be a bit of a slow starter.*

All those nights Gideon and I fell asleep with his hand protectively thrown across my belly, he might have been guarding his own child.

The son he had always wanted.

Tears began to flow as fresh horror overwhelmed me. *How* it happened no longer mattered; all I wanted was the truth. I had to tell Natasha Bray about my suspicions, and she would have to tell the Amblours that they might not have any right to the child in their home. Julien could be my child, my blood and bone.

Gideon had selflessly given his life in the service of his country, but he would never willingly surrender his son to strangers.

If those people had my boy, I would move heaven and earth to get him back.

Because blood trumped everything.

Amelia looked tired when she stopped by to deliver the day's receipts to Mama Isa.

"Mama," she called, coming through the front door. *"¿Donde está?"*

I didn't want her to talk to Mama Isa, at least not yet. I had to show her what I'd discovered.

"Amelia." I found her in the den, caught her arm, and dragged her into the living room.

"What?" A frown creased her forehead as she followed me. "Is something wrong?"

I pulled two photos—Julien's and Marilee's—from my pocket and pressed them into her palm. "I got a card today; the Amblours sent it. Now look at those two photos and tell me what you see."

She stared at the pictures, then blinked. "I see two kids. This is Marilee, and I presume this is the French boy."

"Julien. My baby."

She smiled and looked again. "My, he's getting big. What is he now, three?"

"He'll be two years old tomorrow. And Marilee's two in that picture."

"So?"

"So what do you see? Look carefully—don't you see a resemblance?"

She glanced at the photos again, then she studied me. "Are you okay? You look flushed."

"I'm fine. But these pictures—"

"I see two photos. Two shots of two-year-olds."

"But they look alike, don't you see? Except for the hair."

Amelia studied them again. "I guess they do look a little bit alike—once you realize that they both have two eyes, a nose, and a mouth. Oh, and they both have brown hair."

I inhaled a deep breath, annoyed by her refusal to acknowledge the obvious. "It's more than that and you know it. Look closely—their mouths have the same shape, their noses are practically identical, and their eyes are exactly the same shade of brown."

"Anyone would have brown eyes in that kind of lighting."

I stared at the picture again, wondering if I had missed something. "Are you sure?"

Amelia crossed her arms and narrowed her eyes. "I know what you're thinking, but this kid is not Marilee's brother. I know you'd like that to be the case, but it's not possible. You miss Gideon, so you're pinning your hopes on this kid—"

Ignoring her, I began to pace again. "The thing I can't figure out is why they'd send me a picture now. Unless maybe *they've* noticed the resemblance. They've seen Marilee, they know what she looks like, so maybe they're trying to figure out how this could have happened."

Amelia sighed and lifted her gaze to the ceiling, then seemed to come to a decision. "Wait here," she said. I watched, puzzled, as she left the living room and stepped into the study.

Unwilling to wait, I followed. I found Amelia sitting at Jorge's desk, shuffling through the contents of a drawer. Finally she pulled out a manila envelope. She opened it and removed another vellum envelope, identical to the one I'd opened earlier.

"They didn't *just* send a card," Amelia said, her voice flat. "Tomorrow is the kid's birthday, right? They kept their promise and sent one last year, too. But when we found this one in the mail, Mama and I thought you didn't need a reminder of that awful time. When you didn't ask about the Amblours or mention the baby's birthday, we put the card away."

I stared at the other envelope, trying to make sense of what she'd said. "You kept personal mail from me?"

"We thought you'd ask about them if you really wanted to know how the kid was getting along."

"You kept a personal letter from me," I repeated. "I think that's illegal."

"So take us to jail. Mama and I only did it because we didn't want you to be upset. Getting through the anniversary of Gideon's death was hard enough for you. This would have made it worse."

I knew I ought to be furious with her, but curiosity overpowered every other emotion. I yanked a letter opener from a mug on the desk, then ripped the envelope from side to side. Within a minute I had opened the card and pulled out another photo, this one of Julien at twelve months. The photo could have been a shot of Marilee at the same age.

On the accompanying card, Simone had written a variation of the message I'd read earlier: she and Damien were thinking of me at this special time in their lives, they sent their love, they would always be grateful. And Simone had again enclosed a memento. This morning's card had contained thick little curls, but this envelope held wisps of baby-fine hair.

I pressed my hand over my mouth as a burst of anger tore through me. If I had seen this card earlier, I might not have spent the last year of my life idling in neutral. If a wrong had been committed, I might have had a year to make things right.

"Mandy?" Amelia looked at me, her eyes filled with helpless appeal. "Don't be upset with us. We only did what we thought was best for you."

"How can you know what's best for me?" I drew a long, quivering breath, barely mastering the anger quivering at my core. "I don't know what's best for me, so how can you know anything?"

Amelia's face rippled with anguish, but for once I didn't care.

Between my discovery of Amelia's secret and Mama Isa's call to dinner, I managed to bridle my anger toward my interfering relatives. I knew they hadn't meant to hurt me, and I *had* lived in a dark place during those first months after Gideon's death. If Simone had sent a photo of a blond, round-faced, pale-skinned French boy, their decision to hide the first letter wouldn't have felt like a dagger in my heart.

But the child in those pictures looked nothing like Damien Amblour and quite a bit like Gideon. And that resemblance spurred me to action.

Marilee was attending a Christmas party at a friend's house, so at dinner I commandeered the conversation and made everyone pass around my collection of assorted photographs. Opinion at the table, however, was far from unanimous. While Mama Isa and Jorge admitted that the two children did favor one another, they seemed unwilling to concede that a mistake could have been made under "such scientific conditions." Amelia and Mario flatly stated that the kids didn't look at all alike, while Yanela and Gordon tended to waver, asking confused questions in Spanish and siding with whoever was speaking at the time.

I watched with special interest when Gideon's mother picked up the picture of Julien. Elaine stiffened for an instant, cast a quick glance at Tumelo, and studied the photo again.

Then she snapped the picture on the table like a card shark playing four aces. "*Estoy segura.* I don't need to compare this with Marilee's picture. That is Gideon's son. I would know my grandchild anywhere."

"Elaine," Amelia said, a pleading note in her voice, "surely you're mistaken. This cannot be Gideon's child. These medical people take precautions, they employ sophisticated technologies and safeguards and tests—"

"I don't know much about technology." Elaine folded her hands in her lap. "But a mother knows her son's face, and I see it in this child. *Este es el hijo de Gideón.*"

She looked directly at me, and for the first time in my life I saw respect glowing in her eyes. "You were right to show us the truth, Amanda. Now . . . what do we do about it?"

I stared, surprised by her confidence and her challenge. What were we to do? What *could* we do?

"I—I don't know," I admitted. "I'm not sure what the steps are, but there has to be some kind of procedure for correcting a mistake like this. I suppose I should start at the Surrogacy Center."

"I never thought you should get involved with that place"—Elaine's eyes narrowed—"but if it is what God uses to bring me a grandson, I will trust *el Dios.* He knows what he is doing." Something like a smile lifted the corners of her eyes as she turned toward her husband. "Imagine, Tumelo—after all this time and so much sadness, God has blessed us with a grandson."

He lifted his glass to her, they smiled, and he drank.

When Natasha Bray appeared delighted to see me, I realized she had no idea why I'd made an appointment at her office.

"Mandy!" She beamed as she stepped out from behind her desk. "I've thought about you so many times over the past few months. How are you and your darling daughter?"

I smiled and said Marilee was fine and we were doing as well as could be expected, considering our loss. Natasha's smile vanished at this reference to Gideon's death, but she perched on the edge of her desk and gestured toward an empty chair. "What brings you to see me? Are you thinking about volunteering for another couple? Experienced surrogates are in demand, you know. They earn quite a bit more."

I sat and gripped the arms of the chair. "Actually, Natasha, I'm here because—well, let me begin by showing you something." I slipped the photos of two-year-old Marilee and Julien from my purse and handed them to her. "Notice anything unusual?"

Her lips pursed in a rosette as she scanned the images. "I know Marilee, of course, but"—she flashed the picture of Julien toward me—"who is this sweet lad? One of her cousins?"

"That is Julien Amblour," I replied. "And you see the resemblance, don't you? Looking at these pictures, I can't help but wonder if Julien is my son."

Confusion flickered over her face. "You can't possibly think—"

"I've considered it carefully, and I believe the baby I carried was mine and Gideon's. He was unusually small throughout the pregnancy, I missed a crucial early ultrasound, and we never did any genetic testing."

"We had no need for it. You were healthy, the baby was healthy—"

I waved her words away. "I want to consult with my doctor, and I want the Amblours to do some kind of paternity test to settle the matter. After all, Damien was determined to have a biological child, right? If Julien isn't Damien's son, the Amblours shouldn't want him. And if he's my son"—my voice broke—"I *do* want him. I need to get him home where he belongs, the sooner, the better. He ought to know his real family."

A flicker of shock widened Natasha's eyes and something that looked like panic tightened her mouth. "Get a grip on your emotions, Amanda; we need to think this through. You can't come in here and demand an investigation simply because you believe these two children look alike. I don't see any resemblance."

"You thought they were related."

"I didn't know what they were. I was hazarding a guess."

"Maybe you don't *want* to see how much they look alike."

"Maybe you *do.* Maybe you're so desperate to see similarities that your mind is playing tricks on you. After all, you've just come through a period of mourning . . . and I'm beginning to wonder if you aren't still grieving."

I bit my lower lip, barely managing to rein in my restless emotions. My heart stirred with a dozen feelings, but irritation led the pack. "I will always miss Gideon," I told her, "but I haven't lost my mind."

"I didn't say you had. But you need to calm down, get some therapy, and work through the issues that have confused you. I'm sorry you lost your husband, truly I am, but making trouble for the Amblours is not going to bring your soldier back. If you pursue this matter you're going to rattle a happy family, you could cause serious disruption in a marriage, and you'll probably introduce serious trouble to your own house. How is your daughter going to feel about this?"

"I don't want to make trouble for anyone." I struggled to keep my voice steady. "I only want to know if that child is my biological son, so I'm going to speak to my reproductive endocrinologist about my pregnancy. If you throw up a single roadblock, I'll hire a lawyer. I'll do whatever I have to do to get an answer, and as soon as I get it, I'll make things right and then go away."

"You don't realize—"

"I've realized a lot of things, Natasha. I'm not out to disparage your agency, and I don't mean to make a public example out of anyone. I only want to know—I *need* to know—if Julien Amblour should be living in my home. It's as simple as that."

"What you're describing is hardly simple." Natasha gave me a bland look, but a wary twitch of her eye told me she knew I was leading her toward potential disaster. A scowl darkened her brow. "I have to wonder . . . Why did you wait two years to confront me about this alleged problem?"

"I never saw Julien until last week." I met her accusing gaze without flinching. "I came to see you as a courtesy because I thought I should tell you what I'm about to do. I thought you might have a procedure for situations like this—"

"We don't *have* situations like the one you're describing."

I folded my hands. "Since you don't have a procedure, I'm going to investigate as quietly as possible. But don't doubt me—I *am* going to investigate. If you don't cooperate, I'll have to make a lot of noise."

"You're about to make a fool of yourself." The friendliness in her eyes had frozen into a blue as cold as ice. "We don't make mistakes at the Surrogacy Center. We have far too many safeguards in place."

"Gideon always said every system was failproof only until it failed."

Natasha ignored my comment. "You'll regret ever mentioning this. Have you considered the cost? Lawyers and genetic testing aren't cheap. Wouldn't that money be better spent on your daughter's future?"

"Money's not a problem for us anymore."

"Isn't it?" Her eyes softened with seriousness. "Then think about how people will talk. Surrogate mothers have a hard enough time explaining themselves, but you're about to make things worse. If you claim that child and this case gets any publicity, you'll be about as popular as Marybeth Whitehead. You'll be shredded in the blogosphere."

I shook my head. "I don't care what other people think of me. If Julien is my son, he needs me and he needs to know about his father."

"So your motive boils down to what—maternal feelings?" Her eyes narrowed. "You didn't seem to have many maternal feelings when he was born. You didn't even want to look at that boy."

The back of my neck burned. "I had just lost my husband. I didn't think I could stand to see something else I was about to lose."

"In your preliminary interview, you said you wouldn't be attached to the baby. You sat right in that chair and said you wanted to be a surrogate for financial reasons, pure and simple. You have your money, so why make a fuss? Unless this is some kind of blackmail—"

"I don't want a penny from those people."

"You only want to destroy their lives." Natasha's voice dripped with sarcasm. "The woman who earnestly wanted to help a childless couple is about to undo everything she did for them. Which will only make people wonder why you're *really* doing this—and why you waited two years to make your move."

Heat—pure rage—scalded my lungs. Why couldn't she see that if Julien was my child, I had every legal and ethical right to raise him?

"Let people wonder about my motives; any mother would understand. If Julien Amblour is my son, he's all I have left of Gideon. And that's reason enough for me to pursue this."

I stood and turned to walk out of the office, but Natasha hadn't finished. "I still say you could use some therapy," she called as I strode over the carpet. "Clearly, you're lacking psychological closure."

I stormed past the softly focused wall art featuring smiling couples and babies and pretended not to hear the pretty blonde receptionist who wished me a very merry Christmas.

Dr. Harvey Forrester, my reproductive endocrinologist, appeared surprised to learn that I'd made an appointment to talk about a past pregnancy instead of a future one. "What's this about?" he said, ushering me into his office. "Something worrying you?"

I thought about showing him the photographs of Julien and Marilee, then decided against it. They were a Rorschach test; people saw only what they wanted to see.

"First," I said, taking a seat in one of his guest chairs, "if you've heard about this from Natasha Bray at the Surrogacy Center—"

"I haven't heard anything." He frowned. "She might have called and left a message, though."

"That's not important. I came to see you because I need to know if it'd be possible for a woman to miscarry a transferred IVF embryo and then get pregnant by her husband."

His mouth twisted in a lopsided smile. "Of course it's possible. Both events occur frequently, but not often within days of each other." He leaned against his desk. "What's the time frame in your hypothetical situation?"

"Within a month," I said, pulling the little calendar he'd given me from my purse. "Or a couple of weeks. So close that no one suspects the fetus is actually the carrier's biological offspring until after the baby is born."

His jaw shifted, bristling the silver stubble on his cheek. "This isn't a hypothetical case, is it?"

"No, it's not. I don't know how much you remember about me, but after the pregnancy test I had in this office—"

"No need to go any further. What you're proposing couldn't be possible in that time frame. The six-week sonogram would have revealed an empty womb—no gestational sac or fetal pole. Even if a subsequent conception had occurred, it wouldn't show up on an ultrasound until later."

"But that's the problem—my first ultrasound was canceled and I missed the second one because the doctor's equipment was broken. All the subsequent ultrasounds revealed an unusually small fetus. And when the baby was born, supposedly at forty weeks, he barely weighed six pounds."

"Six pounds isn't all that unusual for a full-term infant."

"But my daughter weighed nine pounds. And my labor could have been brought on by stress because I started having contractions right after I learned—after I heard"—I gulped as an unexpected rise of grief choked me—"after I learned my husband had been killed."

As I struggled to get my emotions under control, the doctor cleared his throat and looked away, probably embarrassed by my tears. It'd be easy for him to dismiss me, to tell me that such things couldn't happen, that I was suggesting a medical impossibility. . . .

"Do you know what you're doing?" he finally said, his voice soft. "And are you sure you want to do it?"

I pulled out a tissue to blow my nose. "I don't care about opening a can of worms."

"But other people are involved. If you're correct in your assumption, this situation won't be easily resolved. And the costs—physical, financial, and especially emotional—"

"Dr. Forrester"—I steadied my voice—"what if the boy we're talking about was yours?"

He drew a deep breath, then promised to pull my file and review my case with Dr. Hawthorn.

A tremor of mingled fear and dread shot through me when I turned onto Mama Isa's street and saw all the cars. Vehicles filled every inch of the paved front lawn, forcing me to park across the road. My pulse quickened as I strode toward the house. Had someone died? Had something happened to Yanela or Yaritza? Maybe Mama Isa had called a family meeting to discuss how to deal with my delusions. . . .

I hurried inside, my nerves tight, and found the family scattered throughout the house. Amelia, who wore a dazed and happy expression, stood in the living room and appeared to be the eye of the hurricane.

"What's going on?" I crossed my arms and watched my cousin accept two stuffed garbage bags from Elaine. "Has there been a national disaster?"

"We got the call," Amelia said, her eyes distracted as she turned and carried her bulky load toward the front door. "We're picking up our baby tonight. Mama called her friends, and they've all donated things. People have been dropping stuff off for the last hour, and thank goodness for that. We're not ready!"

I stepped aside to let her hand the garbage bags to Mario, who had come into the house behind me. "What else, Mama?" he asked Amelia. "I got the playpen into the trunk, but do we need a baby bed?"

"Just put those in the car!" Amelia pushed him with a playful tap and sent him out the door.

I followed Amelia into the family room, where Yanela, Marilee, and Yaritza sat on the sofa, sorting items of children's clothing from a large heap on the floor. "How old is this child?" I asked. "And is it a boy or girl?"

Amelia blinked, then focused on me. "He's a boy, about six weeks old. Do babies that small sleep in a baby bed?"

I recognized the look of mad happiness on her face—I'd worn that look many times when Gideon was alive. That expression, coupled with the earnestness in her eyes, touched something inside me and turned my stubborn sentimentality to mush. Why should I cling to something that might do her a world of good?

"Babies that age *can* sleep in a baby bed," I told her as Mario came back into the house, "but you might prefer something smaller for a while. I happen to have a beautiful cradle in Marilee's room, but you'll have to dump out all the stuffed animals before you put it in your car."

She stared at me, her eyes abstracted, but they cleared as understanding dawned. "Mario"—she smiled, her gaze not leaving my face—"go get the cradle in Marilee's room. But put the stuffed animals on the bed; don't leave them on the floor."

Mario hurried off to haul out the cradle while Amelia wrapped me in an embrace. "Thank you," she whispered. "Thank you for being here because I don't have a clue about what to do."

"You'll do fine." I smoothed her hair and then stepped back. "Now, do you have sheets? You don't need a special sheet for the cradle, you can fold a flat sheet to cover the mattress. Later, when you put up a crib, you'll need special sheets to fit." I turned, trying to remember what I'd done with Marilee's baby linens. "I have some, somewhere. Probably up in the attic. Or in our storage unit."

Amelia shook her head. "We can look for sheets later. Right now I want to be sure the kid has something to wear."

I heard the patter of quick steps and turned to see Elaine enter the room, her face flushed and her arms filled with flannel baby blankets—something the baby probably wouldn't need in Florida unless he slept under an air-conditioning vent. Her gaze moved into mine. "Mandy, what else will she need? It's been so long since we had a baby around here."

"Bottles?" I suggested. "Formula? Diapers? All babies do at that age is eat, sleep, and poop."

"I think we've got those bases covered." Amelia actually *beamed* at me, her face glowing as if she'd never known an unhappy day. "Our social worker called about an hour ago, so I left Jenna in charge of the grocery and came straight over. Everything's fallen into place since then."

I grinned, impressed with the efficiency of the family grapevine. "What did the social worker tell you?"

"We have a little boy," Amelia said, "Latino, probably one of the migrant workers' babies. He was abandoned in south Florida, but when they heard a heart murmur, they flew him up here for an exam at All Children's Hospital. He's fine, so he can come home with us. We'll take care of him, and if no one claims him in the next six months, we can move forward with the adoption. He'll be legally ours. Forever."

Her stipulation—*if no one claims him*—tripped a warning flag in my head, but I knew Amelia wanted to remain positive. She was desperate to believe that God had reserved this little boy for her and Mario.

"That's wonderful," I told her, "and I'm thrilled for you. You're going to love him every bit as much as you'd love your own flesh and blood."

I don't know why I uttered such a cliché—maybe I simply didn't know what else to say. But Amelia didn't hold my lack of originality against me.

"Thanks, cuz. I love him already." She turned to Mario, who'd come back into the house. "Is that it? Do we have everything we need for now?"

His eyes were wild with panic, but he nodded. "I think so."

"Then let's go pick up our baby."

Amelia gave me another hug, Mario kissed Mama Isa on the cheek, then together they practically ran out of the room. "We'll be back soon," Mario called. *"Hasta luego!"*

Mama Isa, Elaine, and I stood in the doorway as Mario started the car and backed out of the driveway. A familiar tightness gripped my stomach and I recognized it as parental anxiety. Amelia would soon learn about this feeling, if she hadn't already.

I leaned against the doorframe, imagining the scene at the hospital. I could almost see the smile on Amelia's face as she opened her arms for the baby, I could almost hear the hoarseness in Mario's voice as he struggled to find the right first words to whisper to his son.

How fitting that they should hear good news today. And how wonderful that their baby boy might soon nap on Mama Isa's sofa with mine.

At work the next day, I answered the phone and heard a familiar male voice. "Amanda Lisandra, please."

My hand tightened on the receiver. "Dr. Forrester?"

"You're right—though the laws of probability are against it, after consulting with Dr. Hawthorn I would have to say it's possible you miscarried and became pregnant with your husband's child. I'm not saying the child *is* your biological son, only that the hypothetical situation you presented is quite credible."

I exhaled a sigh of relief. "Thank you. Now it's a matter of obtaining medical proof, right? And aren't all babies blood-typed at birth? So if we can find Damien Amblour's blood type, and the egg donor's—"

"It's not that simple," Dr. Forrester interrupted. "Let's say one parent is blood type A and the other is B. Even with only those two types, their biological child could be type O, A, B, or AB. Blood typing alone isn't going to prove paternity. DNA is the only way to be sure."

I patted my chest to calm my thumping heart. "Okay—so how do I get DNA results?"

"For a DNA test, you need genetic samples from the child and a parent. The test will either confirm or deny the probability they are related."

"Any idea how I can get—"

"I'm afraid you're on your own from this point. If you want to continue pursuing this matter, your next call should be to a lawyer. I'm afraid I can't do anything else for you."

You can't—or you won't? I didn't speak the words aloud because I suspected he might be worried about me suing him for malpractice.

"I understand." Even as I answered, I wondered if this was the reason I'd been reluctant to spend Gideon's life insurance proceeds or the military death benefit. Maybe my subconscious knew this day would come. . . . Maybe God knew I'd need the money to put my family back together.

"Thank you, Dr. Forrester." I smiled, hoping he could hear how truly grateful I was. "Don't worry, I know none of this was your fault. I only want to make sure the situation turns out the way it should."

"Best of luck to you, then."

"Thank you." I almost added that I didn't believe in luck, but Dr. Forrester didn't want to hear my views on luck versus God's sovereignty. But I knew the truth—if God had given me a son, God would want me to raise that son.

And who was I to question the will of God?

Chapter Fifteen

Two days before Christmas, I managed to snag an appointment with a family attorney who had several offices in the area. According to the ad in the Yellow Pages, attorney Joseph Pippen would do all he could to protect my rights in various family matters, including adoption cases, marriage and property disputes, and paternity testing.

I had a feeling my case could involve everything on his list.

My stomach was a quivering mess as I dressed for my appointment. I had never consulted a lawyer before, never thought about suing anyone for anything. Everything I knew about legal matters had come from watching television crime dramas, and I knew how unrealistic those shows could be. But the Amblours were wealthy, and wealth and power usually went hand in hand. They might be able to influence their local officials, they might even have friends who were judges. They probably kept a family lawyer on retainer and golfed with him on weekends.

So even before I stepped foot into my lawyer's office, I felt intimidated and overwhelmed.

A cheery receptionist in a red Christmas sweater ushered me into Mr. Pippen's office and offered me a cup of coffee. Feeling jittery enough without chemical additives, I shook my head and took a seat, grateful for an opportunity to look around and size up the man who might be instrumental in assuring my family's future.

The reception area had been decked with Christmas garlands and red bows, but Mr. Pippen's office remained free of holiday decorations. His wooden desk and bookshelves gleamed in the light from a pair of brass lamps, some kind of award featuring a golden microphone sat on the corner of his desk, and a picture of a baseball player hung in a niche inside his bookcase. A baseball glove rested on the top of a short bookcase, adding to the baseball theme, and a framed poster of the 1995 Cleveland Indians hung by the window.

I smiled, figuring the man had to be some kind of a radio host and rabid baseball fan from Ohio. A transplant, maybe even a snowbird who'd flown to Florida one winter and decided to stay.

Joseph Pippen entered with long strides and immediately shook my hand. "Mrs. Lisandra, so nice to meet you," he said, smiling beneath a thicket of tousled brown hair. "How can I help you?"

He sat in the opposite guest chair while I attempted to explain my case without using anything but factual terms. "I don't *know* that Julien Amblour is my son," I said, struggling to repress the tremor threatening to creep into my voice, "but the resemblance in the photos certainly suggests he could be. I also have a statement from my doctor saying it's medically possible the boy is mine. What I need, Mr. Pippen, is a DNA test, but I have no idea how to go about getting one."

The lawyer gave me a bright-eyed glance, filled with shrewdness. "You say Julien is supposed to be Damien Amblour's biological son. So if a test proves otherwise, he's your son by default."

"And my late husband's," I added, restating the obvious. "And therefore not related to the Amblours at all."

Mr. Pippen studied my face for a long moment, then he nodded and tapped a pencil against the legal pad in his lap. "Getting DNA from a French citizen might be tricky. Anytime you venture into international courts, you're playing an entirely different ball game, with quite a few different rules. The fact that surrogacy is illegal in France only complicates the matter further."

I closed my eyes, sensing the stealthy approach of discouragement. What did I know about international law? "So this is going to be impossible?"

"Not at all. As my Little League coach used to say, 'If you want something badly enough, there's always a way to win.'"

I lifted my head, wondering how far the lawyer would go to help me get my son. If he exhausted every available legal avenue, did he know international lawyers who could be hired to persuade judges with a sizable financial gift? Or maybe he had connections who knew shadowy agents who might be willing to snatch the boy. . . .

I looked away, afraid that Mr. Pippen would see my wild imaginings in my eyes. Ordinarily I'd obey every law and submit to every authority, but this case wasn't about property or intellectual rights, it was about *my son.* And surely a mother's right to raise her own child was God given and inalienable. Because I had done nothing wrong, no nation, agency, or man ought to be allowed to take that right from me.

And time was of the essence. I couldn't ignore the fact that Julien was undoubtedly becoming more attached to the Amblours with every passing day. The longer we waited for an affirmative response from France, the harder it would be for Julien to adjust to his true family.

I turned and met the attorney's gaze head-on. "Do you really think we can win this fight through the courts?"

"I do. But we might have to play hardball, and the process of convincing the other party to agree to genetic testing could take months. On the other hand, if you're right about how much that couple wanted a biological heir, they may not fight your request for custody if a DNA test establishes that the boy isn't genetically related. But I wouldn't bet on that outcome—the child has been with them two full years, and that's plenty of time to establish a tight bond between parents and child. Mr. Amblour may not feel as strongly about the importance of rearing his biological offspring after living so long with this boy."

My heart rode a roller coaster, rising in hope and plunging in despair with every point the lawyer made. By the time he finished his summation, I felt as though I'd been hanging on for dear life.

But at least I was still on the ride.

Mr. Pippen pressed his finger to his lips, then nodded as if he'd made a decision. "International law can be complicated, but the passive personality principle states that a court may assert jurisdiction over persons outside a nation's territory on the basis that one of its citizens has been harmed."

I stared at the man, my head spinning. "Would you care to explain that in layman's terms?"

The lawyer smiled. "No matter who his parents are, this child is an American citizen by virtue of being born in Florida—and our nation doesn't take kindly to people of other nations who deprive our citizens of their rights. If the boy is your son, we would try to convince a judge that the child is suffering harm by being kept from his biological mother, a woman willing and eager to raise him. If that approach fails and he is your child, then what transpired at the Surrogacy Center is tantamount to baby selling. You were hired to carry *their* son; if he's yours, you mistakenly handed over *your* son for compensation."

I blinked through a fog of confusion. "But Natasha Bray didn't intend to hand over my child. And she took great pains to be sure I was compensated every month for my time and effort, not for delivering the baby. She insisted that no money change hands when the baby was born.

"Doesn't matter. Inadvertent baby selling is still baby selling. Putting a woman's own baby on a payment plan—it's highly unethical."

He stared into the distance a moment more, then sighed in what looked like contentment. "I think we could put together a convincing case and persuade the court to order genetic testing. If the child turns out to be biologically related to his French father, the matter is settled. But if he is *not* related to Mr. Amblour, I am sure we could apply enough pressure to convince the court to order the boy's return to Florida."

Thrilled by his last words, I fisted my hands, but Mr. Pippen shot me a warning look. "This won't be a quick fix. International disputes can take months and involve a lot of lawyers. It won't be easy and it won't be inexpensive. Are you quite sure you want to pursue this?"

I stared at him, amazed that he could even ask the question. "I'm willing to do whatever it takes."

He nodded slowly, then stood and extended his hand. "A pleasure to meet you, Mrs. Lisandra, and a Merry Christmas to you and yours. I look forward to working on your case."

Mr. Pippen's warning rang in my ears as I drove back to Mama Isa's: *International disputes can take months and involve a lot of lawyers.*

Months? I had already been separated from the child who could be my son for two years. I'd missed his infancy, his immunizations, his first steps, and his first words. If he belonged to me, he should be learning to speak English and Spanish, not French. If he was mine, he should grow up learning how to play baseball and hearing how wonderful his father was, not playing in some circular stone tower.

If he was my son, he had no business living in a vineyard. He should be playing with his sister and building sand castles on Clearwater Beach. He should be watching his new baby cousin sleep in his daddy's oak cradle.

I parked in my usual spot at Mama Isa's, then walked toward the house. The tinny sounds of her old piano seeped through the windows as Marilee practiced her lessons. Not wanting to interrupt, I slipped into the living room and pressed a kiss to the top of my daughter's head, then went to my bedroom and closed the door.

I needed time to think. To breathe. To adjust to the idea that I might have to wait a long time before my questions would be answered.

I kicked off my shoes and fell back on the bed, then stared at the ceiling, my mind vibrating with a thousand thoughts. If the Amblours lived in the United States, this process wouldn't be so complicated. If I only had some sort of genetic sample from Damien Amblour, maybe I could somehow expedite the process. . . .

A solitary fact, unanchored and overlooked, slipped into my awareness. I *did* have a genetic specimen, but from Julien, not Damien. I had two birthday cards and two different samples of the boy's hair. And I'd watched enough episodes of *CSI* to realize that DNA could be taken from a single strand.

I opened the nightstand drawer and searched for the vellum envelopes. They lay beneath my Bible, safely put away, and as I opened each of them another tidbit from *CSI* surfaced in my consciousness. A hair that had been snipped from someone's head wouldn't work because DNA wasn't found in the hair itself, but in the follicle. I needed a hair that had been once rooted to the head, which meant my options would be limited to the first card, for which Simone had gathered a few strands of fine hair from a sheet or towel, not a barber's drape.

I picked up several hairs and examined them, then turned on the lamp and held them up to the light. After a moment of searching, I felt a smile spread over my lips. Unless my eyes were deceiving me, a tiny lump remained on the end of at least two hairs, and those lumps were genetic gold mines.

I opened another drawer, found a piece of tissue paper, carefully wrapped the hair in the paper, then folded the package small enough to fit in an envelope. I sealed the envelope, then wrote the date and JULIEN LOUIS on the outside. Satisfied that the sample was safe, I tucked it back inside my drawer.

Now that I had DNA from Julien, I wouldn't need anything from Damien. All I needed was my DNA, and I'd be willing to pluck myself bald if I couldn't find a lab that would swab my cheek.

I was about to reach for the Yellow Pages when I remembered that I wouldn't have to find a lab. Shortly after Desert Storm, the military began keeping blood samples from every member of the U.S. Armed Forces, ostensibly to help with the identification of remains. In Gaithersburg, Maryland, a freezing chamber contained vacuum-sealed envelopes with two drops of blood from thousands of people, including my husband—and the facility would maintain that genetic sample for fifty years.

I sat back on the bed, startled by how simple the answer could be. I could ask Mr. Pippen to pursue a court order if I had to, but I knew Snake Billings, the special operator who could get anything from anyone. If Snake would work his magic and do me this favor, I wouldn't have to visit a lab at all.

I reached for my purse, pulled out my phone, and scrolled through my contact list. I hadn't spoken to Snake since we moved to Mama Isa's, but I knew he'd do anything for Gideon, even now.

If anyone could help me get access to Gideon's DNA and a genetic test, Snake could.

At the Christmas Eve service, I held Marilee's hand during the candle lighting and joined in the liturgical readings. My forearms pebbled with gooseflesh as the choir sang carols that sounded like echoes from a circle of angels. I caught Yanela's eye and smiled as we slipped out of our pew and lowered ourselves to the narrow wooden kneelers for prayer.

Then I settled back for the traditionally short homily. Though I wanted to feel the Christmas spirit, I had other things on my mind—the DNA evidence I'd given to Snake, the test he had promised to obtain, the boy who could be my son over in France.

What did Simone and Damien do to celebrate Christmas? How much about the holiday did little Julien understand?

Unable to find answers to my questions, I pasted on a mildly interested expression and let my mind wander. I was pondering how I should cook the potatoes for tomorrow's dinner when a phrase from the priest's sermon jerked me back to reality: *Mary was a surrogate mother.*

I blinked and lifted my head, then glanced down the pew to see if the phrase had caught anyone else's attention. Mama Isa had her gaze on the flickering candles by the altar and Jorge had already nodded off. I thought Amelia might feel the pressure of my gaze and turn toward me, but she was focused on her baby, rubbing his back as he slept on her shoulder. Mario wore the dazed look of a sleep-deprived father, so he probably hadn't heard a word the priest said.

"You heard me correctly," the priest repeated, squinting out over the packed church. "The other day I was reading a newspaper article about technology and it struck me that Mary was, in a sense, a surrogate mother. She bore a child for someone else; she carried a baby for the world. For you. For me."

I stared at the small priest behind the pulpit. Candles from a nearby candelabrum glimmered on his shiny head, and his spectacles flashed every time he looked up from his notes. The man wasn't much to look at, but his comment had hooked me.

"Mary wasn't the first surrogate depicted in the Bible," the priest continued, shooting a wry smile across the congregation. "In a misguided effort to produce the child of promise, Sarah gave her handmaid to Abraham, thus producing Ishmael, whose descendants have been contending with the children of Isaac ever since. Rachel and Leah, two sisters who were also rivals, each gave her handmaid to Jacob so the servant could bear children for her mistress."

"But Mary had no rival, nor did she seek the privilege of bearing God's only son. Instead God chose her, knowing she had a generous and faithful heart, and then God warned her about the pain her heart would suffer. When she presented the baby Jesus at the Temple, Simeon the prophet told her that a sword would pierce her soul."

Marilee stirred beside me. When I glanced down, she was looking up at me, a question in her brown eyes.

I lifted a brow, silently giving her permission to whisper.

She leaned over to reach my ear. "Did Joseph die, too?"

My heart twisted when I realized that Marilee had linked the Holy Family and surrogacy to Gideon's sacrifice. "No, honey." I slipped my arm around her shoulder and smoothed her hair. "Joseph didn't die; he lived with Jesus many years. For a long time, they were a happy family . . . just like we were."

I waited, searching for signs of confusion in her eyes, but apparently my explanation satisfied her. She settled back in the pew and folded her hands in her lap.

I looked at the priest, inwardly groaning under a load of guilt. Marilee rarely spoke about my time as a surrogate, so I had no idea she had linked it to Gideon's death.

"Time proved Simeon right," the priest continued. "Though Scripture does not record everything Mary endured as she raised the child Jesus, we know she experienced the pain of Christ's birth and his death. She tasted the bitterest agony a mother can know, but for every pain she experienced a corresponding joy. She rejoiced with the angels at Jesus's birth, she rejoiced in her son when he performed his first miracle at the wedding in Cana. And after that bitter, excruciating death on the cross, Mary rejoiced to know that Jesus had risen from the dead and promised to send his Spirit, whose arrival she witnessed at Pentecost.

"Yes, a sword pierced Mary's soul, and yes, she suffered. But she still offered up her son, and no one has greater love than one who willingly sacrifices for another. So this Christmas, as you consider the immeasurable love God has for us, take a moment to consider the love Mary had for God—an unselfish love that resulted in salvation for the world. For whom are you showing that kind of love? For whom are you suffering, and for whom are you willing to undergo the agonizing pain love sometimes requires?"

I sat very still, thinking, as the choir began to sing.

To my surprise and delight, Marilee slept late on Christmas morning, allowing me to snatch an extra hour of rest. By the time we sleepyheads made our way to the kitchen, Mama Isa had pastries on the table, a sausage casserole in the oven, and hot cider simmering on the stove. A CD player on top of the refrigerator played "Jingle Bell Rock" in Spanish as Jorge danced through the house draping silver icicles on anyone who got in his way.

Marilee and I sat at the table to wait for breakfast, but Mama Isa would have none of that. "Get that child to the Christmas tree," she scolded, a happy light in her eye. "Let her open a few presents before all the others get here. If you want to have any time alone with *tu hija,* you had better grab it now."

So we went into the den, where Marilee pulled out the presents I'd wrapped and stashed under the tall Christmas tree. I sat cross-legged on the carpet, a mug of cider in hand, and felt a little guilty for waiting until the last minute to do my shopping. I had every intention of getting an early start this year, but I'd been plagued by inertia until I received the Amblours' cards. Since seeing those photos, my quest to discover the truth about Julien had pushed almost every other concern from my mind.

Fortunately, a week ago Mama Isa reminded me of my duty to my daughter, and shopping for Marilee helped me remember that I also needed to get a gift for the newest addition to the family. Twice I'd driven over to see Johny, Amelia's and Mario's baby boy, and each time an awestruck Amelia had offered him to me as if he were the rarest of treasures.

I wanted to be happy for her, but a current of grief pulled me under each time I took Johny into my arms, a current that intertwined memories of Gideon's death and my baby's birth. I swallowed my misery and cooed to the baby, even giving him a bottle once, but those tasks only aggravated an old wound that ached at any mention of a little one. Because I couldn't bear the raging maelstrom in my heart, I always handed Johny back after only a few minutes.

I suspected that my throat would always ache with regret when I thought about what happened in that horrible December, but the ache would evolve into complete wretchedness if Julien proved to be my son and I wasn't allowed to care for him. In two years I had never given him a bottle, changed his diaper, or sung him a lullaby, but if he proved to be mine I had no intention of missing another day.

"Thank you, Mommy!" Marilee's squeal roused me from my reverie, then she threw her arms around my neck. I hugged her, surprised to see that she had already opened the puzzle, the doll, the art set, and the CDs of classical piano music.

"You're welcome, sweetheart." I kissed her forehead and smiled. "And I hope you're hungry, because something smells awfully good in the kitchen."

We feasted with Mama Isa and Jorge, then laughed and joked with other family members as they arrived—Amelia, Mario, and Johny, Elaine and Tumelo, Yanela and Gordon, Carlos and Yaritza. Jenna Daniels, the grocery's bakery manager, had also been invited, and she brought her boyfriend, a Polish student who didn't seem to speak much English but kept his arm around Jenna's full figure.

Yanela was sporting a new red sweater, complete with sequins, and Elaine modeled a new skirt, spinning so it flared in a circle and delighted Marilee.

When everyone had eaten their fill of Mama Isa's delicious brunch, we moved into the living room for the family gift exchange. Marilee had drawn Gordon's name, and was excited to give him a hand-carved pipe. I tried to tell her that he hadn't smoked a pipe in years, but she insisted that the pipe was pretty, and wouldn't he enjoy just looking at it?

Of course he would. He opened the box and beamed at the beautiful pipe, then called Marilee over for a warm hug and kiss on the forehead. She grinned at me, her *I told you so* expression reaching all the way across the family circle.

Mama Isa had just opened the lightweight sweater I bought her when the phone rang. Jorge answered, then gestured to me. *"Es para ti, Mandy. Creo que es tu madre."*

Mom. Of course she would call on Christmas day, since her busy social calendar hadn't allowed her to drive over this year. And of course she would call right in the middle of the Lisandra clan's gift giving.

I smiled my thanks to Jorge, then went to my bedroom to pick up the extension. Any other time I would ask Mom if I could call her later, but I hadn't yet told her about the photos of Julien. I *wanted* to tell her, but I'd postponed that news, not knowing how to explain a situation that still held so many uncertainties.

But she was waiting on the phone, and I'd run out of time. She'd never forgive me if she learned that I'd known about Julien and said nothing when we talked on Christmas.

"Merry Christmas, Mom." I fell forward onto my bed and propped myself on my elbows. "Are you doing anything special today?"

"Just lunch at the Social Center," she said, "and caroling tonight. I've been seeing one of my neighbors—a real nice man named Mark. I think you'd like him."

"As long as *you* like him." I pulled my pillow toward me, intending to get comfortable. "Isn't that the important thing?"

She asked me what I got Marilee for Christmas and I told her, leaving out the part about how I waited until the last minute to do my shopping. I told her what Mama Isa and Jorge had given me (a nice necklace/earring set), and when I ran out of gifts to describe, I told her that I might have a son living in France.

While she listened in stunned silence I told her about receiving the photos, talking to my doctor, and consulting with Mr. Pippen.

I told her about finding the baby hair and asking Snake Billings to pull whatever strings he could in order to get the hair tested and compared to Gideon's DNA. I talked so fast that my words came out double-time, as if they'd been glued together.

"What—who—are you sure you can trust him to do that?" Mom said when I paused to snatch a breath.

"Mom." I resisted the urge to roll my eyes. "Snake has friends in high places. He told me that taking care of a DNA test would be cake."

"What does that mean?"

"It'd be easy. Simple." I paused, waiting for her to bubble over with excitement at the thought of another grandchild, but her reaction wasn't exactly what I expected.

"You shouldn't pursue this child," she said, her voice flat. "You should leave it alone. Walk away and pretend you never saw those pictures."

My mind whirled at her response, then I swallowed hard, lifted my chin, and gripped the phone more tightly. "Thank you for sharing your opinion," I said, a chill on the edge of my words. "And I hope you'll understand if I don't accept that advice. Because it's obvious you can't understand what I'm feeling."

"Amanda—"

"I've gotta go, Mom, we're opening Christmas presents."

"Amanda, I—"

I dropped the old extension phone back into its cradle, not interested in her excuses and explanations. I sat on the edge of the bed, trembling inside, then picked up the receiver and laid it on my nightstand, leaving it off the hook. I didn't want to talk to her, and I didn't want her to interrupt the Lisandra Christmas. She'd probably try to call a couple of times, then she'd give up and go on to her luncheon, maybe take in a movie with her new boyfriend.

As for me, I had family waiting in the family room.

Because the day after Christmas was a Sunday, after church I decided to take Marilee to see Amelia's new baby. Mama Isa and Tumelo had closed the grocery for the entire weekend, so with no school and no work, my daughter and I felt positively giddy with freedom.

We drove to Ybor City, the heart of the Cuban section of Tampa, and parked on the street. Amelia and Mario's charming one-story home appeared neat and tidy, though I knew in a few months I'd see toys strewn on the sidewalk, a Little Tikes house on the front lawn, and maybe a swing set in the side yard. They had waited so long to be parents, they would delight in their roles as mama and papa. Everyone in the family would be happy to spoil little Johny Guevara.

After getting out of the car, I opened the trunk and picked up the baby food machine I'd brought as a gift. Mama Isa said the machine was unnecessary and too expensive since it didn't do anything a blender couldn't do, but I wanted to get Amelia something unique. As to Mama Isa's objection, television remotes were unnecessary, too, but everyone I knew used one.

Marilee and I walked up the sidewalk and stopped at the front door. Ordinarily we'd exercise the prerogative of family and walk on in, but a new baby could upset even the most reliable family schedule. If Amelia and Mario were taking advantage of the post-Christmas quiet to rest, I hated to disturb them.

So I crept to the window, shaded my eyes, and peered inside. I could see Amelia in the living room, so I tapped my fingernails on the window. She looked up, startled, then jerked her head toward the door.

"It's okay," I told Marilee. "Amelia's awake and so is the baby."

A wistful look filled my daughter's eyes. "Can I hold him?"

"You'll have to ask your aunt Amelia."

We went inside and joined Amelia in the living room, where she was trying to quiet a fussy baby. Marilee studied little Johny for a moment, then dropped to the carpeted floor and turned on the television.

I knew she wouldn't want to hold the baby until he was quiet. I didn't blame her.

"Keep the volume low," I reminded her. "Uncle Mario is probably trying to sleep."

"Mario's worn out," Amelia admitted, patting the baby on her shoulder. "And I'm about to be. Can you take him for a while? He's been fussing for two hours and I have no idea what's wrong."

Where did she get the idea I was some kind of baby whisperer? I set the gift-wrapped package on the floor and took Johny from her, steeling my heart against the incomparable feel of an infant in my arms. The beautiful little boy had a head full of dark hair, eyes like milk chocolate, and a round face, now creased in lines of extreme displeasure. Upon opening his eyes and seeing me, his crying shifted from random fussing to the steady, loud, rhythmic cries of a frustrated newborn.

I propped him on my shoulder and rubbed his back. "Is he hungry?"

Amelia shook her head. "I just fed him and now he won't take a bottle."

"Diaper clean?"

"Just changed it."

"And how old is he?"

"Eight weeks, so he's too young for teething. I think." When Amelia bit her lower lip I understood her frustration. Nothing was more unsettling for a mother than not understanding why her child was upset.

"He *might* be teething," I offered, "because some kids are born with teeth. I always used that ointment that numbs the gums. But this could be colic, and I don't know what to do about that. Marilee never had it."

After a few minutes of patting, jiggling, and cooing, I gave up and offered the crying baby to Amelia. Sighing, she took the little boy. "Maybe he's sad. Maybe he hates being here with us. Is that possible?"

I looked away, not knowing what to say. Could babies that young hate anything? "Maybe he's confused," I suggested. "I don't think babies know much, but they're bound to realize something's different when they're dropped into a new place with new people. But you've had him for, what, two weeks? Give him time. Keep him warm and fed and happy and he'll adjust."

"You'd better be right." Amelia gave me a wan smile, then pointed to the couch and raised her voice to be heard above the baby's squalling. "Have a seat and tell me how you're doing. We didn't get to talk much at Mama Isa's yesterday."

I glanced at Marilee to be sure she'd be okay with staying for a while, but she seemed engrossed in the Home & Garden channel.

"Christmas was fun, wasn't it?" I sat on the end of the sofa and tucked my legs beneath me. "Except for the call I got from my mom, the day was completely relaxing. I haven't had a day like that in ages."

"I noticed you seemed tense when you came out of your bedroom." Amelia lifted a brow, family shorthand for *Spill the beans.* "What happened with your mom?"

"Nothing, and that's my point. She's a lot more concerned about her social life than she is about me and Marilee."

"You think so?" Amelia sank into an old rocker and stroked the fussy baby. "Did you tell her about your latest obsession?"

"I'm not obsessed."

The corner of her mouth dipped. "Could have fooled me. Mama and I talked the other day, and we both think you're making a mistake. But Mama's not going to say anything because you're living under her roof and she wants to keep the peace."

"You think *I'm* obsessed?" I stared, amazed at her audacity. "Who moped around the grocery for months because the social worker couldn't find a baby for her? Who called social services every other week just to hear the woman's voice?"

Amelia sighed. "Okay, I was obsessed, too. I'm not saying there's anything wrong with feeling passionate about something. But you can feel passionate about a thing and still be wrong—"

"Is it wrong to want my own child?"

"You don't know that he's your child."

"I don't know that he *isn't.* Of all people, you should understand how I feel."

I waited for the words to take hold, but Amelia closed her eyes. "I *do* know, I do, and I'm so sorry you're going through this. I understand the pain of desperately wanting a baby, but you *have* a child, you have Marilee. The other baby isn't yours. He belongs to the people who have loved him for two years."

"I can love him forever. And I'll soon know if he's my son—I should have the results of a DNA test sometime next week, if the holiday doesn't slow things down. But I will definitely have an answer after New Year's."

Amelia glanced at little Johny, who had finally quieted. She tossed a thin blanket over his shoulders, then met my gaze, concern and confusion flitting in her eyes. "You were able to get a test without the other couple's cooperation?"

"I didn't need their cooperation to see if there's a link between Julien and Gideon. I had exactly what I needed for that."

Amelia settled into a more comfortable position in the rocker. "I don't know, Mandy. Something about this doesn't seem right. I've been skeptical since the day you first decided to be a surrogate."

The idea of her judging me was so absurd I wanted to laugh, though I felt miles away from genuine humor. My cousin sat in front of me with a baby in her arms, a baby she didn't conceive. She was siding with the Amblours because her situation had skewed her perspective.

But she wouldn't agree.

"What," I asked slowly, "is wrong with a mother trying to retrieve the child she accidentally lost?"

Amelia blew out a breath. "You make it sound like you were on a sinking ship and the baby got lost in all the confusion. That's not what happened. You signed papers and that other couple took the boy in good faith. If that kid isn't their biological son, they were victims, too."

"Agreed. But accidental mistakes can be corrected. The situation can be rectified."

"You're not repairing a damaged car here, you're dealing with people's lives. And though it's hard to put my feelings into words, it seems like you're violating that other family's privacy or something. They're going to be upset when they find out what you're up to. You made a deal, and now you're wanting to renege on your agreement."

I stared and felt a dozen different emotions collide. "You think I *sold* my baby?"

She held her finger over her lips, reminding me of the sleeping child on her shoulder, then lowered her voice to an intense whisper. "Maybe you didn't do it intentionally. But if that kid turns out to be yours, it doesn't change the fact that they paid you to surrender him. Face it—they paid you to have a baby for them; you agreed with their terms and took their money. So I can't see why anything should change just because the boy looks a bit like Marilee. Maybe he's yours, maybe he's not. But he has spent two years with that other family, so they are his parents. How can you even *think* about jerking him out of the only home he's ever known?"

I sat back, unable to believe what I was hearing. Had her adoption experience blinded her to the fact that competent biological mothers had a right to raise their own children?

I understood the depth of desperation Amelia felt only a few weeks ago. She should have understood mine.

"I would give the money back in a heartbeat," I said, my voice low and insistent. "Money's not the issue."

"Mama?" Marilee pointed to the television. "What's happening?"

I looked at the TV. The program she'd been watching had been interrupted by a special report, something about an earthquake in Turkey. Grainy video footage played on the screen: scenes of debris, collapsing buildings, toppling palm trees, and panicked people running for their lives.

"That's horrible." Amelia's voice dropped to a somber note. "Can you imagine being caught up in that?"

I couldn't. Or maybe I could. The old dread reared its head and touched the base of my spine with its cold finger, reminding me of the heroes who rushed to face danger and never came back. My husband had given his life to fight terror, yet here was another kind, caused not by man, but by nature.

Not even Gideon and his elite operators could have made headway against the force of an earthquake.

"Experts believe this to be one of the worst earthquakes in recorded history," a reporter said, his voice playing over the scenes of destruction. "Up to one-third of the victims are expected to be children, since they are the least able to protect themselves against falling debris."

Children? My gaze fell on the back of Marilee's head and my pulse quickened. My son—the boy who might be my son—was out of my control and in a foreign country. Did earthquakes ever strike France? Even if they never had, anything could happen, especially in this age of bizarre weather patterns.

I squared my shoulders and lifted my chin. This tragedy, as horrible as it was, only strengthened my resolve. I would never feel truly secure until I knew the truth about Julien. And if he was my son, I would never feel real peace until he was safe and with me, where I could keep an eye on him. I might not be able to stop an earthquake from endangering my son, but if we were together, at least I could try to save his life.

I leaned forward and called softly to Marilee. "You about ready to go, hon? I think we might need to help Mama Isa clean up after Christmas."

Amelia's expression changed, a wry thought tightening the corner of her mouth. She must have realized I was retreating to maintain the peace between us.

"I'd better go," I said, standing. "You're obviously exhausted from all the changes around here, so I'll let you get some rest."

"I'm not exhausted," Amelia protested. "Only a little less energetic than usual."

"Whatever. Marilee, we need to go." I headed toward the door, then turned. "I hope you like the baby present. Your mama says it's completely inappropriate."

"Then I'm sure I'll like it. And I'll unwrap it as soon as I can move without waking Johny." She gave me a tentative smile as I opened the door. "Think about what I said, will you?"

"Yeah. See you later." I waved and walked toward my car, feeling proud because I'd resisted the temptation to have the last word.

On the tenth day of January, an ordinary Monday morning, Marilee went to school, Mama Isa went to the grocery, and Jorge went outside to tend his tomatoes. After breakfast, I went back to bed with a terrible cold, rousing myself at ten only because guilt wouldn't allow me to sleep any longer. My head felt as swollen as a balloon, my nose dripped like a leaky faucet, and my sandpaper lips demanded lubrication. I couldn't have been more miserable, but when I saw the mail carrier stroll through the carport and drop mail in the box, my gut told me my answer had arrived.

I don't remember getting off the couch and walking to the front door. I don't remember going outside in my pajamas and taking the letter from the box. I *do* remember seeing the name of a laboratory in the return address, and getting a paper cut when I ripped the envelope and pulled out a single sheet of white paper.

I didn't read the letter or study the chart on the page; instead my eyes gravitated to a central paragraph:

Interpretation: Based on the DNA Analysis, the alleged Father, Gideon Lisandra, cannot be excluded as the biological Father of the Child, Julien Louis Amblour, because they share the same genetic markers. . . .

Probability Percentage: 99.9942

I read the paragraph again, then looked up and studied my reflection in Mama Isa's foyer mirror. What was I supposed to do next? Should I faint, scream like a celebrating cheerleader, or weep like Tammy Faye?

What was the proper reaction for discovering that you had a son and you'd given him away?

I tilted my head, wondering how the woman in the mirror managed to remain preternaturally calm, and stared beyond my reflection when Jorge came through the door, his hands smudged with dirt, his forehead streaked with perspiration. He mopped his forehead with a crumpled handkerchief, then squinted at me in the mirror, his face alive with troubled question. "Amanda? *Estás bien?*"

His simple query shattered my inertia. I turned, then crumpled in the middle and fell into his arms, my heart squeezed so tight I could barely breathe.

"I did something terrible, Jorge. I sold Gideon's son."

Chapter Sixteen

Armed with proof that Julien Louis Amblour should be Gideon Lisandra Jr., I met with my lawyer again. Mr. Pippen reviewed the DNA report and my notes on my conversation with my doctor, then he advised me to keep a copy of my pregnancy journal and the calendar I'd used to chart my hormone shots.

"I don't think we'll need anything other than this DNA report," Mr. Pippen said, smiling at me from across his desk. "I'll need to confirm it, of course. But when we take this to court and the judge rules that the French couple must return your son, the opposing attorney may want to know how this mistake could have occurred. And if the other couple—"

"The Amblours," I reminded him.

"If the Amblours decide to sue the Surrogacy Center, it's a sure bet someone will subpoena you and request those items. So keep them safe."

I leaned forward, barely able to suppress my eagerness. "What happens next? And when do you think—realistically—my boy will come home?"

Mr. Pippen pressed his hands together and looked thoughtful. "The first thing we need to do is inform the other couple of these test results. We need to give them an opportunity to face the facts and do the right thing."

"And if they don't?"

"Then we go to the French courts. Seeing the genetic report, I'm almost certain the judge will rule in our favor, and what happens afterward will depend on the other couple's determination to see this through. They might contest the judge's ruling. Their lawyer will almost certainly insist on DNA testing from a French lab. They'll try to establish a genetic link between the child and Mr. Amblour."

"But there is no link."

"I said they'd *try* it. I didn't say they'd prove it."

I sat back, satisfied with his answer. "Then they'll surrender my son?"

He held up a warning hand. "These cases can be tricky, and any time you deal with an international court, you can run into problems. They may refuse to hand the boy over because he's bonded with them and breaking that bond could be detrimental to his mental health. If I were their lawyer, I'd contest the judge's ruling and build a case centered on the best interests of the child. I'd hire child welfare experts and developmental psychologists. I'd send an investigator to learn as much as he could about *you,* and then I'd try to prove that living with the Amblours would be far better for the child than living with you."

I listened with a rising sense of dismay. "How could they do that? I'm his birth mother, and I'm raising his sister. I have close ties with Gideon's family, so I have an excellent support system. I don't do drugs, we're all hard workers, no one's an alcoholic and no one's ever been arrested—"

"But you're a single mother and the Amblours are a two-parent family. You're living with a relative in a home you don't own, while the Amblours live on a large generational estate. You have some money put away, but the Amblours are independently wealthy, with means to provide nannies, tutors, and anything else the boy might need. Furthermore, the child has formed a strong bond with them, and any developmental expert is going to testify about the detrimental effects of taking a child from parents he has come to know and trust. In addition to all that, a judge could view your participation in a surrogacy program as evidence that you never wanted another child of your own; you were only interested in money."

My cheeks flamed. "That hardly seems fair. I never would have surrendered the baby if I'd known he was *mine*—"

"We can't change the past." Mr. Pippen removed his glasses and gentled his voice. "I'm not trying to discourage you, I'm trying to prepare you for a possible worst-case scenario. This situation could be involved, complicated, and expensive."

"Is there a best-case scenario?" My voice sounded small in the room. "Is there any chance this could be easy?"

One corner of the attorney's mouth lifted in a smile. "Sure. They could hire a lawyer who will so thoroughly spell out the difficulties and complications in a worst-case scenario that they decide to do the right thing from the beginning. To spare the boy and themselves from a long and protracted court battle, they could sign away their parental rights and bring the boy to you almost immediately."

"Then that's what I'm hoping for." I locked my hands and tried to steady my voice. "That's what I'll be praying for."

"I'll let you know what happens when they're presented with this evidence." Mr. Pippen made a copy of the DNA report and slid it into a folder on his desk. "From this point, leave everything in my hands and wait to hear from me."

I drew a deep breath and nodded, but waiting had never been easy for me.

Marilee and I had just come through the front door and greeted Jorge when my cell phone rang. I answered, expecting to hear from

Amelia or someone at the grocery, but the voice on the line was hoarse, agitated, and heavily accented. "How could you, Amanda?"

I whirled away from Marilee and stepped back outside, amazed at how quickly Mr. Pippen had relayed the DNA evidence to France. I'd left the report with him only two days before. "Simone?"

"What have you done?"

In the sound of her broken voice I heard the shattering of my secret hope: that faced with the probability of a long and difficult custody battle, Simone and Damien would simply release Julien and let him come home.

"How could I do this?" My voice trembled. "How could I not? He is my son, Simone, and he deserves to know his mother, his sister, and his grandparents. Gideon would want him to grow up surrounded by his family."

I drew a deep breath, wanting to tell her how much I'd suffered since losing Gideon, but inelegant sobs rolled over the phone line before I could begin.

"You will . . . never know," Simone cried, her words muddied and indistinct, "how this has . . . destroyed us."

I closed my eyes, regretting her pain even as I struggled with my own. "I'm sorry," I managed to whisper, "I didn't want to hurt you. I would have investigated sooner, but I never saw Julien's photos until recently, and then I knew." I hesitated as a thought I hadn't considered occurred to me. "*You* must have known there was a problem months ago. How could you look at that baby and not realize that he looked like my family?"

"We love him. We love him and he loves us."

She didn't answer my question, confirming my suspicion that she must have known. Even if she'd told herself that the egg donor was dark-haired and brown-eyed, she must have noted the boy's resemblance to Marilee.

"I love him, too," I told her, "just as I loved his father. I don't know what happened, but something went wrong and I lost your embryos. I conceived and delivered my own baby, and because he's mine he needs to be with me, with his family."

"Amanda—"

"I know this hurts"—I pressed on, talking over the rasps of her anguish—"because I've been suffering for two years. Something inside me died along with Gideon, and I've spent months trying to find my footing because I couldn't manage without him. But when I saw the picture of Julien I knew I had to get my life together. Julien is my son and he needs to grow up with me. I'll give your money back, I'll do anything you want, but I need my son *here.*"

"You are wrong." Simone's voice lowered to a rough whisper, and I suspected that someone else had entered the room where she was. I held the phone closer to my ear, straining to pick up some clue—

A high, clear voice rattled off a few French words that ended with *maman.*

Mama.

Julien.

The realization was like a blow to the center of my chest. My little boy was at the other end of this telephone connection, probably arriving at Simone's side to ask for something. If he were here, I would give him whatever he wanted and more. I would introduce him to a sister who looked just like him, and cousins and aunts and uncles and doting grandparents . . .

"Julien!" The cry sprang from my lips, then I heard nothing but silence. I didn't dare disconnect the call because my son might say something else, might sing a note or run across the room, allowing me to hear his quick little footsteps.

But Simone's voice filled my ear, her rushing words leaving room for nothing else: "We did nothing wrong. We did not cheat you, we did not break the rules. We do not deserve this."

I swallowed hard. "I know you didn't mean for things to work out this way. I'm sorry. None of us deserves this. Accidents happen."

"You will destroy him if you continue with this claim. He loves his home here, he loves us. He does not even speak English."

"Simone." I drew a ragged breath and tried to be patient. "The boy is only two years old. He can learn a new language."

"He has spent his entire life with us at Domaine de Amblour! He knows no other home."

"But he has another home and it's here, with us. And, thank heaven, children are adaptable. He will accept his family because he's one of us. He's not French; he's Cuban-American."

"You are asking for the impossible!"

"I am not." I struggled to maintain an even, conciliatory tone. If I could make her understand, maybe I wouldn't have to spend months waiting for my son to come home.

"Simone," I said, "the situation may be difficult, but the answer is really quite simple. I'm truly sorry this happened, and I'm sorry I have to hurt you. But Julien is my son, and he belongs with his American family. I think this is a hard truth, but there you have it. He's my son and I want him home with me. You would feel the same way if the situation were reversed."

When she didn't respond, I lowered the phone and saw that the call had been disconnected.

Depleted from the adrenaline rush, I leaned on one of the plastered pillars of the front porch and struggled to arrange my face into a calm mask lest I alarm Jorge, Marilee, and Mama Isa. Knowing that the family was divided on the matter of Julien's situation, I had decided not to tell them about the positive DNA test until I knew my boy was on his way home. Then they would rejoice and welcome him, their reservations vanishing like morning mist.

But maybe it was time to give them the complete truth.

That night, as our family dinner drew to a close, I stood, rapped on the table, and told the Lisandras everything that had happened. Yes, Gideon had a son, and I was doing everything I could to bring him home. As I suspected, the family members who had discouraged me from thinking about the baby in France abruptly changed their tune. Julien was no longer a stranger's child, he was *ours,* he was a Lisandra, and he was Gideon's son. As such, he must be brought into the family.

Though all the Lisandras wanted to help me, I didn't know what they could do until we knew if and when Julien would be coming to America. Jorge offered to teach the boy Spanish, but I gently reminded him that the child would need to learn English if he wanted to speak to his mother. Mama Isa volunteered to clean out her sewing room so the boy could have his own space, but I told her the time had come for me to move out and find my own place. If the court awarded me custody, I would have two children, a seven-year-old and a two-year-old, and they would need separate spaces. So I'd need at least a three-bedroom house or apartment, preferably something with a wide lawn and trees an active boy could climb when he was old enough.

I sat and smiled as my family buzzed with excited ideas about where I should live. If Simone and Damien chose to turn my situation into an international courtroom battle, I would need more than a lawyer. I would need allies, and this family could provide me with plenty.

Later that night, I knew they were all on my side when Mama Isa, Jorge, and Yanela stepped onto the front porch. While I watched from my bedroom window, Jorge unwound a roll of yellow plastic ribbon and Yanela snipped the end. Then Mama Isa stood on a stepstool and tied the ribbon around a pillar of her house. Like a silent team, they moved from pillar to pillar, until all six of them bore yellow ribbons that fluttered in the slight breeze.

I smiled through a soft veil of tears. Many American homes and trees bore yellow ribbons for servicemen and women, but these streamers, I knew, were for Julien.

A month later I found myself nervous and perspiring as I walked out of Joseph Pippen's office. The receptionist ushered me into a conference room where an unfamiliar woman had set up a small machine at the head of a long table. In preparation for my deposition, Mr. Pippen had covered the right side of the table with folders and files.

"We've received a copy of your file from the Surrogacy Center," Mr. Pippen said, motioning that I should sit in the empty chair next to his, "and I've read the notes Natasha Bray made after interviewing you and the Amblours."

I took my seat. "They were interviewed, but I don't think they went through nearly as rigorous a screening process as I did."

"Probably not, since they were the ones with the cash." Mr. Pippen gave me a wry smile, then glanced at his watch. "We're waiting for Mr. Bouchard, the Amblours' attorney. I understand his flight arrived a couple of hours ago, so we'll give him time to find the office and get situated."

I had prepared for this deposition with one of Mr. Pippen's associates the day before. That young man had given me pointers as he asked questions from a long list the lawyer had provided. Trouble was, I'd been so distracted by the gravity of the situation that most of his suggestions had gone right over my head.

Now I gripped the armrests of my chair and wondered if I could remember how to spell my name. "Anything I should know before we begin?"

"The procedure is straightforward." Mr. Pippen sat on the edge of the table. "I'm going to ask you a few questions, then Mr. Bouchard will ask you questions. Mrs. Jones"—he nodded at the transcriptionist, who smiled at me—"will transcribe every word we exchange. Before we begin she's going to administer an oath, so you must tell the truth here just as you would if we were in a court of law."

I nodded. "I understand."

"Good. I would caution you to reply accurately, truthfully, and briefly. If you aren't sure of an answer, it's better to admit you're not certain than to guess."

I nodded again and he smiled. "Remember that nods won't work for the court reporter—we need verbal answers. A simple yes or no will do."

"Okay."

"And also remember"—a muscle flicked at his jaw—"we need to give the court a reason to believe the child would be better off with you than with the Amblours. I understand you were once friendly with these people, but you must trust what I'm trying to do."

I lowered my voice to a stage whisper. "They're not bad people. I would never have chosen them if I didn't think they'd be good parents."

Mr. Pippen smiled again. "I'm only going to ask about your impressions, about things you may have encountered during the time you carried the baby. I would never ask you to lie."

I leaned back, slightly comforted even though I had never been so keenly aware of the power of language. Every word I said—and every shade of meaning within those words—might be interpreted by a judge as a reason to approve or deny my request for custody.

Beneath the table, my kneecaps began to twitch.

A moment later voices filled the hallway, then a tall, gray-haired man walked into the room, briefcase in hand. He introduced himself as Girard Bouchard, then shook hands with me and Mr. Pippen.

I folded my arms as he took a seat across from us.

"I wanted to thank you for coming all this way," Mr. Pippen said, "when we could have done this by video conference call."

"I like to see the people I am addressing," Mr. Bouchard answered, opening his briefcase. He lowered his chin and met my gaze dead-on. "I like to meet them face-to-face."

I shifted, my nervousness rising a notch. Did this man expect to uncover something in my eyes?

"Do you need anything?" Mr. Pippen asked. "A glass of water, legal pad, anything at all?"

"Thank you, but I am ready." My heart skipped a beat when he took out a pen and paper, then smiled. "I am eager to get going."

"Then let's begin."

Mr. Pippen nodded to the court reporter, who held up a Bible and asked me to place my right hand on it. "Do you swear to tell the truth, the whole truth, and nothing but the truth, so help you, God?"

I swallowed hard. "I do."

She lowered the Bible, and my lawyer gave me a confident smile.

In all the years of my life I've only been involved in one deposition—and I could die happy never being involved in another. Mr. Pippen began by asking why I wanted to be a gestational carrier, if my husband approved of the idea, and why I chose the Amblours from the three prospective couples whose files I'd been given. I answered as best I could, explaining things in the fewest possible words. I was terrified that I might make a mistake about something as trivial as a date or a small detail—one error under oath could give the opposing attorney reason to call me a liar and question all my testimony.

After covering the preliminaries involved in my surrogacy, Mr. Pippen asked about the early stage of my pregnancy, and seemed to focus on the day I noticed spotting. Just when I thought the questions had become about as invasive as they could be, he asked when Gideon and I had been intimate—and he wanted dates, so I had to consult my pregnancy calendar. The questions were personal and pointed, but I knew I had to answer in order to support the DNA test results we had submitted to the court. My lawyer needed to establish that I had been pregnant twice—once, briefly, with an Amblour embryo, and a second time with Gideon's child.

Next Mr. Pippen delved into the details of my second pregnancy: why I had missed ultrasounds that might have revealed a just-developing embryo, how the ultrasound technician and the doctor frequently remarked that the fetus seemed undersized, and how they excused their concern with Damien Amblour's assurance that the egg donor had been a small woman. Like a mosaic artist, Mr. Pippen laid out fact after fact, pressing each one into place until he had created a complete picture.

Then he asked me about the odd requests that came from the Amblours during my pregnancy. From the tone of his questions I gathered that he wanted to present the Amblours as wealthy eccentrics who might not make stellar parents. So I told him about the recordings I'd been asked to play for my tummy. I talked about Simone's insistence that I not eat shellfish or red meat for the duration of the pregnancy. How they asked me not to pump my own gas. How Simone sent boxes of natural products and hired the Happy Housekeepers to clean my home. And how Damien even had the chutzpah to ask that I not be intimate with my husband for the remaining months of the pregnancy if Gideon ever traveled on a mission to Asia.

Mr. Pippen's forehead creased, though he and I had discussed this before. "Why would he make such an odd request?"

A blush heated my cheeks, just as it had when Gideon told me what Damien was thinking. "My husband explained that Mr. Amblour must have assumed that Gideon would be unfaithful to me if he ever went to Asia, and that he might pick up a sexually transmitted disease that could be passed on to the child."

"Quite a few assumptions in that request, weren't there?"

"Yes." I leveled my gaze at the opposing attorney. "And none of them were valid."

Mr. Pippen shot me a small, triumphant smile. "Did you comply with the intended parents' requests?"

I nodded, then remembered that I needed to speak for the court recorder. "Yes. Whenever possible, I did."

"Even though you weren't legally required to obey their wishes? Is it fair to say you did it out of the goodness of your heart?"

Mr. Bouchard waved his pen. "Objection as to form."

My lawyer adjusted his smile. "I'll rephrase: Did you comply with their wishes because you wanted to please them?"

"I did it because I wanted them to be happy and because I thought I was carrying their baby. So even though those requests weren't listed in the contract, I did my best to put the Amblours at ease. They'd been through a lot with surrogates before they met me, and I didn't want them to worry this time."

Mr. Pippen walked to the window, then glanced at me over his shoulder. "What was your impression of the Amblours after you met them the first time?"

I shrugged. "I liked them. They seemed like a nice couple."

"What was your impression of Damien Amblour?"

I drew a deep breath, knowing that my next words might be critically important. "I thought him nice enough, but he seemed to be fixated on having a biological son. Several times he mentioned how much he wanted an heir from his bloodline to take over the family estate . . . and that's not something I could relate to."

"Yet Mr. Amblour was focused on this aspect of family life?"

"He certainly seemed to be. From what I gathered, his desire for a genetic heir was their chief reason for pursuing a gestational carrier. Otherwise, he and his wife would have adopted."

Mr. Pippen dipped his head slightly, then turned to face me. "What did you think of Simone Amblour?"

I smiled. "I felt a little sorry for her. She was a lovely lady, but she seemed insecure in her marriage. I couldn't help feeling that she believed her husband might divorce her if she couldn't produce a baby for him."

"Objection." Mr. Bouchard's face contracted into a prim and forbidding expression. "A *feeling* isn't fact."

"Let me rephrase." Mr. Pippen folded his hands. "Did she actually tell you that her husband would divorce her if she couldn't give him a son?"

"She never said that outright. But she implied it."

"Did she say why they hadn't been able to have biological children?"

"She was never specific about the reason for her miscarriages, and I didn't want to pry. Simone wasn't a young woman—I thought she must have been around forty—and he was much older. I felt sorry for her when they had to resort to an egg donor."

"But the egg donor wasn't of crucial importance, correct? They were content as long as the child would be related to Damien Amblour?"

"*He* was content—that's what I understood."

"Did Mrs. Amblour express this thought to you?"

"Not in so many words, but yes."

"Objection." Mr. Bouchard smiled. "The witness is making yet another assumption."

Mr. Pippin's smile matched his. "I'll move on." He looked back at me. "Tell me, Mrs. Lisandra—did Simone Amblour ever say or do anything to make you personally uncomfortable? Something that made you question her judgment?"

I shifted in my chair. "Only once."

"Would you tell us what happened?"

I pressed my lips together, then told the whole truth: "On my daughter's birthday, the Amblours sent a grand piano to our house. I thought the gift wildly inappropriate and much too expensive, but my daughter loved it. So I thought I had to keep it in order to avoid breaking my little girl's heart."

"Why did you think it inappropriate?"

"Because Marilee was only five and wouldn't really appreciate it. Plus, I knew I could never reciprocate. Who sends a grand piano to a five-year-old?"

Mr. Pippen gave the other lawyer an easygoing grin with a good deal of confidence behind it. "Do you still have this piano?"

"We sold it when we moved."

"So you no longer felt that you should keep the instrument?"

"No. I was done with the Amblours by then, done with everything. My husband had just been killed, and I . . . I closed down for a while. I moved in with relatives."

My lawyer consulted his notes for a moment, then leaned on the table and looked directly at me. "Mrs. Lisandra, did you and your husband ever talk about having other children?"

"We did—Gideon wanted a son."

"So why didn't you have a baby of your own?"

"Because"—I glanced at Mr. Bouchard, who had begun to write on his legal pad—"because we weren't financially prepared to have another child. Our daughter attends a school for gifted musicians. It's a great school, but the tuition is high."

"Is money one of the reasons you decided to investigate surrogacy?"

"It was one of several reasons; I wanted to help another couple, I knew I carried babies easily and loved being pregnant, and I knew we weren't financially ready to have another child of our own."

"But if you *had* gotten pregnant—let's say you found you were pregnant before you got involved with the Amblours—would you have kept that baby?"

"Of course. Marilee would have had to change schools, though. I don't see how we could have afforded another child *and* my daughter's tuition."

"Are you employed, Mrs. Lisandra?"

"I work at Mama Yanela's Cuban grocery."

"Have you tried to find a job offering better pay?"

"Yes, but I haven't been successful. I've always wanted to be a social worker, but I got married and dropped out of college before graduating. I'll have better luck when I get my degree."

"Thank you, Mrs. Lisandra." Mr. Pippen gave the French attorney a stiff nod. "We reserve the right to question the witness when you have concluded, Mr. Bouchard."

Prickles of unease nipped at the backs of my knees as the opposing lawyer made another note on his legal pad, lowered his pen, and looked across the table as if he'd like to fillet me for lunch.

The Amblours' attorney adjusted his expression and flashed a revised smile that seemed about as genuine as a Louis Vuitton bag made in China. "Do you need a few minutes, Mrs. Lisandra? I understand there is coffee in the break room—"

"I'm fine. I'd like to get this over and done."

"Then we will proceed." He checked his notes for a moment, then pressed his hands together. "Did you like the Amblours when you first met them?"

I nodded, then remembered to speak. "I did."

"You liked them even before you met them, correct? You liked Damien and Simone so much that you chose them from the three couples presented to you?"

"That's right."

"You did not see any problems in their home or marriage during that initial screening period, did you?"

"No."

"As you looked through their folder, did you surmise that they were a wealthy couple?"

I blinked. "I'm pretty sure only wealthy couples can afford to work with the Surrogacy Center."

"So the reason you singled them out had nothing to do with the fact that Mr. Amblour is from a distinguished and affluent family?"

"I knew nothing about his family at that point."

"You did not notice that they seemed to be the most prosperous couple represented in the three files you were given?"

My voice went dry. "The folders didn't contain financial statements."

The attorney shot me a twisted smile. "Very well. Did you see any problems in the Amblours' home or marriage during your first meeting with them?"

"No."

"What about when they came to Florida for the embryo transfer? You spent time with them during that trip, correct?"

"I did."

"Did anything about the Amblours or the state of their marriage alarm you then? Did you see anything that gave you even a moment's hesitation about carrying a child for them?"

"No, I didn't."

"What about when they visited Florida before the baby's birth? In the months between the embryo transfer and the birth of Julien Louis Amblour, were you given any reason to doubt the Amblours' ability to be good parents?"

"No."

"After the birth, then. Did anything make you reconsider your choice to surrender the infant you carried to Damien and Simone Amblour?"

"Well . . . maybe one thing. They had told me they were going to stay in Florida awhile—that their doctor advised them not to travel with a newborn until he was a week old." I tilted my head, surprised the memory surfaced so easily. "I went to see them, hoping to say a final good-bye, but the Amblours had already flown home. They flew when the baby was only a couple of days old."

"So you didn't see the child when you went to see them?"

"No."

"Did you see him at all?"

"I saw them take him from me, but only for a minute, and I saw him briefly a few hours later, when I left the hospital."

"You claim you never suspected the child might be yours until two months ago, when you saw a photo, then you realized that he looks like your daughter. When you studied the newborn right before you left the hospital, did you note a family resemblance?"

I snatched a breath. "My husband had just been killed, so I didn't even want to look at the baby. I had experienced enough loss; I didn't want to feel the pang of losing anyone else."

The lawyer pressed his palms together and brought his hands to his lips, almost as if he were praying. "I was sorry to hear of your husband's passing, especially at such an unfortunate time. But you didn't answer my question—did you note a family resemblance when you saw the child as a newborn?"

I closed my eyes and forced a laugh. "Newborns don't look like much of anyone. Their heads are misshapen, their faces puffy, and their eyes are usually closed. No, I didn't note a family resemblance."

"Let's move on, then. Aside from the fact that the Amblours and their child flew home earlier than you thought they should, during your first meeting, during the months of your pregnancy, and during the actual birth, did you ever see or hear anything to make you doubt the Amblours' ability to be good parents?"

I hesitated, intimidated by the sheer size of the question. The word no rode the tip of my tongue, but it wasn't entirely accurate. "I saw some things."

"Ah. Did you see pictures of inadequate housing?"

"No."

"Did you witness Damien Amblour losing his temper? Did you see him strike his wife or anyone else?"

"No."

"Were you given any reason to believe my clients were not financially able or willing to support a child?"

"No."

He chuckled. "I should say not, especially since they were paying you more than your husband earned in a year."

"Objection." Mr. Pippen spoke up. "The late Mr. Lisandra's salary is not relevant to this line of questioning."

"I'll withdraw it."

The French attorney glanced at his notes, then cleared his throat. "Isn't it true, Mrs. Lisandra, that you had absolutely no reason to fear for the future health or safety of this child while you were involved with the Amblours?"

A lump formed in my stomach, weighing me down. "I had reservations and questions. I wondered how Simone could be happy in a marriage that seemed so . . . stiff. I wondered how Damien could be so fixated on having a biological heir, and I worried that the baby might be a girl—I don't think Damien would have been thrilled with a girl. I wondered what kind of mother thought it was okay to give a kid a grand piano for her fifth birthday. I wondered about all these things, but I believed the child I was carrying was *their* child, so I pushed my hesitations aside. I didn't think I had a right to be concerned."

"What if, Mrs. Lisandra, a subsequent genetic test reveals Julien Louis Amblour to be Mr. Amblour's biological offspring?"

"Objection." Mr. Pippen glared at the opposing attorney. "There is no reason to believe anything of the sort."

"Objection noted," the court reporter said, clicking away at her machine.

"We shall see what the court decides." Mr. Bouchard began again. "If you had these concerns during the pregnancy, why did you wait two years to voice them?"

I faltered in a maze of confusing thoughts. "Like I said, I thought I had no right to express my concerns. I can't mother every child in the world; I can only protect the children God has entrusted to me. I didn't begin to feel responsible for Julien until I saw his picture."

"So you didn't feel responsible for him during the pregnancy?"

"Of course I did, but I saw myself as a babysitter, not a parent. I deliberately tried to remain detached because I thought my responsibility would end when I handed him over to the Amblours. But now that I know he's my son, I *am* responsible for him, make no mistake about that."

The Frenchman's brow lowered. "The matter of his parentage has yet to be settled." He pulled a photograph from his briefcase and slid it toward me. The picture revealed a sprawling estate—green vineyards, a huge stone home, lovely gardens. Without being told, I knew I was looking at Domaine de Amblour.

"Julien Amblour lives here," Mr. Bouchard said, "and he is currently heir to a vast fortune. He is reportedly in good health and happy in his family. Other than you, Mrs. Lisandra, who would benefit from wresting this child from the only parents he has ever known and bringing him to a country that will seem foreign to him?"

Despite my determination to remain calm, his words cut deep, infecting me with doubt. Phrased that way, no thinking person would want to remove Julien from the Amblours' custody. But I had good reasons for wanting my son to come home. Righteous reasons.

"Why should he live in a foreign country with people who are not of his blood?" I met Bouchard's sanctimonious gaze without flinching. "Why shouldn't Julien know the woman who gave him life, and why shouldn't he learn about the brave, unselfish man who died serving his family and his country? Why shouldn't he know his grandmother and grandfather, his aunts and uncles, his cousins? Why shouldn't he live here and inherit a position in the family business? He deserves to know about his great-grandparents' escape from Castro and Cuba. He has a right to know his big sister. He ought to know his father was a hero and he has seeds of greatness in him. Julien deserves all this and more."

As my voice grew louder and more confident, Mr. Bouchard averted his gaze and kept his eyes on his notes. I couldn't help thinking that he didn't care about what I had to say; he was only waiting to take another jab.

Fine, then. Punch away.

"Ms. Lisandra," he said when I'd finished, "according to your medical file, you reported hemorrhaging on the weekend of April sixth and seventh. This is a common symptom of miscarriage, yet you continued to behave as though you were still pregnant with the Amblours' fetus. Why did you do that?"

Troubled by the question, I glanced at my attorney. What was he getting at?

Mr. Pippen nodded, silently urging me to answer.

"Because I thought I was still pregnant—and that kind of

bleeding doesn't always mean miscarriage. I had the same kind of spotting when I was pregnant with my daughter, and it meant nothing."

Bouchard shuffled a few papers. "According to your medical records, you missed two scheduled ultrasounds at the beginning of your pregnancy—one on the eighteenth of April and another on May eighth. Why did you miss those?"

"Haven't we already talked about this?"

"I'd like to hear about them again."

I sighed. "The first cancellation wasn't my fault—the doctor's office didn't have power, so they canceled all appointments."

"Why didn't you set up a scan for the next day?"

"I tried, but they couldn't fit me in the schedule."

"Is it not true that an ultrasound on that date—April eighteenth—would have revealed an empty uterus? That you were not, in fact, pregnant at all?"

"I don't know what it would have revealed." I felt myself flushing. "I'm not a doctor."

"The ultrasound you missed on May eighth—care to explain that one?"

"I was sick, but I kept my doctor's appointment." I pressed my damp palm to the tabletop, repressing the urge to crawl over the table and slap the man. "I was so nauseous I could barely lift my head off the pillow that morning, but I went to the office and we heard a fetal heartbeat."

"Because you were pregnant?"

"Because I was pregnant, sure. But I *thought* I'd been pregnant all along. We missed the ultrasound because the machine wasn't working."

"Were you not concerned about skipping this ultrasound? And if you'd had it, is it not true that it would have revealed only a gestational sac?"

"I'm not a doctor; I don't know what it would have shown. But I wasn't worried about missing the ultrasound because I knew it wouldn't make anything better or worse. I knew I was pregnant, and all I wanted was to deliver a healthy baby."

"A healthy baby . . . which you *did* deliver and surrender almost exactly when the Amblour pregnancy would have been forty weeks. A child you delivered without any great concern. A baby you barely glanced at before you let the Amblours leave the country."

I gripped the arms of my chair to keep myself firmly in my seat. "I . . . was . . . *grieving* . . . for my husband." From the corner of my eye I saw Mr. Pippen straighten. He was probably only seconds away from suggesting that I take a break.

I sank back and covered my eyes, forcing myself to calm down. Was this man suggesting that I purposely got pregnant with Gideon's baby so I could wait two years and then bring a case against the Amblours? Perhaps he thought I could be persuaded to drop the matter if his clients would deposit more money in my bank account.

Or maybe he only wanted the court to hear these details and question my sincerity. Even DNA evidence might not be enough to persuade a judge who believed I had concocted a scheme to blackmail the venerable Amblours.

I looked at Mr. Pippen, who nodded and smiled as awareness thickened between us. All Bouchard had to do was convince a judge that I had chosen the wealthiest clients offered to me, gotten myself pregnant, covered up a miscarriage, conceived my husband's child, and intentionally avoided ultrasounds in order to commit fraud. No one who knew me would ever believe I could think up such a plan, but Bouchard had a way of laying out the scenario so fraud seemed a logical conclusion. He might instill enough doubt that a French court would dismiss my legitimate claim and leave Julien in France, ostensibly deciding in the best interests of the child.

Because what sort of jurist would take a two-year-old from his home and place him with a scheming surrogate?

I crossed my arms and flashed a brow at Mr. Pippen, telegraphing my newly acquired understanding. Bouchard was using this testimony as preamble, a foundation to build in front of the judge before he swept in with his ridiculous claims.

But I would tell the complete truth. When Mr. Pippen cross-examined me, he'd ask questions that went to the heart of the matter, and I'd clearly spell out my intentions: I loved my son more than life and wanted to be his mother. And I'd be happy for the Amblours to keep all their money. I didn't want a penny from them and I'd be happy to return every cent they paid me.

Mr. Bouchard said something else, breaking into my thoughts.

"I beg your pardon?" I smiled. "Could you repeat the question?"

"I said, how much were you paid for carrying this child?"

Resolved to give him nothing but bare and indisputable facts, I gripped the edge of the table and replied.

Chapter Seventeen

The weeks after my deposition passed with agonizing slowness. While I waited, spring bathed central Florida in waves of warmth, coaxing bright green buds from the live oaks and new spears from the palm trees. Caladiums bloomed in pots around Mama Isa's front porch, and Jorge painted the metal gliders in a fresh coat of yellow to match the ribbons on the porch posts. Marilee spent hours practicing for her spring recital, and at the grocery we arranged packages of sunny marshmallow Peeps in cellophane mountains.

I wandered through those weeks in a fog, preoccupied with thoughts of France and my absent son. I was certain I would win my case—how could any judge deny a child to his biological mother? If by some chance the case went as far as an international court, how could France deny the United States access to an American citizen?

The full realization of what victory would mean blossomed in my imagination. I would have to find a way to ease Julien's transition from the Amblour family to the Lisandra clan, but that would be easy because the Lisandras were eager to welcome him. I should probably find a child psychologist to help me ease the baby's transition into a new family and a new culture. And then there was the matter of his name—should I call him Gideon Jr. or leave him as

Julien? Or perhaps I should name him Gideon Julien Lisandra? Which approach would be best for him?

I pondered these questions for hours, writing out long lists of pros and cons about each decision, and nearly every day I thought of some aspect of the transition I hadn't yet considered. How could I comfort Julien without a working knowledge of French? If I hired a tutor for myself, could I pick up enough of the language to help us through our first few weeks together? And how should we manage the transfer? Should I go to France and pick up Julien, or would it be better if the Amblours brought him to me? Maybe it would be less traumatic for all of us if we found an impartial third party to act as an escort on the long flight across the Atlantic.

I downloaded French language lessons from the Internet, but didn't find them practical because I couldn't *see* the words I heard. I bought a book guaranteed to teach me French in only thirty lessons, but since I couldn't *hear* the words, I had no idea how to pronounce them.

Why couldn't I have been a surrogate for a couple from Britain or even Spain?

I also needed a place to live. Marilee and I went to our storage unit and pulled out the dollhouse, then took it back to Mama Isa's. We set it on the coffee table, then looked at the rooms and decided that the colors of our dream house no longer felt right. I couldn't explain exactly why the house no longer seemed appropriate—probably because we had designed it for life with Gideon, and that life was finished. Now we needed to plan a life with Julien, and a little boy seemed to require livelier colors.

Twice I went out with a real estate agent and looked at homes near the grocery, but those were mostly older structures in dire need of present or future repair. Since Gideon had always been our handyman, I didn't want to buy any property that would require work beyond basic cleaning. So I ended up looking at newer homes, but most new developments were in north Tampa and far from the heart of the city. The houses were pretty and spacious, but

I'd be facing nearly an hour's drive in dense traffic if the kids and I wanted to join the family at Mama Isa's on Saturday evenings.

I'm sure I frustrated the real estate agent, but I couldn't seem to find anything that would work for us. Or maybe I simply felt uncertain because my future remained unsettled.

I didn't even know if or how I'd be employed once Julien came home. If the adjustment period went well and I wanted to remain at the grocery, I would need child care. I could always stop working, but our new house would devour a large percentage of the money I had stashed away. So I would soon find myself in a familiar situation—desperately in need of a college degree—unless I found some other line of work.

Could I learn more about the grocery business? And would Tumelo consider leaving his stake in the grocery to me so I could eventually pass it to Julien? But what if my son grew up and decided he didn't want to work in a Cuban grocery?

How long would I have to confine myself to only *dreaming* about my son? I nibbled my nails to nubs, prayed until I began to sound like a broken record, and waited to hear from my lawyer.

Joseph Pippen left for France on Wednesday, April 20. He planned to personally visit with the Amblours and their lawyer, and if he couldn't prevail upon them to surrender my son, he was going to present a petition before a French court. Though I had begged him to give me a date when we might know *something,* he gently refused. "Your guess is as good as mine," he told me the last time we talked. "I'll know something when I know something, and then I'll call you. Some things cannot be rushed."

The Saturday before Easter I sat at Mama Isa's long kitchen table and numbly watched Amelia take charge of the children as they colored eggs for the Easter egg hunt. Five-month-old Johny was too young to understand what was going on, but he sat in his baby seat and waved his arms as Marilee dipped eggs into the brilliant dyes and held them before his wide eyes.

I crossed my arms and felt my mouth curve in a wistful smile.

Next year Julien should be sitting at this table with them, his small fingers struggling to hold the flimsy wire that came in the box of egg dye. Marilee would help him, and both of them would entertain little Johny. . . .

I looked over at Amelia, who was glowing with happiness. Earlier she had shown me the pastel blue suit she bought Johny for Easter, and I teased her about going overboard for the holiday.

"I don't care." She smiled away my comment. "I may have only one kid, so I'm going to do everything I want to do with him. He may be the most overdressed baby in church, but I'll always have a picture of him in his first Easter suit. And that, *prima,* will be priceless."

I had never seen Amelia so content. I was happy for her, but a wasp of jealousy buzzed in my ear as I watched her give Marilee another batch of hard-boiled eggs. God had answered Amelia's prayers, but my arms were still empty.

I tried to hide my resentment, but my expression must have hinted at the turmoil within me. When the children had finished decorating their eggs and Elaine began to clean up, Amelia picked up her son and pulled me aside. "I know seeing me with Johny is hard for you," she said sotto voce, "but you need to use this time to think about things."

I narrowed my eyes. "What things?"

She gave me a warning look, then shifted her baby to her other hip. "You once told me that I would love Johny because love has nothing to do with genetics."

My blood sparked with irritation. "So?"

"You were right. Love doesn't have anything to do with biology, yet you are set on having that boy simply because he has Gideon's DNA. Have you forgotten that those other people love him desperately?"

My irritation veered sharply to anger. "Maybe *I* love him desperately. Why shouldn't I? He has my DNA, too. He should grow up with his *real* mother."

"And what do you think the French woman is, artificial?"

I took a half step back, stunned by her comment, then shook my head. "Don't confuse the issue with word play. He's my son, I love him, and here's the bottom line—that little boy is all I have left of Gideon."

And then, in one of those rare silences in which time slows and the world stands still, my daughter's silvery voice rang out: "What about me, Mommy?"

And an avalanche of guilt crashed over me.

Remorse tightened my throat when I looked into Amelia's eyes and saw myself reflected in them: a resolute, wounded woman intent on obtaining her rights at any cost.

My darling daughter smiled up at me, love mingling with uncertainty in her brown eyes. I squirmed under the touch of her loving gaze as my conscience reared its knobby head. I was Marilee's only remaining parent, but in my all-consuming obsession with Julien I had relegated my daughter to Mama Isa's care and focused my attention on a child I didn't even know.

"I'm sorry, honey," I told her, my voice hoarse as I bent to look at her. "Of course I have you, and you are Daddy's favorite girl. Soon we'll all be together—you, me, and your brother. Everything will be fine then, you'll see."

I had been neglectful, but I would make it up to Marilee. As soon as my baby boy came home.

After the big Easter-egg-decorating party, the women of the Lisandra clan gathered in Mama Isa's kitchen to clean up spilled dyes and shards of eggshell. I joined them, but ducked into the hallway when my cell phone rang. I pulled it out and felt my heart shift into overdrive when I recognized Mr. Pippen's number.

I ran for the relative quiet of my bedroom. "Hello? Mr. Pippen?"

"Congratulations, Amanda. We scored a home run."

A full minute passed before the significance of his words registered, then I blinked in numb astonishment. "Are you saying what I think you're saying?"

"The judge placed great weight on the DNA report. In his ruling, he stated that since the Amblours were motivated to pursue surrogacy in order to have a biological child, they could not credibly make a case for keeping a child who was not genetically related to them. He's ruled that the boy be returned to you."

Shock waves radiated from a nexus in my chest, tingling my scalp and numbing my toes. "Julien's coming home?"

"I'm holding a court order stating that Julien Louis Amblour be remanded to the custody of his biological mother in less than ten days. I'll meet with Bouchard tomorrow to establish how we want to handle those arrangements. Would you like to fly over to meet him, or would you like someone to bring him to you?"

"Could you bring him?" I spoke without thinking, and an instant after saying the words I knew I'd spoken too soon.

"I'm afraid I need to return to the U.S. sooner rather than later, and I'm sure the Amblours will want to take every one of the ten days they were granted."

"Of course they will. Just a minute, I have to think. This is happening too fast." I pressed my hand to my head and closed my eyes, struggling to put my jumbled thoughts in order. If someone brought Julien to me, he'd either have to travel with Simone, Damien, or an escort, and none of those options would be exactly comforting for a two-year-old, especially if Simone and Damien were distraught. Better, then, for me to go to him. A trip to France might benefit me in other ways, too—I could see Julien in his environment, spend a couple of days absorbing the culture, and then bring my son home and introduce him to the family.

"I want to get him. I'll go to France."

"Very well. I'll let you know the details after I've talked to the Amblours' attorney."

I gripped the edge of a bookcase to steady my swirling head. "Are you sure that's the end of it? They won't appeal?"

"They might, but the boy would live with you while they went through the appeal process, so I'm reasonably sure they won't. They'll realize that even the possibility of the child's going back and forth is not in the boy's best interests."

"Mr. Pippen"—I struggled to find words to describe the sense of elation tingling my toes—"thank you."

"It's been a pleasure. Talk to you soon."

I shut off the phone and exhaled in a rush, then looked up to find Amelia, Johny, and Mama Isa peering at me from the doorway.

Amelia arched a brow. "Was that—"

I nodded. "Sometime in the next ten days, I'm flying to France to get my son."

Mama Isa lifted her hands and shouted while Amelia danced through the hallway with Johny on her hip. I followed them to the kitchen, where Elaine, Marilee, and Yanela joined in the celebration.

I sank into a chair and lowered my head into my hands. I had won an amazing victory, yet Mr. Pippen's report left me feeling strangely numb. Perhaps the news hadn't fully sunk in, or perhaps the victory didn't feel completely satisfying because Gideon wasn't around to share it.

But my heart warmed to see the others' happy faces. Tonight the entire family would gather around this table and rejoice because one of our own was coming home.

I opened my eyes and saw a black velvet sky; I curled my fists and felt dew-damp grass beneath my fingers. Night noises chirped and whispered around me, along with the steady tick of a cooling car engine. I groaned and lifted my head, silencing the shrill scritch of the crickets as completely as someone pressing the Stop button on a recorder.

I looked down the length of my body and saw a child's form and figure—pudgy knees, small sneakers, flat chest. And even as I obeyed an impulse and rolled onto my stomach, I knew I was having the dream again. What did they call this? Lucid dreaming. Dreams in which the dreamer is fully aware of his dream state.

Dr. Hawthorn was wrong to blame this dream on pregnancy. I didn't experience it as often as I had during those nine months, but it kept returning in all its crisp vividness.

Reluctantly, I lifted my head and saw the overturned car, heard palmettos rustling their fans, and smelled gasoline. Again I saw my father's outstretched hand, the fingers twitching in spasm.

Obeying the familiar script, I crawled onward, gravel cutting into my knees as I called for my father. A shard of broken taillight sliced my elbow, but I crept forward, determined to changed the dream's outcome if I could. "Daddy?"

I lowered my head, peered into the darkness of the car. My father's bloody face appeared above his white shirt, then he said my name and attempted to smile.

"You need to get away from the car," he said, his voice forceful without being frantic. "Go sit on the grass and wait there."

"I don't want to leave you, Daddy. I won't leave you. Not this time."

"You have to, honey. You have to obey me, right now."

"I can't leave you. And this time things will be different because I'm not going anywhere."

"Mandy, listen to me." His voice held a silken thread of warning. "You have to go. This is the way it's supposed to be."

"But I don't want to. I want to keep you with me."

"Get away, honey. Gideon and I are waiting at the tree by the river. And stop worrying—your questions have been answered and your future firmly settled. You're going to do the right thing."

What was he saying? I was supposed to control the script in a lucid dream, and I had already done the right thing. I had pursued our son and won the right to bring him home.

Surely Daddy was proud of me.

I reached out to take my father's hand, but it melted into empty air. "Daddy?"

Something in the night—a noise?—jolted me awake. I sat up and gulped deep breaths, waiting for the material world to focus. Once my eyes adjusted to the darkness, I recognized my desk, the nightstand, the stack of boxes on the closet floor. I listened, but quiet filled the house. I heard only the distant hum of freeway traffic and the soft tapping of windblown rain on the window.

Rooted again in reality, I lay back down, clutched my comforter, and wondered about the dream. Did God still speak to people in dreams? Amelia thought they did, and Mama Isa would agree. And I would never be able to forget the nightmare I had before learning that Gideon had been killed.

So if God did communicate through dreams, had he spoken to me? Or had he passed on a message from my father?

I exhaled softly. Neither, probably. My imagination had embroidered a recurrent dream, nothing more. Yet Dr. Hawthorn said dreams are the venue through which our subconscious sends us messages—was my subconscious trying to make me feel better about breaking Simone's heart?

Maybe my dream sprang from a guilty conscience. I'd do almost anything to avoid hurting Simone and Damien, but I couldn't see any way around causing them pain. I tried to imagine some sort of compromise in which they could occasionally visit Tampa, but a clean break might be less painful than a couple of awkward annual visits.

I rolled toward the wall, recalling what my dream father had said: that my future was settled and I was going to do the right thing. What on earth could that mean?

Maybe I was missing something obvious . . . maybe I needed to call someone who could help me see through my confusion. But who loved me enough to welcome a bizarre call in the middle of the night? Amelia loved me, but she wouldn't want me to call and wake the baby. Mama Isa loved me, too, as did Elaine, but they wouldn't want to hear about my nightmares at this hour.

A tear slipped from my lashes and rolled down my cheek.

Gideon would have listened to anything, then he would have held me in his arms until I felt safe again. And if he'd been alive . . . I could have called my dad.

I swiped the tear from my face, then turned on the bedside lamp, padded across the room, and pulled my purse from the back of the desk chair. I found my cell phone and punched Mom's name in the contact list. While I waited and listened to the ring tone, I told myself I was being silly; Mom would listen, then she'd probably tell me to take a sleeping pill and go back to bed.

"Hello?"

"Mom?" I tried on a smile. "Sorry, did I wake you?"

"Mandy?" Her voice, which had been thick with sleepiness, sharpened immediately. "Has something happened to Marilee?"

"Marilee and I are both fine." I closed my eyes and released a slow breath. "I know this sounds silly, but I had a terrible dream. I couldn't go back to sleep, so I thought I might give you a call." I forced a weak laugh. "You've always had a gift for making my nightmares seem stupid."

"What on earth"—she cleared her throat—"what on earth did you dream? If you saw me being run over by a semi in the Publix parking lot, maybe I won't go to the grocery store tomorrow."

"Don't worry—there wasn't a semi in sight." I sank to the edge of my bed. "It was the old nightmare about the car wreck. But this time I knew I was dreaming, so I tried to change the script. But when Daddy promised to meet me at the river, he said something about Gideon being there, and that was different from what he usually says. And then he said I needed to stop worrying, that everything was settled and I was going to do the right thing. Trouble is, I don't have any idea what he was talking about."

I expected her to chuckle, sigh, or tell me to pull on my big-girl panties and go back to sleep. What I didn't expect was silence. And in that unearthly quiet, a sudden and inexplicable uneasiness chilled my bones.

"Amanda," she finally said, her voice soft with compassion. "I think we need to talk about the accident. If you're dreaming about it again, something important must be weighing on your mind. I don't know what it is, but maybe you do."

"I don't want to talk about ancient history."

"But apparently you *need* to talk about it. You always have that dream when something heavy is occupying your thoughts—I think it's because you're wishing you could talk to your father."

I grimaced as her words struck home—grateful that she couldn't see my face. "Mom, that's crazy."

"Anyone would struggle with a major loss in a lifetime," she said, going on as if she hadn't heard me, "yet you've had to deal with two."

I turned out the bedside lamp. "Good night, Mom."

"You're probably having nightmares because something is stirring up your feelings of grief and abandonment. And you know what they say—a buried hurt doesn't go away, it festers beneath the surface. The only way to take care of the problem is to open the wound and let it all pour out."

I grimaced as my mind filled with images of scabs and scalpels and oozing goop. "That's disgusting." I switched the phone to my other hand and crawled back beneath my comforter. "Well, sorry to wake you. I'm fine, and ready to go back to sleep."

"Wait, Mandy—I'll let you go back to bed if you will answer one question."

I sighed. "What?"

"Don't you think I know that you felt closer to your dad than to me? I saw how his death devastated you. And I'm sure there were times when you found yourself wishing that I'd been the one to die in that accident."

Staring into the gloom-shrouded room, I lay perfectly still, the phone glued to my ear. How did she know?

Chapter Eighteen

Mom, I didn't—"

The lie that sprang automatically to my lips was swiftly swatted down. "You don't have to deny it, honey," she said. "You were pretty transparent as a kid, and I knew you and your daddy were extra close. The light went out of your eyes when he died, and it didn't come back for a long, long time."

For a long moment I lay in the thick silence of concentration, then I pushed myself up. Mom had been a lot more aware than I realized, but just because I grieved over my father didn't mean I hated her.

"Losing Dad hurt a lot," I admitted, shrugging in the darkness. "And as a kid I probably felt and said some things I'm not proud of. But I was just a child when all that happened."

Mom hesitated, then spoke more slowly. "I know how profoundly your dad's death affected you, and I think I know why you and I haven't been closer over the years."

"We've been fine—"

"Amanda." A gentle rebuke underlined my name.

"We've been okay," I finally said. "We've gotten along better than some mothers and daughters."

"But not as well as we could have. I regret that—I was always trying to break through your shell, but you were a tough little nut.

You didn't want to let me in. The more I tried to reach you, the more you resisted. So finally I stopped trying."

"Mom, I—" I paused, having run out of excuses. "I never meant to hurt you."

A humorless, tired laugh filled my ear. "I know, honey, but that doesn't mean that you didn't. You wanted your dad, and compared to him, I must have seemed like a sorry substitute. I tried not to take it personally—after all, Wayne was an amazing man. But sometimes I wanted to reach out and knock some sense into your head so you'd look around and see that someone else adored you, too. That the parent left behind was trying her hardest to be mother, father, and best friend. But I don't think I ever got through to you. No one did, until Gideon."

My throat tightened as an unexpected surge of grief rose up from my chest. Why was I having this morose conversation? I did not want to be lying in the dark and talking to my mother at 2:00 a.m.; we both ought to be asleep. I had a full day ahead, and she probably did, too. Plus I had Marilee to think about, and Julien to prepare for. . . .

I felt a surge of adrenaline, an instant of déjá vu. Something was on the tip of my tongue, and then it wasn't. Something important.

Or maybe not.

"I have to be up early," I said. "And I have to get Marilee to school. Can we do this some other time?"

"You called *me,* remember? You're the one who wanted to talk about your nightmare." A heavy sigh filled my ear, followed by the sound of movement, as if Mom were making herself comfortable for an extended conversation. "How much do you remember about the accident? You and your dad were on the way home from a restaurant when he braked to avoid hitting a deer. The roads were slick and somehow he flipped the vehicle. You'd taken off your seat belt to lie down in the backseat, so you were thrown out."

I frowned as a pulse of irritation murmured in my ear. "I don't want to talk about this anymore."

"I know you're still struggling with loss, honey. Losing your father was terrible, but losing Gideon traumatized you all over again—"

"Now you sound like my therapist."

She released a soft chuckle. "I knew you remembered. Two years of weekly appointments—that's a lot of therapy, especially for a kid."

Outside, a car turned around in Mama Isa's driveway, sending shadows to dance on the bedroom wall. Mom and I had both had a hard time dealing with Dad's death, but she hadn't had much time to mourn. As a suddenly single woman, she'd had to increase her hours at the pet store and shoulder all the responsibilities for our little family.

A glimmer of realization seeped through my irritation. "Why didn't you ever remarry?"

She laughed. "Somehow it never felt like the right thing to do. None of the men I met could ever measure up to Wayne, so I didn't want to marry again. And, truthfully, I didn't get asked out very often—in those days, men weren't as quick to show interest when a woman came with a kid attached. Especially a kid who spent a lot of time at a psychologist's office."

I brought my hand to my temple as spectral visions played on the backs of my eyelids, colliding and cracking like rolling marbles. I had successfully bagged up the most disturbing memories of my past, but this conversation had loosened the string. Now I recalled afternoons spent in a waiting area reading tattered copies of *Highlights* and a receptionist who set out chocolate-chip cookies on a brightly colored platter.

"I've worried about my daughter," I said absently, still studying the sepia memories that had opened in the darkness. "I loved my husband, but I always wanted Gid to stay safe for Marilee's sake."

"Because . . . you didn't want her to lose her father?"

"Because I didn't want her to think he hated her."

The confession rolled out of me like syllables on a string, hooked by the bait Mom had clumsily tossed at my psyche. As my words hung there in the silence, slick and greasy and unexpected, I don't know which of us was more surprised.

"You didn't . . ." Mom's voice faltered. "Honey, Marilee knows Gideon adored her. His feelings were obvious to everyone."

A flash of memory caught me by surprise, like a white-hot sword thrust through my chest and belly. I gasped, staggering under the pain, and gripped the phone so tightly my fingers went bone white.

"I . . . didn't . . . take off . . . my seat belt." I bit off each word and spat it at the phone. "I never had it on. Daddy was listening to a baseball game on the radio, so he didn't check on me. I tried to buckle it, but I couldn't fasten the thing by myself."

"Mandy?" Concern seeped from Mom's voice. "Are you all right?"

Tears streamed down my face, hot spurts of fury and despair, but I couldn't stop. "I was mad and jealous because he'd rather listen to baseball than take care of me. And then we had the wreck, and I found myself outside on the grass. I crawled over and called to him, but he wouldn't come out of the car. He kept saying he'd meet me at the river, but then the fire started and he started screaming."

"Mandy, you don't have to go through all this—"

"He told me to get away! He shrieked at me, telling me to go away and leave him alone, and sometimes in my dreams I can still hear him telling me to go away. And I'm terrified that Marilee will begin to think Gideon left us because he didn't love her. Death is hard on a family, but it's especially hard on a child."

"Oh, Mandy," Mom whispered, in an aching, husky voice I barely recognized. "I'm so sorry—I never knew you felt that way. Now that you're an adult, surely you understand that he was frantic to get you away from the car? He wanted you to be safe."

I drew a ragged breath, wiped my runny nose on a tissue, and struggled to regain control of my emotions. "Logically, I get it," I finally answered. "But the heart doesn't always feel what the mind knows. Especially when the heart is young."

My head fell into my hand as more memories washed over me

in a cold flood, shivering my flesh. Because I lost my father, I spent two years visiting a nice therapist who urged me to play with her paper dolls and insisted that the dolls talk about the accident. The dolls hadn't wanted to talk, but finally they cooperated, or I would have been visiting the psychologist forever. So I told the woman about what Daddy said, about how I was thrown free of the car because he forgot to fasten my seat belt. I told her I loved Daddy best, so why didn't he love me enough to take me to heaven with him?

Like an electric tingle, an epiphany lit up my nerve endings: no wonder the therapist insisted that I keep visiting her office. With all my talk of going to heaven, she must have thought I had some kind of death wish.

But I never wanted to die. I wanted to know why my dad forgot about my seat belt, and why he died and left me. Most of all, I wanted to know what was wrong with me, why he'd found it so easy to leave me behind.

So many confusing feelings had baffled me then . . . and confused me now.

"Sweetheart." My mom, rarely given to endearments or sentimental sayings, spoke to me with tears in her voice. "Mandy, I know your father loved you every bit as much as you love Marilee. You shouldn't for one minute think that you weren't cherished."

"Sure." I choked back a sob. "I know. I'm a mother, and I understand. But when you're a kid . . . everything is one thing or the other. You don't know what to do with your feelings, and those feelings aren't always logical. That's why I worry about Marilee."

"And that's why you'll tell her over and over that her daddy adored her. And that he's waiting for her by the river."

"I know." I sniffed and wiped my nose again. "I know you're right."

Fresh tears began to flow as another picture sharpened—the woman at the other end of this phone line had sacrificed her life for me. I rarely thought of her as anything but Mom, but when my father died she had been young and beautiful, with her entire life ahead of her. But during the time of her greatest loss, she focused on working hard to support me. She spent years loving and caring for me, a heartbroken and traumatized child.

And I had been ungrateful, because instead of appreciating her, I had chosen to cherish my wounds.

I did not sleep again that night.

After saying good-bye to Mom, I turned on my lamp and went to my closet, where one box held important family documents—canceled checks, previous years' tax returns, my life insurance policy, and our birth certificates. And, in a separate yellowed envelope, copies of two death certificates. My father's and Gideon's.

I sat in the small cone of lamplight and considered the way my world had shifted with each loss. I had been a grief-stricken child who fitfully emerged from therapy, but I had never fully dealt with the stew of anger and perceived rejection simmering in my subconscious. How can anyone deal with a problem unless they know it exists?

I almost laughed as the pieces of my life clicked together like a kaleidoscope, a pattern emerging from the blurred and broken glass. No wonder I chose to major in psychology. I don't know how long I visited therapists as a child, but in college I studied the effects of trauma upon children. Children who experienced a grief-inducing loss were often fearful of being separated from their loved ones, they lacked self-confidence, and they avoided situations that reminded them of the distressing event. They could also have intrusive memories about their loss, often in the form of nightmares. . . .

I had been as blind as a mole. Why hadn't I applied my psychology lessons to my own life? Maybe I'd been trying to, at least subconsciously. But my stubborn conscious self wouldn't listen.

No wonder I never felt terribly close to my mother. I'd been too busy resenting her for stepping in to fill my father's place. And no wonder Mom was so happy in The Villages. She was finally able to experience many of the things she had sacrificed for me.

No wonder I fell in love with the tender warrior who came into my life and charmed me. Gideon had protected, shielded, and adored me, all the things my doting father did until the accident took him away. I never saw Gid as a father figure, but no one but my father had ever made me feel as adored, as special, as Gideon did.

And no wonder I resisted my mother's efforts to help me grow up. I wanted to remain a child, to cling to the time before the accident, so I resisted anything that might involve taking responsibility for myself. No pets for me, no babysitting jobs, no high school band, no collegiate sports. No part-time jobs, until I started work at Mama Yanela's.

Even worse, as an adult I continued to resist responsibility: once Gideon died, I didn't even want a house, so I moved in with Jorge and Isa.

Though it pained me to admit it, moving in with family members had even allowed me to surrender my responsibility to my daughter. Mama Isa made sure Marilee was fed, bathed, and loved. When I used grief as an excuse to check out of my life, Marilee did her homework under Jorge's watchful eye.

I had been neglecting every responsibility until I learned about Julien. I pursued him with the stubborn tenacity of a dog chasing a bone because he was my son. He was someone who had been taken from me, and I wanted him back like I wanted air to breathe and food to eat. I would never be able to bring Daddy or Gideon back, but I could have Julien. Him, at least, I could restore to the family.

Your questions have been answered and your future firmly settled. You're going to do the right thing.

Was I? What would be the result of continuing with my plan? As Amelia had warned, I would rip my precious son from the only home he'd ever known. I would break his young heart as surely as my father's death had broken mine. Yes, he was young, but to a two-year-old, two years was a very long time.

Amelia couldn't know what I knew from experience—that even at a tender age, children were not rubber balls that could slam into tragedy and bounce back without any ill effects. They suffered the effects of loss and grief acutely, particularly when they lacked the verbal skills to express their feelings.

If I continued on my present course, I might cause Julien to regard me with the same emotions I felt for the woman who had raised and loved me—restrained affection, distance, and a vague feeling of incompatibility. My son might grow up feeling that he didn't belong in my home.

How could that result be worth the risk?

On Easter Sunday, after church, I sat with my Cuban family around Mama Isa's table and tried to make sense of jokes and stories in which I still understood only about half the words. But the missing details didn't matter because I could close my eyes and relax in the familiar rhythm of their laughter and their voices, knowing I was well-loved and at home.

Though my eyes are blue, my hair blond, and my skin light, I am part of a Cuban family. I see it in the way Mama Isa cares for Marilee, I feel it in the way Jorge lightly touches my shoulders as he stands behind me and tells a story about a customer at the grocery. I hear it in the way Mario says, "Tell her, Mandy," when he wants me to score a point for his side in a debate with Elaine, and I taste it in the special *pastelitos* Yanela makes just for me because she knows I can't resist those little pastries.

I see it in the way Marilee slips one of her colored eggs into baby Johny's lap so he won't feel left out during the Easter egg hunt.

I hadn't told anyone about my sleepless night and the catharsis that occurred during the call with my mother. I hadn't even told Amelia what I'd realized about Julien, myself, and the remnants of grief that had affected my personality since childhood.

A smile curved my lips as I looked at her. Who was I kidding?

She already knew about my personality flaws, and she loved me anyway. As did my mother. As had Gideon.

Just as Carlos and Yaritza took in Yanela and Gordon so many years ago, Gideon's family had taken me in without hesitation, without caring that I didn't share their history, their culture, or even their language. But they loved me because Gideon loved me. And they loved me still.

Amelia and Mario had welcomed little Johny in the same way. Their acceptance and love for him was evident in the way they cared for him, protected him, and even in the way they looked at him. In his short life he had gone through trauma, too, and if he later developed emotional problems, they would help him cope, just as my mother sacrificed to help me. Because that is what love does.

Two years ago, Damien and Simone Amblour welcomed a newborn baby into their lives. Since then, Julien had known love, acceptance, and stability. The Amblours had loved him, cared for him, and fought for him.

And I had every reason to believe they would continue to do so.

Eight days later I tightened my seat belt on an Air France jet as we glided onto the runway at La Rochelle, a few miles from Domaine de Amblour. My nerves tensed as I folded my hands and considered my mission. I had only packed an overnight case for the long flight; if all went well, I'd spend only an hour or two in La Rochelle.

Mr. Pippen had offered to send one of his associates as a traveling companion, but I no longer needed anyone to help me find my way.

The plane touched down, then turned and taxied toward the airport building. As the flight attendant welcomed us in French, I bent to pick up my purse, which held my travel documents and other important papers. Along with my passport, I carried two sealed envelopes I'd accepted from Mr. Pippen just before I boarded.

The plane settled at the Jetway and the flight attendant opened the door. I gathered my belongings and waited, heart thumping like a punching bag, as we exited row by row.

I walked into the gate area amid a chattering of French, then headed in the direction of *la livraison des bagages.* The Amblours would meet me at baggage claim, Simone had promised. From there, we'd find a quiet room where we could talk.

Coming down the escalator, I spotted my French acquaintances almost immediately. Simone would have stood out in any crowd, and Damien appeared as stately and patrician as he had the last time we were together. But today a dark-haired toddler clung to his hand. I wanted to stop the world and spend an hour or two studying the child, but for now I needed to retain custody of my eyes.

"*Allô!*" I twiddled my fingers to catch the Amblours' attention. "Simone! Damien! *Bonjour!*"

Smiling carefully, they came forward and welcomed me with embraces, but I couldn't help noticing a deep worry line between Simone's sculpted brows. The last several weeks had been hard on all of us, but after today the situation would be resolved. In time, broken hearts would mend.

I purposely saved the best till last. After greeting Simone and Damien, I stooped to regard Julien at eye level. My heart opened as I studied him, drinking in his dark eyes, his perfectly formed mouth, the curly hair that had come directly from Gideon. There was nothing of Damien about him—the boy looked more like a Spaniard than the man of the house. But the current master of Domaine de Amblour clung tightly to the child's hand, his chin resolute and his blue eyes determined.

"May I"—I smiled—"have a kiss?" I held out both hands, but the boy was struck by a sudden attack of shyness and ducked behind his father's leg. I didn't blame him for feeling embarrassed, but his rejection made my heart twist.

"Julien!" His mother scolded him in French, but I shook my head.

"That's all right. He doesn't know me yet."

I stood and finally noticed the dark-suited man standing behind Damien. "Allow me," Simone said, "to introduce our attorney, Girard Bouchard."

Though my memories of the lawyer weren't exactly delightful, I forced a smile and shook the hand he offered. "Nice to see you again, Mr. Bouchard." With the pleasantries out of the way, I gripped my overnight case and looked around. "Do you have a place where we can meet in private?"

The attorney gestured toward the escalator. "All is in readiness. If you'll come this way."

Julien rode on Simone's hip as we followed Bouchard up the escalator to the main floor, then crossed the wide expanse in front of the check-in counters. Finally the attorney opened a nondescript panel in the wall and pointed to another door halfway down the hallway. "Second room on the left, please. The area is ours for the afternoon."

The confidence that had buoyed me when I boarded the plane shriveled like a spent balloon as I walked forward and took a seat at a conference table in the small room. Simone, Damien, and Girard Bouchard sat across from me, three lined up against one. Despite their polite greetings, I knew the Amblours had to be wound as tightly as clock springs.

Fortunately, Julien seemed unaware of the underlying tension in the air. He sat on Simone's lap, his thumb in his mouth and a tattered cloth monkey beneath his arm.

I expected Mr. Bouchard to open the meeting, but Damien spoke first. "I thought," he said, the line of his mouth tightening as if he found the act of speaking to me distasteful, "you would bring your attorney."

I managed a half smile. "Mr. Pippen offered to send one of his associates, but I saw no need to involve anyone else when this really affects only the three of us—well, four, counting Julien."

Avoiding the lawyer's steely gaze, I pulled the two sealed envelopes from my bag.

"What is this?" Mr. Bouchard's expression darkened with displeasure. "Your lawyer did not mention any additional documents."

"This is a letter," I said, handing Damien one of the envelopes. "Inside you will find notarized copies in French and English. But before you open it, I want to tell you something."

Damien set the envelope on the table and covered it with his hand, but his eyes never left my face.

"I've been thinking"—a lump rose in my throat, threatening to choke off my words—"about what love is, and what family means. And like King Solomon, I have realized that the mother who loves best may well be the one who is most willing to let go. So that's what I want to do. Though Julien is my biological son, I want to officially relinquish my right to raise him."

I caught and held Simone's gaze. "When I first got pregnant, in May, I sent you an e-card wishing you a happy Mother's Day for years to come. I will always wish you well on that holiday, Simone—as you and Damien raise our son."

I clenched my hand beneath the table, wondering if the people across from me had any idea what it had cost me to utter those words. Throughout the flight I had considered changing my mind, tossing the notarized documents, and taking my baby home with me. The option tantalized, filling my head with images of Julien and Marilee sitting side by side at Mama Isa's dinner table, bringing me a birthday breakfast tray, and joining me on my knees for bedtime prayers. As I flew over the Atlantic I had prayed and pondered and imagined Gideon peering over heaven's balcony to observe me—what would he want me to do? The best thing for the child, of course. And along with their parents' love, children need stability.

I had assumed that because God sent me a son, I had the right to raise that son. I hadn't seen any other logical possibility, but love had opened my eyes.

I had come to do the right thing.

I gestured to the envelope beneath Damien's hand. "Inside you'll find a fully notarized document stating that I will never contest your right to raise Julien Louis Amblour as your son. For his sake, I want you to continue as an intact family. I want Julien to remain in the only home he's ever known, with the only parents he's ever had. In short, I don't believe DNA is the only thing that binds people together, and I deeply regret the pain this situation has caused you. I give you my word . . . I will never disturb you again."

Simone's eyes filled with tears, but I was more concerned about Damien's reaction. For days I had struggled with his apparent fixation on having a biological heir. Relinquishing my parental rights would be pointless if he could not love my son.

Silence surrounded us, broken only by the quiet rustle of the boy's jacket as he squirmed on Simone's lap. She turned to her husband, silent entreaty in her eyes, and I expected Damien to look to his attorney for advice. . . .

Instead, Damien Amblour stood and pressed his splayed fingertips to the top of the table. In a trembling voice, he thanked me for coming to France. "To be honest," he said, managing a wavering smile, "I was angry when I first heard you were claiming the boy. But not until I learned that you had every right to do so—that he was, in fact, your child—did I realize how much I had come to love him." Damien's smile dissolved into a bewildered expression of hurt. "I could not lose the boy, Amanda, without losing my heart as well. So from the bottom of my soul, I thank you. You have been more than generous with us once again."

If they knew how hard I struggled with my decision, they'd realize I wasn't being generous. I didn't relent for their sakes, but for Julien's.

Simone looked at me, her eyes bright with repressed tears. She wrapped her arms around her son, then reached out and embraced her husband. As the three of them huddled on the other side of the table, I found myself studying Julien's beautiful face and the dark eyes that seemed to regard me with sharp curiosity and a suggestion of humor. Gideon's eyes.

"Bonjour," I whispered, not wanting to frighten him away. *"Comment allez-vous?"*

The boy ducked beneath the safety of his mother's arm, then peeped out at me.

I smiled and wriggled my fingers in a little wave, but could barely see him through the veil of my tears.

I did not fly directly home after leaving France. Instead, I flew through the night to Washington, D.C., and then took a taxi to Arlington Cemetery. Because I'd been giving birth to Julien at the time of Gideon's funeral, I had yet to visit my husband's grave site.

I found section 35, site 2598, in a quiet part of the park, far from the tourists who milled around the Tomb of the Unknown Soldier and the Kennedy grave sites. I sank to my knees in the soft grass and studied the white stone marker: *Gideon Gosling Lisandra, Lieutenant, Joint Special Operations Command. June 3, 1976–December 6, 2008. Afghanistan.*

Gideon had been laid to rest next to a World War II vet, and I knew he'd like that. He used to say World War II and the first few days after September 11 were the last occasions America pulled together, and he feared for the state of our country if we didn't learn how to pull together again.

"Gideon." I whispered his name above an overwhelming rise of yearning for the man who had been my friend, my husband, and the father of two beautiful children. "You'll never know how much I miss you, but I'm finally learning to stand on my own two feet. With a lot of help, of course, mostly from your family. They've been so kind to me, and they miss you terribly. But you're very much with us. You'll always be with us."

I paused to listen to a swallow calling to its mate from a nearby tree. The poor fellow sounded nearly as lonely as I felt.

"I came to tell you something. And if you can't hear me, then I trust the Lord to relay this message." I closed my eyes. "We have a two-year old son. We have a beautiful boy who's growing up in France. He's very much loved by both his parents and he's going to inherit a beautiful vineyard." I swallowed back a sob and shook my head, willing myself not to cry. "They say the Lord works in mysterious ways, and this may be one of his strangest plans yet. I wanted to bring Julien home—you can't imagine how badly I wanted to—but in the end, I couldn't rip him away from the only mama and papa he's ever known. I know you'll understand why."

I brushed my hand over the manicured grass on my husband's earthly resting place. "Simone and Damien have promised that I will always be a part of Julien's life. I'm not sure what that's going to look like, but I'm going to see him every time an opportunity arises. I want Marilee to know her brother . . . and all the rest of *la familia,* too."

I listened to my warbling serenader until the last drop of birdsong faded, then I reached out and traced the granite letters of my love's first name. "I spoke to your mama before I left for France. Though I hadn't totally decided what I would do when I met the Amblours, I think she guessed, because she came over to hug me before I went to the airport. As she walked me to the car, I remembered that she'd lost your sister, so I asked if the pain of losing a child ever goes away. 'No,' she said, 'but the pain changes. And you carry it around like a pebble in your pocket.' "

I slipped my hand into my pocket and pulled out one of the two small stones I'd picked up from Mama Isa's driveway. "I will carry mine in memory of Julien, and I've brought one for you. Remember—we will all be together one day."

I set the little rock on the grave marker, then lifted my gaze to the treetops and the bright blue heaven beyond. "I'll always love you, Gid. I'm going back to school because I have to keep living, but I'll be first in line to find you by the river."

Epilogue

Thanksgiving

Once again Mama Isa's house filled with the sounds of music and merrymaking; once again her kitchen table creaked beneath the weight of a turkey and dozens of tempting dishes. As Marilee and I got out of the car and walked through the men assembled on the front porch, I realized the area seemed smaller than usual—or maybe there were simply more men on the porch. Mario, Jorge, and Tumelo sat on the left side, where Mario and Tumelo played checkers while Jorge cheered them on. On the right side, Grandpa Gordon occupied the center chair while he entertained seven-year-old Johny and eight-year-old Julien with a demonstration of cat's cradle.

"Good afternoon, boys." I kissed two foreheads, then wrapped an arm around Johny's shoulders and ran my fingers through Julien's curls. "Julien! *Où sont ta mère et ton père?*"

"Inside the house," he said, his English far smoother than my French. He gestured toward the front door. *"Dans la cuisine."*

His parents were already in the kitchen? I went inside, then wound my way through the relatives and discovered Simone and Damien working at Mama Isa's table. Simone wore a faded apron and stirred something chocolaty while Damien stood guard over several bottles from Domaine de Amblour. The recently widowed

Yaritza, now ninety-three, sat beside the bottles and watched Damien with a narrow-eyed gaze.

Amelia sidled over, nudged me with an elbow, and jerked her chin in Yaritza's direction. "What do you think? Is she sizing up the man or his European tailor?"

I laughed. "Offer to seat him beside her at dinner. Then you'll have your answer."

"Bonjour!" Damien waved at me before commencing to pour a glass for my mother. "Merry Thanksgiving to you!"

"That's '*Happy* Thanksgiving,'" I answered, stopping to hug my mom. I stepped back and met her gaze. "I'm glad you came. Everything okay up there in The Villages?"

"There's a bit of a controversy over golf cart parking areas," she said, a twinkle in her eye. "But I'm dating the president of the homeowners association, so I've got a great seat for the shuffleboard championship."

I laughed and moved toward Simone, who was staring at the contents of her bowl with a perplexed expression. "Simone, how well you look! When did you get in?"

She glanced around as if searching for a calendar, then shrugged. "We flew in the night before yesterday, and came here straightaway. Madame Alejandro has been so kind to give us her guest rooms—"

"She'll be offended if you don't call her Mama Isa," I said. "After all, you're part of the family, too."

"I keep telling her to be less formal," Damien said, looking younger and more relaxed than I had ever seen him. "But she forgets."

"After all these years, she ought to remember." I grinned and ran my finger along the edge of her bowl, then tasted the dark batter. "Yummy. What is it?"

"I am not certain," Simone confessed. "But after it is mixed, I am to put it in a square pan and bake it."

"Probably brownies." I squeezed her arm, then went to help Elaine and Yanela with the pig roasting in the backyard.

Later, when we had all gathered around the long pine table at the end of Mama Isa's rectangular kitchen, I looked around the circle and couldn't stop a smile. Somehow, against all odds, we had become a family. When I surrendered my right to claim my son all those years ago, I never dreamed we would come together like this.

Now Jorge, acting as host, thanked God for the food and our family. After his amen, we passed heaping bowls of deliciousness around the table. As we served ourselves and the noise level rose several decibels, I glanced at Marilee, who was sitting next to me at the grown-up table now that she'd turned fourteen. "Have you had much of a chance to talk to Julien?"

"Not yet"—she crinkled her nose—"'cause he's acting like such a *boy*! Do you know what he and Johny were doing outside? A burping contest! I thought the French were supposed to be more civilized."

I laughed and assured her that boys would be boys, no matter where they grew up.

Thank heaven for that.

Reading Group Guide

QUESTIONS AND TOPICS FOR DISCUSSION

1. Before reading this novel, had you ever given much thought to the ethics of surrogate parenting? What about the ethics of in vitro fertilization?

2. What do you think about Mandy's motives for deciding to become a surrogate?

3. At one point, Mandy thinks, *And, unlike Millie, I hoped my lifetime would hold far more significant feats than having someone else's baby.* Knowing what you know about Mandy, what do you think is the most significant thing she has accomplished thus far?

4. If you were in Mandy's situation, what would you do about the child you suspected of being your biological son? Would you let him remain where he was or would you want to raise him yourself? Do you agree with Mandy's decision?

5. Do you think Mandy really chose the best answer for Julien? What was the best answer for her?

6. When Mandy first finds out about Julien's resemblance to Marilee, she believes "blood trumps everything" even though she wouldn't have applied that principle in the situation with Amelia, Mario, and the three-year-old foster son they were forced to surrender. If you were a judge in family court, how would you rule in situations like these?

7. Did you enjoy the first-person writing style? Do you wish you'd had a peek into any other characters' heads?

8. Who was your favorite character? What did you especially like about them? Which character did you like the least?

9. Did you experience any sort of emotional trauma in your childhood? How did the incident affect you? How are you different today because of the event? Are you comfortable talking about the trauma as an adult?

10. What do you think the future holds for Mandy? For Julien? For Marilee?

11. Have you read any of Angela Hunt's other books? How does this novel compare to the other books you've read?

A CONVERSATION WITH ANGELA HUNT

What kind of research did you conduct on surrogacy and adoption for *The Offering*? What did you discover about practices in the United States versus other countries?

I did quite a bit of research on surrogacy—I read a book written by a surrogate mother, plus I read several recent articles about the increase in surrogacy among military wives. As referenced in the novel, I discovered that surrogacy is easier in the U.S. than in many European countries. As to adoption—I've lived that!

In *The Offering*, Mandy considers the cultural repercussions of carrying another man's child since she is part of a large Cuban family. What other cultural implications do you think exist, both inside and outside of Cuban culture?

I do think that most cultural objections to surrogacy rise from misunderstanding—people don't realize that gestational carriers are carrying a child that is completely unrelated to the pregnant woman. The Mary Beth Whitehead case, where the child developed from Ms. Whitehead's egg and so was her biological child, forced many parents to abandon true surrogacy and opt instead for a gestational carrier.

How did you use faith and religion to inform Mandy's and several other characters' decisions? What kind of role does faith play in your own life?

I believe that God created every life for a purpose—so we should behave responsibly toward unborn children even if they are only at the blastocyst stage. Too many doctors don't fully inform parents about "discarded embryos" and too many IVF parents don't realize—or don't want to know—that they may be asked to "discard" fully human lives. I have no problem with IVF or surrogacy as long as everyone involved fully understands the bioethical issues and resolves to preserve all human life: that would mean no freezing of embryos (because half of those embryos probably won't survive the thawing procedure) and fertilizing only as many eggs as a woman is willing and able to carry in a pregnancy.

Have you ever heard of the kind of mistake that happened with Mandy's pregnancy?

Fortunately, no. But I have read about IVF cases where a woman gave birth to two babies who were supposed to be her genetic offspring but weren't. I've also read about a British couple whose last frozen embryo was implanted in another woman who, upon learning of the mistake, aborted the baby she was carrying. I've met an American family whose frozen embryo was implanted in another woman, but she chose to surrender the child to the biological parents at birth. Some heartbreaking mistakes have occurred in the field of reproductive medicine.

In *The Offering*, some of the characters seemed judgmental of Mandy's chief motivator—money—for participating in surrogacy. Do you think that's a good enough reason to participate in such a significant and potentially devastating task? If you were giving advice to a friend considering surrogacy, what would you tell her?

Money is not the root of all evil—the love of money is, and Mandy was not in love with money, she was simply trying to help her family. Her motivation was no different from mine when I show up to work each morning. But if someone I knew wanted to be a gestational carrier, I would warn her that the chief ethical danger is the cheapening of human life. If a doctor or the intended parents intend to treat IVF embryos like spare parts, or if they even mention selective termination (aborting one or more babies because too many embryos implanted), I would urge her to find another place to fulfill her desire to serve a childless couple.

***The Offering* feels like the intimate trials and musings of a close friend, and it's difficult to shake the feeling that you're reading someone's journal. How personal did the book end up being for you?**

As an adoptive parent, for years I have had a keen interest in life and parenting issues. And as someone who worked hard to add children to our family, I must admit that I wanted Mandy to get custody of her baby boy. When I discussed my book-in-progress with some friends, I was stunned that they thought Mandy was being selfish. My goodness, why wouldn't she want to raise her own child? I'd fight tooth and nail to have my baby back in my arms. But when I considered that the Amblours were good parents, and because I know the first two years of a child's life are crucial for healthy development, I realized that Mandy would have to consider what was best for Julien. And sacrificing for the child—isn't that what motherhood is all about?

In some states, the birth mother of an adopted child has a certain amount of time into the adoption where she can change her mind and essentially take the baby back from the adoptive parents. We saw this possibility come up with Mario and Amelia. Do you think this is fair?

I think it's hard. Terribly hard on the adoptive parents who have given their heart to a child only to have the child—and their hearts—ripped out. It's especially hard when the biological parents don't seem to "deserve" the children who had been taken away. But if I were a young woman who surrendered my baby because I felt hopeless and helpless, I would hope and pray that I would be able to turn my life around and be granted a second chance with my child. So for the sake of young women like that, I do think the "revocation of consent period" is fair. Some agencies will not place a baby with an adoptive couple until after this period is over—if excellent foster homes are available, that might be the best approach.

According to your Web site, one of your interests is photography. How do writing and taking photographs compare? Which gives you more creative fulfillment?

They are very similar when it comes to marketing, branding, and selling, but they're quite different when it comes to creating art.

Yet both require a thorough knowledge of equipment and technology, and both deliver occasional surprises for the artist. Both are focused on eliciting emotion from the reader/viewer. Both have levels of competency: beginning, amateur, and professional. Both require the artist to see the world in new ways. Both, I suppose, can change lives and hearts. But photography doesn't require nearly as many hours to produce a single polished product. That's refreshing.

You've written more than 115 books. Where do you find your inspiration for writing fiction?

I find inspiration everywhere, but mostly from daily life. I'll read something interesting or hear something intriguing and think, "What if . . ." and I'm off.

What is your favorite genre to write?

I really don't have a favorite. I find that writing is like building, and as long as a writer can skillfully use the appropriate "tools" and follow the genre blueprint, he can write anything from a novel to a screenplay. Just as a builder would grow tired of making dog houses all the time, I'd be bored if I had to write every book in the same genre. I love mixing things up.

Do you have plans to write another book? Will we be seeing Mandy again?

I always have another book on the calendar, and I'm busy writing now. But I don't think we'll be seeing Mandy again . . . unless she shows up at my desk and insists that I get busy.

References

I owe a debt of thanks to Dr. Harry Kraus, surgeon and novelist, who answered my questions about whether the scenario described in this book is possible . . . and yes, it is. I also owe a bundle of thanks to Natasha Rodriguez, who helped me with my Spanish—if you find any errors, they are mine, not hers.

For the record, I do have an attorney friend named Joseph Pippen, but to my knowledge he does not have dealings with shadowy characters, nor would he ever attempt to bribe a judge. He is, however, a good sport, and I trust he will forgive Mandy's musings about his namesake character.

Also for the record, I realize that U.S. Special Operations Command is located in Tampa, Florida, while most of the special operators themselves live around Fort Bragg, North Carolina. But one of our family friends is a special operator, and though he lives in North Carolina most of the time, he's also a local boy and we're proud of him. So I hope you'll excuse me for having Gideon and his family live in the Tampa area.

These two books were also very helpful:

S. F. Tomajczyk, *US Elite Counter-Terrorist Forces.* Osceola, WI: Motorbooks International, 1997.

Stacy Ziegler, *Pathways to Parenthood: The Ultimate Guide to Surrogacy.* Boca Raton, FL: BrownWalker Press, 2005.

Look for *The Fine Art of Insincerity* and *Five Miles South of Peculiar*, more great reads from

ANGELA HUNT

ANGELA HUNT

New York Times Bestselling Author of THE FINE ART OF INSINCERITY

FIVE MILES SOUTH OF

Peculiar

A NOVEL

"Only Angela Hunt could write a relationship novel that's a page-turner! . . . Come spend the weekend in coastal Georgia with three women who clean house in more ways than one!"

—**Liz Curtis Higgs**, bestselling author of *Here Burns My Candle*, on *The Fine Art of Insincerity*

"Angela Hunt has penned another winner! From the opening scene, she had me wanting to find out what would happen next to the people of Peculiar, peculiar and otherwise."

—**Robin Lee Hatcher**, bestselling author of *Heart of Gold* and *Belonging*, on *Five Miles South of Peculiar*

Available wherever books are sold or at SimonandSchuster.com

HOWARD BOOKS
A Division of Simon & Schuster
A CBS COMPANY